MEET THE AUTHOR

TEASERS,
TRAILERS & MORE...

The Last Love Note

A NOVEL

EMMA GREY

Zibby Books
New York

Library of Congress Control Number: 2023934653

Paperback ISBN: 978-1-958506-28-8
Hardcover ISBN: 978-1-958506-29-5
eBook ISBN: 978-1-958506-51-6

Book design by Ursula Damm

Cover design by Sarah Horgan

www.zibbymedia.com

Printed in the United States of America

10 9 8 7 6 5 4 3 2 1

To Jeff
In this case, you're why I write

And to Mum and Dad
Whose love notes spanned 72 years

PROLOGUE

Two years ago

My phone erupts into Darth Vader's "Imperial March." I scoop Charlie off the polished concrete floor and lower him into the shopping cart, shove AirPods into my ears, and brace myself.

"Mum?"

The custom ringtone was Cam's idea. An attempt to cheer me up, after one of Mum's cyclonic visits. She means well, and I love her dearly. But there'd been some bumps as we morphed into mother and grandmother. Cam thought the ringtone would give me a laugh the next time she called, and it did.

Then he went and got sick. And now I can't bring myself to undo his joke.

I can't undo anything. I'm still paying his phone bill, just to hear his voicemail. A copy of Bruce Springsteen's autobiography is still facedown and spread-eagled on the bedside table, partially read. I can't even declutter all the sticky notes he left strewn all over the house and through my car and in my handbag. Even his handwriting brings me to my knees . . .

"I'm at the supermarket," I announce once I finally have Mum's attention. She has a habit of calling me just before she's actually available to speak—usually while she's finishing a conversation with someone else. Cam called it "conversational limbo."

I reach for his favorite soap. Inhale it. Pass it to Charlie in the cart. He sniffs it too.

"The *supermarket?*" Mum repeats, as if she's flabbergasted. Everything I do, no matter how mundane, seems to come as a shock to my mum. Always has.

"Apparently life goes on . . ." I explain, before looking into my nearly empty cart. It's evidence that life has in fact come to a crashing halt.

Before he got sick, Cam and I took turns at being hunter and gatherer. He was stellar at both. Shopping aficionado. Home-grown master chef. And now that I've assumed both roles full-time, I can't seem to assemble an actual meal.

A ponytailed woman in activewear brushes past me in a cloud of perfume and competence. I watch as she selects a pack of tampons and a bar of soap, drops them into her basket, and crosses them off her list with a flourish.

Was I *ever* like that? That blasé about soap? These people carry on as if the whole world has not been irrevocably shattered.

"Listen, Kate, why don't you and Charlie come with me to my Probus meeting tomorrow?" Probus is Mum's social universe. But she can't seriously think I'm in the mood to attend a retirees' club mixer with a three-year-old while on bereavement leave?

"Shirley Delaney's husband just died too," she explains.

"Mum, he was eighty-seven." I know this because she's already told me about his lingering death in more detail than a newly bereaved person, or indeed anyone, would ever want to know.

"Widowed is widowed," she proclaims, and tears spring to my eyes again. I'm thirty-eight years old. The term "widow" should not apply to me. I need to get out of this conversation before Mum dismantles me in front of her impressionable grandson.

A teenage shelf-stocker, dragging an enormous cart packed with shampoo and conditioner, starts kicking cardboard boxes out of the way on the floor near us. Our gazes meet, in the eye of my crisis.

"Can I help you?" he offers, reluctantly.

I shake my head. It's clear that neither of us wants to be here. Nor does he genuinely want to help. I'm just in his way. *Hopelessly lost,* I want to confess. *And not just in this supermarket.*

Charlie has capitalized on my distraction by seizing a bottle of shaving cream from a display stand. I notice it just as one of the playgroup mums rounds the corner into my aisle. A friendly face!

I think she sees me, but she acts like she's suddenly remembered dog food or toilet cleaner or frozen peas—*anything*. She reverses her cart and shoos her twins back out of the aisle, away from the inevitable awkwardness of my existence. So now I'm a widow *and* a social pariah.

I look back at Charlie. He now has the lid of the shaving cream off and is pushing down hard on the pump with the heel of his hand, squirting foam all over his *Fireman Sam* top, tracksuit pants, sneakers. . . .

"Mum! I've got to go," I say, searching for some tissues in my bag. I pull out the wad of envelopes I'd grabbed from the mailbox on the way out. Sympathy cards. Bills. Something from the electric company, addressed to Cam, which it shouldn't be; I'd spent a frustrating half hour on the phone a few days ago, attempting to solve the seemingly insurmountable problem of our account being held in his name only.

"The account holder is *dead*," I'd clarified miserably after the operator had told me twice that she was authorized to speak only with him. Really, I couldn't have made it any plainer. "How do you expect me to bring him to the phone?"

Where are the tissues?

"Charlie, don't put that stuff in your mouth!"

I stop rummaging when it dawns on me that the envelope, addressed to Cam, has the words "We're sorry to see you go" emblazoned across the front.

I tear open the seal and unfold the paper. *Dear Mr. Whittaker,* it reads. *We're sorry you've decided to leave us. Please take a few minutes to help us know how we might have better met your needs. . . .*

And there it is.

Rock bottom. Slamming into me in the men's toiletries section, thirteen miserable days after the worst day of my life—brutal letter to my dead husband in hand, raft of personal items he'll never use taunting me from all sides as the truth of my situation really lands. Properly. For the first time.

The man I love does not exist.

Does. Not. Exist.

He didn't "decide" to leave the electric company. Didn't decide to leave any of us. And now there's no need to buy this soap, and too few names on our accounts.

"Oh, Charlie! What a *mess*."

I'm all-out sobbing now, the way I've longed to sob since the funeral and haven't been able to. Of course the tears would come *now*, just as I'm trying to wipe shaving cream off everything using the envelope.

Some other time, it might be cute that he's slathering foam on his cheeks and pretending to scrape it off his face with an imaginary razor. But not now. I flash forward to a time when I'll have to teach him how to shave for real. I don't know what I'm doing now, and he's only three. The idea of raising a teenage boy without Cam's insider knowledge fills me with dread.

"Look at me, Mumma!" Charlie's bright blue eyes are alight with mischief, dimpled smile beaming through the white foam. He takes my hand and places it flat on the side of his face, just like Cam used to let him do when we were helping him shave.

"I'm Dadda!" he says, laughing.

Oh, God.

I don't think I can do this.

1

The present

"Grace, *please* come away from the window!"

She's pulled back the curtains in my front room, flooding it in late-winter sunlight. Ensconced in the window seat with a glass of sauv blanc in hand, she's brazenly gawking at the guy moving in across the road.

Charlie's been playing something other than Minecraft for more than ten minutes, and I feel like an excellent mother. It's such a rare victory that I've celebrated by reopening the manuscript of the literary novel I've been pushing uphill since the Neolithic Age, about five words at a time.

"Your new neighbor *rocks* a flannel," Grace says. With ash-blond hair backlit by the setting sun, she is ethereal. I watch as she stretches her long legs across the window seat and adjusts her forest-green maxi dress over high-heeled boots, and I wonder how I ended up with such a glamorous friend.

Grace and I are so close, I struggle to believe I've known her only six years, since Cam and I dragged ourselves away from Melbourne and moved to Queanbeyan, a town in the southeast, near Canberra, so he could lecture at the Australian National University. Meeting her at basketball in our mid-thirties was like finally discovering the Diana to my Anne. The Louise to my Thelma. The Diaz to my Barrymore.

"Wonder if he's DTF," she muses, before taking another sip of her wine.

"Department of Treasury and Finance?" I ask. "Wait, no. That's two separate departments. . . ."

She drags her focus away from the man across the road for long enough to properly observe me, incredulous at my naïveté.

"What? Oh, is that some Tinder acronym?" I ask. I have zero intention of mastering online dating. Or any kind of dating at all. Online or off, speed, double, group—I'll have none of it, much to Grace Randall's everlasting disappointment.

"Yes, obviously DTF is a Tinder thing, Kate. It means Down to—"

"*Shush!*" I say, pointing in Charlie's direction.

"That man does *not* look like a public servant," she observes. Grace has been public sector–averse ever since a bad date with Gerry from the Australian Fisheries Management Authority, who mansplained commercial fish statistics over a shrimp cocktail, even though she'd already told him she was vegan, and allergic to math.

"There are attractive public servants," I argue. "I used to be one myself, remember? A public servant. Not—"

"Shut up, Kate, and just *look!*"

I'll get no peace until I join her at the window, so I save my document and set the laptop down. As I cross the room toward her, I slide black-rimmed reading glasses down my nose and fold my arms in preemptive disapproval. *Here comes the Fun Police.*

She gives me the once-over and frowns. All right, yes, there's nothing glam about black leggings, mismatched socks, and a sky-blue penguin Snuggie, but if I can't be comfortable in my own house, where can I be? I've twisted unmanageable auburn curls into a bun that's loosely held in place by the pencil I've been using to handwrite a list of inconsistencies in my novel. Thanks to rapid-fire interruptions, the list is almost as long as the novel itself. *How do other mums do this?*

I look out the window.

"Don't let him see the penguins!" Grace instructs, glaring at the Snuggie. "Kate, you look the complete opposite of DTF right now."

I *am* the opposite of it. I'm about to remind her of the reason for my multiyear celibacy streak, when the object of Grace's fascination emerges from the truck. Sandy blond hair. Five-o'clock shadow. Ripped everything—jeans, six-pack, biceps. There's something very Jon Bon Jovi in *Moonlight and Valentino* about the way he's getting the job done. No fuss. Unintentionally gorgeous.

"I know you're grieving, Kate, and Officially Not Interested, but come on, now. Surely even *you* can't fail to appreciate this."

He tilts the king-size bedframe he's carrying, and we tilt our heads in unison, hypnotized. *Gawd!* I feel instantly guilty and take a step back from the window into the shadows.

"You *are* allowed to notice other men," Grace says, more gently now. "The whole world knows you'll love Cam forever."

Yes. "Till death do us part" was just the start of it.

I thought love would fade, the way grief does. Was terrified it would, at first. Scared a day might come when I'd forget the exact shape of the hairline at Cam's neck. Or the way the scent of Aramis would announce his presence behind me, fresh from a shave and a shower, towel wrapped around his waist, drops of water falling from the tips of his hair onto my skin as he kissed me.

I needn't have worried. Once the sharpest angles of early grief softened and blurry glimpses of a new life without him began to come into focus, my love for him only intensified exponentially, rendering all other men incomparable.

Even Grace's guy across the road, now coming back out of his house. He bounds up into the truck and drags a chest of drawers carefully down its ramp on a dolly, shifts a few boxes to make a path for it, and disappears back inside. Capable. Focused.

"Good work ethic," I note. From the expression on Grace's face, I can tell the observation falls flat.

People tell me I'm still young. They say I'll meet someone else. They point out that, at forty, my longest relationship might still be ahead of me. I get it, intellectually. But Cam is an impossible act to follow. Ours is an impossible vibe to re-create. It's why I cannot be standing here at my front window, leering at some flannel-clad, DTF non–public servant as he wields half of IKEA out of a truck, solo.

"It's been two years," Grace reminds me. I bristle at the implication that I should be over my grief by now. Or that it might be time to "move on." The thought of doing that panics me. How would I even conduct a first date with some unsuspecting victim who hasn't been properly briefed on the extent of my brokenness? Why would anyone sign up for what can only ever be a half-share of me?

"I'm not ready, Grace. I'm not even interested in the idea of it, academically. I've got Charlie, and the novel, and Mum, and work—"

She silences my catalog of excuses with a gentle hand on my arm. "You're scared."

Grace should be scared, too. Her backstory wasn't easy either. A grand romance that swept away most of the last decade and spat her out, at thirty-eight, straight into an IVF clinic with borderline unviable eggs and a dream so tenacious even the fertility specialist's "five percent chance" hasn't dulled her hope. I don't know how she isn't terrified of relationships now, like I am.

Of course, just as I'm about to retreat to the safety of my manuscript, the guy across the road glances up at my house and catches the two of us ogling. *Fantastic.*

"To hot new neighbors," Grace says under her breath, waving her wineglass at him through my window as if we're admiring him across a bar.

"Why did Daddy have a grenade in his study?" Charlie asks, materializing beside me.

But this is no time for war games. In the interest of future neighborly relations, I'm mentally searching for plausible explanations as to why Grace and I have been all but dangling out the window. Neighborhood Watch?

"Er, DEFCON 1," she whispers.

"I know. I'm *mortified.*"

"No! Not Jon Bon Jovi across the road," she says. "Charlie!"

I look down at my son. He's got his dad's golden curls, his freckles, his mischievous blue eyes . . . and his *grenade?*

Cam might have taught English, but his real love was history. He was always collecting souvenirs from overseas battlefields. Bullets from France. Random bits of gun shells. A little vial of sand from the beach at Gallipoli. And apparently the very legitimate-looking grenade that's currently in the hot little hand of our excitable five-year-old.

"Let me see that," I say, lifting it off Charlie's palm as gently as possible. Of course, there's no chance it's *live.* Cam only ever bought artifacts from bona fide collectors and registered antiques dealers. If he were here now, he'd crouch down beside Charlie and explain how it worked, Charlie would graduate from the conversation slightly more knowledgeable, and I would have one less thing to explain about the world. The thought of all the lost conversations between them makes my heart ache as much as it hurts my head trying to bridge the gap.

"This is Peak Kate," Grace says, snapping a photo of me holding the grenade. She crops it so it's just my Snuggie-clad forearm and hand in the frame and has it uploaded to Facebook before I can think straight. I know she tags me in it, because my phone flashes with a notification on the sofa. I've got my settings locked down for situations exactly like this, where Grace's love of drama clashes with my desire to not invite my entire friends list to witness every single episode of my mayhem.

"It's fine," I reassure her. "It's Cam!" Thorough, dependable Cam, who would never store a live weapon in the house. The very idea that this thing could be genuinely dangerous is laughable.

Nevertheless, I *am* an aspiring writer. My imagination has not only stayed intact through my grief but been actively fed by it. I'm forever inventing dire scenarios in which something else is snatched away from me. Some*one*. And finally, the mother in me gets her head together.

"Grace, why don't you take Charlie somewhere? Drive-through soft serve?"

"Epic!" Charlie shouts, dancing on the spot. He's so excited about the ice cream and bonus time with Grace that I have to side-step out of his way so he doesn't knock this thing out of my hand.

It's a testament to our friendship that Grace has a car seat for Charlie permanently installed in her car. But before they can go, we're interrupted by Siri, informing Grace of an incoming FaceTime call.

"Give me a minute, mate," she says, as she touches her screen to answer. He's barnacled to her leg, trying to drag her toward the door, and I have to call him off.

"Where are you?" a woman's voice says as soon as the video connection cuts in. I can't see the screen, but her voice has an edge to it. "Grace, listen to me. I'm in the sandpit. . . ."

Charlie releases Grace's leg and pulls at her arm so he can see this sandpit, but I know from my short-lived public sector career that she means she's posted somewhere in the Middle East.

"I've just shown your Facebook post to my colleague here," the woman explains. "He's an ammunitions engineer. Look, I don't want to alarm you, but you need to call the police."

There's a knock at the door and Grace and I flinch.

Is that them? No. What? We haven't even phoned them yet.

I tiptoe carefully down the hall, past the boxes of Cam's clothes I finally sorted through on the weekend. I thought two years had been long enough and I Kondo'd the daylights out of his side of the wardrobe while comfort-viewing *Bridget Jones* on the laptop. But I overestimated my ability to let them go. To let *him* go. It turns out I might want to look through them one more time. And possibly wear them. Potentially forever.

When I open the door, it's lucky I don't drop the grenade on the spot and blow up half the street. *Gosh*, he's good-looking. It's verging on ridiculous, up close. For just a second, I bask in the magnificence that is my neighbor's chiseled face. And body. The whole ensemble that is his person, really. And I forget I have something in my hand that could potentially detonate.

"Hey," he says warmly, wiping his hand on his jeans and offering to shake mine. When I don't accept, his attention drops to the grenade in my palm and he falters, then says, "Sorry, is this a bad time?"

I mean, sure. I am standing here swamped by a penguin-themed wearable blanket, clutching an apparently genuine, potentially live, unexploded device while high-powered expats in the Middle East crisis-manage from the next room . . . but I extend my free hand anyway. Niceties need not fly out the window just because we're at Code Red.

"I'm Kate," I tell him confidently. "Welcome to Braxton Street." I peer past him, beyond the apple box eucalyptus in my front yard, all the way down the street and across the suburb, until I catch a glimpse of the purplish haze of the Brindabella Mountains in the distance.

What am I looking for, exactly? His white horse?

"Saw you and your friend in the window," he says. *The shame.* "Thought I should say hello. I'm Justin."

"I'm Charlie!" My inquisitive little boy pushes around me and stands directly in front of him. "What is DTF?"

Seriously? This whole neighborly meet and greet has been a PR disaster. One I have to rectify, fast, if I'm ever to look this man in the face again.

"I have a grenade," I blurt, holding up the evidence for Justin to scrutinize more closely. As distractions go, it's a precision strike. He seems bamboozled. "But it's okay!" I rush on. "A friend of a friend knows a military weapons expert. I'm sure she's overreacting—but now Defense is intrigued, and half of Facebook is onto me, so I'm going to have to follow through and get the police involved."

It's too much information, far too soon. Justin looks both alert and alarmed, as well as romance-novel-cover hot, but I don't have the bandwidth to develop a crush right now.

Cam would have found this whole situation riotous. He'd have dined out on the story for years. *Did I tell you about the time my wife caused a global security incident with a replica grenade I picked up at a militaria emporium in Vietnam?*

"It's not mine!" I explain quickly to Justin. "Don't worry. I'm not a terrorist."

I can hardly wait for Grace to dissect this conversation later. I know she'll want to coach me on my substandard banter. *Look, Kate, the main thing is to avoid giving him the impression that this is a hostage situation. . . .*

Justin stares at me as I place my phone down on one of Cam's boxes, put it on speaker, and click on the number for the local police station. What with him looking so spectacular and eyeballing me so intently, I briefly wish I did look a bit more DTF. But there's no time for regrets. I try to pull the pencil out of my hair in case I need to write instructions, but it's stuck in a knot of curls and now I'm just yanking knotty hair instead of allowing it to tumble dreamily over my shoulders like it would if I was anyone but myself.

Focus! I have to get my story straight for the authorities.

"Hello?" I say hesitantly when someone takes my call at the station. I wave Justin in over the threshold, shut the door behind him, and follow him as he threads his way carefully past the boxes of Cam's things, like he's stepping through a minefield. To be fair, he might be. We make it into my 1940s-inspired living room—fireplace, bookshelves, old-fashioned armchairs, magazine racks bursting with notebooks and novels—and Grace couldn't be more delighted to see who the penguins have dragged in.

She ends the call with her Defense contact, beams at Justin, and readjusts her entire demeanor as I gather myself and attempt to sound more like the experienced academic fundraiser that I am in my day job. Less criminal.

"My husband was obsessed with military history," I begin, by way of setting the scene for the constable. "He died two years ago, and I haven't been able to bring myself to clear out the things in his study yet. . . ."

"Ma'am, you've phoned the Monaro Police," the officer says, interrupting story time. "Is this a prank call?"

"Oh, no," I gush. "I wish it was! Not that I'd do that, obviously. I absolutely value the work you do."

Grace shakes her head and sends me hand signals to get on with it. It's all right for her; she's not the one confessing.

"It's just, well, a funny situation, really," I say, even though there's nothing remotely amusing about it. "Essentially, my five-year-old son found a grenade in his deceased father's study and now I'm holding it in my hand."

I usually say "dead." Not "deceased." Not "late." Not "passed." Once, in a stressful social interaction, I described Cam as having "left" Charlie and me, only to have a woman trash-talk him for ditching us.

There's a moment of silence while the police officer processes my story, during which I worry that Justin might have stopped breathing.

"Would you mind holding?" the officer says, and I'm switched to smooth jazz, which seems at odds with the nature of our call.

"Grace, this is my neighbor, Justin," I explain brightly, as if we've all run into one another at the theater. "Justin, this is—"

I can't finish, because a more senior police officer comes on the line now.

"Ma'am, did you say your husband was in the military?"

"No—he was an English professor."

There's a sigh. "So not a trained weapons expert, then?"

I see what they're getting at, but Cam wasn't stupid. This whole thing is a massive misunderstanding on the part of Grace's over-zealous Defense friend.

"My husband's specialty was medieval literature," I inform the officer. The shelves behind us are chock-full of hundreds of books that can back up my claim. "But when Cam collected this stuff, it was only ever from reputable sources. I'm sure it's just a replica. We're only phoning it in because my friend put a photo on Facebook and had an urgent call from a weapons engineer in the sandpit." I feel immensely official, using that term.

It's like we're living on the set of an action flick. Privately, I'm thrilled to be providing Justin with such Class-A entertainment on his first day in the neighborhood. Now that he's over the initial shock, I can tell he's invested. His brown eyes are bright with adrenaline.

"Do you think you could possibly leave the device somewhere out of the reach of children?" the officer asks.

Mother of the year.

"We'll have the bomb squad out to you shortly, and some personnel from unexploded ordnance in Defense."

I glance out the front window, as if the squad will miraculously appear—Special Forces plunging into my azaleas from helicopters overhead—even though I'm yet to confirm my address. And that's when I notice my boss, Hugh, in his unmissable, steel-gray Audi sports coupe swinging confidently into my drive.

Bloody brilliant.

2

I pass the grenade to Justin so I can deal with Hugh. Even though I'm 99 percent certain it's nothing to worry about, I haven't handed over something so gingerly since the first time I offloaded a sleeping Charlie into Cam's arms in the maternity ward. Back then we were tentative. Protective. Terrified that we'd somehow drop him. Instead, it was Charlie and me who somehow dropped Cam.

Grace seems more ruffled by my boss's impending visit than she is about the bomb. I wish I could shovel the inevitable awkwardness out of her path, but all I can manage under pressure is an apologetic smile and a wordless promise to debrief later, as she rounds up Charlie's shoes and jacket, suddenly motivated to evacuate.

I throw open my front door just as Hugh is about to knock. He's standing there, looking like he'll never be adequately compensated for what he's had to endure in the four years since he hired me as a senior alumni giving coordinator at the university.

"Rough day?" he inquires. I could fire back the same question, except I know I am part of his problem. There's been another data breach at the university, so the internal servers are down. He's carrying the briefing papers for tomorrow's meeting in Far North Queensland, a three-hour flight from here. It's with regional CEOs and scientists about an upcoming fundraising campaign. We would have had more time to prepare if I hadn't taken today off on personal leave, but I feel so guilty traveling for work as a sole parent, I stayed here to keep things calm on the home front leading into my departure. Suffice to say that plan is not going well. And now I feel bad that Hugh has driven so far out of his way. This *juggle*!

"It's a bit of a story. . . ." I begin. It always is. And I'm starting to feel claustrophobic in all this fleece. Anyone would, surely, with an impending visit from the bomb squad, so I secure the hem of my T-shirt with one hand and whip the Snuggie over my head with the other. It catches on the pencil in my hair, so I spin to face the garden briefly while I free it with two hands, in case the T-shirt rides up, which it does.

By the time I turn back to face Hugh, shaking out the mess of curls that fall over my shoulders like I wanted them to earlier, he has made himself comfortable, leaning his six-foot-two frame against the iron veranda railing. The paperwork is pressed to his chest by casually crossed arms, while he settles in for the details. I note that his blue eyes have dulled to that deep gray, the way they always do when he's exhausted. Also noteworthy is the loosened tie, top shirt button undone, and thick, dark hair recently raked through, possibly in frustration, likely about me. I bet he's been tweaking our departmental project plan, lightening my load by taking on more of the stakeholder engagement himself. And I suspect I'm about to push my ever-patient boss beyond what has historically been a very high threshold for my wild excuses.

"Are you going to tell me this story, Kate? Or am I waiting for an interpretive dance?"

"Is that the cops?" Justin calls from the living room, not having mastered my art of breaking things delicately. Momentary surprise flashes across Hugh's face at the sound of his voice. My own expression mimics Charlie's when I catch him in the cookie jar before dinner, even though Cam is the real culprit here, surely, for dying on me, leaving loose ends.

Salt stings my eyes at the rare, uncharitable thought about my husband. *Never speak ill of the dead, Kate*. It's another impossible standard to which widows are held while they slip and falter across the unstable ice of grief, hoping it will hold.

"Are you in trouble?" Hugh asks. The muscles in his jaw have tightened, and I'm sorry I've worried him. There have been very few personal crises over the last four years that Hugh hasn't shown up for. That said, this is the first to involve the authorities.

"It's not how it sounds." I step through the doorway and out into the cold shock of crisp winter air. "It's not the cops, exactly. . . ."

I know that chin tilt. Blue-gray eyes bore into mine, wanting the truth.

"Technically, it's the bomb squad," Justin clarifies, eavesdropping through the hall.

I need to manage this unfolding situation. So I opt for the same matter-of-fact tone I use in our Monday meetings, when I update Hugh on the progress of our philanthropic pipeline over a latte and a double-shot long black in the café near our campus office.

"Look, we're just waiting on a small team of military experts from the explosive ordnance cell in Defense. Charlie found a vintage grenade in Cam's study. I'm sure it's fine, but everyone has totally lost their minds." *Would you like sugar with that, Hugh? How was your run this morning?*

"Who's that inside?" he asks, as if he's missed the central thesis of my story. We have a bomb! Have my emergencies become so predictable that the most noteworthy aspect of this is the strange man inside my house?

"That's Justin." *Why am I blushing?* "He's taking care of my explosive."

The police hadn't told me exactly what to do with it; I doubt the Queanbeyan station gets many calls from local mothers on this topic. They just said to keep it away from kids, which is obviously Lesson A in Grenade Ownership 101—a subject I appear to have very much bombed.

Hugh dumps the manila folders in my arms. The tired gray leaves his eyes almost instantly, replaced by steel blue. It's the color I notice sometimes during difficult negotiations at work, when the stakes are high and he's entirely switched on. Those eyes sweep over my face now, checking whether I'm serious, just as a patrol car flashing red and blue lights drives purposefully up our street and pulls in at a jaunty angle on my nature strip, as if to reinforce my story. Why must I always have an audience when things get so decidedly out of control? This audience, in particular.

Hugh steps toward me, and I freak out about Grace and place my hand flat across his chest, blocking his entry. He shuts his eyes for a second, as if summoning patience from a deity, then looks into my upturned face.

"Am I an accessory after the fact?" he asks, deadpan. Here is a person who's become clinically desensitized through repeated exposure to myriad crises over the course of our whole professional relationship. "This *is* a false alarm, Kate. Isn't it?"

"Oh, I'm not worried about the grenade." Cam's got this. Or he did have it, years ago.

I lean in so close I pick up the echo of this morning's cologne on Hugh's neck. "Grace is here," I admit, in a whisper.

And there's that familiar catch in his breath.

3

Constable Wentworth seems very green, both in experience and in skin tone. So green, I wonder if this is his first ever call-out, and whether he needs a bucket. I glance into the house and notice that Justin has moved the "crime scene" from the living room into the kitchen area out the back, where there's more room.

"The team from explosive ordnance is about five minutes away," the young constable advises, looking over his shoulder for backup from his partner, who is forensically scouring my weed-ridden yard. "The important thing is not to panic."

He seems to deliver this pep talk to himself. Is he even old enough to carry a gun? I'm at the age where new professionals are starting to appear impossibly youthful, but this kid seems fresh from high school.

He leads me and Hugh through the front hall and straight into the fray: two days' worth of dishes piled high in the sink, a herd of clothes horses staggering near the window, LEGO bricks just . . . *everywhere*.

"Uncle Hugh!" Charlie squeals, bounding in from the lounge and leaping into my boss's arms, almost knocking him off balance.

Grace's entry into the room, and into Hugh's presence, is frostier. What's that saying again? Never play matchmaker and dip your best friend's pen in your boss's ink? No. That's not it. Is it the other way around? I'm trying to rearrange the analogy in my head when the officer says, "Right. Where is this object?"

Justin reveals the grenade on the kitchen bench like he's a model on *Wheel of Fortune*. He's sensibly placed it in a melamine Peppa Pig bowl left over from Charlie's afternoon snack.

The constable looks into the bowl and says, "That actually looks like a grenade."

I don't know what he expected. Why would I make this up?

Hugh can't help himself. He moves closer, and now it's the three of them bent over my kitchen bench, heads together, examining the evidence like they're on a Boy Scouts Adventure.

"These items are sold to enthusiasts all the time," Hugh says while the constable takes photos. I imagine the pictures being tendered in court as evidence and wish he'd let me tidy up a bit.

"If you can just stand back, please," the officer says, pulling out a notebook. "It's not going to explode if we don't pull the pin?"

It's unclear whether that's a statement or a question. I place the pile of submissions on the distressed pine table, pull out a chair, and sink into it. The sudden injection of testosterone in my kitchen fills me with nostalgia. I used to sit there at that same bench, sipping wine, eating cheese, flicking through the weekend papers and solving the world's problems with Cam as he ad-libbed something incredible for dinner. A ghost of that memory seems superimposed on the image before me now of the constable, Hugh, and Justin, and I wonder how in hell I got from point A to B.

Stand back from Kate, everyone. Don't pull the pin. . . .

If I lost this house, I'd lose Cam all over again. His presence is cemented into the very foundation. It's painted onto the walls and sewn into the fabric of the soft furnishings. He's everywhere, in every room. Even in the tired sticky notes he used to obsessively label everything when he got sick, in a way that, years later, is helping Charlie learn to read. I trace one now, stuck to the back of the chair beside me, reinforced with tape. I flick the hot-pink paper where the edges have curled and faded in the sun. The word "chair" is written in Cam's solid handwriting, and I move my thumb across the individual letters, trying to sense the pressure of his pen on this inconsequential little note, made magical because Cam once touched it, too. It's a thing his eyes once focused on, like mine are now, as I try to align us through time and space and somehow bring him back.

"I've secured the weapon," the constable reports into his two-way radio. I'm not sure Peppa Pig is a suitable guardian for Cam's grenade, but okay. Then he looks across the room at me. "What were you doing when your son wandered out with this?"

His question plays into every insecurity I hold as a parent. *Well, Officer, my bestie and I were drinking wine on a school afternoon, translating Tinder acronyms, and perving on the Adonis to your right.*

"Grace and I were in the front room," I answer.

Do NOT lie to the police.

"We were just—looking out the window and . . ."

Don't reference a Greek god, Kate.

Justin straightens, blond hair shining under the halogen down-lights, as if he's presenting himself as Exhibit A.

"We were birdwatching," Grace says simply.

It could be true? The suburb is surrounded by bushland and backs onto Mount Jerrabomberra. I wake to birdsong every morning, do I not? I don't even get my ten thousand steps in spring, because I'm fearful of all the swooping magpies.

"It's like Hitchcock around here sometimes," I add, for emphasis.

Justin coughs, to stifle a laugh.

"And you were where, exactly?" the officer asks him.

"Directly opposite Kate's front window." *Is it my imagination, or is he flexing his muscles?* "Hitchcock Central."

Hugh chuckles, and I have an uncomfortable flashback to my crush being revealed in front of the entire class in Year Nine. The police officer writes these details in his notebook, while the four of us stay silent. From mortification, in my case.

"Note to self," Hugh says quietly, after a long pause. "Buy Kate binoculars for Christmas."

My hand finds Grace's abandoned glass of wine on the table beside me. I want to scull it, except, as irresponsible parenting goes, it's probably bad enough that I seem to be harboring some sort of bomb.

"So, your son was playing with it?" the officer queries again. He's like a dog with a bone. "While you were occupied at the window in the other room. *Birdwatching?*" He frowns at Justin.

Yes, yes. I think we've fully established I was in the grips of a galloping infatuation while my child played unsupervised with bombs.

Hugh is studying me closely. His scrutiny urges me to stand up and tip the rest of Grace's wine down the sink. Such a waste! I straighten a pile of bills and other papers on the bench, then fuss over a drying rack of laundry beside him.

"Use your time wisely and well," Mum always says. Might fold a load while we're waiting for the Defense Department . . .

But that's when it dawns on me that literally all my bras, minus the one I am wearing, are dangling off the drying rack. All of them!

Who needs to wash this many at once? And since when did I own such bland underwear? Not that I'm trying to impress anyone here. Not in that way, at least.

I must say, Justin is very collected in a crisis. He's like an off-duty Bond, lounging against my kitchen bench. Perhaps he's moved to Canberra to work at the Australian Security Intelligence Organization. The writer in me would quite like to live opposite a spy. Hugh catches me staring, leans in close, and whispers, "Give me advance warning if you're going to swoon."

The sound of his voice startles me so much that the drying rack I'm fiddling with buckles and collapses against his leg. *Ugly bras ahoy!*

I drop to the floor and snatch my unmentionables right off his beautifully polished, black R.M. Williams boots. He doesn't even flinch. And that's when I decide that the five of us—me, Charlie, Hugh, Grace, and Justin—are going to evacuate ourselves in the absence of any proper leadership from the establishment.

"We'll wait outside, if that's okay," I announce. "It's safer."

Charlie scoops up some LEGO bricks and I push him in the direction of the front door while I grab the pinboard off the kitchen wall and follow the others out into my front garden. The constable's partner keeps an eagle eye on us, like we're a newly minted terrorist cell.

If there are two things I couldn't stand to lose if the house exploded—which is not a risk I'd seriously contemplated until this evening—it's Cam's notes and our map of the world on this pinboard. He'd left me in bed one rainy Sunday afternoon more than a decade ago and ducked to the shops, only to delight me later with an informal presentation on *Kate & Cam's Excellent Adventure.*

"Red thumb tacks for everywhere we've been," he'd said, pointing out cities with a drumstick from his nearby kit. "The obligatory Contiki tour through Europe—which we should redo, Katie, and not be permanently hungover this time. Youth is wasted on the young."

"Twenty-four is still young," I argued.

"There will be an opportunity for comments at the end," he said before tapping the drumstick on New Zealand, Thailand, Tasmania, and the Great Ocean Road, along which we'd camped and hiked and fallen irreversibly in love, that first summer after we met at Melbourne Uni.

"Now, for the audience participation section," he announced. "I need a volunteer to stick green thumb tacks on all the places we want to go."

I crawled to the end of the bed and knelt in front of the map, while he dished out thumb tacks and I pinned them on New York City, Prince Edward Island, and Florence. Technically we'd already spent a morning in Florence, but I wanted a week. Then I took another one and pinned it on Norway.

"I thought this might happen," Cam said, grinning, and he put the thumb tacks down and produced a sheet of gold and silver stars. "That's for the aurora borealis."

Always number one on our bucket list.

Still top of mine.

4

I surface from the memory and crash back into my domestic security incident, flushed with something that feels like homesickness but can't be. Justin is inspecting the half-constructed LEGO set with Charlie. Grace is giving her details to Constable Wentworth's partner, with Charlie's backpack in hand. Hugh notices me blink back tears and pull myself together again. That's the problem with grief. It's not packed tidily in a box that you can bring out in appropriate, private moments and sort through. It's threaded inconveniently through everything.

"What've we got here?" Justin asks Charlie, with genuine interest.

"It's the Minecraft Jungle Abomination," Charlie explains eagerly. "And see, this is the articulated plant and the enchanted creeper."

"This is an Iron Golem, right?" Justin picks up some kind of creature. *What is he? The Minecraft whisperer?*

Grace walks over and nudges me, nodding at the two of them. I know exactly what she's thinking. Charlie doesn't usually warm to strangers this fast. Ever since his dad died, he's been inherently wary of any strange men around me. I've been wary of that myself.

But thinking about Cam just now, and our adventure list, I sense the distant rumblings of a rather unwelcome epiphany. Ours was always an adventure list for two. Not one. Have I really lost all interest in living the big life we imagined together now that he's gone? Is the plan just to go to work and drag Charlie through every school week, pining for Cam, on rinse and repeat until we get from kindergarten to Year Twelve? And then what? Charlie leaves too? Who will I be without both of them?

It's only now, standing on my front lawn, adventure chart lit up by a disco of police lights, that something profound strikes me.

All the green pins were mine.

Cam grew up in the UK. His parents are in their eighties now and live in a town called Wallingford, between Oxford and Reading. They traveled a lot together when Cam was a kid. In our family, it was only Dad who traveled, until distant shores lured him away from Mum and me permanently. So that rainy Sunday when Cam had held out a handful of green pins, it felt like he was offering me the world.

The sight of an attractive new man—or any man—talking Minecraft with our son while I stand here having a midlife identity crisis brings on heart palpitations. I don't know what I'm doing. Don't know what I *want*. Don't even know who I *am* anymore, minus Cam.

"The estate agent promised me this was a nice, quiet street," Justin says conversationally, almost as if he is not talking to a rudderless woman with six bras and a pinboard in her hands and a bomb in her kitchen. He gives me a teasing nudge, and the brief touch of his skin on mine makes me jump. My physical response to Justin sets off a counterreaction in Hugh, which freaks me out in turn, until we're all so skittish I wonder if we're hooked up to the same invisible circuit.

The military team arrives and several uniformed officers stride past us and enter my house. As we step farther out of the way to facilitate their delicate weapon-seizure operation, I stuff the bras behind a potted magnolia and Grace glares at me for being weird in front of men.

"What should we do with Charlie now?" Hugh asks. He's the kind of hyper-responsible man you can throw all your underwear at during a weapons crisis and he won't even notice.

"I was trying to get him out of here just before you arrived." I *am* a responsible parent, despite this evening's solid attempt to disprove that.

"You didn't think to remove yourself at the same time?"

I can tell he's frustrated. But then so am I. This entire situation and the personal epiphany it's provoked are snowballing in ways he couldn't begin to imagine.

"I had every faith in my husband."

I straighten to my full five-foot-seven and challenge him to an argument he can't win. Battling with my logic would equate to accusing Cam of putting his family in danger, and Hugh would never do that. The two of them were tight. I'd introduced them at one of our work barbecues early on, after which I used to joke about being the third wheel in their bromance.

The real answer to his question about why I didn't think to remove myself from danger is something I dare not admit aloud. Since Cam died, I've secretly walked a dangerous tightrope. I know I need to stay alive—for Charlie. But if an accident befell me, well . . .

Hugh looks from me to Justin, and it occurs to me I've forgotten my manners.

"Justin, this is my long-suffering boss, Hugh Lancaster. Justin is my, er . . ." *Crush? Hero?* "Neighbor."

THE LAST LOVE NOTE

"Your savior, did you say?" Hugh responds, a picture of innocence. The man is starting to get on my last nerve.

"Expect a lot of after-hours entertainment," Grace warns Justin, somewhat redundantly. Is anyone here on my side? The idea of Justin becoming tangled in my after-hours anything sends a bolt of heat straight to my face and, as if to draw unwanted attention to it, my hand shoots to my cheek in a failed mission to cool the area.

They all notice it. I frown at Grace and Hugh and wonder again why my matchmaking tanked, when they're so clearly on the same wavelength.

"Kate and I have only just met," Justin explains, sweeping in to rescue the conversation. "Just landed here today actually, from Adelaide. Can report the festival state has nothing on Braxton Street."

Grace finds this vastly entertaining, and Justin lights up at her feedback.

"What brings you here?" I ask, keen to steer us off the topic of my drama.

"Twelve-month gig in Finance," he says. "I'm an actuary."

A public-sector actuary? I can virtually hear the cogs in Grace's brain rapidly reworking her policies on both public servants and math.

"Imagined we'd start off with a neighborly drink, Kate," he says. "But this whole Tomb-Raider-SWAT-team experience is . . . equally captivating."

I laugh aloud, properly, for the first time in ages. His brown eyes sparkle, and I warm to him even more.

"She has a knack for first impressions," Hugh observes, almost under his breath. I silently implore him not to excavate that deeply into our shared history, and certainly not to do it publicly, in front of a stranger I have to live opposite.

"So you're just here for the career stuff?" Grace quizzes him. "Tell us you're not a trailing spouse with a wife or girlfriend in the area?"

Her unveiled motivation is hair-raising.

Justin grins and looks at me, when he should be looking at her. "Not yet," he says.

Lord!

I'm still analyzing his comment when Constable Wentworth appears and says, "Right, which one of you is Kate's husband?" He has a clipboard and pen poised to record official details.

It's one of those unexpected moments when I'm sideswiped. Grace stops the playful flirting and looks crushed for me as the officer's question cuts deep. Emotion I've buried, repeatedly, gushes to the surface again, white hot.

Justin steps back as if to distance himself and Hugh steps forward, beside me, his arm briefly touching mine. No physical jolts at *his* touch. Just a much-needed sense of understanding and solidarity.

"Did the dispatcher not tell you?" I ask, clearing the emotion from my throat. "My husband died."

It's a line I've delivered countless times, but it still sounds like fiction escaping my mouth. I've become good at disguising the grief in my voice. Good at managing other people's discomfort when they ask about my partner or query what Cameron does for a living. Once, on a work trip in Sydney, when an Uber driver asked about my husband, I pretended he was still alive.

"He's an English professor," I'd said, luxuriating in the present tense. "And a great dad. He loves to cook. He makes this incredible Thai chicken dish. . . ."

"The grenade is no doubt a defused battlefield souvenir," Hugh is saying beside me. "Cameron was careful. He would have made sure it passed every regulation."

He can't have seen the tears that have sprung into my eyes during his defense, and I know he doesn't need to. The earlier teasing is over now and we're a united front. Hugh tunes in to my emotions like he's conducting a symphony. The nuanced tones. The look on my face. Even the way something takes my breath away. I swear he knows what I'm about to feel before I do. Like right now, when I really don't want to explain Cam's death to a stranger for the millionth time.

"Thanks for calling this one in," one of the military members says, while his colleague carries the grenade down my front steps.

"We've examined it," the officer says as she walks past with the weapon in hand. "You're right, it's not live, but in the wrong hands it could provoke a serious terrorist scare. They'll take it up to a base near Sydney for safe destruction. I'm sorry about your husband."

"So am I," Justin says, the thrill from our twilight weapons raid drained right out of him. "Kate, I'm really sorry."

I don't want the new guy pitying me. I don't want anyone doing that. I just wish this conversation would change direction by magic.

"You going to stand around playing CSI all night or read that paperwork?" Hugh asks on cue. "Can't wing this one, Kate. You're leading the presentation."

Work. A safe topic.

"You know I'm on top of this," I say, even though right now I most certainly am not on top of it. Not any of it. He'd be alarmed if he knew how out of control I really feel—about everything.

"Thanks for coming," I say, exhausted. It's a general thank-you to all assembled. *Thanks for coming to my show.*

"Come on, Charlie. Let's pack your bag for your sleepover at Nanna's!" Grace says, taking his hand. This is the part where he normally gets clingy. But as he turns to go with Grace, he shoots

Justin a massive smile. Grace, in turn, shoots me a knowing look that's meant to be private, but that the entire viewing public can't possibly misinterpret.

"Work trip," I explain to Justin. "Shall we rain-check that welcome drink for when I get back?"

He taps me playfully on the arm. "You can tell me all about your passion for ornithology."

Hugh snorts.

I have no words.

Then Justin glances deliberately at Hugh before he leans forward, puts a hand confidently on my waist, and brushes my cheek with a kiss. I'm getting intoxicating notes of hard physical labor and Giorgio Armani, a scent that lingers even after he breaks away and walks across the road to his house, carrying my attention with him.

"See you in the morning, then," Hugh says beside me.

When I don't respond, he snaps his fingers in front of my eyes and says, "Hey, Lara Croft!"

I return to him with a mental thud. "Paperwork." *Boring.* "Got it."

I really need this mini holiday from All The Things. All the things except work, of course. And Hugh, who comes with that territory. And who, now that I finally look at him, is staring at me as if I've just handed Justin a rose on *The Bachelorette*.

5

At four in the morning, I make an executive decision to give up on sleep altogether. I was still taking notes on the briefing papers at two, and now the whole project is making me nervous. It's an ambitious fundraising campaign to attract donors for scholarships in the university's climate change research programs. My idea. A cinematic film showcasing the achievements of our alumni scientists, interwoven with words by the university's preeminent writers and poets, set to a piece of music composed by a grad student in the music school after the summer bushfires a few years ago. I want to send donors the message that we're in this together. Arts. Science. All of us. And the university is bigger than the sum of its parts.

Hugh thought the idea was beautiful. He backed me a hundred percent. Sank a large chunk of our fundraising budget into this one campaign. And now his belief in me is giving me the heebie-jeebies.

"It's a feel-good story," I'd argued late one Friday afternoon after the rest of our team had bolted to happy hour at a local bar. "But if we can't demonstrate a direct boost to donations, I'm worried it will be your head that rolls."

"You're shaping a bang-for-buck appeal that aligns with the university's strategic objectives. You've brought several faculties into the spotlight on a global water-cooler topic. Give them cold, hard science and pull at their humanity. What's not to love, Kate?"

But now, in the hours before dawn, it all seems too complicated. After I toss and turn about work for a while, I can't move on from the idea that I've had one of Cam's treasured possessions seized from the house for destruction. I imagine it being blown to smithereens, over and over. Symbolic of our tragedy.

I roll over in bed again and, as if to cheer itself up a bit, my mind ambles across the road. I tell myself it's not disrespecting Cam's memory to invent an imaginary little bedtime story involving my new neighbor and the fascination he develops in me, not in spite of my bumbling single-mother-widowhood but because of it. Yes. I make him that sort of man. Attracted to the flaws. The history. The stretch marks and scars plastered on my body and soul. I almost drift off in a kaleidoscope of muscles and king-size beds and explosives and mind-boggling actuarial math. In my fantasy, Justin doesn't leave when I need him most. Not like Cam.

Don't think that!

I sit up, slammed by guilt. Cam died against his will. What sort of person lies here, grief-stricken over her beautiful husband, fantasizing about another man falling helplessly for her stretch marks and history and flaws? Worse, a man who isn't some distant Hollywood heartthrob like usual but the very accessible hero next door.

Now I'm wide awake again, and another disturbing thought rushes in: Hugh will sack me if I fall asleep in this meeting. Well, he won't actually sack me. I've done worse than fall asleep at work. The man is a saint! But the thought of letting him down again undoes all of Fantasy Justin's work in soothing my troubled mind.

Eventually I get up, shower, and throw last-minute toiletries into the oversize tote I take on flying interstate visits. This should be a relatively straightforward, if hectic, trip. The first of several mad dashes to meet with the cast of thousands now involved in the project. Today it's Far North Queensland to see a bunch of interested company directors, then various university-affiliated environmental scientists who can strut our stuff and attract millions in financial support.

I sit on the window seat in my front room, blanket around my knees, sipping tea, killing time, and wondering how I got stuck here, in the wrong life.

I'm meant to be a writer. *Am one*, at heart. But cannot possibly live the life of one—not even part-time. The way the cards have fallen, I can only grasp for words in stolen moments. Pull them onto pages in fits and starts around the very real challenge of keeping a roof over Charlie's head until he's old enough to do that himself.

With Cam, I always had the space to write. He ensured that. Even then, though, I clung to my day job, scared of really putting my work out there. Terrified of rejection. I even struggled to show Cam my work. An English professor, of course, so professionally equipped to judge it.

"Why do you write?" he'd asked me once. I'd been pushing words around the pages of a short story for weeks and was staring down the last few hours until the deadline to enter it in a literary award. I'd shown him my work mid–crisis of confidence, needing to hear it was good enough.

We'd had a blazing row.

"I'm not one of your students!" I'd shouted.

But he'd defended his question. "Seriously. I'm asking you why you write. What drives you?"

"Cam! I want to know what you *think*," I'd cut back. "About *this* piece."

His face was racked with emotion. Love, mainly. Fear of hurting me. And professional integrity. "I think it's good," he'd said quietly. "But Kate, I don't think you've found your place yet."

His feedback struck a nerve. I'd been wanting to write serious literary fiction since Cam and I first met as undergrads. But trying to force beautiful words into serious stories and onto pages *just so* was sucking all the joy out of the process.

I drain my cup of tea and hug the blanket. This is why I don't do "silence." Other mums crave these rare moments alone in the quiet when nobody's demanding anything. But with Charlie at Mum's twenty minutes away, the quiet just scares me. What if my grief is worse than I think? Maybe I'm distracted on purpose, and I've subconsciously engineered a frantic, overcommitted, hectic whirl so I can always put "busy" center stage, and grief can only ever hover in the wings.

It's a workday. Keep it together.

I check the time and get up and rinse the mug. I've determined that it's cheaper to pay for two days of long-stay parking at the airport than to get a cab or an Uber from here, and I find it less stressful than waiting around for people who might never come. I've got enough to worry about with my flying phobia.

Locking up, I toss my bag in the passenger seat of my trusty red Mini. My previous car had given up the ghost one day in that problem-plagued six months after Cam had died. I'd over-whelmed myself on the car sales websites that evening, wishing he was around to help me decide. "Just give me a sign, Cam," I'd pleaded. The next morning, I'd driven to the local shops and swung into a park beside an impeccable late-model red Mini

Cooper with a for-sale sign on the dash, low mileage, and a price tag under ten grand.

The windshield is iced over now, but I'll get the heater going and scrape it with a credit card. I push the start button and . . . nothing. I turn the key manually. The engine chokes, like it's in the last wheezes of the death rattle—a sound I wish I didn't have the experience to recognize.

My heart pounds as I check the time. It's too late to call a spontaneous ride and make it to the airport in time. That's the problem living in a place where sprawling suburbs weave through the bush and farmland. You can't just stand on a street corner and hail a cab.

I have the phone in my hand, ready to break the career-limiting news to Hugh that I'm not going to make the flight, followed by unpalatable groveling and another empty promise to be more on my game in the future, when a light flicks on out the front of Justin's place.

Hmm. Have I become the kind of woman who'd pass a virtual stranger her grenade and then beg for a second, totally unrealistic favor in the space of eleven hours?

Rhetorical question.

A message pops up on my phone. *"Nearly here?"* It's accompanied by a photo of a long black on a glass table in the airport lounge. My blood sugar plummets.

I grab my bag from the seat, close the door, lock the car, and march across my front lawn, across the road, over Justin's frost-covered nature strip and up to his doorstep. I can't overthink this. I just knock and silently resolve to become a far less clingy neighbor upon my return from this trip. A more reliable employee, too. Just better, in several key aspects.

Justin's house is shaped like a bunker. A rendered, gray box of a place that I've always wanted to snoop through. After a minute or so, I hear the bolt unlock and the door creaks open. Soft light spills out from the entryway and Justin stands there and yawns, messy blond hair, smooth skin illuminated like one of Michelangelo's sculpted angels—in a pair of black boxers and nothing else, blinking his warm, caramel eyes.

Not already awake, then. *My bad.*

It's also my bad that there's a significant delay in explaining the purpose of our predawn catch-up, while my eyes adjust to his gloriousness. It's been an incredibly long time since I've been this close to a man wearing so few clothes. Particularly one with a physique like an Olympian. I was flustered enough to begin with, what with the broken-down car and the screaming travel deadline, and now I barely know where to look.

He has no such trouble himself, eyeing me, standing expectantly on his doorstep, overnight bag in hand, as if I'm about to move in. "Morning, Kate," he drawls in the low and gravelly voice of the rudely awoken. "Something else you want defused?"

I blush red. Again. "Actually, there *is* a small logistical problem—"

"It's the battery," he diagnoses, before I can continue. "Heard the engine failing to turn over from bed."

I imagine him, starfished on the mattress in those boxers, listening to my ailing vehicle. *Stop it!* There's no time to call for roadside assistance. No time for any conceivable option beyond begging this man for help. "Hugh is in the airport lounge," I tell him. "He's probably ordering me a latte as we speak." I'm so churned up now, the thought of dairy makes me nauseated. "Of course, he sensibly lives in a high-rise apartment just minutes away from literally everything—"

"Does he?" Justin pulls me across the threshold into his bunker out of the cold. "And miss the charms of suburban life?"

I almost lunge at him. "I'm so sorry to be banging on your door. The front light came on—"

"It's a sensor."

"You must be exhausted from moving in yesterday." I gesture at the moving boxes piled high on polished floorboards all around us. It's like he's hauled it all in and run out of steam to unpack anything. Or maybe he ran out of time, given last night's furor. "Justin, I am an incredibly desperate woman!"

He draws his mouth into a slow smile. "Are you?"

There isn't a minute to spare. We cannot stand here, the only two people awake in the southern hemisphere—apart from Hugh and hopefully our pilot—exchanging flirty innuendo about my apparent level of desperation. This is an emergency. The second emergency, in fact, of our brief and dramatic acquaintance.

"Why don't I give you a lift?" he suggests.

I could kiss him. Of course, now I'm picturing exactly that, and exhibiting the social graces of my inner bookish teenager.

"Give me two minutes," Justin says. "Pull up a box. Make yourself at home."

6

Justin saunters down a long corridor and my trance is broken only after he's completely out of sight. I scrabble for my phone, bash out a quick message to Hugh: *"Car trouble. Getting a lift."* Then try to distract myself admiring the warm neutrals of Justin's bachelor pad. Lined up along the gallery-styled corridor are some large, framed prints underneath where they'll presumably be hung. They're incredible landscape photographs—driftwood on the beach at sunrise, a forest waterfall in long exposure, an old tin hut in the outback with leading lines of cracked red soil. The box beside me is labeled *camera equipment* and wrapped in tape marking it as fragile.

Is he a photographer, too? Oh, I hope so. I've graduated from my phone camera to a proper one, and I'm still at the stage of being discombobulated by the exposure triangle. Perhaps he'll tutor me.

Last night's flannel shirt is lying where it was tossed on top of a box of dumbbells. I pick it up, just for a second, and turn the fabric over in my hands. It's reminiscent of two days ago, when I'd spent three hours sitting on the floor of my bedroom picking up every one of Cam's shirts in turn. I pored over each one, searching for even a hint of Cam's scent, hugged it, thanked it for its service, and even *then* I couldn't let go.

Dots on my phone screen indicate Hugh is typing something back. Then they stop. Then start again. His dithering is making me nervous, and I stick the phone on silent and toss it into my handbag, because I'm a rebel. Or a coward.

When Justin returns, he's back in his fabled ripped jeans, boots, and a fresh white T-shirt under a well-worn brown leather jacket.

"Wow," I gush, before I can stop myself. My situation is not helped by the fact that I'm still holding his shirt, like some teenage fangirl at a concert. This is worse than the birdwatching debacle. *What did you do next?* Grace will ask. *Get him to autograph your boobs?*

"The leather is just . . ." I stumble on, deflecting my enthusiasm toward the garment instead of the man who is modeling it. My fingers get in on the ruse and reach out to massage the sleeve of the jacket while I examine the stitching closely, like a Florentine leather connoisseur who isn't very late for a flight.

Justin smiles kindly, a cool kid making amends in one simple transaction for all the attention I didn't receive from Out-of-My-Leaguers in high school. The internal access to the garage is blocked off with furniture, so we head back outside, where he locks the house and then clicks a button for the garage door. I check the time on my watch and calculate that we'll just make it. And then I stand there, gaping.

"It's a motorcycle," I inform him.

He takes the tote and my phone and keys out of my hands and stores them away in the saddlebag.

"This is not just a motorcycle, Kate. It's an Indian."

I don't know what that is. I just know I'm not getting on it. Granted, the matte black and polished chrome complements the whole late-'90s Jon Bon Jovi experience he's offering, but this is just not for me.

"But you're an actuary," I argue, as if his sensible career choice somehow precludes him from the bad-boy archetype.

"And you're late." He produces a second leather jacket from the trunk and holds it up while I thread my arms into it.

As I zip up the front, I can't help wondering who wore it last. Some Hells Angel in figure-hugging, black leather pants instead of the classic black business skirt and tailored white shirt I'm wearing. At least my knee-high boots are vaguely protective, I guess. I figured they'd keep me warm until we got to Cairns, and then I could swap shoes and be good to go for the presentation.

Justin tosses me a heavy black helmet. "Nice catch," he says.

"Seven years of basketball," I hear myself answer inanely, feet still planted firmly on the concrete floor of his garage while my plane takes off and my boss fires and replaces me and I lose the house.

He swings a leg over the seat and pats the space behind him. I'm meant to climb onto it, I realize, but I've never hoisted myself onto a motorcycle before. Is it just like a horse? Although, what am I saying? I couldn't easily mount a horse in this skirt either. He hits the keyless ignition and the engine roars to life, scaring the daylights out of me and probably waking half the street.

"Come on!" he yells over the top of it. "You're late for Hugh."

He's found my kryptonite. I approach and place one hand tentatively on Justin's shoulder, pull my skirt up with the other, and throw my right leg inelegantly over the seat. The skirt is affronted. It threatens to split at the seams but opts instead for riding way up my legs, just as he reaches back, grabs my hands, brings them around his waist, and slides me forward on the leather saddle.

Right. Michelangelo's angel is now clamped between my thighs. Pressed up against him, I'm sure I'm leaving nothing to the imagination, but he has exorcized my free will and I can't move to adjust things.

"Is this outfit even legal?" I yell while I work out the helmet. Shouldn't I be wearing more protective gear?

He glances over his shoulder at my knee-high boot, bare leg, and skirt hitched to the rafters, kicks the stand, and yells, "It shouldn't be."

I'm still reeling from the compliment as he sweeps us out of the driveway, down our street, past the village center, and onto Lanyon Drive, glimpses of snowcapped mountains reinforcing how chilly it is as first light brightens the sky. We rush past a winter fantasyland of frost-covered farms, fog lifting in patches into a lightening blue sky, and my heart rate bolts. My thighs clench tightly around his hips with surprising force for a set of muscles that haven't seen the inside of a gym in four years. When we reach the highway and I cling tighter around his waist, he opens the throttle and I know he's showing off now.

Wait! I am a sole parent. I shouldn't be taking such risks! Getting on a motorcycle with a virtual stranger, without proper protective gear? But it's too late now. Temperature below freezing, giddy smile frozen to my face, I let out a couple of loud whoops, which only encourages him to floor it.

I feel more alive right now than I've felt in *years*. Maybe it's because, on the back of this bike, I feel closer to death than I ever have before. A fraction of a second of lost concentration is all that lies between Cam and me. Such a fine line. Infinitesimal.

Justin roars through the early-morning traffic, weaving in and out of cars. Cold air slices through me until I'm numb, and when we finally cruise past the airport hotel and into the passenger drop-off loop, I'm disappointed the ride is over. I can see Hugh standing at the curb in his suit, briefcase placed beside him on the pavement, checking his watch. *What happened to the Qantas Club?*

Justin sees Hugh, too. I know this because he revs the engine unnecessarily as we pull in right beside where Hugh is standing. Hugh doesn't even register it's me until I take off the helmet and shake my tangled curls loose with a flourish of thoroughly gratuitous drama, to the tune of 1,000 revs per minute and some perfectly timed lighting from the sunrise.

By the time he clocks who I am, his gaze has helped itself to an unprecedented and unprofessional roam through my windswept hair, all the way down to my leather boots and up my thigh again, where it finally stalls.

Justin swings the front wheel of the bike into the curb to steady it and leans it onto the kickstand. He takes my helmet and extends his hand as if I'm Daphne Bridgerton alighting from a horse-drawn carriage at a nineteenth-century ball. As I prepare to dismount, I realize those Regency women had longer and more voluminous skirts and didn't inadvertently flash everyone behind them in the drop-off queue like I do as I swing my leg over the back of the enormous bike, stumble backward over the gutter in a poorly executed Fosbury Flop high jump, and tumble into the waiting arms of my exceedingly unimpressed boss.

Hugh steadies me, sighs heavily, glares at Justin over my head, props me onto my own two, very uncoordinated feet, and bends down so we're at eye level. "Are you drunk, Kate?"

The nerve!

"Excuse me, I haven't had more than half a glass of anything in weeks. You saw me tip Grace's glass down the sink last night in front of you."

Alcohol doesn't mix with grief, I've found, so I've been largely avoiding it. And that thought brings me up sharp. For twenty or so liberating minutes, I'd actually forgotten that I am heartbroken. No, it's worse than that. You're heartbroken after a breakup. You can grieve a breakup, too, and grieve someone's absence from your life, but when someone dies, it's soul-deep. An impossible-to-grasp, endless absence not just from you, but from the entire world. You won't run into them by accident in the supermarket. You can't stalk them on social media. Your best friend won't furnish you with gossip about their next steps. There's just nothing. Forever.

Justin hands me my bag, pulling me from my thoughts. I step back and admire the bike properly now. On the back of it, for the very first time since the night Cam died, there'd been a sliver of time free from obsessing over the sheer awfulness of it all. Obsessing over Cam. And how much I miss and adore him and can barely gasp for air sometimes in his absence. What a precious escape this ride was.

Reality chases the dream. I'm definitely thinking about Cam now and feeling really bad about how effortlessly sexy I imagined myself to be just then, perched behind Justin, all leather and legs and Biker Chick Energy . . . before misjudging the dismount, obviously, annoying Hugh and snapping straight back into the real world.

I start to unzip the leather jacket, but Justin grabs my hand and pauses the action at my chest.

"Nobody's going to need that before you get back," he explains, still holding on to my hand. "Keep it. You look hot."

I glance at Hugh. If I'm scouting for a second opinion, I'm not going to get it.

When I pull out my phone, Justin lifts it straight out of my hand and inputs what I assume is his number, whether I want it or not. Hugh and I watch silently as he saves the contact, hands it back, and says, "I put it on speed dial." This is a man who has clearly experienced very little social rejection. He must have godlike status in the largely introverted actuarial world.

"We board in ten minutes," Hugh says, his tone brisk. I toss the strap of my tote over my shoulder and mumble an inadequate thank-you to Justin, launching myself at him for a lightning-fast hug.

He hugs me back so tight I'm breathless. Then he readjusts the strap of my bag, which is now all caught up in the zipper of his jacket somehow. Hugh sighs as I peel myself off my neighbor, and a police officer wanders over and says, "Move on, please." This is strictly a drop-off area, and not a place for awkward and premature public displays of affection, regardless of how cinematic this scene looks in my imagination. There's always been a lot of *Anne of Green Gables* about me, imagination-wise.

"Two police incidents since we met," Justin observes, swinging his leg over the bike again and kicking the stand. "You'll get me in trouble, Kate."

He makes an exit as dramatic as our entrance and I stand on the pavement, staring after him and trying to turn off my inner Anne. Of course, she's well on her way and by the time I catch up with Hugh, who's had it with the whole performance, he's removing his belt for his second pass through security this morning. He hands me a tray for my phone and laptop and another for the jacket and my bag, which is bulging with the latest Elin Hilderbrand novel and one of Emily Henry's gems. I have a personal rule never to run out of book chapters in the air, without a backup.

"Buy yourself a Kindle," Hugh mutters. I would mount a defense of physical books, but the security guard is eyeing my generous bounty and sighs, very deeply, as though he hates people. Hugh picks up one of the novels and I grab the rest, only to be beckoned over for a random explosives check, which doesn't seem random in the slightest, because I'm stopped for it every time.

"No gunpowder residue from last night," Hugh notes, as I'm released, clean, and we stride toward the gate. "That would have been interesting."

"That whole thing was a complete overreaction," I remind him. Secretly I'm relieved, because I hadn't even thought about the grenade and don't know how I would have explained it to the police if Charlie had smuggled it into my bag or something, instead of showing me.

"This is an announcement for passengers Lancaster and Whittaker, on flight QF1456 to Brisbane. Please proceed to Gate eleven, as your aircraft is preparing for departure."

We are the last two to board the plane. Hugh is definitely a "first to board" type of person. We jostle ourselves down the aisle and my bag won't squash into the overhead locker, because it's already full with the bags of the punctual people.

Hugh watches my struggle, until he can stand it no longer. He reaches over my head and gives it—and by extension, me—a hearty shove. We're put in our place, my bag and I, and he shuts the locker door, stands back, and offers me the window seat, which I slide into.

"How long is this flight?" I ask. I can't get out of here fast enough.

"An hour and forty minutes to Brisbane and about two and a half hours to Cairns after that," he replies as he shuffles in next to me. He might as well be describing his life sentence.

"I got to the airport as fast as I could," I explain. "I'm sorry. I didn't get a minute's sleep last night."

He glances at the whole helmet-hair-meets-bed-hair situation, swallows, and says, "Really?"

"Oh, God," I say, so loudly the white-haired woman in front of me turns to her husband and tut-tuts. I grab Hugh's arm with both hands and he flinches. "Forgot the Valium!"

This is dire.

I've tried counseling and hypnosis and the Fear of Flying course the airport runs, but nothing works. Valium takes the edge off, though, so I don't spend the entire time floundering in an anxiety attack.

I can't help that this is how I was raised. Of course, my parents didn't intentionally give me a phobia, but I'm from a family of pioneer aviators. Two of my great-uncles died in plane crashes. One of their planes simply broke apart mid-flight in the 1930s. It's the stuff of family legend.

"Planes don't break in half in midair these days, Kate," Hugh says, demonstrating how many times he's been the audience of one for my "unresourceful runway self-talk script," as the psychologist calls it. Normally I'm way less freaked out about this than I am right now, because normally I'm way more medicated. I couldn't grip Hugh's arm any tighter if I was having a transition-stage contraction and it was too late for the epidural.

Don't picture Charlie's birth! Delivery suite memories lead to emotionally perilous memories of Cam. I can picture his face so clearly now that it's like he is right here, up close, forehead pressed to mine, our tiny baby in his arms, whispering, "Thank you, sweetheart. You're amazing."

Stop it.

"It'll be okay," Hugh says quietly, extracting each of my fingers from the sleeve of his now creased white shirt and bringing the armrest down gently between us. He's probably wishing it was something more substantial. Cone of silence. Force field.

I turn away from him and stare out the window, desperately seeking composure. The captain announces that the doors are armed and instructs the crew to cross-check and be seated for take-off. I need a happy place. Stat.

Wish I was back on that bike.

7

As the plane lifts into the air, my body starts to shake. The sight of the tarmac falling away makes the anxiety even worse. So, as Lake Burley Griffin and Mount Majura shrink out of sight in our wake, I go to plan B: staring at the headrest in front of me and doing the breathing exercises the psych taught me, which always work so well in her office when I'm not technically anxious at all.

Staring at the headrest, however, only draws my attention to the card in the seat pocket containing safety instructions in the event of a crash. I shove it behind the in-flight magazine and the sick bag, which I'm going to need in a minute because I'm close to hyperventilating.

I look at Hugh. He's plan C, and a picture of ease, leaning back against his headrest, eyes closed, unflappable. *How does he do it?* He's habitually in command.

This is so different from when I used to travel with Cam. I was never anxious then. If anything, I was the risk-taker. The one missing the last bus at some remote beach just for the perfect sunset photo, even if we had to walk miles back to the hotel in the dark. I was always angling for mystery flights and spontaneous mini breaks and off-grid adventures.

We had Christmas Day in Paris once as students. It was right at the end of our trip, and we'd drained our budget and couldn't afford a proper Christmas lunch in a café. So we spent the entire day walking the streets with nothing but a baguette and a wheel of Brie between us. We sat on the Pont des Arts, freezing our butts off while we invented stories about the couples who locked padlocks on the bridge.

"We didn't have to come all this way, you know," Cam had said. "You make a trip to the local supermarket fun. But, Katie, I'm seriously cold. Do you want to go to church?"

"*Pardon?*" I'd replied in a bad French accent. Had he found religion?

"*Voudriez-vous aller à l'église?*" he'd stumbled through, using an English–French translation book, pre-smartphones. "*C'est gratuity.*"

"Free?"

"And warm," he argued.

We spent the next three hours sitting on a wooden pew, huddled over an electric bar heater in some understated, crumbling little chapel, losing track of time, just talking, until we were finally thrown out by the nuns, who apparently had more of a social life than we could afford. It was never flashy with Cam. It never needed to be. Once he'd swept me into his orbit, I'd barely notice we were in the sky.

But it's not Cam beside me now. It's Hugh. And he's shut down, so I'm completely lost. Not for the first time, I wish things with Hugh were more like they used to be. Something big went down between Cam and Hugh, near the end. Neither would ever speak about it, no matter how much I begged them to let me in. All I know is, after it happened, the landscape of our friendship shifted.

I watched the walls go up between the two of them and felt the tremor of a new fault line beneath Hugh and me. It never stopped him from being supportive, but it's hard to be totally at ease with a person who holds a secret my husband took to the grave.

The plane's captain introduces herself over the intercom and I pay attention like I'm her star student. She maintains that she's looking forward to flying us to Brisbane this morning and I marvel at the fact that she chooses to put herself thirty thousand feet above the earth as a job.

"She sounds about sixteen," I whisper.

Hugh still has his eyes shut, but his mouth twitches.

"We're expecting a few little bumps from some upcoming weather," the woman says.

I'd googled the interstate weather warnings this morning and can only assume she is drastically underplaying the situation. "I'll keep the seatbelt sign illuminated until—"

Nothing. Silence.

"Until what?" I ask nobody in particular. The pilot's introduction is suspended and the interior lighting flicks off and back on. I have visions of her getting distracted by something unforeseen and alarming on the weather radar, instruments going haywire. Or by something worse. Bird strike. UFO.

"Get some sleep, Kate," Hugh says wearily, having opened his eyes and apparently decided I am overthinking. "You look exhausted."

I look at him as if he hasn't been listening. "I told you, Hugh, I was—"

"Up all night. Yes, I know."

"I'm totally worn out," I say. But instead of thanking me for my dedication, he sighs, pulls out a folder of climate change project summaries he's already read, and flicks through it—pointlessly, as far as I can tell. Maybe I should follow his example. I dig into my laptop bag and pull out my notes, but my eyes swim on the page. I'm basically pretending to read, like I'm three, Hugh is my overbearing older brother, and I'm playing copycat.

"You did do a bit of work last night, then," he says, glancing at my notes on the page.

"A *bit* of work?" I flick through pages and pages of carefully considered background notes on the attendees. "This took hours! What did you think I was doing all night?"

He looks chastised. "Oh, I don't know. Binging Netflix? Astrophotography tutorials on YouTube?"

He knows about the astrophotography? I thought I'd kept that obsession to myself.

"I'm kind of offended you think I'd mess around with that stuff instead of—"

"Maybe you gave Mad Max a private housewarming after I left," he says, more guardedly.

Wow.

Hugh is a person who has sat there and held on through various badly timed emotional meltdowns at work when everyone else just made themselves scarce. He's let me cry without ever trying to fix it. He's seen me at my very worst. Utterly destroyed. Seen things no ordinary boss would, things even close friends are barely privy to. When I think of the way he was there for me the day Cam died . . . this is someone who has picked up pieces that were never his responsibility to reassemble.

But despite that closeness, we rarely stray onto the topic of each other's love lives anymore. Not my now nonexistent one, nor the top-secret and highly populous one I always imagine him having.

And we particularly don't go there since the fiasco with Grace. If we talk about relationships at all now, it's always in the context of my suddenly not having one and the resultant single-mother logistics that frequently run rampant through the team schedule.

"Sorry," he says, as if he's reading my mind again. "It's none of my business."

He is visibly uncomfortable right now, trapped on a plane with me, seatbelts fastened, incoming turbulence, regrettable topic opened, but I refuse to let him slam it shut the way he's clearly dying to. He's practically squirming under my gaze, and I'm not going to pretend there isn't a small part of me that loves this sliver of uncharacteristic vulnerability.

"I'm in love," I make clear. "With Cam. And even though I'm perfectly at liberty to do so, I'm not going to succumb to Justin's unarguable charms and have a fling with him on his first night in his new house as a neighborly thank-you for his assistance with the missile crisis."

"Grenade."

"Or even just because he's undeniably gorgeous. I am human, after all, and technically unattached. And you saw him. But—"

Hugh shuts his eyes for a second. "It's all right, Kate. This is not my area."

"There is no *area!*"

The tut-tutter in front of us turns around and frowns at me. I pass her frown straight on to Hugh, as this is directly his fault. He rolls his eyes and leans closer so he can lower his voice, as if he's finally accepted that the fastest way out of this conversation is through it.

"It's just, you turn up on the back of a motorcycle at sunrise looking like . . ." He's struggling for the right descriptor. Deep blue eyes flit over my face and drop to the silver zippers on the borrowed leather jacket and back again, and I'm reminded of how I felt on that bike with Justin. Reckless. Liberated. Exhilarated.

It's very different, I realize now, from how I felt watching my boss on the footpath, all responsible and executive and frustrated at my tardiness as usual . . . until he noticed me.

Confession: If being welded to Justin made me feel like a bad girl for the first and only time since I got detention for a momentary lapse in judgment in the school chapel in Year Eight, that wholly unexpected, unprofessional once-over from Hugh had felt *wicked*.

I hope he can't read my thoughts now. They've gone to a place they've never dared occupy before. We're still locked on each other's eyes, stuck in the flashback, and I try to convince myself this isn't about Hugh. It can't be. It's about the way he made me feel, looking at me as though I am something more than the overwhelmed, falling-apart widow he works with, complete with a devastated child, trying to make ends meet and keep everything afloat. For all Justin's accomplished flirting this morning, it was turning the head of straitlaced, always aboveboard, declare-your-conflicts-of-interest Hugh Lancaster that had jostled that long-relegated experience of feeling *desired* to center stage. Because Hugh doesn't do this. I don't know what came over him, to be honest.

"Looking like what?" I prompt, not ready to release him from this agony. "Calamity Jane?"

He takes an almost imperceptible breath, and his eyes darken even more. "No."

And that's all he'll say about it, too. It might be barely eight in the morning, but he casts a forlorn glance in the direction of the drinks trolley, which is grounded for the anticipated turbulence. Then his attention is redirected—not on me, but on his work folder, checking that everything's in order, which it always is, so there's no need to check at all, but he always does. He'll be berating himself for having said too much and crossed a line he shouldn't have and likely never will again. He might be generous with his duty of care for his colleagues, but he's also a stickler for exemplary behavior at work. Sexy motorcycle shenanigans don't fit the brief.

Which is totally fine because it's not Hugh I'm theoretically interested in. But as soon as I think those words, I feel sick. How can I be interested in *anyone?*

They say it's just like having a second child, falling in love again. That when you've lost a partner, you can eventually love two people at the same time. But the idea of that is so distant from me right now that I can't accept it as true or understand how it would work.

You're allowed to notice other men.

I know Grace is right. I know it's natural to face loneliness and wonder *what if.* To imagine what it might be like to fill the abyss of Cam's absence someday. But I haven't wanted to imagine it. Not once since he first started showing neurological symptoms and I began that drawn-out, yearslong, pre-grieving before we even started closing in on his actual death.

Grace thinks I have some arbitrary "rule" about when I can start dating again. "What are you waiting for, Kate?" she challenges me. "The deathiversary to hit double figures?"

I see other widowed people dipping a toe back into the dating scene and, whether it's been six months or six years, they're *always* judged. "I couldn't do it," people say, loved up and secure in a relationship they think is bulletproof. But until you're in a situation like this, you can't conceive of the loneliness. You can't know in advance how you'll grieve. Can't understand that time doesn't operate the way it used to. Seconds are hours. Days are years.

Your person was *just here*. Now they're flung beyond the fringes of the universe.

When Justin showed up yesterday, suave as all heck, with his big actuarial brain and his creative photography and that *bike*, he nudged open a door I've kept slammed shut.

I met Cam at nineteen. That makes me one of the least experienced adults I know. I don't have a "type." Not unless you count the type I fall for in rom-coms. Mark Darcy over Daniel Cleaver. Mr. Knightley over Mr. Darcy. Gilbert Blythe over every man in existence, living or dead.

Perhaps my celibate life along with last night's domestic security incident, and the sleep deprivation, and the flying phobia, and the anxiety attack, and the dangerously thrilling commute to the airport this morning are all combining to give me sex hallucinations. *Is that a thing?*

"What are you thinking about now?" Hugh asks, hopefully out of professional interest but possibly because my filthy expression betrays me.

Kate, I'm begging you, do not use the term "sex hallucinations" with your boss.

The plane drops to the bottom of an air pocket with a thud. I push Hugh's elbow off the armrest—it's everyone for themselves—and grip it as if it'll somehow prevent me from plunging to my death. Then there's another huge thud and several of the overhead locker doors fling open. Bags and coats fall into the aisle and onto people's heads. This is my worst nightmare. No, actually, I'm already living one of those, but this is right up there.

Finally, I see everything with a near-death clarity. These uninvited thoughts about Justin. The wild ideas of impressing something upon Hugh other than my capacity for missed deadlines and stranger-than-fiction excuses. I don't need this type of complication interrupting what should be my sole focus: Charlie. My darling child. Thrown too soon into a world of grief he shouldn't have known until he was much, much older. He doesn't need his mother gallivanting about on motorcycles with virtual strangers, feeling reckless and sexy and inventing fictitious love triangles to boost her plummeting self-confidence.

"Charlie's biggest fear is he's going to lose me too," I divulge. If he doesn't start each night sleeping in my bed, he always ends it there. "He asks me what will happen if he comes home from school one day and I'm dead."

Hugh's face falls. He couldn't love Charlie more if he was his own nephew.

"And I can't promise I won't be. You can't lie to kids who have been forced to become miniature death experts."

I feel this immense responsibility to stay alive.

"Kate." Hugh puts his hand on my arm, which, of course, with all his boundaries and rules and standards and irreproachable work ethic, he's never really done before, even when things were at their worst. Because we're about to plunge to our deaths, I allow it. There are no boundaries when you're falling out of the sky.

"I know this must seem hypocritical after the motorcycle this morning, but that was risk management," I explain. "I was more scared I'd let you down than I was of crashing."

This admission makes him wince. We both work hard, even if my hours are all over the place, but he has never been the kind of hard-nosed boss who wouldn't understand that car trouble is just a thing that happens.

"So when the car wouldn't start, I knocked on Justin's door," I explain.

"At six in the morning?"

My cheeks flame as an image of Justin lounging in the hallway in his underwear presents itself.

Hugh smiles. "And the poor guy just capitulated?"

Yes?

"You didn't think he deserved a sleep-in after lugging a houseful of furniture and being dragged into your ballistics predicament?"

"The porch light went on," I argue weakly. "In hindsight, it was probably a cat."

"I think this story tops the way we met."

He has to be joking. Nothing tops that.

8

Four years ago

One-year-old Charlie pops off the breast, disgusted.

"Look at him. Screwing up his face like he's a food critic sending a dish back to a five-star Michelin kitchen." Cam flings a suitcase on the bed and zips open the lid.

I've never been great in the kitchen, so it doesn't shock me that what I'm cooking up here is falling short of expectations. I sit Charlie up on my lap and rehook the clip on my nursing bra, defeated. He's been fussy for days.

Charlie reaches straight for Cam and says, "Dadda!" Cam groans as he picks him up, pretending he weighs a ton, and I take in the two of them. Charlie's a genetic miniature of his dad. Dark blond curls, intelligent blue eyes. Same dimpled smile that Cam flashed at me in second-year uni, which Charlie now flashes at me when he should be asleep in the middle of the night.

"I think it's called a 'nursing strike,'" Cam suggests, reading from a breastfeeding FAQ page on his phone.

"Oh, no you don't, buddy!" I say, and Charlie giggles as Cam lowers him to the floor of our bedroom. "We didn't put ourselves through that feeding gauntlet just for you to reject Mummy now."

By "gauntlet," I mean cracked nipples, blocked milk ducts, several bouts of mastitis, and an inpatient stay in a maternal and baby health center, during which I almost lost my mind. "How can something so natural be so *painful?*" I'd cried, as a lactation consultant manhandled my stinging nipple into Charlie's mouth for the umpteenth time, unsuccessfully. She reminded me of that string group on the *Titanic*, determined to keep playing, even though the ship was very clearly sinking.

Cam throws his phone on the bed and starts folding shirts. He's packing for the Congress of Medieval Literature conference in Rome. I watch as he folds slim-fit, textured layers of brown, green, and gray into neat piles on the bed and imagine him wearing the very same clothes at the Trevi Fountain, where we once tossed in a coin and wished for the baby who's now crawling around on our floor.

I'm trying to hide just how petrified I am at the thought of him being on the other side of the world. Ten days might seem like a fast turnaround to the person having an intellectually stimulating whirlwind trip to one of the world's most fabulous cities, but it's a lifetime in stay-at-home-mother minutes.

But I can't ask him to stay. He'd had to cancel a Parisian research trip earlier in the year because things had hurtled so far out of control on the maternal health front that the doctor was threatening to admit me. I'd always been so good with other people's babies, so it had come as a huge shock when I couldn't seem to operate my own child on instinct.

"Postpartum depression can cause this lack of confidence," the doctor explained as she filled out a script for antidepressants that are safe to take while breastfeeding. Over the next few months, slowly but surely, the days became less fraught. I stopped counting down the minutes until I heard the garage door go up, signaling that Cam was home and I wouldn't be messing this up on my own for the next few hours. It finally became an exercise in falling in love with my baby. Which I did. Hard.

"What time are you heading to the gym?" Cam asks. It's a sentence he's never uttered previously, but Grace has dragged me into her campaign to conceive. This apparently includes a seven p.m. BoxFit class at a strength-and-conditioning torture chamber in Kingston, at which she's a card-carrying cult member.

"I so rarely get time out from Charlie," I say to Cam while I'm rifling through the back of the underwear drawer, looking for some semblance of a sports bra. "Why would I choose to spend it getting punched?"

My idea of fitness is losing track of time in the bush with my camera. At the moment, that's just the camera on my phone, but once I'm back at work and we're a little more flush, I'm going to buy a secondhand mirrorless crop sensor and really get into it as a hobby. It's the only activity in the world where I truly lose myself.

"What if going back to work upsets the apple cart?" I ask him as I pull on some leggings. "I feel like we've only just got our act together as a family. I don't even know if I can remember how to do my job."

Cam's not much better. He's sifting through a drawer, searching for the international power cord adapters he's already packed. I point them out and he rolls his eyes. *What are the two of us like?*

"I don't think you just forget how to deliver multimillion-dollar campaigns," he argues. But he hasn't spent nine months growing a human and another twelve keeping it alive via trial and error, until he can barely recall the Netflix password.

Before having Charlie, I'd fallen into fundraising via comms. I'd left a temporary public service position for a job with a heart research institute, pulling together their monthly newsletter and managing their social media accounts. I was always on the hunt for good news stories and spent a lot of time interviewing elite scientists on the cutting edge of heart research—something I loved.

But then their full-time copywriter succumbed to an auto-immune condition and was off work for weeks. I was thrown into interviewing grieving families and creating those sob stories that end up in mailboxes to prod open the hearts and pockets of potential benefactors. I'd never seen such devastation. "She was *our age*, Cam. And a *widow*!" I'd said, crying into my parmigiana on one of our weeknight dates. "Her husband had been in peak fitness. No warning signs. Nothing. And he dropped dead at the kitchen table in front of their two kids. Literally dropped dead in the time it took her to walk to the front door and pick up their Uber Eats."

Cam had taken my hand across the table. "I'll try not to die of a heart attack," he'd promised, and I'd made sure of that by booking us both in for checkups at the GP. We were reassured that everything was fine, but the longer I worked at the institute and the more damaged families I met, the more anxious I became.

"There's a job going in the expansion team at the uni," he says now.

I have no idea what he means.

"Hang on, it's not 'expansion.' Another word like that . . ."

I wait, while he consults his enormous mental thesaurus, but he draws a blank.

"Come on, Cam, you're the English expert."

"It's on the tip of my tongue. But imagine that, Red. You and me, re-creating the university romance of our youth. Same stunts. Different city. Lazy picnic lunches on Fellows Oval outside the Chifley Library . . ."

"Oh, yes. Wouldn't that go down well," I challenge him. "Professor Whittaker rolling around on a picnic blanket in full view of everyone in the School of Literature . . ."

"Exactly!" He pulls me toward him by the waist and kisses me, tossing me onto the bed like he did when we were twentysome-things, and less likely to trigger a bout of sciatica. But his neat piles of clothes start toppling, my head is butting up against the lid of the suitcase, and Charlie wants "up," so we forget the romance, drag our baby into a group hug, and laugh at what's become of us.

"Well. This has been lovely, but Mummy has to go to the gym now," I announce, jumping off the bed and catching sight of myself in the full-length mirror in gray leggings and a blue tank top, pausing for a moment of self-doubt. Nothing is quite where it used to be. There's just a little bit more here. A little bit less there. General deference to motherhood and gravity all over.

Cam props himself on one elbow on the bed, resting his blond head in his hand and admiring me. "Best decision of my life, passing you a love note in that lecture."

"Best decision of mine, overlooking how unoriginal it was and going out with you anyway."

I thwack him on the shoe, and he picks up Charlie and chases me out of the bedroom, suddenly joined by our excitable black spaniel, Mr. Knightley, as we tear down the hall, through the kitchen, and toward the front door, which I throw open, squealing, only to run right into Grace, who is standing on the porch like a fitness model.

"Remind me how long you two have been together?" she asks, shaking her head and smiling.

"Sixteen years," Cam brags. "Don't break her on the treadmill!"

There are only two free treadmills. They're in the corner beside each other, and I step onto the one next to a guy who's running at a pace I'd personally resort to only if I was being chased by a wild animal. He's intimidatingly fit and so focused he doesn't even glance my way as I step up beside him. If he missed his step, he'd be shot clean through the back wall of the gym at this speed.

Grace hits "Quick start" and immediately accelerates and sets an incline. She's one of those people with absolutely no time to waste. Seconds later, not only is she already jogging, but she's kicking straight into a life update, the likes of which you'd normally reserve for a less public setting, unless, like us, you rarely had toddler-free chat time.

"The doctor said I have a poor ovarian reserve," she reports.

"Oh! I'm sorry. What does that mean, really?"

"Fewer eggs, lower quality, higher rates of chromosomal abnormalities and miscarriage, failure to fertilize, failure to implant, failure to thrive . . ." With every point she makes, she gives the speed button a corresponding push, until she's sprinting. "Basically, it's a five percent chance," she practically shouts over the sound of the machine. "She said it would take a miracle."

It's hard to know what to say. I know the IVF struggle well, but I'm one of its success stories. I feel like Charlie and I should come with one of those warning labels, saying results may vary.

"It's a good thing I believe in miracles," Grace goes on between quick breaths, and I can't decide whether it's kind or cruel to buy into her hope. "Obviously I need to ditch the man."

Her long-term partner, Max, has wielded smoke and mirrors year after year to distract her from his consistently unfulfilled promises to "get serious." He's a man-child with a commitment phobia and no intention of giving her the baby-making opportunity he's been falsely advertising for nearly a decade.

"It's the sunk cost that got me," she explains. "Like when you stick with a movie you hate because your former self invested so much time in the first act. I kept hoping he'd change his mind. *Ugh.* So over it. Let's talk about you."

What to say, though? Cam and I got six straight hours' sleep last night? Charlie tried his first ice cream at a mums' group party the other weekend?

"Gosh, let me think." I increase the speed on the treadmill slightly as I rack my brain for non-baby-related content. "All Cam and I do lately is talk about how tired we are, whose turn it is to wash up, and whether it's too early for two adults to go to bed yet. And not for any fun reason."

I know I shouldn't be traitorously whining about our sex drought in public, but something about Grace's romantic and reproductive plight drives me to underplay how great things actually are between Cam and I, temporary lack of sex notwithstanding.

"I don't buy it," she says. "As if you can keep your hands off that *delicious* man, even after sixteen years."

"It's seventeen, actually. My so-called delicious husband forgot our anniversary last month and I haven't had the heart to tell him."

She's right, though. He is delicious. And funny, and kind, and intelligent, and a great dad. . . . We might try each other's patience at times, but he is a jackpot of a husband, and I was lucky enough to hold the golden ticket.

"Anyway, Grace, I'm applying for a job."

She glances at me to check that I'm not joking. "Okay, wow!"

"Sensible, right? I mean, I can barely function *without* a job, so . . ."

"You'll eat it for breakfast. You won an Australian Philanthropy Award, Kate—own it!"

The pre-Charlie, award-winning me feels like a whole different person. "All I can envision is Charlie starting childcare and coming down with every illness in the pediatric encyclopedia. And then I'll use up all my leave and be forced to bring the stomach flu or hand, foot, and mouth disease into the office. . . ."

"Isn't that for cows?"

"No, that's a different thing. And you know how women typically undersell themselves? I get so nervous in interviews I go the other way."

"You don't!"

"I don't mean to, but I lose my cool and slightly inflate my abilities. I'm worried I'll get the job and then spend the whole time trying to live up to the slightly better version of myself that they're all expecting."

The runner beside me starts reducing his speed to a walk, and then to a stop. He wipes the treadmill down with a towel and takes a big swig of water from his drink bottle.

"I'm pretty sure the correct answer to 'What motivated you to apply for this job?' isn't 'So I can go to the toilet in peace,'" I admit, and I'm musing on that when the sudden arrival of a seriously magnificent young woman throws us for a loop. She's curvy and fit, in matching, bright purple designer gym gear, with a sleek black ponytail and a complexion so flawless it seems to come with its own filter.

I don't mean to stare. But everything about her is perfect. And very unlikely to be rejected by a future baby. Or by anyone.

The woman catches me staring and rightly scowls.

"Sorry! It's just . . ." But before I can defend myself by explaining the whole nursing strike situation, I've lost my balance.

Grace slams the emergency stop button on my treadmill. It's too late though, and I'm flung violently off the back of it onto the carpeted floor in an ungainly heap, derriere first, à la Downward Dog, right at the feet of the guy who'd been running so capably beside me.

"I'm so sorry!" I say, rolling over into a sit. Sorry for what, I'm not sure, unless it's about offending him with the general spectacle.

After taking a moment to gather himself, he offers a hand to haul me up, and I take it and scramble to my feet, then dust myself off.

"Are you all right?" he asks.

He's giving off serious Derek "McDreamy" Shepherd vibes, what with his dark hair and attentive bedside manner. Concerned blue eyes conduct a full-body sweep of my potentially injured skeleton. Things do hurt, here and there, but I'm not going to make any more of a fuss than I already have. Then I watch as the man's attention snags, briefly, on my left breast. Then the right.

Perhaps I've still got it, after all.

But his eyes dart away uncomfortably, and his lips part as he expels a pained sigh, like he's sort of . . . baffled.

I do not want to own the kind of breasts that baffle men. And cannot believe his nerve. See, this is exactly why I avoid places like this!

Grace dismounts her equipment and checks on me too. As does Purple Pants. All three are examining me now, like a team of beautifully toned specialists in the ER.

Grace clears her throat and nods at my chest. But the tingling is already alerting me to the problem.

Of all the times for my dodgy milk supply to rally, it's chosen *now*? Two ever-increasing wet circles radiate through my blue tank top while the four of us stand there, in the middle of the gym, in our very own private circle of hell. Nobody knows where to look except Purple Pants, who can't keep her eyes off me as if this whole experience is thoroughly educational. As for the man, he's impassive and walks off toward the locker rooms.

"You've got to admit, this is a little bit funny, Kate," Grace says, hiding a smile. I'll admit no such thing. All my insecurities rush in at once. This isn't just about an embarrassing moment; those are a dime a dozen in my world. It's about the struggle I'm having, *again*, to feed Charlie. The fear of being solely responsible for him while Cam's away. The sight of all the überfit bodies here, compared with the squishy model I'm in, and a sudden inferiority complex at the thought of all the glamorous European women with whom Cam is about to professionally mingle, while I'm here, looking like this, *being* like this . . .

Grace notices me wobbling and puts a hand on my shoulder in comfort, just as the treadmill guy jogs back over from the locker room. I wipe my eyes and pull myself back together.

"Here." He passes me a clean T-shirt. Brumbies rugby. I hate rugby. But in this moment, I love him. So does Grace. So does Purple Pants.

I pull it over my head and it falls onto my body, bathing me in the scent of pine laundry detergent.

"Thank you. Really." Words are inadequate.

"OMG. Hashtag dad hack," Purple Pants gushes, and I cringe on her behalf. "You must have kids?"

He shakes his head.

"Girlfriend?" she plows on.

"Not really."

"String of one-night stands, at the very least?" She says this with a hand on his biceps and a silent contract to assist in that department, if desired.

He laughs at this. "Probably nothing as entertaining as you're envisioning. Anyway, it's been, um . . ." He looks at me, lost for words about how it's been. "Goodbye," he settles on eventually. "And good luck."

"You too," I answer nervously. What am I wishing him luck for? His one-night stand? "I'll return your shirt to reception?"

But he's already walking away, and the three of us stare after him—Daft Punk's "Harder, Better, Faster, Stronger" pumping, gym equipment clanging around us.

"Not all heroes wear capes," Purple Pants says dreamily. And she picks up her drink bottle and chases him out.

9

I'm nervous as hell walking into my job interview a few weeks later.

The philanthropy team is based in one of Acton's red-roofed, white weatherboard heritage cottages, built over a century ago when the capital city was first established. I wish we were meeting in one of the futuristic, towering, glass-walled buildings near the main student hub. You can be anonymous in a building like that. This cottage is the sort of place you'd expect to order Devonshire tea and buy a souvenir tea towel. The floorboards creak, announcing my arrival as soon as I cross the threshold, and a very big part of me wants to abort this mission.

I used to find fundraising hard. I was the kind of person who had to buy all the charity chocolates myself rather than sell them, because I hated asking people for money. But, over the years, I just found my way with it. Turns out it's all about stories. People's personal experiences, shared respectfully, drive up donations. The families I worked with felt like they were contributing in an area where they once felt powerless. I ended up in quite a senior role at the institute and thrived in it. And, as Grace reminded me, I won awards for it.

But that was all before becoming a mum. Having a baby really knocked the wind from my sails. It took us years of trying before Charlie finally came along. Infertility shredded my confidence, and eventually the complicated process of bringing a baby into the world just sort of swallowed me whole. By the time he was born, by emergency C-section after a difficult labor because he was breech, I already felt like I'd failed as a mother several times over. And that was before the milk came in and he refused to attach while I scavenged for truth among so much conflicting advice that I barely knew which way was up.

"You must be Kate," a young woman says, coming out into the corridor from one of the office areas. She's vibrantly dressed in a neon-yellow blouse, swishy black pants, and bright red boots to match the frames of her glasses—fashion choices that seem out of place in the heritage surrounds. "I'm Sophie Lawrence. They won't be too long. Would you like a cup of tea? Glass of water?"

"Scones with jam and cream?" I say, forgetting she wasn't aboard my earlier train of thought. "This is that kind of building, isn't it?"

She's not entirely sure.

"Thanks, Sophie. I'm fine." I smooth the creases in my black jacket nervously and take a seat on a brown leather couch. Dressing in a business suit this morning had felt like a game of pretend. The clothes had also felt considerably tighter than they had the last time I'd worn them, which was right up until I started showing with Charlie at fifteen weeks. Maybe I should join Grace more regularly at the gym. Avec breast pads next time.

When I'd arrived home after the gym incident in a strange man's rugby top, Cam thought it was hilarious. He'd tried to drag me along to games once or twice, before we mutually agreed it would be more fun for both of us if I wasn't present. I'd felt so guilty about the "sex drought" admission at the gym that I'd initiated a "one-night stand" of our own before his Italy trip. Given the infrequency of opportunity before or since, and the threat of interruption throughout, it had all the hallmarks of a few stolen moments with a stranger, which after seventeen years was *quite something*. Every time I think about it, I can't wipe the smile off my face. . . .

"They're ready for you now," Sophie says, pulling me out of my reverie. She guides me down the corridor toward what must have once been a formal dining room, but which is now being used as a small boardroom.

Three people stand up to greet me. One of the women introduces herself as Angela, Head of Advancement, which was the word on the tip of Cam's tongue the other week. She gives me a strong, welcoming smile, and I like her on sight. The man, Simon, is from the Human Resources Division. The other woman is the scribe, and she shoots me an encouraging smile, as if she's zeroed in on my obvious nerves.

They all seem very nice and I'm about to sit down, when a second door into the boardroom opens. I turn around. And I feel *sick*. In my defense, the man walking in looks equally disconcerted. He pales briefly at the sight of me, then pulls himself together and extends his hand for me to shake.

"Hugh Lancaster," he says as he holds my gaze with the dark blue eyes I'd last observed darting away from my chest during #lactationgate. "Head of Development."

"Kate Whittaker," I respond, dazed and following his lead. *Officer in charge of Perpetual Mortification.*

Our hands shake for slightly too long, as if they're supposed to be causing a diversion while we regroup. I've heard legends about this city's "one and a half degrees of separation" but hadn't believed it until now. Eventually he lets go of my hand, pulls out my chair, and motions for me to take a seat, while I have a flashback to him throwing me his rugby top. I wonder if he's always this chivalrous. And then my flashback takes a turn for the worse and leaps to my conversation with Grace on the treadmill. A conversation during which I basically armed him with a professional horror story about myself, right down to the highly contagious diseases I planned to spread around the office like some kind of biological terrorist.

I want to throw up. Or run. Or both.

Hugh reaches across the table to pour a glass of water for me. And one for him. I wish it was something stronger. I'd even take orange juice at this point for the sugar hit. But thinking of orange juice makes me nauseated again. My goodness, I haven't felt that way about juice since . . .

Oh my God.

An unspeakable thought barges into my brain. *But could I be?* Surely not. Cam and I had our one-night stand only a couple of weeks ago. No, it was longer than that. Before Italy. And he's already been back two weeks. . . .

Accidentally getting pregnant is not in our playbook. Our narrative is that we struggle. We have to throw everything we have at the task, financially, emotionally, and physically. Even then, the odds are low for us. And isn't it true that you're less likely to get pregnant while you're breastfee— *Oh, holy* . . . the nursing strike.

"Could you perhaps begin, Kate, by telling us a little about yourself?" Angela says warmly. She has no idea what she's asking. Hugh does. He looks frightened.

I think I'm pregnant, I want to say. *I haven't had a period in months. You hear of these people who struggle with their first and then fall without even trying second time around. Are my boobs sore? This can't be happening. . . .*

But instead of saying any of that, I clear my throat and wonder if it's too early to ask for pain relief.

"Kate?" Hugh asks. He's looking at my hand plastered to my chest, no doubt wrongly guessing my problem and thinking he's running out of clothes to throw at me. *I'm way beyond that, Hugh. Thinking of upgrading to a peoplemover.*

I stare at him, horrified. There is a great pause, into which I am supposed to be inserting a dazzling explanation of my experience. Hugh nods, as if he's trying to will me on. *I'll forget what I overheard on the treadmill if you can,* he seems to be saying.

"Angela, perhaps I should speak a little about the role, first?" he says, in response to my silent existential crisis.

I take the glass to my lips for a sip of water but feel like it's going to come up again if I swallow, so I place it back on the table without drinking anything.

Angela looks confused, and jots something on the paper in front of her.

"We deliver strategic, large-scale annual appeals designed to build the university's capacity to respond to some of the world's biggest challenges," Hugh begins.

Like the fact that Cam and I are operating on a twelve-month sleep deficit already, which we're about to compound.

"We want someone who'll inspire stakeholders to be excited by our energy and vision."

We are SO drained.

"You'll plan and deliver comprehensive fundraising campaigns."

I don't think I can fit a second car seat in the turn-of-the-century Mazda and still concertina the pram into the boot around the anchor strap. No, it's worse. We'll need a bigger stroller.

Cam has been talking about dropping to part-time when I return to work, so we can share the childcare more equitably. He doesn't want to miss out on Charlie's preschool years. It's always been family first for him. I can't deny him that. I have to get this job. *Have* to.

I sit up straight, as an avalanche of fake confidence comes over me, like this is drama class and I'm in the leading role. "Thanks for that introduction, Hugh. I'm excited by the idea of contributing to the impact and reach of the university. I applied for this role because . . ."

I want to go to the toilet on my own.

I can't face any more weeping widows at the heart institute.

I drive a 2001 Mazda.

". . . coming from a world-leading research institute that really has one broad objective, I'm attracted by the idea of building strong campaigns across diverse programs and helping advance one of the world's top universities heading into one of the most challenging periods in human history."

I don't even know what I just said or where it came from, just that Angela is nodding, and Hugh is staring at me as if he's trying to reconcile Professional Kate with the klutz from the gym.

"What would you say are the key barriers to higher-education philanthropy?" he asks.

I pause to gather my thoughts. "Well, there are the broad challenges facing fundraising in general—fierce competition for donors and dollars, trying to cut through excess noise in an exploding comms space."

"Mmm?" He nods, shoving me toward a better answer.

"We're seeing global trends with higher education grappling with additional financial and enrollment challenges, cuts, and reforms."

Angela ticks a series of boxes, writes some notes, and shuffles her page, ready to ask the next question.

"What else?" Hugh says, leaning in. He acts like he's operating on personal curiosity now, as if the other three aren't in the conversation.

His colleague looks surprised, and flicks back to the page before.

I dredge my mind for the "X-factor" response he seems to be angling for. *What would Cam say?* "Well," I begin, an idea forming almost as it leaves my mouth, "a more nuanced theme that I think is worth considering in the broader tertiary sector is the decades-long culture war between arts and science, and the impact of an institution's strategic research priorities on the potential further devaluation of the arts, specifically."

His expression is inscrutable. "Our campaigns tend to be necessarily targeted and specific. Drawing funds to the university involves tough choices that make economic sense."

I shrug. "I get that it's a harder sell. Fifty years from now, we want to hope there's sufficient scientific brilliance to reverse us out of the corner we're painting ourselves into, climate-wise. But without developing sufficient artistic brilliance to capture the poetry of that human experience and make connections and meaning from it all—what are we fighting for?"

He hasn't written a single point on the blank page in front of him. "Right," he says.

"That's a challenge facing tertiary-sector philanthropy," I go on. "Asking what you're fighting for, strategically, and why. Looking beyond the low-hanging fruit and ensuring there are people on your team with the energy to reach higher. If you always go for the easy sell, you'll shoot the Renaissance Man in the foot."

We lock gazes and he narrows his eyes, impossible to read. Maybe all I've done is thrown a spanner into the works, but I suspect he likes the challenge.

As for the rest of their questions, a string of answers fall out of my mouth and I can't be stumped. It's like I'm channeling some god of desperate, potentially pregnant working mums. Hugh must find me totally unrecognizable. Technically irrelevant as it is, I feel like I'm holding out on them though, by not telling them about the unconfirmed baby. They know about Charlie—I was open about this being my return to work from parental leave. But they don't know about this next one. Of course, nobody does. Not even Cam.

"Do you have any final questions for us, Kate?" Hugh asks. He's been looking at me strangely since I painted the whole "Renaissance Man with a shot foot" visual.

Probably wondering if he's being pranked. Or *was* pranked, at the gym.

I know you're meant to have a question prepared, but right now I can think of only one. "Could I be excused?" I say, and I run out of the room with my hand over my mouth.

10

When I get home, Cam is lying on the living room floor in front of the bookcase, reading *Jane Eyre for Babies* to Charlie. He's got him the whole series—*Pride and Prejudice, Moby-Dick, Wuthering Heights* . . .

"Look at Daddy, filling your head with all that nineteenth-century nonsense!" I say to Charlie as I throw my bag on the couch and flop down on the floor with them.

He giggles, and flings *Jane Eyre* across the room, in favor of *Paw Patrol*.

I kick off my shoes. It's the first time I've worn heels in more than a year, and I'd forgotten how much I hate them. I wriggle over and lie down, resting my head on Cam's outstretched leg. Charlie clambers on top of me, loving this family pile-on. For just a few more seconds, I pretend our world isn't about to be rocked by a force I'm not sure I'm going to withstand, emotionally.

"Did he sleep?" I ask. We're obsessed with Charlie's naps at the moment. He's trying to give up the afternoon one, and we're on a mission to preserve the status quo, including strict adherence to afternoon cot time, even if he doesn't technically shut his eyes.

Cam looks slightly taken aback. Then guilty.

I sit up again, annoyed. "Oh, great! You're *hopeless*, Cam! Why do I have to be bad cop?"

Charlie picks up one of my shoes, dumps it in Cam's lap, and laughs. I watch as Cam turns it over in his hand, then looks back at me.

"How did the interview go?" he asks, as if the shoe has jogged his memory about why he'd had to rearrange his Tuesday lecture to be home with Charlie.

"Actually, it went pretty well. They're phoning references," I tell him. "Miraculous, really, given I threw up at the end of it!"

"Oh, no! Nerves?"

I consider ending the story here, as he continues.

"Were they good about it?"

"It was that guy from the gym."

"Rugby dude? You're kidding!"

"Yes, except he's not a dude. He's the Head of Development, and my potential boss."

I watch Cam's face light up with pride about the possible job. He doesn't care about the extra money, because he doesn't fully appreciate how many children we have, but he's happy for me. I can tell.

"What's wrong, then?"

I take a deep breath. "I think I'm pregnant."

Saying it aloud brings home everything this would mean for me. I already feel incompetent as Charlie's mum. The mistakes I have made in the first year alone! What if the mild PPD gets worse? What if I really, deeply, fully lose my grip?

I can see that Cam is trying to disguise his excitement. Maybe he should stay home full-time with this next one. A flash of guilt slices through me at the thought that I could already be rejecting a baby that, right now, is at its tiniest. The thought of the defenseless little thing inside me makes me tear up. I'm all over the place.

"I picked up a test on the way home," I tell him. "It's one of those early-response ones, so we should know."

When you've grappled to hold your mind together while looking after a helpless human, the idea of doubling that responsibility is terrifying. If I'd had any inkling that it wasn't going to take several rounds of treatment and several thousand dollars to reach this point, we would have been more careful.

I look up to meet his eye, and my voice cracks as I say, "What if this is the thing that pushes me over the edge?"

He stands up, pulls Charlie off me, and hoists me to my feet and straight into a hug. I burrow into his T-shirt and focus on the scent of his earthy cologne. Whatever else happens, everything feels possible with him by my side.

But then I'm gripped by a grisly and totally irrational fear that I could lose him. It comes out of nowhere and I am horror-struck at the concept. It was bad enough when he was in Rome for ten days.

He releases me from the hug.

"Take the test," he says. "I'll be right here."

In the toilet, I don't look at the stick. Can't look at it. But inside I know. I can sense the life within me the way I sensed Charlie before any test did.

I wash up and come out to Cam, who's giving Charlie his bottle. A huge pang of love for them both spreads through me, and I hand the test to him. "Over to you," I say. If only I could delegate the entire pregnancy to him as well.

Charlie's little face lights up when he hears my voice, and he turns to see me, eyes bright, milk dripping down his chin while he smiles at me. His love undoes me. He holds out his arms, wriggling to move from Cam to me, and I go to him, needing his weight against my body, wanting to squish him too tight because there's no way for me to express how desperately I adore him. And then I'm tearing up again.

I can't look at Cam's face. It will be even greater proof than the test in his hand. I stare into Charlie's eyes while he feeds from the bottle. This is the upside of feeding this way. Such perfect eye contact. Every time I glance at him, he lights up. Every time. He's my greatest and most loyal audience, my most reassuring cheerleader. Nothing I do—no doubts I have—can stop him from loving me the way he does.

"Charlie," Cam says, approaching us for a three-way hug. Charlie breaks away from the bottle and looks at his daddy expectantly, and we both laugh. "You're going to have a little brother or sister."

Charlie has no idea what Cam is saying, but he beams and giggles. Cam looks into my eyes and finds tears and terror and knowing. And love.

He kisses me on the forehead, and Charlie reaches up and tries to push his face away from mine. In this moment, he won't share me. My heart breaks for the rude awakening he'll receive in a few months, when he has to.

"How will we do this?" I whisper.

Cam rubs my arm. He's even more relaxed than he seemed the first time around. "One day at a time," he suggests. "Love you, Katie. I think you're incredible."

I wish I understood why. Wish I felt within myself even a modicum of the faith he has in me. "But, Cam . . ."

He puts a finger gently to my lips and draws me into a long hug, which ends only when I release him.

It's not until a few hours later, when I come into the en suite to brush my teeth before bed, that I find a note stuck to the bathroom mirror, using the old nickname he gave me when we met: *We've got this, Red. x*

11

Day one in the office about a month later and I've thrown up twice before my boss even gets in. It's partly the morning sickness, partly the unintended briefing session I gave him about all the ways I'm sure to make a hash of this. That thing I said at the gym about slightly exaggerating my application and constantly falling short of my colleagues' expectations has kicked in even before I've been given my first task. I need to have a conversation with him about all of that and clear the air, or I'll spend eight hours a day drowning in rampant imposter syndrome. Oh, and as I can't keep *anything* down, I need to tell him about the baby. *Great.*

"You're reporting straight to *him*, yeah?" Sophie is freaking me out the way she's whispering and looking paranoid and calling him "him," as she motions toward his office.

"I believe so," I say, breathing through another wave of nausea.

"Everyone here would walk over hot coals for that guy," she confides.

Walking over hot coals seems easier than having to undo the professional ineptitude I demonstrated on the treadmill.

"Everyone's also got a massive crush on him," she adds delightedly. She's gone full-blown fangirl over this guy like he's Harry Styles. Then she slams down the paper she's using to fan herself and spins her chair back to face her computer monitor. She clears her throat loudly, basically drawing attention to the fact that she, and by association me, has been gossiping about Hugh as he approaches our desks.

"Morning, Sophie," he says, probably aware of what's going on and ignoring it as he should. "See me in my office, Kate?"

Already? I pick up a notebook and pen, and my nerve and a handful of tissues in case of emergencies, and I follow him into an immaculate office that takes minimalism to a new level. The guy needs an indoor plant or something.

"You okay?" he asks. "You look peaky."

Tell him about the baby. Tell him about the baby.

"Er, big weekend," I admit. It's technically true, in that I ended up being rehydrated on a drip at Queanbeyan hospital on Friday night.

He looks at me as though I've just stumbled in from a bar-crawling bender. "Baby keep you up?"

Which one? "Something like that. How was your weekend?"

Visions immediately spring to mind of that gorgeous woman from the gym and her equally ripped posse of sensational twenty-somethings, parading through his bachelor pad.

"Worked most of the weekend," he explains. "Kate—"

"Hugh—"

We speak on top of each other. He tells me to go ahead.

"About the gym," I begin. He shakes his head, but I insist on continuing. "I'm mortified about, well . . . *so much*. Obviously, I didn't plan on seeing you again, or I wouldn't have . . ."

Practically sprayed him with breast milk?

His big swivel chair creaks as he adjusts his position, awkwardly.

"Hugh, I have to tell you something else." I close the office door and grab a chair, then try to center myself. When I look at him again he seems to be reconsidering his professional choices. "I know it's my first day here, but honestly I feel so nauseated, I can't possibly keep this a secret until twelve weeks."

He is speechless.

"I'm so sorry about the timing. I figured out what was going on during the interview, would you believe, because of . . . various symptoms."

His eyes flick to my chest, but not in a lecherous way, then snap back to my face. "Well, congratulations," he says at last, kindly. He also rubs his forehead. I think I've already worn him out. "When are you due?"

"Oh, it's *really* early days. The baby is basically the size of a green olive! We're not entirely sure of the date officially." *This is your boss, Kate, not the obstetrician!*

I hope Hugh is not doing mental arithmetic. Exactly seven weeks have elapsed since my sex-drought admission on the treadmill, and I silently will myself not to overshare the captivating little anecdote that this baby was in fact conceived while I was still wearing his rugby shirt.

"Pretty early to be announcing it, isn't it?"

I agree. "I'm just deathly sick. I can't believe I've even dragged myself in here. I've thrown up in the staff toilets twice already."

He's silent.

"I'll understand if this is too much. Honestly, if I'd already had confirmation before the interview, I would have said something."

"Kate. Get your head around the legislation. It makes no difference whether you're pregnant or not if you're the right person for the job. Which you are." He considers me closely. "Charming though all that self-deprecation was at the gym, it's at odds with the way you handled yourself under pressure. Your references backed you to the hilt. Apparently, at your last gig, you were instrumental in facilitating the biggest donor grant in the institute's history. Your interview performance was, in the main, extraordinarily strong. Once you pulled yourself together, you were the standout applicant, hands down. Why do you think we offered you the role so quickly? Have some faith in yourself."

It's probably the hormones, but I want to cry. Faith in myself has been in short supply lately. "Why are you looking so concerned, then?" I ask him.

"I'm not concerned. Just thinking. What do you need from us to make this easier?"

I don't know what he means, and it must show on my face because he continues. "Would it help if we set you up a home office for a while? Take away some of the stress of having to act more well than you feel?"

I have to stop myself from clambering over the top of his desk and hugging him out of gratitude.

"We'll have a conversation with HR about flexible hours. We could potentially spread your three days out over five if that would make things easier. Leave it with me."

Take me to the hot coals.

"For now, just take your time settling in. First day, it's all about working out who people are and where everything is. I think we're gathering for an informal morning tea soon—about fifteen people? I'll introduce you then. We'll meet in a day or so and talk through strategy for the donor program. How does that sound?"

I'm still back at the offer of a home office, trying to unpack his magnanimity.

"And, Kate, if you're too sick to be here, just let me know and take yourself home."

I thank him profusely, for the opportunity and the support, and when I come back out of the office, Sophie catches my eye and winks. I get the fangirling now.

The real mystery is why a man like Hugh is still single. All those one-night stands must get very tedious. If only I knew a truly wonderful single woman in search of a deserving man to assist in her quest to prove the fertility doctor wrong about that 5 percent chance. . . .

12

Cam and I go for an ultrasound at eleven weeks because my hormone levels are a little off where they should be. We're holding hands and feeling weak with anticipation and fear as we watch the image of our tiny child come into focus on the screen, and even though there's a strong heartbeat and the sonographer doesn't look worried, I can't shake an inkling that something is off.

The technician starts capturing images and measuring various things, including the tiny heartbeat. My own heart is pounding with nerves. I've had a rapid immersion in second-time-mummy love for this teeny one. I'd been so terrified about doing this, and suddenly my terror is all about not doing it.

"Everything looks good so far," the technician says with a smile for me and Cam, who looks worse now than he did when I was in labor with Charlie. "This your second, Dad?"

Cam's still staring at the screen. I squeeze his hand. He doesn't squeeze it back.

"Yes, we have a son," I explain for him. "He's fourteen months."

"Two under two, eh? Brave!"

"We'll be okay," Cam says, smiling at me. Squeezing my hand now. "How does everything look?"

The radiographer glances at me and repeats her info. "Great so far."

"We're going to have two under two," Cam explains, and the technician looks at me again. I wonder what could possibly be more important to Cam than this ultrasound in this moment. Why won't he pay attention?

Everything checks out and we finish up and pay at the desk and Cam suggests coffee in the little bistro next to the radiology center.

I check my watch. "But don't you have an eleven-o'clock lecture?"

He frowns. "Lost track of time," he admits.

We get in the car and he backs out of the space carefully and drives out of the parking lot, hesitating at the T-intersection slightly too long.

"Could have gone," I say unhelpfully, turning my attention back to the little printout of our baby's first photo in my hands—such a delicate little bean of a person.

Cameron jams his foot down and accelerates, fast, across the intersection. There's nowhere near enough space or time for an oncoming car to swerve, and it clips us on Cam's side, spins us around, and slams us up onto the concrete Jersey barrier on the median strip.

There's steam hissing out from under the hood. I've dropped the photo of the baby. I'm silent, in the passenger seat. He's holding the steering wheel and staring forward.

"Katie . . ."

"I'm okay. You?"

He looks at me, his face contorted in pain. He seems nineteen again, and twenty-four, and thirty, and every other age I've shared with him, all at once. Whole years seem to pass before his next words. "I think there's something wrong with me, Red."

Everything around us slows down. At first, I think it's because we're an obstacle on the road, facing the wrong way, but it's not just the cars slowing down and the pedestrians dawdling so they can look. It's our future, coming at us in nightmarish slow-motion. Cam and I and Charlie, and our unborn baby. Every moment up until now collides with every future moment, as if we are warping time.

He is not okay.

I entertain myself with a fantasy that it's because he's been injured in the crash.

We sit here, for what feels like countless lifetimes, until the helpers arrive. They open each of our doors and ask us questions. But I don't want them asking questions of Cam. If they don't ask, he can't fail.

Sirens wail in the distance. It's the sound that never comes for us. Always for other people. The people on the other end of bad things happening. *Not us.* Since the moment I got pregnant with this baby, without even trying, we've been in a bubble. Perfect. Safe.

"She's pregnant," I hear Cam tell the paramedics minutes later. "Check her first."

"How many weeks?"

That stumps him.

"Eleven," I respond, fighting tears. "We just had the ultrasound, minutes ago."

The paramedic nods and suggests his partner check me out, while he shines a light into Cam's eyes and looks at his pupils. "Did you hit your head?" he asks.

Cam doesn't know. Like he doesn't know how many weeks our baby is. And like he misjudged the space between cars at the intersection and couldn't pay attention in the ultrasound.

There are other things too. Things I'd noticed and brushed aside over the last few weeks. Moments of forgetfulness. Missteps. A faraway look in his eyes that he worked hard to wrestle back to the here and now whenever I caught him.

This accident is the universe's way of forcing me to face facts. There is something very wrong here. We're about to be put in two separate ambulances and carted off to the hospital and that's when they're going to find it: the thing in Cam's brain that has been gradually stealing my husband from me, one little slipup at a time.

We're brought in and parked on gurneys in a corridor out the back of the Emergency Department at the Canberra Hospital in Garran. Nursing teams are hovering around both of us, putting cannulas in our hands in case we need fluids or surgery. It seems an overreaction; we were barely hurt. They're treating us as if we'd had internal injuries anyway. Maybe it's protocol.

Cam is parked just across the corridor. For my entire life with him, every time we've looked at each other since we first met way back in that lecture theater, I've felt secure. Certain. Protected. And so has he. With our necks immobilized right now, we can't turn our heads, and that connection is cut. Even worse, I think the connection was already interrupted before the accident.

There's something missing in the way he's been looking at me. I've been noticing it for weeks. I'd even wondered the unthinkable: had he met someone? He seemed distracted and quiet and just not himself. I saw it in the ultrasound room, and again in the car. Add to that all the forgetful little incidents—missing our wedding anniversary, forgetting Charlie's sleep routine, looking for stuff he'd already packed, too many words on the tip of his tongue. . . .

The lights are on, but my incandescent husband is not a hundred percent home.

"What's happening?" I ask, grabbing the arm of a nurse as she hurries past.

"Someone will be with you as soon as we can."

"Can you tell us your name?" a doctor is saying across the hall.

"Cameron Edward Whittaker."

Thank God.

"Date of birth?"

He rattles it off, and I'm feeling comforted. I have an active imagination. Always have had. Maybe I'm making things up. Perhaps it's the PPD and the unexpected pregnancy and the new job causing me to be overly anxious and invent things.

"Can you tell us, Cam, what day it is today?"

Monday the eighth. Monday the eighth. Monday the eighth.

Silence. "Umm . . ."

"Just the month is fine," the doctor says. "Or the year?"

Come on, Cam. You can do this! Think!

"Is it . . . I don't know."

They check his pupils again. "Can you tell us who is with you today?"

"Yes," Cam says, and I can hear the smile in his tone. "That's the love of my life. Mother of my child."

I melt. The nurses melt. Everyone within earshot melts.

"Aww, how old is your child, Cam?"

"He just had his first birthday."

Well, a couple of months ago, but okay.

"Any plans for a brother or sister?"

I put a hand over my nonexistent bump and think of the ultrasound photo. *Where is it?* I feel quite panicked. It's the only real proof, apart from my morning sickness, that I'm pregnant.

"No plans," Cam says, confidently.

If I wasn't already lying down, I would fall down. I'm dizzy. Hot. And scared witless.

"Cam—"

A nurse puts a finger to her lips, asking me not to say anything.

"Do you remember where you were just before the accident?"

I hold my abdomen protectively and *will* him to know. Despite all the clattering in Emergency, I can almost hear him trying to concentrate.

"We were at . . ." Recognition flits into his voice, briefly. "Katie— are you pregnant?"

I start to cry and imagine his face lighting up the way it lit up when I showed him the early pregnancy test. It's like he's learning this news for the first time.

The more excited he sounds, the more terrified I become. I don't know what's wrong with him, but I know it's serious.

"Out of an abundance of caution, I think we might order a CT scan," a young resident says. "Nothing to worry about at this stage. It's likely a concussion."

"Will I be having one?"

"Not at this point, no."

"Because of the baby?"

She looks at my stomach, then back at my eyes, kindly. "No."

Because I'm *with* it, aren't I? I can answer basic questions. There's clearly nothing wrong with my brain.

"Let's get you thoroughly checked out, Kate, and then you can probably hop off this bed."

Subtext: I can quit being the patient here and start being my husband's support person.

*

An hour and a half later, I am officially discharged. I sit in Cam's empty cubicle, unable to go anywhere near radiology, obviously. They said it could take a while.

Being alone here, waiting, makes the whole thing feel even more enormous in my mind. I need time to think before I call anyone and make this real. It's the first time I try out the words. *What if Cam has a brain tumor?* Even thinking it makes me instantly sick, and I belt down the corridor to the nearest toilet.

My phone lights up and I can see it's Hugh, probably wondering where I am. I can't talk about work right now, so I decline the call. *No.* If Cam's sick, I have to keep my job. I hit the button on the missed call and, when he picks up, I barge into the conversation without preamble, as though we've been working together for years.

"We've had a car accident," I blurt out. "We're at the hospital. Cam's having a CT scan now."

"Is he okay? Are you and Charlie?" Hugh asks. "The baby?" Somehow the fact that Hugh can rattle off a complete roll call of my nuclear family makes Cam's forgetfulness seem even worse.

"I think he's got a brain tumor!" I blurt out.

"What?"

"Cam. He's not right. He can't answer basic questions."

There's a pause on the line. "Where's Charlie?"

"Childcare." It's been less than a month since he started, and he still cries every time we drop him off. That should be his biggest problem. He's too innocent to have a seriously ill parent.

"Who's waiting with you? Can your mum come?"

My mum is not an "emergency" person. She *is* the emergency, much of the time. Even the idea of having her here raises my blood pressure.

I don't speak because I don't want to sound pathetic. Grace is at a social work conference in Sydney, though of course I'll text her next.

"Do you want me to call in?" Hugh asks, into my silence. Any human on the other end of this phone call would have to say that.

Yes.

"I'm fine," I lie. I'd like to think I'm overreacting, as usual, but every cell in my body seems to know this is not a rehearsal for some distant future diagnosis, decades from now when we're old and tired and ready for it.

"I'm not convinced," Hugh observes.

"Don't make a special trip." I haven't known him long, but I suspect a special trip is exactly what he will make.

"I'll be there in twenty minutes," he promises.

I pass the time between our call and his arrival googling brain tumor symptoms on my phone.

Headaches. *Check.*

Vision problems. *I suspect so.*

Confusion. *Yes.*

Personality or behavior changes. *Yes.*

It's been little glitches. Introversion, when he's normally so gregarious. Frustration, instead of his usual patience.

I can't keep reading. I was hoping it might be comforting, might tell me there's something else, much more innocuous, behind all of this. A virus, perhaps. Some totally treatable infection.

I lock my phone and up pops the photo of my boys on the lock screen. Cam with Charlie on his shoulders. Daddy's boy. Cam is the fun parent. He's the fun spouse.

My heart sinks again and I blink back tears.

"*Listen, Grace,*" I type. "*I'm fine, but we were in a car accident. Cam is having a CT scan. Something's very wrong.*"

"I can hire a car and be home in three hours," she types back. *"Let me get out of this session so I can call you. . . ."*

"Hugh is on his way in," I type.

"Boss of the year?" she writes.

Something like that. He fixed the problem at the gym. He fixes everything at work. There's a part of me that hopes he'll stride in and fix this too. Wave a magic wand and make it all go away. Or at least open up a manageable path through it, with the happily-ever-after ending Cam and I are supposed to get.

13

A lovely nurse bustles in just as Hugh arrives. I try to ignore the unsettled expression he clears as he enters the cubicle.

"There's a bit of a queue at radiology," the nurse explains. "Now would be a good time to pop out and get something to eat. I've got your number and I'll call as soon as Cam gets back."

An orderly had wheeled Cam away on the bed and this empty cubicle—everything unplugged and switched off—feels like a harbinger of doom.

I look to Hugh for leadership. That's what he's paid for, after all. And I hate the compassion I meet in his eyes. Compassion is for people with something terrible going on. This diversion is way off script for *Kate and Cam's Excellent Adventure*.

"I can't think of food," I tell him.

"Let's go for a walk."

We make it out of Emergency and as far as the hospital foyer. I don't want to stray too far in case the nurse rings.

There's a discarded magazine on one of the lounges. I take a seat and flick through pages of "inspiring" interviews with "brave" women who've made it through unimaginable tragedy. I do not want to join them. I'm not the heroic type. I'm more the falling-in-a-heap type.

Hugh sits down beside me, catches a headline in the magazine, and confiscates it. "You know they invent most of that stuff," he says definitively. "Come on. You need to eat. There's a café across the road and we could sit in the sun for a few minutes."

"I'm not hungry."

"Come and watch me eat, then."

He stands up and starts walking. I find myself following him out of the foyer like he's the Pied Piper of Hamelin. Must be the Hot Coals Effect.

Canberra has the audacity to have turned on one of its peerless autumn days for this experience. The crunch of red and brown leaves, the soft breeze and twinkling sunbursts through the trees want to trick me into believing the high-tech environment of machines and alarms and tubes and cords that we've just exited does not exist.

"What about some soup?" Hugh suggests when we reach a small café in the private hospital across the road. It's populated by staff in scrubs, and shadow families—gaunt, pale humans, living a half-life while a loved one suffers. *Are these my people now?*

"Really can't eat," I tell Hugh.

"Come on. You don't know how long you'll be in here with him. Keep your strength up."

"I don't want to talk about Cam, or my strength. The two are not currently compatible."

"Two bowls of soup, please, and bread rolls on the side." He pulls out a credit card from his wallet and says, "You're stronger than you think, Whittaker."

"You've known me all of, what, nine weeks?"

"And what a fascinating nine weeks that has been."

When he smiles, it lights up the whole café. My body absorbs the light, desperate for the flicker of warmth.

"Listen. I'm not going to tell you everything is going to be okay," he says as we find a table outside. "I do know Cam is in the best possible hands. You're not alone."

I'm not *alone*, but I'm also not overwhelmed with Canberra friends. Most of my friends are back in Melbourne or scattered around the world. Between them, Cam and Grace tick so many boxes for me, I haven't worked too hard on expanding my circle further here, particularly when I spent most of the first two years struggling through pregnancy and new motherhood. A local mums' group has been nice, but it's been a bit fractured since some of us returned to work and others haven't.

"Apart from Grace, who you met at the gym, and who's on her way home from Sydney, most of my friends are interstate," I admit. "Or overseas."

"Well, you've got your colleagues," he states calmly.

"Who've known me five minutes and definitely have somewhere better to be than a hospital bistro."

Saying that makes my heart race. I want him to stay. The idea that Cam is right now having tests that could upturn our entire future, and that I will have to handle this alone, utterly unnerves me. Being the only adult, caring for Cam if he slips further from Charlie and the baby and me, is a waking nightmare I simply cannot entertain.

"Can we change the subject?" I ask, taking a sip of the soup. Its hearty tomato flavor is as out of place in my mouth as the autumn trees had been in my hospital reality.

"As long as we don't talk about work," Hugh says, pulling a small white roll apart and dunking it into the soup. "Such a bore."

I force a smile.

Hugh and I have had several coffee meetings in the last few weeks, but we haven't shared so much as a sandwich in the work kitchen yet. Everything about having a meal with a relatively unfamiliar man amplifies all the ways in which he is not Cam. Cam doesn't dunk bread. Unlike my husband, Hugh scoops his spoon away from him in the bowl like you're supposed to. I watch as he lifts the spoon to the line of unfamiliar lips. Dark stubble on his neck that he's missed in his morning shave, where I'm used to seeing blond. . . .

Stop this, Kate. You'll go mad.

I need spoken words to drown my internal chatter. One of those buoying, distracting conversations people dance through in waiting rooms when they're really miles away, worried as hell.

"What do you do in your spare time, Hugh, apart from picking up strange women at the gym?" I'm referring, of course, to myself, and the fact that he picked me up from the floor after I was discharged from the treadmill.

"You're technically the only woman who's thrown herself at my feet lately," he replies and takes another sip of soup. And a bite of his roll.

Looking at him, I find that very hard to believe. "You know that woman in the purple gym gear chased after you."

"Yep," he explains. Full stop. He takes a convenient glance at his lock screen, checking for missed messages.

I see.

"Did she ever get the tea on your relationship status?"

His spoon hovers in midair.

"The tea? What's that? Some sort of millennial slang you've appropriated?" He knows exactly what I'm asking. He's just refusing to engage.

I push my bowl of soup aside. "Can't you just play along, if only to take my mind off Cam for a few minutes?" Setting Hugh up, like some off-camera, real-life love project, could be exactly the distraction I need. "I know people," I tell him. "In case you're looking for . . . you know."

I don't mean sex! I sound like my boss's pimp.

"I mean in case you're looking for a love story," I clarify. "Like I have with Cam."

The comparison slips out before I can edit it and rips me straight back into a world of pain. I imagine Cam, right now, being fed brain-first into a CT machine, even more frightened than I am about what's happening to him.

"She'd have to be all in," Hugh says steadily. "I want that 'two of us against the world' thing. She needs to be funny. Unpretentious. What you see is what you get. . . ."

He checks he's got my attention back. "I'm telling you this purely because I know you're feeling sick about Cam right now and want to be distracted, okay? Not as permission to go rogue and start matchmaking."

I sit up straight. "Do I seem like the kind of person to go rogue?"

"Yes, frankly."

I pretend to look offended. And think of Grace. She's funny. And also recently single, now that she's turfed Max.

"I want someone caring," he continues. "Generous."

Check. Check.

"Do you want kids?" I ask bluntly. Because if he doesn't, Grace is a no.

He looks more uncomfortable than I did in the job interview. "With the right person," he says. "That would be wonderful."

Hugh and Grace and their future babies are as happy in my head as I am bereft, on my own, with my two. I've never been so envious of two people in all my life.

"You look like you've seen a ghost, Kate," he says. "You all right?"

No. I'm not. It's hard to explain why, but I feel like I've lost my husband and my best friend and my boss, all in one fell swoop.

My phone rings.

"Kate? I'm Dr. Wilson. I'm a resident in the Neurology Department, just taking a look at your husband's preliminary test results. Are you still in the area? I'd like to speak with you."

This is the call. Our lives are about to implode. I look at Hugh, watching me, concerned, and I have to restrain my hand from moving itself across the table to grasp his.

"I'm coming now," I tell the doctor.

14

Cam is in the bed, looking as concerned as I feel. Dr. Wilson drags an extra chair into the cubicle and asks me to sit down. I do not want the kind of news that I can't receive standing up. I take Cam's hand nervously.

"Okay. Now, as I understand it, you've presented here due to a car accident, with some concern that Cam may have hit his head. We've done a structural imaging scan and there's no sign of trauma from the accident."

"As I thought," I say quietly.

"But there are still a few unusual symptoms. Some cognitive difficulties, some confusion, and memory issues. Is this something you've been noticing for a while?"

"I just put it down to a busy life and stress," I say, feeling neglectful. "He's so healthy."

"We're going to need to do some more tests to find out what's going on. To begin with, Cam, would you mind standing up and walking down the corridor and back?"

Cam gets off the bed and stands. He's so tall. Those floppy, blond curls. That relaxed attitude that drew me toward him the second I saw him stride into that first lecture, smiling with his friends. He'd been unaware of the hold he had over me from that very first second, long before he passed that first note.

He walks down the corridor and back. Nothing out of the ordinary as far as I can tell. Surely there can't be anything seriously wrong when someone looks as good as he does now.

Dr. Wilson performs a couple of tests on his reflexes and muscle coordination. He passes with flying colors. She asks about nutrition and alcohol use and scribbles notes on Cam's file.

"I'd like you to draw a clockface with all the numbers correctly positioned," she says. "And please show the time as ten past two."

He flashes me a confident grin and does as she asks.

"Now, Cam. I'm going to ask you to remember three items," she says. "Table, shoe, and Richmond Street. Got that?"

Cam winks at me. "Table, shoe, Richmond Street."

"Great. Now, what day is it today?"

"Monday the eighth."

Relief floods through me.

"What's your wife's name?"

"Kate."

"Name and ages of your children?"

"Charlie, he's one. And Kate is pregnant, just a few weeks along. We had the ultrasound earlier."

I feel like giving him a standing ovation. I've never been so proud! It must have been a bump to the head, surely? Can't we call it a day?

"What were those three items I asked you to remember?" Dr. Wilson asks, after a few more basic questions. She puts the file down and looks at Cam carefully.

Confusion.

"I recall you asking me to remember some things."

"Take your time. There were three."

Table, Cam. Shoe! RICHMOND STREET! How can this be so hard?

He looks at me, tears in his eyes. "I'm sorry, Katie."

His remorse over failing this test is the single most tragic moment I've ever witnessed. My blood runs cold as I feel our relationship slipping away from us already, ushering in a bleak new reality that's dark and confusing and something I don't feel remotely equipped to handle.

"We'll get to the bottom of this, but you'll need to be admitted," the doctor says. "There are lots of tests to come. I'll hand you over to the nursing staff to make that happen."

With Cam finally settled on the seventh-floor neurological ward by eight p.m., I'm made to leave so he can get some proper rest. And so that I can too, apparently, even though I know for a fact I'm not going to sleep a wink. I've been updating Grace and Hugh all afternoon, and I'd had to phone Mum earlier to fill her in and ask her to collect Charlie from childcare midafternoon.

"Neurological ward?" she'd repeated just now when I called again. "But Cam is such a brilliant man, Katherine!"

"Brilliant men do get sick, Mum," I'd answered impatiently. "Being clever isn't an immunity idol."

"A what?"

"Never mind."

"But his brain, *of all things*?"

Thankfully Grace was due back about now and should be at home with Charlie soon, waiting for me. I really need a nonconfrontational face.

I walk into the elevator and push the button for the ground floor. The doors close and I feel temporarily cocooned. Of course, as soon as the doors shut, the tears come. *What is going to happen to us? What about this baby?*

Moments later, the bell pings and the elevator doors open and I have this fleeting wish that my fairy godmother will be standing there, ready to transform the entire situation. But it's some other crying family, going up. This place is horrible.

I've never felt more alone than I do walking into the hospital's main foyer, which was buzzing earlier in the day but is now dimly lit and eerily quiet. When I see him, I stop in my tracks. He's sitting on the lounge alone, illuminated by his laptop, tie undone and draped around his neck, shirt sleeves rolled up. Diligent. Patient.

When he sees me, he shuts the lid of the computer and stands up. I walk straight over to him, not even trying to disguise the fact that I'm upset. I want to fall into his arms and bawl, but something stops me. It's not the fact that he's my boss—in this moment we are just two humans having a very real, grown-up experience. It's the invisible wall he keeps around himself, which I noticed the first time we met. It commands respect.

"Why are you still here?" I ask.

"I went back to work in the interim," he explains. "But you gave me a comprehensive list of all the support you don't have. Your best friend is at home with Charlie. You crashed your car. I figured you'd need a lift home eventually."

I don't know what to say. It's extraordinarily kind of him. "I would have caught an Uber."

"I know. But you'll be up for some hefty medical bills and a lot of uncertainty. It's one small thing I could do to help. I'd have been working at home in Kingston, ten minutes away, anyway. This is just a change of scene."

Does he ever stop working? I wait while he packs up his things and we walk outside into the crisp night air, where I breathe deeply.

"This has been the worst day of my life," I tell him bluntly. I immediately feel guilty, because today was also the day we saw our baby for the first time, and that was temporarily gorgeous.

We're walking slowly back to the parking lot. It's the speed you'd saunter in the twilight if you had all the time in the world—or were trying to string out the sweet spot between one horrible reality and another, as I am. Being here, with all this medical testing horror, and being at home without Cam. I'm dreading getting through Charlie's night-waking and calling out, invariably for Daddy, who he seems to favor at the moment. *Gosh, now more tears.*

Hugh walks beside me and must be well aware of my crying but is doing nothing to cheer me up. It's the perfect response. So many people can't handle someone's discomfort, but this gentle strength is exactly what I need right now. Of course that makes me cry even more. . . .

"Will Grace be able to stay over?" he asks.

Oh, I hope so.

"Obviously, don't give a second thought to work," he adds.

I hadn't given it a first thought.

"The doctor doesn't know what's wrong," I say. Hugh hasn't intruded, but I need to talk about it. "He said they need to do a lot more tests. The CT scan didn't show anything obvious."

We've reached Hugh's Audi now, and he clicks the central locking. I swing myself into the leather passenger seat and notice how immaculate it is. No mashed cookies and random grapes worked into the upholstery. I try to imagine Hugh as a dad, and think he'd struggle a bit with the mess.

Not like Cam, who revels in it. If anyone was born to father children, it's my husband. The parental instinct runs strong in him, and I often wish I could borrow even a fraction of it, instead of second-guessing every move I make.

"This is really kind of you. Thanks. I think I would have sobbed all over an Uber driver, and it's bad enough with you."

Understanding blue eyes acknowledge my plight. "Put your address in here," he says, "so you don't have to think about it."

I tap it into the GPS and send Grace a message to say I'm on my way. Then I lean back on the headrest and shut my eyes. It feels like I'm carrying today's exhaustion, plus all the provisional exhaustion from the future.

Our companionable silence is broken only by the occasional sniff from me. I look over at him at one point, his eyes focused on the traffic, face lit up by the passing streetlights, and realize he's one of those quality people anyone could call, day or night, and he'd be there.

The darkness of the Monaro Highway cloaks my agony, and I wish the drive home would suspend reality for longer than twenty minutes. Eventually Hugh pulls up in our driveway and cuts the engine just as my outside light flicks on and Grace appears in the doorway. My other angel. She comes down the path and gives me an enormous, silent hug, then wipes the tears from my face and her own.

When she's composed herself, she looks at Hugh and extends her hand. "Hello again."

He smiles and shakes Grace's hand, and she falls in love with him on the spot and they live happily ever after. The end. Seriously. I've seen that look in her eyes many times. Usually, it's directed at totally the wrong guy. But this time . . .

"Nice to see you again, Grace," he says.

"How's Charlie?" I ask.

"Go inside and see him, Kate. He's fallen asleep in the most gorgeous position in the cot."

I turn to walk toward the house and pause to thank Hugh for everything. When I spin around, the two of them are just standing in silence, watching me, and looking spectacular together. I almost feel superfluous to this gathering, and I'm swamped by a wave of sadness, missing Cam.

Hugh puts his hand gently on Grace's arm, as if willing her to go to me. He hasn't touched me at all, even when I was distraught, so matchmaking-wise, this is a promising sign.

"Should we exchange numbers?" Grace asks. "Keep in touch?" He ducks back to the car to get his phone and I watch as they swap details, mutually helpful. Of course, my vivid imagination takes this moment and runs with it all the way to my matron-of-honor speech at their future wedding. *It all started late one night, when Grace led Hugh up my garden path. . . .*

I see myself toasting this, happily. Toasting them. It's all so crystal clear in my mind's eye.

And then I turn to clink glasses with the man who is always by my side, who I'll acknowledge in the speech as having inadvertently brought Grace and Hugh together during his alarming but ultimately innocuous health scare.

But that's where the daydream starts failing me.

15

By the time I've dropped Charlie at childcare the next morning, found a hugely expensive parking garage at the ends of the earth, and walked miles into the hospital and up to Cam's ward, he's had an MRI scan and some other pathology tests and is sitting up in bed eating a tub of fruit.

"There you are!" he says warmly, the second I appear through the gap in the blue curtains and drop my bag on the end of his bed. "The love of my life."

Yep. That's me.

"You okay? How's Charlie? I missed you both!"

It's all the wrong way around. I should be asking about him, but I'm too scared to.

"Did you get any sleep?" he asks.

"Not much. You?"

"Can't sleep without you."

"Me neither."

We are the cutest. Honestly. It's a beautiful thing to be one half of "Cam & Kate." At least, it is when that pairing isn't being threatened. Suddenly, I wonder if I haven't been dinking on the back of our relationship. Too much "Cam & Kate," not enough "Kate"? It's too anxiety-inducing to contemplate.

"Any more news?" I finally build the courage to ask.

"They said the doctor will come around with the results of the scans as soon as possible. I'm really sorry I'm putting you through this, Kate."

Do. Not. Cry.

"How are you feeling?" he asks. "How's the morning sickness?"

He remembered. Actually, now that I think of it, there's been none this morning. I must have turned a corner.

"Do you want the rest of my fruit?" he offers, and I shake my head.

Though the bed is narrow, I squash onto it next to him and I doze on Cam's chest, listening to his heartbeat. In each other's arms, nothing can touch us. We're safe. It doesn't matter if my identity is one part struggling new mum, one part frustrated writer with fundraising talents, and eight parts in love with Cam Whittaker. The whole equation works. If he's well.

"This reminds me of that single bed we crammed ourselves into the first night we slept together," he says. "Remember?"

I shudder. How could I forget? My twentieth birthday. *Way* too many spritzers at the party. Each of us basking in the other's starlight, barely able to keep our hands off each other. My gorgeous boyfriend. *Everyone* loved him. I loved him so much I fell to my knees at one point and drunkenly proposed marriage in front of everyone, just as a joke. He said yes. Also joking. One giant hangover and seventeen years later, here we are.

"Why did you say yes?" I ask him now. "Even as a joke?"

He squeezes my shoulder. "The debauchery and disorderliness were disarming."

I laugh.

"Nuh, it was that what you see is what you get. You were totally unpretentious. . . ."

"Excuse me, Kate? Cameron? I've got some results we need to talk about."

All the romance comes crashing down around us, falling into a splintered pile at the doctor's feet. She's petite and serious, with a dark pixie cut and black-rimmed glasses, wearing Docs. Sensible footwear for walking along hard hospital floors all day, changing people's lives, one way or the other. I know from the expression on her face that she's about to change ours, and I watch as she switches on a lightbox and pulls some printed films out of one of the enormous envelopes she's carrying.

"Okay." Dr. Wilson sighs, as if she's centering herself in this moment, in this room, in our lives. "As I said yesterday, the structural imaging didn't show anything that might explain the symptoms. No tumor that we can detect. No stroke. No trauma to the brain. So, I think we can confidently rule out those causes."

This is good news, surely? They're the main things to be terror-stricken about. The things that kept me awake all night, worrying.

"The bloods came back clear for thyroid disorders or vitamin deficiencies, which can sometimes play havoc with cognition."

I have a feeling she's about to get to the punch line.

"Now, because those tests came back clear but we're still observing symptoms, we ran some functional imaging," she says, pulling the results out of the next envelope. It's like she's about to announce Best Actor at the Oscars. She sets up the scan on the lightbox and checks it, as if to confirm what she's about to say. "This is where we can measure things like glucose metabolism and the amyloid deposits in the brain. Tests like this can be useful in cases where memory and cognition have been impacted quite quickly, and at a relatively young age, when there's no other obvious explanation."

We're both silent. Cam's grip on my hand loosens, but I pull it back. I won't allow him to let go. Not even to *think* of letting go.

"We'll need to do more testing, including a battery of neuropsychological tests, but we're confident enough at this stage to give you a possible diagnosis, and I'm sure you're keen to know our thoughts."

"'Keen' isn't the right word," I mutter.

The doctor smiles bleakly. She looks like she's about to hand down a death sentence. "Look, I'm sorry to break this news, Cam. I suspect what we're dealing with here is early- and rapid-onset Alzheimer's."

We're stunned.

"I'm so terribly sorry," the doctor says, met with our blank stares. *This can't be happening. This isn't even possible, surely, at his age!*

"Prognosis?" Cam asks. I don't recognize the clipped tone in his voice, and I want to run out of the room before I hear the answer.

"It's a bit of a 'how long is a piece of string' question. You're young and fit and otherwise healthy. Some patients live another fifteen or even twenty years."

"And others?"

I wish he would shut up.

"In cases of rapid onset of the disease, and that's what I suspect you may have, Cameron, it can be two or three years."

All I'm hearing now is white static, as the ground gives way and my severed heart hemorrhages all over our beautiful life.

"There's nothing you can do?" I think it's me who asks this, but everything is swimming.

The doctor sighs. It's not good. "I'll refer you to a specialist neurologist in Sydney," she explains. "What I'll recommend is that we hook you up with a social worker who can help you access services to navigate this. I know it must feel overwhelming."

Overwhelming? I was prepared for a brain tumor. But this totally untreatable, galloping monster arriving several decades before it's due seems so much worse.

"Cam is only thirty-eight!" I argue with the doctor. "He's a father! I'm pregnant! There must be some mistake!"

She refuses to accept any of my arguments, and my heart breaks again as the sickening thought descends that Charlie is going to lose the rock-solid center of his world. How will we ever break this to him? As for the baby, I don't even want to think about the implications. They might never remember their dad at all.

Wave upon wave of unbearable realization crashes over me, the more people I imagine being swept into this juggernaut. This will *break* Cam's parents. You're not supposed to bury your child. Not at any age. And they're too frail to travel here from the UK now. They were so ecstatic about our baby news two nights ago, and now this.

"It's hard to accept, I know," Dr. Wilson says. "The earlier you're armed with information, the better for you. In the meantime, there are some drugs we can try. In some cases they slow the progression of the disease. We'll need more tests before we start those."

"But the drugs don't cure it?" I ask, already knowing the answer. My grandmother died from Alzheimer's, as grandmothers often do. She was ninety-two. It was horrendous.

It's so stuffy in here. I get off the bed and start pacing and fanning myself. Breathing too fast.

The windows won't open. I need air. And a healthy husband who isn't going to lose his fucking memory before he's forty.

"Katie," he says, with altogether too much grace. "We'll get through this."

And that's when I lose it. Only one of us will be getting through this, and that person is me. Why does it have to be *Cam* who is sick?

I get an impeccably timed text from Grace. *"Any news?"*

I look at Cam, who I promised to love until death parted us, assuming we meant some time in our eighth or ninth decades. Not *this* decade. Our baby hasn't even been born yet, and one of its parents is . . . well, he's . . . I can't even say it.

"SOS, Grace. It's fucked."

16

Our first instinct is to adopt a "business as usual" approach. No admitting defeat. No brooding. We'll keep ourselves active and distracted while all of this sinks in.

Complete denial, in other words.

"*Alzheimer's?*" Mum probes, when I call in to break the news.

"Early-onset, obviously," I explain. "You can get dementia at any age."

A chilling fear rises within me that it's something that could strike Charlie, too. He could well be genetically predisposed. And not just Charlie. The baby.

Would we have so carelessly conceived if we'd known?

"Katherine, this is unfortunate," Mum says. It's the first time in my life I've known her to underplay a situation. It shows how out of her depth she is that she can't muster more of a frenzy.

When Cam and I sit ourselves down in front of Zoom to tell his parents in England, their beaming faces come into view and part of me wants to hold off. I have the ludicrous thought that maybe Cam can wait out their deaths. We don't know how long it will take for more symptoms to develop. They're in their late seventies now and can't travel all this way. Why can't we hide this from them? Spare them the agony. Maybe they would get Alzheimer's themselves and there'd be no point telling them at all . . .

"How are you feeling, Kate?" his mum asks. She's warm and grandmotherly, and I wish we lived closer. I desperately need one of her hugs.

I'm at a complete loss as to how to answer her question. She's talking about the pregnancy, of course, and last they knew, everything here was going swimmingly.

"Mum, Dad, there's something we need to tell you," Cam says. "And I wish it was better news."

They're instantly worried and move closer together at the kitchen table.

"Is it the baby?" his mum asks, and we shake our heads.

"Not Charlie?"

"Charlie's fine," I say quickly.

"I've been having trouble with my memory lately," Cam begins. "Little things, mostly. Errors of judgment . . ."

We already agreed to leave out the bit about the car accident. Why worry them with unnecessary detail?

"The doctors think it's Alzheimer's," he says, and I watch as my in-laws are suspended in time. The laptop screen looks frozen but isn't. They look at Cam like he's still the six-year-old boy who used to climb trees in their back garden and trample mud onto the freshly mopped linoleum in the kitchen. Not the internationally lauded professor, near the top in his field.

Then their faces fall. Apparently, the British stiff upper lip does not apply when your incredible son tells you he has an incurable brain disease. And nor should it.

*

I'm in the toilets at work only days after his diagnosis, staring at my reflection in the mirror, adding up pregnancy symptoms. Actually, it's more that I'm adding up the number of symptoms I did have and now don't.

Nausea? *Gone.*

Sore boobs? *Gone.*

Ligament twinges? *Gone.*

Exhaustion? Still exhausted, but as my husband has just been diagnosed with a terminal disease and I'm in the process of rewriting our entire future, I give myself a bit of leeway.

I had the first hint of a crampy, dragging feeling about an hour ago, and now I'm standing in here, scared to look. Surely the universe wouldn't be so cruel as to remove half of my little family in one week. Since the diagnosis, I've been struggling with the idea of raising Charlie and the baby on my own. I don't know how to do parenting without Cam. He's the composed one. The intuitive one. *What if I brought this on myself?*

I remember the day I got my first period on my thirteenth birthday, at my horse-riding party, being terrified to look, scared of the evidence, trying to pretend this wasn't happening. I'd have twice as many periods for the rest of my life if I could just avoid seeing evidence of bleeding this one time. I'm not religious, but I find myself bargaining with whoever's listening.

But I think I've used up all my favors. I've already spent a week bargaining about Cam. I started small. *Save him and I'll give up coffee for life. Spare my husband and I'll never eat chocolate again. Never have wine. Never buy another book.*

Then I ramped it up a notch. *I'll give up everything I own. I'll live alone. Save Cam and I'll give him up.* I would do almost anything to keep him alive.

Save my baby, I think now. *And you can have Cam.*

I rush into a stall feeling sick, horrified at my own thoughts. Terrified that I've put some curse on Cam. Equally horrified that I've chosen this baby over the love of my life. An impossible choice, yet I've made it, in an instant. I didn't even think too hard. I'm starting to wonder why it's Cam or the baby at risk at all. Why not me? The type of woman who would sacrifice the devoted father of her one-year-old for a baby we haven't even met yet. One I was initially terrified to have and now feel more connected to than any other human, because it's the only part of Cam's future that's still tracking on an upward curve. Or was.

Baby, please hold on.

I'm already crying when I brave the investigation that proves within seconds that all is lost. Huge, heaving sobs come from a place within me that I didn't even know existed. So much grief, I can't stand it. *I can't do this.* It's impossible to be alive and feel this wounded, and now the bargaining is all about me. *End this. I can't be here. This is beyond me.*

"Kate? Is that you?" It's Sophie's voice, as she enters the bathroom. Bright. Young. Still-enchanted-with-the-world Sophie.

"I'm okay," I explain quickly. With all the crying, the defense sounds weak, even to me. "Actually, Sophie, do you have a pad?"

"Sorry, I use menstrual cups," she says. *Of course she does.* "But Kate, aren't you—"

"I need a pad, specifically. Otherwise, there's a risk of infection."

I hate that I know this without having to look it up. Hate that my encyclopedic knowledge of all things infertility didn't come from books, but from heartbreaking experience over several years.

"I'll find one," Sophie says. Her voice has lost its bubble. I feel bad to have flattened her effervescence.

After a minute or two, there's a knock on the main door to the bathroom. "Kate?" It's Hugh's voice, in the corridor.

Bloody Sophie!

"Please leave me alone," I say, in a voice that can't hide my agony. "I need to go home," I add, my voice shaking. "Via the doctor."

I fold up a bunch of toilet paper to use in the interim, flush the toilet, unlatch the door, and wash my hands. Then I close my eyes for a second, building the courage to open the door into a world without my baby. I pull the handle and step into the corridor, then stand there with Hugh, in a state that couldn't feel more vulnerable if I was giving birth right in front of him.

His expression seems to echo my pain. "I'm sorry," he offers.

Everyone is nothing but sorry, in every direction, and it makes no difference to how heinous everything is. People say, "I wish there was something I could do" and "I don't know what to say" and that's because this is The Impossible. This whole thing. Cam. The baby. Me facing a future without either of them. And now I feel guilty about Charlie. That he's not enough. My innocent, darling child. Not enough to stop me from wishing my own life away.

I'm thinking all of this and hoping none of it is being subliminally communicated. Hugh is standing there, looking traumatized on my behalf. The perfect man. Hot Coals Hugh.

"How are you so freaking *together* all the time?" I find myself sniping at him, very unfairly. "You always know what to say. You're constantly doing exactly what's needed. You cope with everything, no matter how hard. Your life is just this shiny, untarnished, extraordinary, seamless, *easy* experience and I am envious as hell."

I will myself to stop this verbal battering. But there's a circuit misfiring in my brain. I actually want to throw something. No. What I really want is for the physical pain that's about to ramp up in my body to escalate faster and overpower this impossible emotional agony. What is *wrong* with me, taking this out on innocent bystanders when they're only trying to help? And here come hot, plentiful tears. About losing Cam. Losing the baby. Losing my job? Just losing . . . everything. This is all just so *hopeless.*

"I'm sorry," I say, anguished. "Please don't sack me."

If you have to be pathetic and place your fate in the hands of someone else, it's a good move to pick Hugh Lancaster. He is still here. Still standing. Letting me pummel him with the anger I really want to direct inward. In this moment, it's abundantly clear that I have lost my way. And yet I seem to have his full permission and support to be recklessly emotional and say all the things he knows I'll regret, without any judgment at his end. And without the pity I've read on the faces of every single other person who's been privy to the first half of our horrible news. I can't bear the thought of the double helping of pity that will be incoming when people hear I've gone and lost the baby too.

"Your job is safe," he confirms quietly.

Safe.

The very thing I do not feel.

I stare into his eyes for a second, though everything's blurry through tears, and I hope he can read my apology and my thanks. Just having had this outburst has taken the edge off my rage. And I realize that's exactly what Hugh is letting me do. I need to unleash the full force of my despair on someone other than my husband, because you don't shout at a terminally ill person about losing his child.

"'Losing' is such a stupid word for what happens when someone dies," I tell Hugh. "I haven't misplaced my baby. Didn't leave it lying around somewhere, or on the bus or in the trolley at the supermarket. I'm not absentmindedly going to lose my husband. . . ."

Hearing these words, I realize how utterly unfair this whole situation really is. One of these things alone would be almost too much to bear. But *both*? Now I'm pitying myself and that's something I promised I would never do.

"What am I going to do?" I whisper desperately.

"I'm going to call Grace. . . ." he says.

"No, please don't!" I say quickly. "You heard her on the treadmill oversharing about her ovaries. This would be triggering for her. I'll need to tell her gently."

"Your mum?"

"I don't have the strength—"

"I'd ask Sophie," he says, "but Kate, I just don't think she's up to this. I don't think it's fair."

He's right. Let's not devastate the kid. She's sunshine, and don't we all need that?

"Cam isn't allowed to drive, even if he hadn't written off his car," I explain. "Just till they get the full picture from the diagnosis. Although after our accident, I don't think—"

It's déjà vu. The whole idea of needing more medical help so soon after the last lot.

The pain is doing what I'd wanted it to. Ratcheting up, quickly. I invite myself into Hugh's office for somewhere to sit down for a minute, where I won't traumatize Sophie, and I double over.

"Then I'm going to drive you to the hospital, and you're going to see a doctor, who can tell you for sure what is happening and what to do next. Then I'll take you home. And if it's as you fear, you will tell Cam in the kindest, gentlest possible way that this baby is gone. You will cry. He will cry. It will be as bad as you're imagining, or even worse. But you'll hold each other and Charlie and get through this."

I'm silent. And stunned.

"You'll take as much or as little time off work as you need. You'll go back to your GP and see a psychologist. You'll be a mum and a wife, and you'll do things a mum and wife should never have to do and, even when you feel like you can't go on like this anymore, you will, Kate. You won't feel strong, and you'll mess it up sometimes, but you'll do this anyway, because you have no choice. Okay? No choice."

This is the opposite of a pep talk. It's Hugh outlining in excruciating detail just how bad things are going to get. But somehow it's exactly the leadership I need in this moment. I'm too gobsmacked by the inherent sense in what he's saying to even speak.

We collect our things and walk out to the parking lot, and he drives me to the Emergency Ward, where I stand at the reception desk, contemplating the tragic fact that my Medicare card is supposed to have four names on it in the future, but will have only two.

The woman on the admissions desk confirms my details and takes me through to triage. I'm ushered into a private cubicle and Hugh waits outside, while there's an empty chair beside me, where my husband should be.

I lie on the bed and a doctor checks for a heartbeat she can't find and beams on a screen a blurry picture of how empty I am. Did this little soul take one look at the carnage it was entering into and beat a retreat? And then I succumb to a desperate grief I wish wasn't so familiar.

Eventually, Hugh walks me back to his car, opens the door for me, and passes me the seatbelt and I wonder what the point is. I imagine him crashing the car and sending me flying through the windshield. And that is that.

But he doesn't crash it. He carefully drives me home, pulls up in my driveway, and before I get out of his car, he tells me I can do this, as hard as it is.

And, as it turns out, I don't have to. Because as Hugh drives away and Cam opens the front door, he takes one look at my face, draws me into his arms, and sobs.

17

Cam and I spend the entire weekend, more or less, in bed. Charlie scrambles in and out when he's not banging DUPLO bricks on our wooden floorboards, or climbing all over us, squashing us together as if he knows something's wrong and is trying to glue his family back together.

Knightley seems to possess a sixth sense about our pain. He won't leave my side, curled in a fluffy black ball on our bed beside me. And time passes in a haze of flannel PJs and cotton sheets, coffee, and binges of *Black Books* and *Castle* while autumn sunlight plays across the sunshine-yellow walls in the bedroom, necklaces and earrings glittering on my grandmother's mahogany antique dresser.

It's a weekend of "just us" as a family, which we'll always remember. At least, I will.

Late on Sunday morning, with Charlie having a nap and my fingers still sticky from Cam's signature breakfast in bed of pancakes and maple syrup, I steal a glance at him and wonder when the tendrils of dementia will first seep into the kitchen. How many more Sunday breakfasts will he make me? Will the tradition just drop off his radar one weekend, and I'll find myself hungry at midday, tipping dry cereal into a bowl?

He's still in such an early stage of the disease, half the time we can almost pretend it isn't happening. We can make excuses when he slips up and repeats himself or forgets why he came into the room. I can pretend he's not getting enough sleep, or he's stressed at work, and that's why his mind is fragmented. If I try really hard, I can even indulge a fantasy that we're going to grow old together. Or even properly middle-aged.

"Katie, I need you to know how much I love you, even when I can't express it," he says as we lie in bed, facing each other, close enough for me to study every fleck in his blue eyes. Every freckle. Every pore. My fingers travel up the tapered sides of his dark blond hair into that mess of curls on top, while he traces my face and neck and collarbone. Familiar choreography. We're lost in each other, the way we used to be at nineteen when we were first exploring. But now there's a different urgency. We're imprinting every contour, every line, every blemish deep into our collective consciousness.

"Remember this moment," he urges me. "Burn this into your brain, that I adore you. Have always adored you." His eyes fill with tears.

"Cam, I don't think you're going to forget me overnight." At least, I hope he isn't. Surely it's going to be more gradual than that?

"Never doubt it," he continues. "Never doubt us. I will never give up on you, Kate. I will always find a way to reach you. I want to remember you until the very end."

We both know that's not how this is going to play out.

I tortured myself with Dr. Google one afternoon last week while Cam was at a seminar. I'd gone down a rabbit hole in a younger-onset dementia carers' forum and asked for frank advice on what a newbie should expect.

He'll forget all the mundane things first. Make mistakes. Get confused.

He'll start to forget what you did that day, and then that hour, and then that minute.

He'll forget people he doesn't see much, and then the ones he does.

He'll forget your child.

He'll forget you.

He'll forget who he is and how to eat and take care of himself.

One day, he'll forget how to breathe. . . .

It was a crash course that taught me this determined, steamroller of a disease is going to shut Cam down, one function at a time, like someone's pulling the switches from some random control board, turning off the lights one by one until it's pitch dark and there's nothing left.

"Right, that's it," he says, reading the expression on my face. He gets out of bed and drags the duvet clean off me. "I'm not moping around in here with you another minute!"

I roll over, face-first, away from him, and put the pillow over my head.

He takes me by the hips. Pulls my body toward the foot of the bed, spins me face up, and climbs over me. He takes my hands in his and pins them above my head on the mattress, fingers interlaced, and brings his lips to mine, kissing me like he hasn't done since we were teenagers. Wildly. Urgently. As if it's the first and last time we'll ever do this and someone might catch us, any minute. I wrap myself around him as the kiss slows and stops, leaving me breathless and crazily in love.

"Remember, Kate," he says in a low voice, holding my gaze, and my hands, and my heart. "I'm not dead yet."

*

A few Fridays later, the three of us head to Black Mountain Peninsula for a barbecue with my colleagues. They say it will be one of the last warm days of autumn—still warm enough for some people to swim in the lake, not that I do.

"Not enough chlorine or salt in the lake for my wife," Cam jokes when Sophie asks if I'm going to take a dip.

Hugh eventually pulls up, late, swings into the nearest dirt lot among shady eucalyptus trees, pops the boot, and retrieves a cooler of alcohol and soft drinks, to a grateful round of applause. He walks over and sets the box down on the concrete barbecue, while one of the accountants, Andi, fires up the grill and runs some paper towel over it before it heats.

I'm standing with Cam and corralling Charlie between my ankles, feeding him bits of avocado from the salad we brought, most of which he's mashing into my jeans, while I attempt to hold a conversation with our Comms manager, Isobel, about our shared love of true-crime podcasts.

Hugh starts passing out craft beer to anyone who wants one, including Cam, who he hadn't noticed at first.

"Thanks, mate!" Cam says, and Hugh realizes it's him and lights up. He comes around the barbecue and they share a firm handshake.

"Cam, good to meet you! Glad you could come."

They pat each other on the shoulder, and then Hugh notices Charlie between my legs and crouches down to say hello to him, too.

"Decorating Mum's jeans?" he observes. "Wow, you are cute! Yes, I'm talking to you. Hello, Charlie!"

It's always slightly disconcerting seeing work colleagues in personal settings. My team has had a rapid immersion in the Whittaker Saga, as Grace and I have already come to refer to our various recent misfortunes. It slashed a shortcut through some of the early "getting to know you" period at work.

It's not long before Cam and Hugh break off and engage in some terribly intellectual-sounding conversation about the future state of university strategy or some other thing nobody wants to get into at a picnic, except those two. Hilariously, they've both dressed in linen shorts—Cam in brown, Hugh in gray—and white T-shirts. It's like they got on the phone beforehand to organize some masculine equivalent of the "jeans and a nice top" dress code. Wherever the conversation moves to next, it's funny and vibrant and almost enough to trick me into forgetting this Goose and Maverick friendship they're striking up here is destined to burn out early.

Cam looks incredible. He's a man in his prime, physically, intellectually, career-wise, as a dad . . . just in every conceivable dimension. Grace had said he was "delicious" and she was right.

Maybe the doctors got it wrong? Surely they did. Cam is nothing like the partners of those people on the caregivers' forum. Those poor people lost control, fast. But look at him. Listen to him. He couldn't possibly be sick.

I get the idea they're talking about me now. The way Cam looks at me when we're out socially always makes me feel so connected to him. And makes me feel gorgeous, whether I'm wearing mashed avo or a wedding dress.

"Ears burning?" Hugh says as I approach with Charlie on my hip. Cam extends his arm and draws us in.

"Should they be?"

"Should what be?" he asks brightly.

"My ears," I say.

He looks at me, confused. "You've lost me, Kate."

No, not yet.

And just like that, the joy of seeing him so vital and engaged with Hugh is wiped and replaced with another piece of evidence that his brain is faltering, despite appearances.

"I'd better do another round of drinks," Hugh suggests tactfully. As he walks past me his eyes meet mine and his lips curve into a half smile. It doesn't make me feel beautiful at all, like Cam's smile does.

It makes me feel seen.

"I need to duck to the bathroom," I tell Cam as I glance around the park for the facilities. Charlie is standing up, holding on to my leg for security, and I pry his little fingers off my jeans and latch him onto Daddy's leg instead. They look so comical standing together—Cam over six feet tall, Charlie his mini doppelgänger.

"Charlie! Look at Mumma!" I say as I take a photo on my phone of the two of them beaming. My phone has thousands of photos of Cam and Charlie, and almost none of Charlie with me. Cam used to complain that I was incessantly capturing moments instead of just enjoying them, but now thousands of photos don't seem nearly enough. One day, this will be all Charlie has. Photos to hold on to, instead of Daddy's leg. And I will zoom in on them, desperate for familiar details—laugh lines around his mouth, the set of his jaw. Nothing will ever be in high enough resolution.

The toilets are a long way through the park, well beyond the playground. In truth, it's good to have a few moments to myself. I'm still finding "normal life" confronting, while we're trying to adjust to Cam's diagnosis and the miscarriage and also working through ways to make the most of our time. At work, only Hugh knows the specifics about the diagnosis. I haven't reached a point where I can talk about it without going to pieces, so all the others know is I've lost the baby and there's something else going on.

The latest round of tests indicated that things are progressing at the faster end of the prognosis spectrum. The more we learn, the more likely it seems that this won't be one of those slow-developing cases that takes years. Charlie's not even eighteen months old. I'm desperate for Cam to stay alive and "himself" long enough for his little boy to be able to pocket some memories of his own. I can't stand the idea of him having to spend a lifetime cobbling together a representation of the man his father was, entirely from secondary sources.

I run into Sophie in the toilet block, and she takes me aside, eyes alight.

"Oh my *God*, Kate. Your husband is fit AF!"

I laugh at her exuberance.

"And your baby is squishable! I want to eat him! If I end up with even half of what you've got, I'll be a happy woman."

Half of what I had is exactly what I'll end up with. And I'll be miserable.

"Though, if you saw Tinder, you wouldn't like my chances. . . . How lucky are you never having to go near online dating," she says.

"Lucky" isn't a word I've applied to myself recently. But as Sophie prattles on, praising my little family, unaware of the festival of faux pas she's stumbling through, I realize she's right. I *am* lucky, in a sense. Some people never get to experience what I have. They never find that great love. Never adore someone with even a portion of the untamed intensity that still exists between Cam and me seventeen years after we met. At my mums' group, the others sometimes complain about their partners. That they're not hands-on enough as parents, or they're hopeless communicators or just lazy or distant. They describe themselves as housemates sharing a roof, but not a life.

And then there's Grace and the scores of pregnancy tests she's taken, imagining she sees a second line that never materializes, no matter what kind of light she holds it under.

Am I selfish, to wish for more?

"I hope Tinder rallies for you," I say to Sophie as we wander back.

Cam is back talking to Hugh again, on the fringes of the pack. It's so good to see him comfortable, socially. The diagnosis has already dented his confidence. He's not convinced he's properly following conversations, and he's worried he's repeating himself. Both are true, but I can't bring myself to agree with him.

"Who's got Charlie?" Sophie asks suddenly, and we both freeze.

My eyes scan the group. Nobody has him. I can't see him! Every organ in my body plunges in terror. "Hugh!" I scream blood-curdlingly across the park. "Where's Charlie?"

I hate that I've automatically gone over the top of Cam's head, relegating him to the role of an unreliable witness.

Everyone drops everything and flies into a frantic search of the peninsula—with water in three out of four directions. This level of panic feels almost incompatible with life. *I cannot lose three of them!*

"There!" Sophie yells, after what feels like years but must be only seconds. She's pointing at the water's edge, where Charlie is toddling around, splashing in the shallows, chasing a family of ducks—and now all I'm aware of is Cam and me, sprinting toward him, and toward each other, both splashing into the water together, falling into it, scooping Charlie up into our arms together, crying.

I am *furious*.

It takes every ounce of self-control for me to silence the white-hot rage within me.

Could you not just focus, Cam, for FIVE MINUTES!

"I'm sorry, I'm sorry, I'm sorry," he's repeating. "I thought he was with you. I don't know what happened. . . ."

The rest of my team is gathered on the sandy verge now, witness to the forced disintegration of trust in our marriage. It's not his fault. I know that. But from this moment on, I can't leave him alone with Charlie. He'll forget something on the stove and burn the house down.

He's crying, I'm crying, Charlie's crying—though mainly because we've confiscated the ducks. We splash out of the water together and walk slowly back to the picnic spot, where I sit on the bench at the picnic table, Charlie and I wrapped in somebody's towel, rocking back and forth, hugging him tight to my chest, vowing never to let him out of my sight again.

I want to go home. This has been a disaster. I'm embarrassed that everyone saw that.

I look up in time to see Hugh put a hand on Cam's shoulder. In this moment, I'm angry with him, too. He's the only other person here who knows about the Alzheimer's. What could possibly have been so important about their conversation that it justified letting his guard down?

But mostly, I'm angry with myself. It was me alone who misjudged Cam's capacity. It's a harsh preview of the fact that I'm the one who is increasingly going to shoulder all responsibility for the three of us, undoing years of mutual effort.

And Sophie thought I was *lucky*.

"This is killing me," Cam says after we've put Charlie to bed at home. He hasn't forgotten what happened. He's at some in-between phase where there's no rhyme or reason as to which experiences successfully penetrate into his long-term memory and which are lost.

I'm afraid to speak. I'm over my anger now and feel terrible for having blamed the man I love for something beyond his control, even if I kept it to myself.

"I'm going to abandon you," he says, his face twisted in pain. "I'm going to leave you and Charlie. So young. Both of you."

We're both welling up again now. This is horrible—this grieving somebody while they're still here. Grieving a beautiful relationship that had decades of richness left in it, knowing what we have now will gradually be downgraded to some unutterable situation more akin to carer and patient. It's awful, seeing him this sad for us, when it's *his* life that's going to be cut short.

"I need you to promise me something," Cam says, turning to face me and taking both my hands in his on the couch. "I don't want you locking yourself away forever after I'm gone."

"Cam—it is *way* too early for this conversation!" His faculties are still 90 percent sound, and he's talking like it's over already.

"Let me say this, Katie, while I can. It's important to me."

I know where he's going, and I don't want to hear it.

"You're young," he argues. "You could have fifty more years to live. That's longer than you've been alive. Think about it. We were kids when we met. There's so much more out there for you to experience. Don't stop living just because I do."

"Do you regret that?" I ask. "Settling down with your first real girlfriend?"

He laughs. "I just mean there's so much more of *you* to discover. I want you to do that. You and Charlie."

Okay.

"But don't close your heart off, okay?" he says.

"Cam, stop it." He's asking the impossible.

"I'm saying it now because you need to know I was in completely my right mind when I told you this."

I sense exactly the promise he's going to ask me to make. And I don't want to.

"Kate. Find your way to someone who'll love you and Charlie just as much as I do."

I don't want to think about this. I'll never love someone else like I love Cam. It's just not feasible even to imagine it. I touch his cheek and pull him toward me so we're forehead to forehead. "I've had a more amazing love story with you than some people get in a lifetime," I tell him. "And that's enough."

He kisses me on the forehead, which is always somehow so much more beautiful than kissing me anywhere else. I just want him. For *years* more.

"Listen." He takes my hand in his, brings it to his lips, and kisses it. "One day you'll find yourself in a situation where you're feeling something again. And I know you. You'll let the guilt get to you and you'll want to run."

Yes, I will. This premonition rings true.

"When that moment comes, please remember this one. Remember I wanted this for you, with all my heart. All of it. In that moment, don't look back."

He takes my hand and places it on his chest. His heart is beating erratically. *How can he let me go like this?*

"No one can replace you," I explain desperately. "Know that."

We sit there for ages, and I just want to slow everything down. I want us to stay in this bubble forever, where Cam is only mildly confused and partially forgetful, and there's no fictional other man in my horribly grief-stricken, lonely future without him.

18

The present

Somewhere north of Newcastle, tray tables and overhead lockers shake and shudder. After the next shock of turbulence, I ask Hugh straight up: "Are we going to die?" There's a directness in my tone that he can't ignore, and his expression becomes serious in a way that scares me.

Then, worse, he puts his hand over mine—another first. He must be about to break bad news, or why would he do that? I watch in horror as my fingers waste no time in threading themselves through his, like they have a life independent of my brain.

Seeing my hand like that, entwined with a man's after two years spent on its own, reminds me of all the touches I've missed. Cam never passed me a glass of champagne without his fingers brushing mine. He'd touch the small of my back with every "Have you met my wife?" I'd feel his hands on my hips, gently shifting me aside in the kitchen, or tucking the tag of my shirt into the collar at my neck. He'd grab my hand and pull me away from traffic and crowds and into bookshops and cafés. We *craved* each other's touch, even after life got hard. Especially then.

But now my hand is in Hugh's, where it doesn't belong. My fingers are interlaced against unfamiliar skin. Even after working together for years, his hand forms a shape I don't recognize, his touch foreign.

It's too different, and I get spooked and let go, despite my desperate fear that this plane is lurching out of control.

"I think we'll be okay," he tells me, clearing his throat. "She's diverting us from the storm. I know this is your worst nightmare and you're worried about Charlie, and that's understandable, but I have a strong feeling the pilot is much older than sixteen. I think she knows exactly what she's doing."

He knows exactly what he's doing. I want to bottle him and bring him out in every other moment when life feels treacherous. The way I always do with Cam's notes.

Folded inside my purse are the emergency messages I've carried through everything. In fact, I don't know why I didn't reach for them as a Valium substitute earlier. I take out my purse now and sift past receipts and shopping lists and find the notes tucked carefully into a pocket.

"You know how he used to leave me these?" I say to Hugh. "Not the ones around the house that you've seen. Other notes that he'd slip into my car or bag or suitcase. He was always doing it. Passed me the first one back in a lecture on eighteenth-century romantic poets at uni, the day we met."

"Sentimental sop," Hugh teases.

"If only! All it said was 'Hey, Red . . .'"

Hugh laughs. "Smooth, mate. Expected more from a future English professor."

"Young Cam relied heavily on his good looks and boyish charm," I explain, laughing. I love talking about this. Gorgeous images of my first love play across my memory. Gosh, I fell hard for that boy. "Resistance was useless. Anyway, I just remembered this one about you. Funny, I've never thought to show you this earlier. I found it in my handbag on the day of my job interview, wrapped around the lipstick he knew I'd use to touch up before going in to meet you. Read it and weep, Lancaster!"

Hugh takes the yellow sticky note from me and clears his throat, while I go back to gripping the armrest. "KW: If this guy doesn't see the incredible woman I do . . ." He trails off as his eyes track over the rest. "If he lets you slip through his grasp, it will be the biggest mistake of his career. Be brilliant!" There's an unexpected catch in his voice, and he needs a fraction of a second to compose himself. It's not surprising. They were very close. "That's more like it," Hugh says. "God, I miss him."

He looks at me straight. No bravado. Visible grief.

Don't cry.

Too late.

"Right, I'm ordering you not to cry," Hugh says. "It's contagious."

Gallows humor. Perfect.

He might be ordering me not to cry, but he's also lifting the armrest against regulations—both the airline's and his own. And my body involuntarily shifts into the space he opens up between us, with no resistance from him. *Is he more alarmed by our situation than he seems?* Because this is not what we do, inhabit each other's personal space.

Hugh is no stranger to having me go to pieces in his company, but he always keeps me at a careful distance on the other side of his desk. He closes the door and plies me with tissues and tea, but he never hugs me or anything. Not even at Cam's funeral, when I seemed to hug every other person I'd ever met.

"I'd offer you a cup of tea," he says now, "but the service around here is atrocious."

There's another huge bang and a drop and a thud. People scream. I don't care who he is on the organizational chart, I simply invite myself into his arms.

The side of my face is pressed against his chest. His hands float above my body, as if he's unclear how to deal with this development. I try to block out all the chaos and listen for his heartbeat as a distraction. Of course, it's so noisy I can't hear anything, but if I press my ear hard enough against him, I can feel it thumping through his shirt. Unfortunately, it's beating quite fast, betraying his coolheaded demeanor, and that scares the hell out of me.

"You're freaking me out with your heartbeat," I accuse him. "I thought you weren't worried?"

"I'm not."

"Why the racing heart, then?"

"Geez, Kate. Let me adjust that for you, shall I?"

Am I this demanding? I smooth his business shirt under my fingers, and the hard lines of his chest underneath it make me feel like I'm prying. I don't get to touch people anymore. I read something once about "skin hunger." It's an actual condition and, the more firmly I plaster myself to Hugh's torso, the more certain I am that I'm riddled with it.

He braces against me in response. His muscles contract. He doesn't share my skin starvation, nor does he want this level of proximity.

"You miss your desk," I say cryptically.

"What are you talking about?" he asks, his hand finally coming to land on my arm when the plane lurches again.

"Your desk. The barrier. You know, the wall. The blockade . . ."

He's still puzzled.

"I want to be friends with you again," I blurt out, the way a person would do only if they thought time was running out and they wanted to hurriedly make amends and seek forgiveness and dot all the "i's" and cross the "t's" in an otherwise doomed relationship. "Proper friends, I mean. Without this giant obstacle between us."

"What are they piping through these air vents?"

I won't let him evade this with humor. "What happened between you and Cam?" I demand.

I lift my face to his, up close, in time to catch his expression progressing from consternation through recognition, to pain, and settling on the usual resolute distance, whenever this topic is raised.

"Please don't ask me," he says finally. He means business and meets the desperation in my eyes with a hard no. If he won't tell me now, when it feels like our minutes are numbered, he never will. This secret is doomed to stay wedged between us for the rest of our lives. It's why, despite all the early bonding we were forced into when Cam's life was impaled on the Alzheimer's diagnosis, we operate at a slight distance now. It's sad.

Maybe he's right about the air vents, though. *Something* is obviously going to my head because for one wild moment, despite my frustration with his relentless disengagement on this, perhaps because of the stark vulnerability in his expression, I imagine what it might be like to kiss Hugh Lancaster.

Is this a near-death thing? Maybe the libido is the last thing to go.

I'm instantly alarmed at the thought. Where men are concerned, I've had a one-track mind focused on Cameron Whittaker since that very first English lecture. Even more so since he got sick. Certainly since he died. And yet, this morning I've already imagined kissing Justin *and* Hugh. Is this some midlife widowed reawakening?

I push back from him. What if I lose all rational thought? It's that same strange impulse I get walking over bridges, thinking, *What if I irrationally lose my mind and throw my phone over the guardrail? What if I step out into traffic? What if I break into song in this meeting?*

What if I kiss my boss . . .

"I think the turbulence is settling," Hugh says, disentangling himself from me but holding eye contact while we pay attention to every tiny movement of the plane. Moments pass while we stare at each other, alert for that falling sensation.

It never comes. We're through the storm. He moves back and pulls the armrest down between us again.

Nothing to see here, Anne with an "e."

19

The Ballina Byron Gateway Airport has nothing on the bustle of Brisbane, but after the nightmarish flight, I don't care where we are, so long as we're on firm soil.

My phone springs to life with eleven missed calls from Mum. We're still sitting on the plane waiting for the doors to open and the queue to move when I click on voicemail and settle in for what I suspect will be a masterclass in escalating hysteria.

". . . and then I said, as if I don't have enough on my plate already, Gwen, now I'm contending with a sulky camellia! Oh, hello? Hello? It's gone to the voice message. Katherine! Kate?

". . . Are you there? Can you hear me? Hello? She can't hear me, Gwen. Lordy, that girl and her tragic life, but as I've tried to tell her, it doesn't mean she should neglect the washing—

"KATE! Now listen to me! A 'once-in-a-hundred-years storm' has hit the whole east coast! Didn't we just have this? What is going on with the weather? Is it the coal? Those poor librarians in Lismore already threw all the books out the window that other time—

"They've GROUNDED A FLEET OF PLANES at Brisbane airport due to a 'freak hail event.' Good grief! It's end times! I'm going to phone Hugh. I'll get more sense out of him!"

Please don't, Mum.

"Mary!" Hugh says calmly, answering his phone and winking at me. "Kate's here. No, we just landed safely in Ballina. Unscheduled stop, but everything's fine. How's Charlie?"

If my new neighbor is the Minecraft Whisperer, Hugh must be the Mary Whisperer. He has the same anxiety-reducing effect on Mum as I get listening to one of those sleep stories on the meditation apps, read by Matthew McConaughey or Regé-Jean Page. It's exactly the level of composure we need now that we seem to be unexpectedly stuck in subtropical paradise more than one thousand miles short of our final destination.

"Why don't we call you back once we figure this out?" Hugh says, standing up and pulling our bags down from the overhead locker. "We haven't had a chance to sort out a plan just yet."

I stay seated a few seconds longer, silently basking in the way he's taking charge. It's been so long since someone has done that in my life. Shared the problems. No matter how tired I get, or how supportive someone is, I always have to be switched on. I'm the only person in the world who loves Charlie the way a parent would. The only daughter Mum has. The only breadwinner. The only one doing the endless washing and cleaning and cooking. What I wouldn't give for someone—I don't care who—just to step into my life and take the reins, for even a second.

"Ready?" Hugh says, and he stands back in the aisle to let me out.

The post-storm tropical humidity slams into us before we even reach the steps of the plane. I know we're in the wrong place, with meetings in disarray and no way we can drive twenty hours to meet with the scientists on site in Far North Queensland, but a big part of me is atypically unfazed. It's probably the same part of me that's incomparably exhausted. Inside the airport, it's chaos, with crowds pushing for answers on diverted flights and unplanned layovers, kids having meltdowns, adults raising voices at people doing their best in the latest in a long line of "unprecedented" circumstances.

"How ironic is this weather event given the purpose of our trip?" I say, and Hugh has to lean toward me to hear me over the din.

Neither of us has checked baggage, and it's pretty obvious nobody's going anywhere in a hurry. When I look at him, he nods in the direction of the exit.

Minutes later we're in the back of an Uber fleeing the scene like Bonnie and Clyde, heading for the Bangalow Bread Co. to assess our options over coffee.

"Best jam doughnuts north of Sydney," our driver boasts.

Coming from chilly Canberra, I wind the window down and let the warmth wash over me as we rush past fertile dairy farms, Bangalow palms, and thick clumps of the invasive camphor laurel. I don't know how long this forced diversion will last and I'm deter-mined to soak up every second of it while I can, in case we're back on a plane, by some miracle, this afternoon.

I glance at Hugh, sunlight streaming in the car window, wind in his dark hair, lines on his face seeming to uncrease in real time. It's easy to forget you're not the only one with problems. Particularly when people assume a death in the family trumps everything else, as if it's a problem competition. He looks like he needs a break from our usual life as much as I do.

"You here for the writers' festival?" the driver asks.

My heart quickens. "That's this weekend?" I hadn't realized. We weren't meant to be stopping anywhere near Byron Bay, and now it's just minutes away.

"Kicks off tomorrow," the guy answers. "You a writer?"

Now my heart really starts hammering. *Why is this question always so hard?* Once you tell someone you're writing a novel—feeling like a total fraud when you say it—they want to know what it's about. They expect you to be the expert on a plot that feels so wholly out of your own control, it's alarming.

"We fundraise for a university," I say instead, and there's a quiet sense of regret. If I don't believe in my own dream, how can I expect a publisher and future readers to buy into the fantasy?

Hugh looks disappointed in me. Or maybe *for* me. He knows I write. I used to do it every lunchtime there for a while. I ran it past him, of course. Not the novel itself. *Shudder*. The man did not need to suffer through my fledgling attempt at being the next Margaret Atwood. Particularly not since Cam had told me I hadn't yet found my place. Grace, on the other hand, labored through various drafts. She was abundantly encouraging, even though she's more of a Marian Keyes fan herself.

"Other writers have beta readers," I told her once. "You're my alpha." Everyone needs someone glowing, who'll rein in all constructive feedback until your fragile ego has fought its way through at least one full draft.

"When will you own it?" Hugh says unexpectedly. "The writing?"

This question is beyond his remit. It's hard to admit just how long I've been tussling with this manuscript. How hard I've been fighting it, while words trip me up as they fall into the enormous gap between how I imagine it could be, if it was any good, and how it really is.

"If you don't tell people about it, the writing dream stays untested," my grief counselor once told me. "It stays intact." She went on to pronounce my relationship with words and literary rejection as "toxic." "It's gaslighting you," she told me bluntly. "All this 'What's wrong with me? Am I really this bad?' It's not healthy."

"Anyway, we won't be here at the weekend," I explain to the cab driver, ignoring Hugh's question. "We're not meant to be here at all. We'll sort out flights back—"

The cabbie chuckles. "Not in a hurry you won't. The whole east coast from Melbourne to the Sunshine Coast is in chaos. Hundreds of hail-damaged planes. Thousands of stranded travelers. Make a weekend of it. Romantic little Airbnb in the hinterland. Go chase your dream at the festival."

"We're not together," Hugh interrupts, as if it's vitally important to clarify the situation with a guy we'll never see again in all our lives. Even Hugh seems surprised by the intensity of his own protest and glances at me almost apologetically.

"Heartbreaker!" I whisper jokingly. At least I hope he knows I'm joking. Now it's me surprised by how much it matters to me that he doesn't get the wrong idea.

What my heart is really breaking over is the way a child-free weekend in this paradise is being dangled in front of my eyes, and I cannot think how to realistically make it happen. Logistics like this are my nemesis. Mum can't handle Charlie for more than a night or two, and I've never been away from him longer than that. I don't want to ask Grace—it would take a whole weekend out of her mission to find Mr. Right Enough and get pregnant before Christmas.

"What do you want to do?" Hugh asks. "I think we've got a few options."

THE LAST LOVE NOTE

We do? I angle my body to face his in the backseat so he can walk me through them, because from where I'm sitting, it's all too hard.

"We're going to have to reschedule the meetings, either way. So cut that out of the picture."

Right. That's a relief.

"Realistically, we probably can't fly anywhere today, so cut that option." He rushes on because he can probably see the anxiety rising within me about Charlie. "If you really need to get home for Charlie, we could hire a car. It's a twelve-hour drive though, and you haven't slept."

It feels like we're rapidly running out of feasible choices.

"You need a break, Kate," he says. "You're fragile."

Fragile? Doesn't he mean "strong"? Everyone else tells me I'm strong! *I don't know how you do it! You're amazing! I could never be as strong as you!*

It's an exhausting reputation to uphold. I've given up trying to explain that it's not the way it seems. I'm not strong at all. I just have no choice. The idea of collapsing in a heap, drinking myself into a stupor, and retreating from the world seems like a fantasy, but I just don't have that luxury. Every day, I have to get up and be two parents, even when every part of me wants to stay under the covers and hide from the experience that swept away my entire future.

"I mean that with respect," Hugh explains gently. "The fragility. Anyone would be . . ."

Grief almost beat me, once or twice. I wanted to die just to make the pain stop. Landed in his office on one occasion, at wits' end, shut the door behind me, and lost it. "I can't do this anymore!" I cried, between gasping sobs. "I've tried. It's too hard. I miss him too much. I just want to be with him, Hugh. Wherever that is. Even if it's nowhere."

The mother guilt that flooded in after I'd admitted that was on a scale of its own. And Hugh had listened and let me talk and cry and fetched the bin for me to fill up with a million tissues. Then he'd popped his head out of the office and asked Sophie to bring more tissues and clear his calendar for the rest of the day. He and Cam had been thick as thieves. Hugh would have done anything for him.

"Are you safe?" he'd asked when I finally ran out of words. "Are you thinking of hurting yourself?"

He was the only person ever to ask me that directly. Even the doctor had glossed over it when she'd increased the dose of my antidepressants. Telling Hugh had been sensible. Close as he had been to Cam, he kept enough professional distance from me to cope with the information. Mum or Grace would have fallen to pieces over it and somehow made it worse—and they had enough to worry about just dragging Charlie and me through daily life. Hugh organized a psych through work. Gave me easy projects I could do in my sleep, or difficult ones I could get lost in. What-ever I needed. And he didn't once complain if I just sat at my desk, accomplishing nothing.

I *am* fragile. Just too exhausted to allow it. Sick of being sad all the time and stuck in an endless rut where the game plan is simply "holding on." Surviving. With no glittering prize if I make it through. Just raising Charlie, then seeing out the course of my natural life, minus Cam.

The Darth Vader ringtone shatters me back into the present and Mum launches unconventionally straight into a conversation. "Katherine! Right. Grace and I have been in cahoots," she begins in a businesslike manner. "I told her about my conversation with Hugh about your being stranded there with no fixed address and no plans right in the middle of a natural disaster—"

"It's not quite that bad," I say, my face basking in brilliant sun-shine through the car window.

"Why on *earth* didn't you tell me about that disastrous attempt you had at matchmaking?"

What?

"I don't know *what* you were thinking. Hugh and Grace? Entirely unsuited—you're as bad as Emma Woodhouse."

Does she have an actual point?

"Anyway, is Hugh there? Put the phone on speaker."

"That depends, Mum. Are you about to change the topic?"

"Yes, yes. I have *news!*"

"Brace yourself," I whisper to Hugh as I hit the speaker button.

"Look. Both of you. We'll have no argument about this," Mum starts. "Grace and I have organized everything, and it's all settled and paid for."

Okay, now I'm nervous. Hugh catches my eye, wary.

"You'll be staying for three nights in a two-bedroom beach house in New Brighton."

My stomach flips and I look at Hugh, dismayed. *What have they done?*

"Grace said you'll want to go to the Byron Bay Writers Festival, and I said I couldn't think why. Of course, you were always scribbling away as a teenager, but I thought you were over that now that you're an important executive at the university."

Hugh somehow maintains a straight face.

"There are two separate bedrooms, Kate . . . and this is your first proper child-free break. All I'm saying is you're a young, single woman and it's time you started acting like one."

"Mum! *Please!*" I can't even look at Hugh.

"Nonsense! If you're at the beach and you happen to hit it off with some aimless young Byron Bay vagabond . . . it doesn't have to be a Hemsworth brother."

"MUM!"

Even the cabbie's shoulders are shaking now in the front seat. *How is this my life?*

"Grace is going to move into your place on the weekend with Charlie. She's got some ludicrous scheme to overhaul your front garden, not that the poor girl would recognize a weed if she tripped over one in all that Gucci."

I get a mental picture of Grace flailing around in my rock garden in this season's chambray denim Valentino overalls and patent Prada boots, Fendi bag swinging from her shoulder, developing an urgent data science quandary requiring the assistance of a mathematical genius.

"I told her there's no point tidying the yard. You'll only let it go to rack and ruin again because you're addicted to that machine. What do you *do* on there all the time, Kate? I'm sure it's not work. Is it an internet beau? Just make sure he's not one of those puffer fish. I saw a story about that on *A Current Affair* and they prey on desperate, lonely women."

"Mary," Hugh interrupts, taking the phone out of my hand altogether. "It's thoughtful of you and Grace to organize this for us."

"Oh, *Hugh*, it's our pleasure," Mum says, her tone transformed.

"Now, we won't have either of you paying for it," Hugh explains firmly. "I'll sort that out with Kate when we get back. No arguments. But a break is probably what we both need, for different reasons."

Hugh has reasons? Have I become so absorbed in my own problems that I've neglected to check in on his? I know he errs on the side of undersharing his personal life and seems to have it all together, nearly all the time, but I feel like a very bad friend if I've missed something important. Perhaps a weekend away could fix a few things.

"Mum, what if Charlie isn't on board with this plan?" I ask. I couldn't possibly relax if I knew he was pining for me.

"Oh, he'll be ecstatic about a weekend with Grace. I must tell you, he made up a distressing story about you having had some sort of police incident over a bomb, Katherine. Said he would have brought the bomb to school for show and tell but it exploded in Sydney. Do you think he needs more counseling?"

No, but I think I do.

"Where the child inherited this propensity for dramatics I'll never know," she adds, wrapping up the call as the cab pulls up along the main street in Bangalow. "Maybe *he'll* be the writer in the family."

Two hours later, we've caffeinated and confirmed that Bangalow bakery is indeed a state leader in jam doughnuts, caught an Uber to a Byron Bay car rental company, and picked up a cute little convertible. Back on the highway again, we head north. In the distance, the silhouette of the ancient volcanic plug of Mount Warning rises out of the haze.

"I hope that's not a sign!" I nod at the mountain as I drive.

Hugh flicks through a tourist brochure he picked up at the car rental office. "It's okay. It's not known as Mount Warning anymore," he explains as he reads. "To the Bundjalung people it's Wollumbin. The scars on the mountainside are said to be the battle wounds of warrior spirits."

Battle wounds of warrior spirits.

Something within me longs to emulate that mountain. Wants to erupt with such violence and heat and force that the very foundations can't hold. An inevitable collapse. A changed shape rising out of falling ash—scarred, strong, and with an afterlife so fertile and mineral-rich, luscious rainforest springs from the soil for millions of years . . .

The knowledge that I'm not there yet—that I haven't erupted and collapsed and cooled and grown solid after all this time—stings. I've worked *so* hard. Wanted so much to intellectualize and overcome my loss. I've read the literature. Joined support groups. Had counseling. Yet, here I am, years in, still pushing myself up the wrong side of this mountain.

Car window down, I gulp warm air and blink back tears behind dark glasses.

"Have you ever felt homesick for somewhere you've never lived?" Hugh asks, intruding into my thoughts as I head up the highway, watching for the turnoff to Ocean Shores.

"This hinterland reminds me of Ireland," I tell him. I sound as if I'm an authority on the subject, despite never having been. "My great-grandparents were from County Fermanagh. They eloped when their parents disapproved of the match."

"Plucky. I like it."

"Three generations in a row eloped for the same reason. I can't work out if that makes our family incredibly romantic or incredibly judgmental. Either way, yes. I'm homesick for Ireland."

"It wasn't on your Adventure list," he informs me. "Not in red or green."

Surely it must have been. It's in my *blood*. It's not just a desire to visit. It's a calling, across time. Hugh must be wrong.

We pass Brunswick Heads, cross the river, and wind through wide streets and alongside Marshalls Creek until we reach the beachside hamlet of New Brighton. I'm still thinking about Ireland as I pull the car onto Terrace Street and Hugh directs me into the driveway of the house Grace booked. It makes an unassuming first impression. Garage frontage and a rickety wooden fence lined with grevilleas and agapanthus.

"Sit tight while I grab the key," Hugh suggests, and he heads into the neighbor's place to collect it—no fancy lockbox arrangement here.

I stay in the car, door ajar, one foot on the ground, leaning against the headrest and listening to the raw energy of the waves as they pound the nearby beach. Late-winter sun beats through the fabric of my lined skirt until it's so hot I have to move my leg into the shade. Having come from such an icy start, for me this is T-shirt weather.

I pull down the visor and check my face in the mirror. It's official: I am one of the walking dead. Pale skin, dark circles, drawn face, hair still flattened from the motorcycle helmet. Chances of snaring one of Mum's hipster vagabonds for a sneaky holiday romp: nil.

"Ready?" Hugh says, rounding the car and waving the key at me.

Not as such, no. I don't think we gave this harebrained scheme enough consideration. Regardless, I get out of the car and pull my bag from the backseat. I'd packed for one night, not three. My plans for this business trip had included two quick meetings (same skirt, two shirts, shoes) and room service and Netflix (PJs, toothbrush, deodorant). I can't turn up to a beachside writers' festival in a business suit and heels. Or in pajamas.

We push through the gate and follow stepping stones past a segregated guest room and up to the two-story, treated-timber beach house. Firewood has been tipped into an iron drum on the veranda, beside a doormat that reads *beach people*. Kindred spirits. And as Hugh turns the key and pushes the door ajar, I step inside and fall in love at first sight.

It's a converted fishing shack from the sixties. Rustic, cozy, and extended in sections, with much of it genuinely untouched rather than deliberately retro. Deep velvet couches sit on wooden floor-boards beside the freestanding fireplace. Mismatched bookshelves line the walls, crammed with dog-eared copies of Grisham and Christie and Steel. Old boardgames are stacked in frayed boxes with split corners, held together by masking tape. Decks of playing cards wrapped in rubber bands lean against DVDs of Richard Curtis rom-coms, *Midsomer Murders*, and *Yes Minister*. Macramé decorations, crafted long before Pinterest made it cool again, hang from pieces of driftwood on the walls.

Nothing is "on trend." It's as if generations of a big extended family have decorated this house gradually across decades, infusing it in sunscreen and stories, sleep-ins, and growing pains until it is impossible to tell where the family ends and the house begins.

And that sound. Waves crashing on the beach just over the sandhills.

"I love this," I whisper, grateful to the strangers who couldn't know they've shaped exactly the haven I need. But it's what *isn't* here that hits me hardest.

Cam's notes, fixed all around my own house and in my wallet and car and everywhere else, have kept him visible in my life. They've scaffolded my grief. Provided hard evidence that he lived, and thought, and wrote.

I wasn't prepared for the unexpected lightness of being here without them. Tangible relief from the daily onslaught of memories that have been suffocating the fire of my grief, holding me at a place in time when he was still here, instead of letting it rip.

I drop my bag near the wood-paneled kitchen and run up the open staircase to explore. The upstairs bedroom opens to a cov-ered balcony in the treetops. Timber furniture is scattered across the deck, while a cotton hammock sways in the afternoon breeze. I close my eyes at that first whisper of ocean spray on my face.

It's an instant relaxant. This is exactly where I'm meant to be, I'm certain.

Cam had his hands on these arrangements.

That's a game I like to play. Others look for feathers or rainbows or coins. I look for unexpected magic. Small miracles sparking out of black holes. Perfect parking spots. Chance meetings. Stars aligning for subtropical mini breaks and festivals . . .

Hugh follows me out onto the balcony. He leans on the banister, inhales the salt air, and exhales about six months' worth of stress from the office. Compared with the dryness of Canberra, the post-storm humidity seeps into your lungs here, even in winter. The air pulses with the invisible vibrations of life and the ocean itself seems to reach over the rise, caressing your skin with its spray—pulling you toward it, irresistibly, like the moon pulls tides.

"This do?" Hugh asks.

One look at the expression on my face and he smiles, relieved. I'd told him in the car that, freak storm or not, I was uneasy about the whole idea of taking a spontaneous long weekend like this—especially with him.

"I'll stay out of your way," he'd promised. "I've got a uni mate up this way. We'll have a beer and catch up while you're at the festival."

"What would you have done if I'd said no?" I ask him now, but I already know the answer. We'd be halfway to Coffs Harbour by now, gearing up for a milkshake at the Big Banana.

"And pass this up? I'd have kidnapped you," he says. He eases into the hammock, testing his weight against the heavy rainbow-colored fabric before swinging his legs into it, in a way that I'm positive he hasn't done since he was a child.

Who is this relaxed man, and what has he done with my perennially industrious boss?

"You'd have held me hostage in this hideous holiday rental?"

"Yep. Let you suffer the cursed ocean with its endless racket on your private balcony."

"Did we already decide I get the balcony room?" I ask.

"This is a luxury kidnapping, Kate, with only the best views."

"What if I just want to sleep in and devour 1980s romance novels for two straight days and can't even make it to the festival?"

Please make me go.

"That festival is nonnegotiable," he says, stretching his arms up behind his head. "Don't mess with me or I'll force you to watch a sunrise on the beach."

"Is that really within budget?"

"Kate, sunrises are free. You need this holiday more than I thought."

I pull at the ropes of the hammock, and he startles, as if he'll be tipped out. If this is what beach-house Hugh is like, then I can think of worse things than being holed up for an unplanned mini break in his company. He should let this side of him out in the office.

"I'll have to work a bit while we're here, too," he says.

"Mate, that's boring. Don't you need the break as well?"

There's a beat before he answers. "Yeah, probably."

And there's that glimpse again of whatever is troubling him.

"The problem is, I've got this lazy team member. Chronically late. Leaves things till the last minute. Makes ridiculous excuses—even calls in the bomb squad to avoid the office. Loses sleep catching up on work overnight, then snores for hours on the plane, distracting me from my spreadsheets."

"Hello. That was not me."

"Tell that to the busybody in front of us," he suggests. "She kept turning around and glaring at me. Asked me to wake you up at one point or she'd report you to the steward for being a public nuisance."

"She didn't!" I'm half amused, half secretly worried he's serious. Maybe I do snore at high altitudes—

He smiles at me. "It's all right, Kate. You didn't snore."

Relief.

"It was the sleeptalking that really threw me off."

Please, God, not the sex hallucinations.

"I made a deal with unconscious Kate," Hugh says. "We're keeping our conversation private. She was very funny."

Am I not funny awake? Maybe I've lost my sense of humor. *Ugh.*

"I hate how grief reduces you," I admit.

He looks at me, bewildered. "*Reduces* you? Is that what you think?"

20

I'm under the beach's spell without even setting so much as a toe on the sand, and it's time to rectify that. I kick off my boots, peel off Justin's jacket, toss it on the wooden table, and run down the outdoor staircase in bare feet. From the garden, a short path leads me over the rise and onto pristine sand.

There it is. My ocean. I've taken Charlie for day trips to South Coast beaches as often as possible since Cam died. Each time I stand on sand, near waves, I feel a tiny bit more human. More myself. Or some new version of me that's a little less heartbroken and a little more together. There's something about the unstoppable rhythm, no matter how bad things get, that comforts me.

Hugh doesn't follow me. I think he instinctively knows I need this moment.

The wide beach stretches north, and south all the way to the iconic Byron Bay lighthouse, standing on the most easterly point in Australia, above Wategos Beach. The once sleepy coastal town is now a popular backdrop for the Instagram stories of Hollywood celebrities and influencers peddling plant-based collagen powder, hemp oil, and crystals in front of ring-lit tripods.

It's unseasonably warm for late winter, and there's another storm brewing to the southwest, toward Lismore. I walk toward the shore, the sand getting firmer and wetter beneath my feet, and step out a little way into the cold water, deep enough to have to dig my feet in solidly to keep my balance.

It's a lot like grief, standing here. You're dragged from the shallows into the depths where it's dark and heavy and you can't see or hear or breathe. There were times over the last two years when, if I screamed, grief would swallow up the noise. It was bigger than my voice. A whirl of emotion for which there's no sufficient word in the entirety of the English language.

I take a few steps farther out until the water laps the hem of my skirt. It's icy and clear, a stark contrast to the warmth of the sun on my shoulders. Every so often a bigger wave hits and I sink deeper and dig my toes farther into the sand to keep my balance.

Suddenly, there's a much bigger wave coming and no time to back away from it. I'll be saturated in my dry-clean-only skirt, but I don't care. I know it will knock me off my feet and drag me along the sand unless I dive under it. And when I do that, fully clothed, I feel reckless and crazy, and shockingly cold.

Sometimes I flirt with death. It's just a fleeting glance. A blip, somewhere on the outer edge of my radar. A faint, comforting reminder it's always there in case I need it.

A mother shouldn't have these thoughts.

I don't know how long I stand there, soaked through, after that. There are no more waves that big. I think the tide is going out. I'm frozen. Stuck. And I want to cry, but I can't. The afternoon breeze is increasing, clouds are billowing, and now I'm shivering. I take a few steps backward until I'm back on dry sand. Spent.

I know he's standing there before I even turn around. I can sense him. Watching from a respectful distance. Protecting me. Letting me lose it, right to the edge, but not quite over it.

I close my eyes and in moments he is standing right behind me. Close enough for me to feel his energy.

Cam.

He never lets me down at the beach.

"*I miss you,*" I breathe, and I feel his energy slip away again. I said too much. Felt too viscerally. Spooked him. Spooked me? Now he's gone and I'm standing alone again, looking at the ocean, frozen to the bone. Desperately in need of a warm shower, a long sleep, and a stretch of time when no one expects a single thing from me.

But I can't bring myself to leave this spot, where Cam was. I rub my arms, wet shirt and skirt clinging to my body, the wind covering me in sand and goose bumps.

Footsteps cut into the sand behind me. Real footsteps this time. The towel is large and warm and wrapped tightly around my shoulders and across my front. I can't even move my hands to grasp hold of it, I'm so cold. I just turn around and stand there shivering, teeth chattering, looking at him, feeling utterly bedraggled and the lowest I've been in a very long while, yet unable to articulate that. Or anything else.

He pulls the towel tighter. I want him to hug me, for physical warmth, but he doesn't. Maybe I want it for emotional warmth too.

"I'll light the fire," he says, and on some primal level, I feel taken care of.

There was so much help in the beginning. They say grief changes your address book and it surprised me who stepped up, and how. I found that I'd completely underestimated Canberra, making the classic mistake of thinking it was a sterile city, full of politicians. Instead, we were embraced by new friends, friends of friends, neighbors, strangers. . . . And it went far beyond casseroles and lasagna. It was sitting beside me at the bank while I closed his account. Fixing towel rails and running loads of recycling to the tip. Late-night hot chocolates in pajamas when we couldn't stop crying.

A composer friend heard about Cam's death while she was on an interstate bus and was moved to write a piece of music, then and there, that captured the full force of our love so exquisitely, I had it played at the funeral.

And then that first Christmas, a group of random friends joined forces over social media; when Charlie and I drove in after the end-of-year concert at childcare, our whole house was twinkling in fairy lights. In that moment, I felt like the richest woman in the world.

But at some point people have to go back to their own lives. You can't expect them to sit with you forever or be there for every leaking tap or flat tire. As that first wave of support retreats, you're forced to turn into the single parent you never signed up to be.

So, when someone does something thoughtful now, no matter how small—like light a fire, when it's usually you in charge of the heating, the electricity, the food, the homework, the actual work—the kindness just seeps into your skin. Right now, it shocks me out of this trance, enough to find my feet again, take one backward glance to where I felt Cam for a few seconds, and walk back over the sand with Hugh. Stumbling over it. Covered in it.

We reach the back door and I know I can't trample straight into the house. There's an outdoor shower with a tap down low, and Hugh turns it on so we can stick our feet under it, standing on the grass. I pull the towel tightly around me and he leans down and brushes sand from his calves.

"Hold still," he says, on his haunches beside me. He takes my heel in his palm and moves my foot gently under the flow of water, brushing the sand away. I reach for his shoulder to balance, while he does the same with my other foot and I have an out-of-body experience because this is my boss, Hugh, *washing my feet*. It should be a hundred times weirder than it is.

"I'll run the shower," he says, shutting the tap off and standing up again. "Inside."

He grabs a towel he'd left at the door and dries his feet. I step inside and stand on the rattan doormat, water still dripping from me and no energy to deal with it.

"Kate?" he calls from the bathroom a minute later.

I feel disembodied. Is this shock? No. Surely it can't be, two years after the event.

I'm shivering. Steam is swirling out of the downstairs bathroom, through the doorway in the corridor. Hugh emerges from it.

"You coming? Water's hot."

I can't.

He dries his hands on a towel and crosses the room. When he reaches me, I want to speak, but no sound comes out. I'm locked inside my own body, horrified by the realization that's crashing into my consciousness, very belatedly.

"He stays dead," I whisper.

Even though they're barely audible, Hugh catches my words. Holds them.

"He keeps on not coming back," I continue, as if discovering this truth for the first time. Hearing my own words, I start to panic. So much of my grief has been about Charlie losing his dad. Nowhere near enough of it, I realize now, has been about me losing my husband. It's like I've woken up on the crest of a roller coaster I didn't know I'd boarded, I'm not strapped in, and we've just come over the peak.

"I'm so sorry, Kate." He's said it before, of course. At the time. Everyone has said it. It's the phrase we're socially contracted to put ourselves through when someone dies, before normal interaction can continue. But this time, I feel it.

He is sorry. Deeply, empathetically, heart-wrenchingly sorry.

Through his eyes, finally, after two years of this relentless absence and half a day of space, I finally see my situation from the outside. And I feel sorry for myself, too. Achingly so.

What an inconceivable loss.

Water is pelting onto the shower floor. I follow him across the living room, into the bathroom. He checks the temperature and dries his hands. "Okay?" he asks.

I drop the towel and step into the shower. Fully clothed.

Warm water runs over my face and saturates my clothes again. I back up against the tiled wall and sink slowly until I'm sitting on the floor, thoroughly miserable.

Maybe *this* is my rock bottom. I'm forever adjusting the measure. Once, when I was particularly distraught, I took out Cam's X-rays and scans from various injuries over the years and laid them out on the living room floor in the shape of a person. Then I got down and lay on top of them, desperate to be close to his body. And when I put them away, in my mind's eye, the ghostly images of his heart and lungs seemed to move and beat and breathe. I couldn't destroy the X-rays. It would be like obliterating him all over again.

Normally I go away for only one night. Day one of three feels so much more expansive. It's been the first opportunity to really gasp oxygen away from the child I've protected from the worst of my grief, all this time. Grief that is rushing to the surface safely in Charlie's absence. I can't upset him from here. Can't scare him. I can fully lose it and he won't know. I feel like I've never had this much space, nor this much emotion to tip into it.

I look up at Hugh through water and the steam, wondering if he regrets this. He probably wishes he'd brought the university-sponsored counselor along for the ride. But, as our eyes meet, I realize he's hanging in there. He's strong.

I am fragile.

He was right. And as the warm water thaws my skin, the unguarded tears are allowed to flow at last. He watches my face crumple, and he crouches outside the shower, nearer to me. Tentatively, he reaches in and offers me his hand through the waterfall, his white shirt sleeve sodden and transparent.

I take his hand, expecting him to pull me up and get me out of here and do something sensible with me—cup of tea, perhaps—to stop whatever this is.

But this is beyond tea. He knows it. Only fragile, desperate individuals dive fully clothed into oceans and sit in showers wearing work clothes on business trips.

He lets go of my hand. Removes his watch.

"Hugh!"

But it's too late. He steps into the shower and sits down beside me, propping himself against the wall under the water, suit pants wet, white business shirt clinging to his body like mine is to me, water dripping off his dark hair as he looks at me in silence.

I am floored. Nobody has ever done something so, self-sacrificially kind. Hugh doesn't do stunts, and this definitely qualifies as one. In fact, I vaguely recall Daniel Craig doing it once, as Bond, no less.

After minutes of this, I find my voice. "Is this the weekend you had in mind?"

"This is it to a T," he says, leaning his head back against the tiles and closing his eyes. Then we just sit there, side by side, in companionable silence, enjoying communal water therapy, while I cry, and cry, and cry.

This is letting grief rip.

Eventually the water starts running cold and he reaches up and shuts the taps off and we're bedraggled and dripping and I realize this is one of the most intimate moments of my life, second only to giving birth in front of Cam.

Then he suggests we pull ourselves to our feet because there's no food in the house, and not enough dry clothes, and we should do something about both problems before nightfall.

21

"Grace! Firstly, *thank you*. A million thanks. I don't know how, but I'm going to make this up to you somehow. I promise."

She laughs it off. "Pay it forward, Kate. You know I love hanging out with my favorite little person. Practice for my five-percent baby."

I'm walking to an Ocean Shores thrift store that we drove past on the way in. Hugh is back at the beach house, following up on the meeting cancellations with personal emails. Perhaps we both needed space, too.

"Right, before we begin . . ." It's as if I'm calling this phone meeting to order. "Is this an Alice O'Donoghue situation?"

Grace's friend Alice had told us a story once about the time she launched into a massive rant as soon as her partner walked in from work, detailing for him the minutiae of a frustrating day. Tech glitches. Parking ticket. Cardigan repeatedly catching on door handles. That kind of thing.

"Anyway, how was your day?" she had finally asked him, almost as an afterthought, having thoroughly exhausted her list of complaints.

"My father died," he'd told her.

Grace and I nearly died ourselves when she told us, from vicarious mortification. *There, but for the grace of God . . .*

Ever since, before one of us is about to throw ourselves into a long-winded but not life-or-death story, we check that this isn't an "Alice O'Donoghue situation," before safely proceeding.

"All is well here," Grace assures me. "Please go on."

I hardly know where to begin. It's like we've entered a parallel dimension since I last saw her, not twenty-four hours ago. "Okay, this is the executive summary." I need to maximize the debrief portion of this call. "After the police left last night and you all went home, I got no sleep, the car broke down, Justin answered the door at six a.m. naked, practically, and conveyed me to the airport on the back of his Harley-Davidson. No, it's not a Harley. Wait, I can't remember the genre of bike. . . ."

"They're not books, Kate. But forget the bike!" Grace exclaims. "Can we circle back to the part where Justin was naked?"

"No, because I just had a shower with Hugh."

There's an extended pause while Grace recalibrates her understanding of the known universe. "Sorry, *what?*"

I know how it sounds. I just don't know how to explain it. "Neither of us was naked." This only serves to make it more absurd.

"Kate, stop. This needs to be a video call. You're speaking gibberish!" Her very confused face lights up my screen within moments. "Okay, my first suggestion is *do not* tell your mother *any* of this," she advises. It is of course a moot point.

"Oh, I forgot that part. Mum told me, on loudspeaker with Hugh and the cabbie, that I should have a hot fling with a random Hemsworth substitute while I'm here."

She explodes laughing. "Well, you seem to be progressing at breakneck speed toward that goal."

It wasn't like that. Not any of it. But sometimes it's hard to wedge the truth into Grace's imagined narrative.

"Some other time, I'll tell you about the shower thing, Grace. Whatever you're imagining—it wasn't that."

"O-*kay*."

Because it was elemental. Raw. A defining experience between two human beings that I'll remember always. I'm a bit sorry I mentioned it, now.

"Side note: are you wearing pajamas?" she asks.

I pan the camera down my body to confirm it. I hadn't planned for this shopping trip. I'd both swum in the ocean and showered in my business attire. So yes, I'm in aqua-and-blue check cotton shorts and one of Cam's oversized T-shirts, rescued from the donations box.

"There was a *small* hiccup as I was leaving the beach house."

"Tell me."

"It's one of those exposed staircases, with full view from the upstairs landing into the living room below—you know, like on the *Brady Bunch*?"

"Got it."

"Hugh was on the couch, working. I think because of the shower thing, I was disconcerted. . . ."

"Understandable."

"And self-conscious, due to the pajamas. Or maybe it was just to lighten the mood. Anyway, it felt like a good idea to stage one of those Old Hollywood Grand Entrances."

Grace frowns.

"So I pivoted on the spot, but the strap of my shoe got caught in the other and as I spun, I misjudged the top step and stumbled, grabbing hold of the banister to steady myself on the way down until I finally regained some semblance of poise on the second bottom step."

"I see. And Hugh?"

"Watched me wordlessly, then said, 'What am I supposed to do with that?' It was my second grand entrance of the day, and I somehow managed to look more drunk than I did falling off the motorcycle this morning."

"You fell off the motorcycle? Gawd, Kate—are you okay?"

I take a deep breath. None of this is relevant to the purpose of my call. Something's been niggling me about being here with Hugh, even though I'm not here *with* him.

"I keep thinking about you," I admit. "With *The Whole Hugh Thing*." That's what we've labeled the ill-fated matchmaking fiasco.

She shakes her head. "Kate, there was never a *Whole Hugh Thing* with me, was there? He's a lovely man, but he just wasn't into me that way. I think I was into the idea of him for a while, but that was really just the version of him that you'd painted. I barely got to know him. It wasn't your fault the chemistry was missing for us."

At the time, we'd blamed the lack of vibe on the twentysomething, strikingly hot Singaporean student one of my colleagues caught him lunching with at a yum cha restaurant near the university. I'd been crushed for Grace. I'd suspected he was dating other people, which was fine—he and Grace hadn't even had a second date. I just hadn't understood how a woman half his age could eclipse the supernova that is my best friend.

He'd gone all quiet then too. Lots of closed-door phone calls and unusually early knockoffs. When he'd told Grace he didn't think it was going to work out between them, he'd said he was "preoccupied with something personal." Some*one* personal, he should have said. She kept popping up for months! If not at yum cha, in the work car park, the coffee shop, on his phone screen—even in email notifications once, when he was sharing his screen during a meeting with the vice chancellor! Ruby someone. *Annoying*.

"Has it occurred to you that the reason Hugh and I are always so awkward with each other around you is that we didn't want to disappoint Cupid? You were more upset about it not working out between us than we were."

That's because of me? Had I imagined the heartbreak and resentment?

"So let me be perfectly clear," she says firmly. "If you want to have any more showers with Hugh, that's totally fine by me."

She has this *so very wrong*.

"Right," I say awkwardly. "Also, Justin gave me his number," I confess next. I should have brought a clipboard and checklist to keep all the discussion points sorted.

This time something does pass across her face. It's not as strong as envy, but it's there. Disappointment, I think.

"It's normal for neighbors to exchange numbers, isn't it?" I ask. "In the likely event, in my case, that there's ever a problem to report?"

"Perfectly normal," Grace agrees, but her upbeat tone is forced.

I'm going to text him straight after this call and somehow convey the message that he will definitely not be receiving a rose from me, no matter how spectacular he looks on a motorcycle.

There's so much more I want to cover. All the grief stuff. The ocean thing. The Adventure Board epiphany. Ireland. The writing agony. Cam's notes, and the fact that they're not scaffolding after all. They're a cage—and sometime soon, I need to break free.

"Mate, this conversation would dismally fail the Bechdel test," I observe. "Bloody men!"

She laughs. "Okay, tabled for our next discussion: donor insemination—pros and cons. Talking about sperm doesn't count, re:

Bechdel, does it?"

"It's permissible. And I do, very much, want to discuss that with you, Grace."

In fact, it's more than that. I've been mulling over a big idea now for ages. I know we're roughly the same age, but perhaps my eggs are more viable? They were never our issue when we had treatment. And with Cam gone, my opportunity for further children has passed. I'd give Grace this gift in a heartbeat if she needed it.

"I love you, Grace. So much."

"Forever," she replies.

22

I'm in the fitting room at the thrift shop when I text Justin. *"Thanks again for the lift,"* I type. *"Apologies again for waking you."*

He starts typing back almost immediately. Dammit. I don't want to get into a conversation. I just want to get these words out.

"Change of plans here," I draft. *"We're away till Sunday. Good news though, Grace is staying at mine all weekend with Charlie."* Should probably stop there, even though I want to add, *"Maybe you should have that ornithology discussion over a drink with her."*

Let me think about how to position this. . . .

I whip off Cam's T-shirt and the PJ bottoms so I can try on a dress.

"Heard you're staying the weekend there," he writes back, too quickly for me to structure the essay I'm typing. "Your mum called in to pick up something for Charlie. I was out the front . . ."

There is nothing worse than a hanging ellipsis when someone's about to share a story about Mum. There's a big pause. He's not elaborating. I hope he didn't tell her about the grenade. Or the motorbike. Although, what am I, fourteen? I don't have to fill Mum in every time I cause a security incident, or talk to a boy.

My phone springs to life with an unexpected FaceTime call from him and, even though I've been a smartphone owner since 2008, I still jump at the immediacy. Unless I'm talking to Grace, I prefer messages. Add to this that I'm already on tenterhooks and wrung out from the earlier ordeal in the shower—plus the fact that I'm reaching that point where you start swaying with sleep deprivation—and that's my excuse for the fact that I accept the call even though I mean to decline it.

"Kate," he says, coming into view.

The other thing in view is me, in a change room in my underwear! I grab the dress I'm about to try on and hold it up against my front. I'm meant to be dousing any potential flames here, not sexting him!

"How was Mum?" I ask, on edge.

"Actually, she was really sweet," he responds, popping the cap from a beer bottle in his kitchen.

We are talking about *my* mum, aren't we?

"Ended up inviting her in for a cup of tea and Tim Tams, because she was a bit upset."

Upset? Mum experiences many heightened emotions. Frequently. But she's never "upset." I don't think I've ever seen her cry, even when I was a child and she was on her own with me.

"Charlie was at school, so we talked for an hour. She told me the whole story about Cam. It sounded awful, Kate."

It was.

"Must be so hard for a parent to watch a child go through that."

It is.

"I asked if she'd ever sought help—she said people her age just get on with it. . . ."

Hang on, back up. I thought we were talking about me, and how hard it is for me to watch Charlie go through life without his dad. I've been so laser-focused on that, it never occurred to me that Mum must be feeling the same way, watching her child go through life without her husband.

Mum needs help? I'm not prepared for the anxiety this thought gives me. Or the regret.

Someone shared a psychological model with me once about the inner circle of grief. It was all about supporting the people closer to the center of the loss than you are, dumping your own stuff on those further out in the circle from you. Maybe Mum's struggle seems alien to me because she never "dumped in." A haunting image pops up of Mum, alone, crying herself to sleep.

"What did she say that worried you, Justin?"

He looks hesitant, like he'll be breaking her confidence by saying any more.

"Well, she fell apart," he explains.

Fell apart? I flop into the chair in the corner of the cubicle. Whenever people talk about family trauma, it often seems to go the other way. Trauma in the older generation, inherited by the younger. People talk less about instances in which something deeply upsetting travels back up the metaphorical umbilical cord and infects the mother.

There are thirty-two years between Mum and me. Is that enough time for an adult to develop the wisdom and pragmatism to process their adult child's loss? Not just an adult child. A grandson, too. I remember asking my grandfather once when you start to feel old in your mind. He told me you never do. Mum must have been at such a loss when life threw this at us.

"This reminds me of when Knightley died," I tell Justin. "He was our dog." My throat constricts with emotion even uttering his name. "Cam had a policy of only getting rescue dogs, but I made him come with me into a pet shop on the way home from a week-end in Sydney, just to hold Knightley for a minute or two. That's when they told us he'd been rejected by his biological mother. . . ."

Justin recoils, hand on heart as though he's been shot with an arrow.

"We hadn't factored in a dog at that point. Toilet-training a puppy that would tear up the whole house hadn't figured in our plans for the honeymoon period. So we reluctantly handed him back, drove off, and all I could see were tragic images of this rejected little puppy being rejected twice over."

"Stop it, Kate! This is worse than talking to your mother!"

"No, wait. A few minutes down the road, Cam pulled the car over unexpectedly, shuddering to a stop on a gravel verge. Then he swung it around in a U-turn and said, 'We're going back for that puppy.' I think it was the most romantic moment of our entire relationship."

Gosh. I need to pull myself together.

"The reason I'm telling you this story is that only a few months after Cam died, I had to take Knightley to the vet."

Pretty sure the woman in the next cubicle is sniffing now.

"Don't break my heart," Justin says.

"Charlie loved him. He'd grown up knowing him, of course, but Knightley had congestive heart failure." I'm still trying to convince myself I made the right decision—such a difficult one to make on my own.

"I'm sure you did the right thing," Justin says, guessing my mental torture.

Dogs know things. Knightley seemed to know Cam was sick before we did—he got clingy with him, weeks before Cam's diagnosis. And I think his heart failed in part because his beloved owner was gone. I hadn't been prepared for the double whammy of grief I would experience. All the way to the vet's, I was having flashbacks to that heroic moment when Cam swung the car around, wishing I could swing it around now. Pushing myself to drive forward, only to sever another link between us, as if Cam's death and Knightley's were inextricably tied.

"I told Charlie we would pass Knightley straight into Daddy's arms." I can barely get these words out, Lord knows why I'm insisting on doing so. "But watching my already grief-stricken little boy hug somebody else goodbye was some of the worst pain I've ever experienced. Like Mum must feel watching us!"

What I don't tell Justin is that when Knightley's beautiful head sank peacefully onto the vet's table as he slipped from this world, I'd whispered, "Tell Cam I love him." And I rested my cheek on the top of his head, wanting to be as close as possible to the veil between this world and whatever lies beyond it. So close I imagined I could reach out and touch Cam, as he reached out for Knightley. So close I could almost slip through too.

"I'm sorry about your dog," Justin says.

People blunder through in early grief. "I know just how you feel," they say, when you've lost a human being. "I lost my pet."

At the time, I found it breathtakingly offensive. But the day Knightley died, the grief was off the charts. The aftershocks turned out to be nowhere near as powerful as losing Cam; the bounce-back was light years faster. But that initial passing devastated me in a way I hadn't anticipated.

"Your mum was okay when she left," Justin says, to my relief.

Poor Mum. My heart hurts. How could I have been so wrapped up in things that I missed this? For a woman with no filter, she has expertly hidden her deeper thoughts.

Oh, dear. This is not why I messaged Justin. This is meant to be about Grace. I can't raise that now, though. Not after he's just done our family a massive kindness.

Why is everything so complicated?

23

I turn and face the mirror, feeling demoralized enough already without also being confronted by a full-length reflection of my semi-naked self under stark fluorescent lights.

It's not about appearance. Not completely. I've done enough work on body acceptance since having Charlie and losing Cam to be grateful for a body that gave someone life and has also managed to keep itself alive, despite all the trauma and stress it was forced through.

Watching Cam degenerate, physically, as the disease ravaged him, gave me a perspective on the workings of the human body that transcends image. Once you've watched a strong man fade, when you've borne witness to a body in peak physical condition spiraling until it's unable to will itself into one more day, it's harder to care whether breastfeeding has deflated your boobs or a miracle growing within you has graffitied your skin. And when you've spent a few minutes with a body that no longer houses a soul, so still and lifeless and *empty*, you really see it for what it is, and how incredible it has been, no matter how it looks.

At least, that's the philosophical position I'd arrived at before everything got messed up on that motorcycle. And now I feel like a hypocrite. With confidence issues. I'd reached that comfortable place with Cam where he loved me the way Mark Darcy loved Bridget Jones: just as I was. He'd seen me in the delivery suite during childbirth and looked at me like every moment of that experience brought us closer together. Since he died, I've been perfectly content going about my post-Cam life living vicariously through Grace's dating capers, but now I have a vague recollection that there are things a body can do beyond haul sadness around. And a vague idea that perhaps I might want to do those things again one day.

The bell tinkles over the door to the shop. As the door opens and shuts, the breeze blows open a slight gap in the changing room curtain. Peering through it, I see Hugh looking around the store, searching for me. It's strange seeing him so relaxed here, in jean shorts and a black T-shirt. Strange to be here with him at all, in a setting like this.

Behind this flimsy curtain, which looks like it was hung in the 1980s and could disintegrate at any moment, I feel more exposed than ever. I pull the two pieces of fabric tightly together and press myself up against the side wall of the cubicle. Catching my breath.

"Can I help you?" someone says. It's the old lady looking after the store.

"I'm looking for my colleague," he says, before correcting himself. "Friend."

It's a subtle distinction, but one I'm glad he's made, even if it's nothing to this woman whether we work together or hang out socially. I think once you've spent time under a shower with someone crying her eyes out, you've moved well beyond workmates.

"You must mean the lady with the dog," the woman says. Apparently, everyone in the shop heard that entire conversation. "Are you that wonderful man she was talking to on the phone?"

"Er, I think you mean someone else . . . My friend doesn't have a dog."

I make a tiny slit in the curtain and look through it.

"Well, not anymore," the lady says. "Poor Knightley."

Hugh's expression changes. He knew Knightley well.

The old lady takes him by the arm and, *horrors*, starts leading him toward the fitting rooms.

I clear my throat and grasp the curtains even harder. "In here!" I call out, wishing I'd spent more time trying things on instead of having an existential crisis over body image. Now he's standing so close I can see his canvas shoes underneath the curtain and I am almost naked and shaking.

"Kate?"

"What you did for her mum today was really beautiful," the woman goes on. "Inviting her in for Tim Tams? From an old lady who has felt very alone at times, let me thank you, Justin, for being so thoughtful."

The shoes step back.

This is *out of hand*! I step into the bronze halter-neck maxi dress and tie it up at the neck, fling open the curtain, and reach behind myself to do the zip, fumbling with it.

"Hugh! Hello!"

I pick up the PJs I was wearing and scoop up some shorts and T-shirts and a long skirt and blouse, a cardigan, and a couple of other things that I know will be fine without trying them on, stuff my feet back into the sandals, and pick up my phone and sunglasses. The zipper is stuck, I think. I can't budge it.

"Fix that for her, dear, while I tally these up," the manager tells Hugh.

I read her name badge, ready to protest. "Mrs. Davis—"

But Hugh has stepped in behind me already. His fingers brush the skin of my lower back while he gently nudges the zip and slides it slowly up over my skin at a pace my distracted mind is going to replay, later. Several times.

"My first husband died," Mrs. Davis says, just as we were about to make our break. "I was about your age."

"Mrs. Davis, I'm so sorry."

She puts her hand on my arm. Two vastly different life stories. Both on the same page. I ache for her.

"If I didn't volunteer here six days a week, I'd spend all my time staring into the space he once took up in my life."

The space he once took up. Space that can never be occupied. Space destined to be carried forever, everything else forced to expand and grow around it.

"When you walked in here, I could tell you had suffered a great loss. It's all over your face. Your posture. It's in your voice."

This bit I get, on an instinctive level. I feel like such a forty-year-old wreck because of the grief I'm lugging around. Less so, granted, during the zipper moment.

"Take it from a very old woman. No amount of sadness is going to bring your husband back. Did he want you to be happy when he was alive?"

"Blissfully."

She smiles. "Don't take that away from him, then, in death."

I'd never considered it quite this way. Staying sad and half-living this life since he died. It's all I've been able to manage and what I thought people expected. But it's not me. Am I betraying his greatest wish for me?

"You feel him, sometimes, don't you?" she asks me.

I think of the beach and nod.

"He knows what's best for you."

"I felt him today. He stood right behind me. I felt him protecting me." I don't even care that I'm saying this in front of Hugh.

"And then what?"

She watches me closely, and I can see her respond to the recognition that must pass across my face as I look at Hugh, who leans across the desk to pick up my bags.

Then Hugh came and Cam just sort of . . . stepped aside.

24

A few months ago

"Kate, no. You're not wearing that again," Grace says, rolling her eyes at my go-to LBD and walking back to her car.

It's one of the first few big, critical work events I've had the courage to attend since Cam died. High profile. Maximum glam. Several very wealthy potential benefactors will be there, including one who I know is keen to support some cutting-edge university research into the genetics of Alzheimer's. And it's made my job personal. With a son potentially carrying the gene mutations that will lead him down the same path as his father, I'm driven to do everything I can to influence a different result for him, including having a strong interest in research. I will take this right up to the line where a conflict of interest would exist. And Hugh will hold me back from crossing it.

"You need your game face on tonight," Grace instructs as she sweeps through the front door, brandishing a long garment bag and her hair and makeup kit.

First things first. The dress. She hangs the coat hanger on the doorframe, unzips the bag, and sighs rapturously. "You're going to say yes to this dress," she says, eyes sparkling. "Tonight is about getting attention, Kate, and I know you hate that, but this is your job."

"It's about getting attention through having important conversations," I start to protest, but she is revealing a fitted, strapless emerald-green vintage gown that falls away at the waist into delicate folds of floor-length chiffon. The dress is stunning. Striking. Romantic. Dusted with sparkles that are so sparse and delicate, they almost look like a trick of the light. It's certainly a "look at me" dress.

"Well?" she asks, thrilled with herself.

"It definitely says, 'Give me five million dollars for scientific research immediately.'"

"I know, right? I love it. And with your red hair!"

"Auburn, please."

"Own it, Kate. The dress you're wearing now is screaming 'grieving widow just walked in from the funeral.' Take it off!"

I duck into our bedroom—my bedroom, I suppose, these days—and slip off the black dress. The part of me that wants a generous donation to the cause is at war with the part of me that wants a block of chocolate and six hours in my PJs in front of Netflix. When did I lose my love of nightlife and fundraising galas and dancing? I used to lose myself in the rhythm of music, not long before I lost myself in a different way to Cam's illness and the baby I will always wonder about. *Is my spark ever going to return?*

Grace walks in and helps me step into the gown. She shimmies it up my body, and I hold the bodice in place while she zips it up at the back, tight.

I turn to the mirror. Well, it's regal. Can't fault it. She passes me a pair of diamond-and-emerald pendant earrings and places an antique-look statement necklace around my neck. It's not something I'd normally wear, but it perfectly suits the strapless gown. The clasp is a bit tricky, but eventually she gets it, then digs out a pair of silver heels from my wardrobe.

"Now, hair up tonight," she says, and I immediately feel exposed.

"Can't I have it down? Cover up a bit?"

"Not with your shoulders, no."

She pushes me onto the stool by the vanity, which is covered in books, and goes to work, wrangling my long curls into an elegant updo that she's apparently learned from some teenage hair genius on TikTok. She's always had artistic flair, and tonight we need every bit of it.

By the time she's done my makeup, we're cutting it close to being late. She and Charlie are going to drop me off, and I feel increasingly nervous as we pick up my things, lock up, and head off.

"You'll be fine," Grace says, delivering the encouragement I need. "There was a time when you did these kinds of charity schmoozes every second week. You can talk millions of funding dollars out of a donor with your eyes shut. Besides, you won't be on your own, will you?"

She means Hugh, but we rarely speak of him by name ever since my matchmaking crashed and burned. She pulls into the driveway outside Old Parliament House, and I kiss Charlie goodbye and thank Grace again, for everything, then get out of the car and wave them off.

I turn to face the building. Striking First Nations artwork is projected onto the white walls as part of Canberra's gorgeous Enlighten festival. Access to the building is off-limits to the public tonight, but crowds are standing over at a temporary fence, taking photos of the light show.

My heart is racing at the foot of the steps. Professional nerves, I assume. That and having what feels like a throng of paparazzi snapping shots nearby. Not used to being this dressed up anymore, I place a hand on my chest, close my eyes, and inhale deeply to settle myself down. It's a technique I learned in an online parent workshop from the grief camp for kids who've lost a parent, but I can't dwell on that or I'll get upset again.

When I open my eyes, I smooth my dress down, fiddle with my hair, and glance up the steps. Hugh is standing on the landing, in a dinner suit, watching me. My heart thuds again, and I pick up the long skirt and walk carefully toward him. If I can just manage myself in these heels and this dress without tripping, at least until I reach the top of the steps, that will help.

Golden light is spilling out of King's Hall, and I can see fairy lights glittering inside. It's a life-affirming sight, and I'm smiling when I reach Hugh's side.

For a few seconds, neither of us speaks. I'm utterly self-conscious in this getup, and his lack of words is unsettling me further.

"You, um . . ." He glances over me and takes a breath. "This is different."

I laugh. "You can thank my fairy godmother for that," I say. "Except she's not speaking to you on account of your rejection of her for mysterious reasons!"

He looks wounded, and I'm forced to rescue him because he's so genuinely sorry about it not working out with Grace. "Don't worry, Hugh. I'm sure she understands."

He pulls a regretful face. "I hope so. Please pass on my regards, won't you? And send her my compliments on tonight's work."

I roll my eyes.

"Come on. These funds aren't going to raise themselves." He offers his arm and I thread my hand through it, instantly noticing the warmth of his body through his suit. My breath catches. Being this close to a man who isn't my husband feels strange. Too foreign. Even if that man is only Hugh.

I slip my hand out again quickly. Tonight is not for falling to pieces, and if I stand here and compare the nuances between the feel of Hugh's arm and Cam's, that's exactly what's going to happen. As it is, a memory of our wedding has presented itself, me taking Cam's arm to walk out of the church, him picking me up in the cloister way, spinning me around, veil flying, then kissing me, like 120 people weren't watching.

"S-Sorry," I stammer, now, blotting a tear that's threatening Grace's eye makeup. Hugh steps aside a little, giving me space, and we come across a security guard with a scanner, which I set off as soon as he waves it over me. It's probably the shoes. Or maybe the antique necklace.

I stand aside and the guard apologizes while he runs the scanner all over my body, which only draws attention to all the parts of me that feel exposed. Neck, shoulders, imposter syndrome, never-ending sadness . . .

"Would you mind removing your necklace, ma'am? I think it's that."

I will oblige, yes, just as soon as I can work out how to undo the latch. After watching me struggle with it for a few seconds, Hugh steps close. I drop my hands as he picks up the clasp and unlocks it easily, his fingers brushing my shoulder as he drops the necklace forward carefully and allows me to duck out from under his arms.

I'm impressed, but unsurprised, with how dexterous he is with women's jewelry. I drop the necklace into a plastic basket and am scanned again, this time without problem. The guard passes me the jewelry, and we stand to the side while we sort ourselves out.

There's a light breeze from the open doors, and I shiver as I hand the necklace back to Hugh. He leans in, so close I can sense his breath on my skin, dangles the chain over my face, and drops it lower, fastening the ends at my neck.

"There you go," he says, and he clears his throat.

I say nothing, because I feel like the throat-clearing might be contagious.

We start up the main staircase, and the wooden floor is slippery, my skirt is difficult, I'm clutching an evening bag, and hundreds of VIPs I've never met are coming into view. I reach for Hugh's arm, involuntarily this time, and he doesn't skip a beat.

Once in King's Hall, we're almost immediately swamped by familiar faces. Familiar in that I've researched them thoroughly, not that we've met. They've known Hugh for years, of course.

"General Delaney," I say confidently, extending my hand. "I'm Kate Whittaker. I've been so looking forward to meeting you."

The man is in his late eighties and still carries himself like he's currently serving. He shakes my hand, bone-crushingly.

"I'm glad we bumped into each other at the door," I say. "I'd hoped we'd have a chance to chat. We have some shared interests!" I'm talking, of course, of his wealth and our university's research study into patterns of inheritance in early-onset dementia. I know he lost a brother and a nephew to this insidious disease.

"Can I get you a drink, General?" Hugh asks, waving down a server. "Kate?"

"Lancaster!" the general says, ignoring Hugh's question and slapping him on the back. "Why am I only just now meeting this gem of a woman?"

Ugh. He has no way of knowing whether or not I'm a "gem." And he hasn't met me because normally I'm on my couch, howling into my ice cream, wishing my husband was alive. He just likes my dress.

"Kate has initiated plans for several of the university's most successful funding partnerships of late," Hugh explains. It's true. And my success has been directly in proportion to the extent to which I've needed to escape my life by throwing myself at various projects.

"There's one project that I'm particularly invested in right now," I say. "I'm not meant to have favorites, but . . ."

"Go on," the general says. "I'm intrigued now."

It's a bold move to launch straight into fundraising talk. This is meant to be about easing into rapport. But while there's no known cure for a disease that might conceivably take my son in years to come, I really don't care for conventions.

"We have a promising research project on early-onset familial Alzheimer's disease," I say. I place my hand on his arm briefly to communicate that I know about his family history. One of his nieces wrote an article in the national press about losing her father and brother to the disease. "I lost my husband, too, about a year and a half ago."

He stops short and looks at me, clearly shocked. "Oh, dear, I am sorry. I lost my brother and my nephew. Dreadful business. Awful! And look at you, widowed so young. Look at her, Lancaster! It's not right."

I don't want anyone looking at me, not least Hugh, and feeling sorry for me. This is the very thing he knows I go to great lengths to avoid, in case I slip into a sinkhole of despair and never climb back out of it, and he is looking apologetic. He's probably sorry this is exposing a wound. What people don't get is the wound is *always* exposed. You can't be reminded of something when it's all you think about, even after you learn to go about the business of the day simultaneously.

"I'm so sorry for your losses, General. That must be incredibly difficult."

His eyes glisten just for a moment and he straightens up again. I know not to push him to say any more.

"I would love to introduce you to our scientists one day," I say. "If that's something you'd be interested in."

He nods. "Arrange it, please. My sister-in-law wants to erect some godawful monument in honor of Stanley and Joe. I'd much prefer to see the family's funds channeled into something that might actually help. Now, if you'll excuse me, I just have to—"

He gets it. And he needs a second to pull himself together.

Once he's out of earshot, Hugh takes my elbow and leads me into a side corridor, where it's quiet.

"I have to tell you, the last guy in your job was useless at this. I'd bring him to an event and either he'd blunder through from one social faux pas to another or he'd clam up. I think he was terrified of speaking to prospective donors. And to people in general. He preferred spreadsheets."

I laugh.

"When I have these conversations myself," he says, "it takes effort to build the rapport. If I appeal to them, it's usually after months of groundwork. And often after a lot of drinks on their part. You just launch straight in."

I can't pretend it doesn't feel wonderful being bolstered by this feedback. I've spent so much time feeling distracted of late, it's nice to remind him why he hired me. "I don't know, Hugh. It's so much easier just being yourself. We could have tiptoed around General Delaney for months, but that's not saving lives."

"This isn't just a job to you, is it?"

The question surprises me. "Fundraising for the university? No, it's magic. Think of the difference we're helping brilliant people to make." As much as I dream of other things, I mean this.

He nods. "You're very good at this, you know."

"I wish you saw more of this," I say. "And less of Grief Kate."

He smiles. "Poor old Grief Kate has been through the wringer."

"And feels like it."

I turn to go back in, but he stops me.

"Doesn't look like it, tonight," he says.

Hugh's compliment startles me. It's so unlike him to break the impenetrable fourth wall of his professionalism and acknowledge me not as a fundraising professional, a colleague, a mum, the grieving wife of a dead husband . . . but just as a *woman*. It's been so long since I've felt confident in how I look, or even had the emotional space outside personal emergencies and just surviving to pay any attention to that. I'd forgotten how it felt to be acknowledged not just for tragic reasons.

I break away from him and back into the hall, determined to "work the room" and show him that tonight's potential victory wasn't a one-off. The event is filled with people who I know are interested in their future legacy or want to make something of the legacy of people they've lost. I feel uniquely placed to understand that, and to gently float ideas about how they can make a difference.

Hugh works just as hard. I'm aware of him across the room, understated charm offensive in full swing. It occurs to me what a strong team we make when we're totally on our game—or when I am. It's rare for him not to be.

The evening evolves with the arrival of a band, and a few people drift onto the dance floor. I haven't danced since the last time I was out with Grace, just before everything tumbled. Being out tonight, Charlie-free, dressed to the nines and feeling confident for the first time in years, I am itching to get out there.

"Do you dance as well as you network?" I'm asked by the app developer I'm chatting with, Arch Jacobs. He's been an overnight sensation, making a small fortune with an intuitive podcast app that apparently cuts postproduction in half.

"I can't remember!" I say, hoping it's like riding a bike.

He takes my hand and pulls me into the center of the room. The band is catering to the older demographic, playing a range of hits from Glenn Miller through to Elvis, and this is exactly the dress for the task. I'm loving the way it feels as I move, loving all of it, really: the music, the freedom, the temporary holiday this night is giving me from Charlie and all the sadness.

Eventually we peel off for a drink and sit down. I feel like I've exorcized months' worth of stress in just one set of songs.

"That was great," Arch says, still catching his breath as he places a gin and tonic in front of me on the table. "Where'd you learn to dance like that?"

"School of life," I reply, and he laughs.

"What's your story, Kate?" he asks. "Married? Kids? Divorced?"

"Widowed," I answer. Even now, it feels unnatural to utter the word.

Like most people when I break the news, Arch looks immediately uncomfortable. He's searching for words to wrap around a situation like ours. "Oh, no. I'm so sorry. I didn't know. I'm sorry for reminding you."

"How could you have known? And thanks." *I hadn't forgotten!*

The air is charged with a type of awkwardness I've come to accept. I'm forever having to smooth this over for people, help them navigate the topic and reassure them it's okay. On top of everything else involved in grief work, it's just another layer of difficult.

I want an excuse to leave, the spell of the evening broken now. I catch sight of Hugh, who's having a conversation with someone at the back of the room. He looks over and responds to my subliminal communication. I watch him wrap up his chat, shake the guy's hand, grab his suit jacket on the way past his table, and walk to ours.

"Hi," he says to Arch. "I don't think we've met. Hugh Lancaster. Amazing app, mate. Well done."

Arch seems relieved for the change of subject.

"You ready to head off soon?" Hugh asks me. "No rush."

I nod. "Thanks. Arch, it's been lovely to meet you. Thanks for the dancing! Hope to see you again at another event."

He smiles, then goes in for an unexpected hug, crushing me to his chest while he whispers in my ear, "I'm so sorry again, Kate."

When he releases me, I nod, pick up my bag, and follow Hugh out of the room, down the stairs, and through the exit into the cool evening air.

"Thanks," I say. "Grief convo. Awkward as usual."

"Yeah. But it looked like you were having a good time before that?"

I was. The first good time I've had in a really long time. And I'm sorry the evening is over.

Hugh opens the Uber app. "Do you feel like going home?" he says. "Or would you like to make the most of your freedom? We could get a drink somewhere?"

The idea of going home feels horrifically lonely. No Charlie, who's sleeping over at Grace's for a treat. No Cam. No distractions.

Just me in the house. I don't think I'm ready for it.

"Let's get a drink," I blurt. "I don't know where. It's been so long since I've been out in the world after dark. I don't know half the bars in town these days."

"I know exactly the place," Hugh says, booking the car.

Chapters is a new bar on the corner of an old street in the redeveloped central suburb of Kingston, not far from Hugh's apartment. It's tastefully art deco–inspired, with worn leather couches, colored-glass panels, metal accents, and high ceilings. The lighting is warm and the music soft enough to speak over. I think I'm in love with the place and, best, the drinks are named after classic authors. I take a photo of the drinks menu and send it to Grace by way of an update on my evening.

"Chapters? You'll love it! Please tell me you met a hot guy at the gala and you're about to have a wild night of drunken debauchery and merry-widow sex."

"Everything okay?" Hugh says, returning from the bar with our drinks—the "Austen" for me and a "Thoreau" for him. In a flap, I drop the phone on the low table right beside where he's placing my glass. It lands face up, of course, with Grace's message broadcasting from the screen, the words "merry-widow sex" blaringly obvious.

I snatch the phone back, flustered, and check his expression to assess the damage.

"Grace doing okay with Charlie tonight?" he asks. He is the world's best actor. I pick up my glass, tap it against his, and take a sip.

"She didn't say," I respond.

"Other things on her mind," he says, and snorts with laughter.

Kill me.

I glance around the bar, desperate to find a talking point, landing on nothing of note until my eyes rest back on Hugh. He's watching me from the other end of the couch, one leg crossed lazily over his knee at the ankle, arm spread along the back of the couch. He is a picture of someone perfectly at ease, starkly contrasting with me, the picture of anxiety.

"Hugh," I begin, unsure of exactly where I'm taking this.

"Yes, Kate?"

"I am not a merry widow."

He uncrosses his leg and angles his body toward me. "I know."

"I don't have nights of drunken debauchery," I explain, for who knows what reason, as it's unnecessary. "Last time I did that, I ended up marrying the guy."

He nods.

"I do not have . . ."

Stop. Talking. Kate.

"I don't meet hot guys. Or *any* guys. It's just Grace. You know what she's like." Of *course you do, I made you date her.*

"Kate, relax. It's none of my business," he says.

"Yes, but I don't want you to have a mental picture of me cavorting through late-night drinks establishments with random men, when in reality, I spend every single night streaming crime dramas and scrolling social media until it's so late and I'm so exhausted it's safe to get into bed and fall asleep before I notice how empty it is."

Somehow this feels like an even worse topic to have raised than the debauchery. Now it's him who takes a sip of his drink.

"Grace nags me to get back out there," I go on. "Not for anything serious, just—because life is short."

"Life *is* short," he agrees. "And maybe the time will come when you feel ready for that, but there are no rules. There's no rush. Everyone responds differently. You can't expect anyone to understand how hard it is unless they've actually been there."

I shake my head, trying to process his words. "You always get it. I don't know how."

He puts his empty glass down on the table. "The point is, it's your life. Your decision. Your timing. You might resist it now, but you'll know the moment when it comes, and not before. And then you'll realize the bigger risk is not taking a risk."

25

The present

When we arrive back at the beach house from the thrift shop, I spend a while taking macro photos of tropical flowers in the garden. I've got a special lens attachment for my phone that helps you get right up close and capture the detail. I don't know enough yet about the big camera to lug it with me for what was going to be only an overnight trip. Pity. I could have watched YouTube tutorials and figured out the settings while we were here.

After a while, I make my way upstairs and ease into the hammock on the balcony, listening to an episode of the podcast *So You Want to Be a Writer*. It's one of hundreds of interviews with successful writers about how they got their big breaks. From what I can tell the secret seems to be to put actual words on pages. Any words at first, regardless of quality. If only the writing process was as easy as it feels when I'm emailing Grace chaotic stories about Mum or Charlie or work. Or when I'm writing about Cam in my journal and the story tells itself, like it's downloaded from some deep, subconscious source.

A video call from Mum breaks into the podcast. This will be Charlie, home from school. His beautiful face fills the screen and my heart melts. Being so many hundreds of miles away from him is a wrench, though truthfully the hammock and afternoon breeze are going a long way toward soothing that.

"Mummy! I want to go as a dinosaur for Book Week."

God, when is that?

"Nanna has this *all* in hand," Mum says, coming into sight.

I get a flashback to Book Week in Year Four, when she sent me to school decked out in Poland's national dress, carrying a nonfiction book about Poland, even though we aren't Polish and I had wanted to go as Pippi Longstocking. Preferably with a horse.

But now, as a mother myself, I get it. I was not genetically blessed in the fancy-dress department. Cam was always so gung ho about costume parties—he'd have excelled at Book Week. Yet another event in the school calendar that I've been dreading, surrounded by all the mums and dads. I guess it's not as bad as Father's Day will be. I think we'll play hooky when that rolls around.

Bluey's theme song kicks off in the background. Charlie says, "Bye, Mum!" and rushes away, perfectly content in my absence.

"Gracious, Kate, you look glorious!" Mum observes. It's not like her. "What's changed?"

I'm on holiday? It's warm? New dress? Massive emotional meltdown?

"How are *you*, Mum?"

Now that Justin's told me the truth about Mum's struggle, it's easier to spot the cracks in her façade. Practiced happy face, hyperefficiency, quick turnaround when the conversation sneaks in her direction.

"Oh, I'm having a *wonderful* time! Charlie is divine when I have him all to myself. How's Hugh?"

"He's fine." Although I'm not sure that's strictly true either. He's on a beach walk now, but he's been quiet since the thrift shop. That's the thing with Hugh. He's generous with everything but his own story. Maybe this is just what he does after work. Goes for walks. Who knows? He's a closed book.

"What happened to that man?" Mum asks. It's an odd question.

"What do you mean?"

"The obvious question, Kate!" she says. "Who broke him?"

Broke him? I didn't know this was a question that needed answering, or why even the thought of it fans a flame within me that I hadn't realized was even smoldering. Hugh Lancaster could be commander-in-chief of the enduringly unattached. Surely it's *him* doing the heartbreaking. And even if he does have relationships, they're never significant enough to mention at work, not even Yum Cha Ruby, who he kept seeing for *months*.

Which is when it hits me. Maybe it's not his relationships that are never significant enough. Maybe it's us. The team of people at work. Me, Sophie, the finance and comms people, and those who work on raising funds for specific areas of the university, here and overseas—all of whom he regards well professionally, there's no doubt. Hugh might be in my inner circle, I realize now, but I am not necessarily in his. I'm not cleared for this highly sensitive material. The details of Hugh Lancaster's love life exist on a need-to-know basis, and his colleagues do not have that level of approval.

I do have a want-to-know, though. A really-want-to-know.

"Oh, I don't know, Mum. He never talks about that stuff," I finally say.

"Broken men play their cards close to their chests," Mum explains, playing fast and loose with stereotypes as usual.

She needs to stop talking about him being broken. I simply cannot have that.

"But if you can push through that wall, a man like Hugh will give you everything."

That's fine, but I don't want Hugh's everything.

"I'm not the woman for that job," I argue. "We just work together, Mum. Remember?"

She finds this hilarious, apparently. "Just colleagues? You can't be serious! He was Cam's close friend. Charlie calls him Uncle. You tried to matchmake him with your best friend. Even I've got him in my phone contacts. This is not a normal professional dynamic, Katherine. There are only so many ways you can try to insert the poor man into our family, and you've exhausted nearly all of them."

That's not what I've been trying to do. *Is it?* I start to feel woozy. Must be from the sleep deprivation. Or maybe from rocking in the hammock. I stop that at once and sit upright.

"When Grace said you'd want to go to the writers' festival, I told her you'll never make that leap. Becoming a successful writer would involve giving up the day job. Which would sever the connection you and Hugh Lancaster have developed over the last four years."

I plant my feet more firmly on the deck. "Mum! Stop! You've been watching way too much *Dr. Phil.* The reason I'm not a writer has nothing to do with the threat of losing Hugh." *Surely I'm not that messed up?* "It's because I'm fecking *terrified!*"

It comes out fast and forthright and chased by hot tears of frustration. At myself.

Even Mum is temporarily silenced by this volcanic admission. She's also unimpressed by the language and would usually tell me to *have some decorum, Katherine,* but manages to hold her tongue.

I think of the hundreds of episodes on the writers' podcast.

Hundreds of other authors who were no doubt equally scared to put themselves out there and risk being shot down in the flames of criticism and rejection. But they put themselves out there anyway, didn't they? That's the difference between them and me.

"Kate, your husband died at thirty-eight," Mum says, as if I need reminding of that fact. "If that isn't enough to clarify the consequences of *not* taking these chances while you can, nothing will be."

Are we still talking about the writing? It's hard to argue with her logic, anyway. At least on this one point.

"Well! Enough chitchat. Must sort out Charlie's dinner and catch up on *Grand Designs*. Oh, that Kevin McCloud. *Utterly* dreamy man." She ends the call abruptly on that note and leaves me stunned. I feel like I've been involved in a hit-and-run.

The point about not taking chances while I can is irrefutable. But the part about letting my day job—and Hugh—stand between me and the only true career dream I've ever held couldn't possibly be right. Why would anyone willingly place themselves in such a self-limiting situation?

And if it *was* true, the only sensible path would be to resign, surely. And work somewhere where I'm far less . . . entrenched, while I really throw myself at my book. Perhaps then I could shift gears with Hugh so it's more of a run-of-the-mill, out-of-work-hours friendship. If he'd even want that?

But even thinking about resigning makes me feel shaky. And maybe that makes Mum's point too.

Then I watch as Hugh's tall frame and familiar gait trudges toward the house over the path from the sandhills in the twilight. Dark hair, brooding expression—all very Matthew Macfadyen traipsing toward Keira Knightley over the moors at the end of *Pride and Prejudice*.

And something unfamiliar clenches in my stomach.

"Hey," he says, stopping about three steps before the staircase meets the balcony, while I lean on the railing with lashings of trepidation.

It's a level of informality to which the two of us are not accustomed. He never says "Hey." It would normally be "Hello" or "Hi" or "Evening, Kate."

It catches me off guard, as do the grains of sand caught in the stubble on his chin. I fight an intense desire to reach over the railing and brush the sand off his face.

As if he can read my mind, he steps back and leans against the railing behind him, folding his arms across his chest, looking up at me with those penetrating blue eyes.

"Nice walk?"

He nods contemplatively.

"What demons are you wrestling?" I hear myself ask. It's a perfectly normal conversation-starter, surely. No stranger than a lot of the other things I've said to him over the years.

What I specifically want to know is *who broke you?*

I thought he might laugh, but he doesn't. Nor does he furnish me with a straight answer. "What game are we playing, here?" he asks. "Truth or dare?"

At the very idea of that, and before I can stop it, I find myself taking in the full length of him. Sandy feet. Long limbs. Athletic torso, up through that dark stubble and back to those blue eyes, now with an amused twinkle I don't see nearly often enough.

"You're staring at me like I just pulled up on a motorcycle," he says with a cautious nod to the elephant in the room. He pushes himself off from the banister and takes another step up, arms outstretched, gripping the railing on both sides. Now it's me who wants to take a step back from him.

I almost feel sorry for myself. So starved of romantic attention, I'm fantasizing about having briefly entranced untouchable Hugh Lancaster: confirmed bachelor, workaholic. A man who is inexplicably single at forty-two because, according to my mum and her wildly outdated and frankly misogynistic theories, some invisible woman "broke him."

He doesn't look broken to me. He seems more assured and in control than ever.

I, on the other hand, am spiraling, fast, with the arrival of a fresh new theory on the blurry concept of having any kind of future relationship—with anyone. I thought I was scared of having to learn someone from scratch. Telling my whole story to a new person. It seems as exhausting as the idea of changing psychologists right now.

But when I look at Hugh, something else lands entirely.

It's not intimacy that scares me. *It's loss.*

The breeze picks up and I shiver, breaking the moment. His eyes flit over my bare shoulders and he bounds up the last step, touches my elbow, and leads me back inside, through my bedroom.

There are none of Cam's colorful labels here. No notes on the bedside table, not even being used as bookmarks. Just the perfectly blank slate of crisp white linen. Clean lines, no creases.

Hugh catches me contemplating the bed.

Do not pass go. Do not collect $200.

DO NOT lose your heart again, Kate. It will kill you this time.

I hurry us along, straight past the bed, through the door and onto the upstairs landing, where I can breathe again. "I don't understand Gantt charts," I blurt, turning to face Hugh. "Or any type of charts. Numbers in general, really. I've been cheating with the finance team all this time."

He laughs, loudly.

"It's something about critical paths?" I scramble.

What am I doing? Trying to get myself fired?

"Do you really want to talk about Gantt charts? Not sure if you've noticed, but we're in subtropical paradise."

Waves pound into the silence between us.

"But you should know the financial reports are not why I keep you around," he adds.

"Is this a performance discussion?" I ask.

"Do you want it to be?"

No.

We take a few steps down the indoor staircase, and he stops and turns to face me. "You know, that young guy in your job who had the schmoozing skills of a doorstop was a technical genius," he reminds me.

How is this helping?

"He set up all the project tracking schedules and made the whole process flow seamlessly. We always knew exactly where we were. Reporting was a breeze—"

The less we say about how reporting goes now, the better. He subdues me further with every sentence.

"Then you came along, and the focus was no longer on data. You set up meetings with researchers and scientists and writers and engineers and artists and musicians—experts all over campus. You found out what they really do. You asked what they need, and really thought about the impact of their work. And you did the same with the alumni and benefactors. By the time I was briefing the vice chancellor, you'd given us such a thorough head start, the meetings were almost a done deal. And when we pulled off a substantial donation, you put your writer hat on and blitzed the comms. How you did all of this with your world falling apart, I will never know. So, Kate, understand that I didn't lie awake at night worrying about whether or not you could handle a spreadsheet."

I'd spent so much time feeling like such a mess, worrying I'd melt down during inopportune professional moments. It was exhausting keeping that stormy inner world from leaking out into the public constantly. But, somehow, I had done a good job?

A shadow passes across Hugh's face. "I know how debilitating it is to carry big problems into work every day and still function."

What problems?

"Why don't you ever trust me?" I ask, and it's like I've winded him.

The graying temples and extra lines on his face have snuck up on me. And I watch as pain flits across his features for the briefest second. Deep pain. He shuts it down, fast, but it's there long enough for me to see him in a different light. A little bit broken, perhaps, like Mum said, when he's meant to be whole. Always emotionally together. Hugh is the lighthouse. Never the storm.

"I do trust you. And I will tell you. But let's just close the loop on this conversation first," he says. "I've been thinking about you a lot this afternoon, and your work. And mine. And there's something I need to get off my chest."

The house itself seems to still in this moment, as if even the walls are listening.

"I know you think you're dropping the ball all the time, but you make up for it with your creativity. This film project is unlike anything we've ever done, at least since I've been involved. The universal disconnect and rivalry between faculties over funding has been a thorn in the tertiary sector's side for decades. I know we're not going to fix it with one project, but it's the spirit of the strategic thinking that could open up some exciting new directions."

"This doesn't sound like a problem," I say.

"It's the opposite. But you've got so much self-doubt. And it's very badly placed. You know you're crucial to me, Kate?"

I do not know that. Not in so many words.

"But here's the quandary." He pauses, like he's deliberating whether or not to forge through the rest. "This job is holding you back."

Something in his tone silences my inevitable protest. Or perhaps it's that his statement echoes Mum's.

"I didn't ever want you to feel like you owed me for the flexibility or feel in any way guilty for wanting something more than I can ever offer."

He's never made me feel that way. This feels like we're breaking up. Again, making Mum's point!

"The thing is, Kate, you're the only person in the organization who I'm genuinely scared to lose. But you're also the one I really should stop trying so hard to retain."

26

I've spent the last two years trying to build a fortress for me and Charlie, clinging to the idea of certainty and safety and security. I guess that's what people do when chaos wipes them off their feet and they lose control of everything. Suddenly it all feels precarious.

"The future I imagined just *combusted*," I tell Hugh. "It was my own personal apocalypse. And then I was forced to stagger to my feet and pull Charlie out of the rubble and rebuild everything from scratch. I've had to cling hard to my own life. I've needed help to stay in a world that felt impossible to exist in without Cam."

He knows this; he's provided some of that help. He rests his hand on the banister and waits for more of the monologue that I sense is about to pour itself out of my runaway mouth.

I sit on a step, clearly settling in to deliver quite the lecture. Hugh lets go of the banister and props himself against the wood-paneled wall, putting more space between us. Giving me the floor.

"Mum said something to me tonight and I can't shake it. She said the fact that Cam died at thirty-eight should scare me into going out and getting the things I really want. She thinks I've—"

No, don't go into the dependence-on-the-connection stuff!

"She thinks I've gotten *comfortable* with you. And vice versa." It's an incredibly ironic statement, given that right now I feel like a cat on a hot tin roof.

"I think she's right," Hugh agrees. "Don't you?"

Of course she's bloody right.

I feel like I've arrived at a clearing, in full sunlight. No shadows here to hide in.

"With Charlie and the house and all of Cam's notes at home, being here I finally feel uncaged," I reply. "I feel like Kate, the woman. Not the widow. Not the wife. Not the mum. Not the employee. Just a woman, with a blank page in front of her."

He nods.

The emptiness of that blank page that was so confronting two years ago is starting to feel like this *delicious invitation* to write the next part of my story. A tantalizing glimpse of how it might look to have purpose and forward momentum into a new life.

I look at Hugh. "I know I'm *crucial* to you," I tease, pulling myself up on the step again. "And to all your charts and spreadsheets and whatever the hell all those data schedule things are."

He laughs.

"But sometimes I wonder, seriously, if I'm just staying around because you make it so easy for me."

He shrugs.

"You know, if you see me sitting there, staring into space, don't always assume I'm upset about Cam. I am, about seventy-five percent of the time. But I reckon twenty-five percent of it, I'm actually dreaming up the plot of a novel. The other five percent I'm wrecked from dragging Charlie around with a camera at midnight trying to capture the Milky Way."

He laughs. "Is this a three-hundred-and-sixty-degree feedback session?"

"Maybe?"

"In that case, I need bonus points for overlooking your deplorable math."

"See! Even now, faced with concrete evidence of your staff member's lamentable professional skills gap, you're letting yourself become hopelessly charmed by her above-average public-speaking abilities."

"Which are seriously underused in her current position," he finishes.

"Another oversight. I mean, have you been paying attention *at all* over the last four years, Mr. Lancaster?" I have my hand on my hip now, fishwife style.

His scrutiny flicks down my arm to my waist, and back to my eyes. "I've paid attention every second," he answers succinctly. And now it's him taking a step up, so we're at eye level.

If this was one of my incomplete novels, he'd forget his professional ethics at this juncture, put his hand on my waist, and pull me into the kiss I imagined this morning on the plane, and several times since, if I'm honest.

He smiles. "You're an open book, Kate."

I hope not!

"If I was doing my job right," he explains calmly, "I'd take everything you've just said and schedule a career-planning session with you at your earliest convenience. A good boss would help you maneuver yourself to where you want to be."

His eyes are High-Stakes-Negotiation Blue, and my appetite for doing something irrational and impulsive is at an all-time high.

"What would a bad boss do?" I ask fatefully.

They say your life flashes before your eyes when you're going to die. Apparently, mine flashes before my eyes when I'm about to dust off the old feminine wiles and unleash them, full throttle, at the innocent man who employed me. Somewhere early on in this highlight reel, I realize none of it is familiar. It's not my past that's flashing before my eyes at all. It's my future. *Am I psychic, suddenly? What is this?*

Halter-neck dress on the stairs. Tangled sheets. Ardent blue eyes. Sunrise. Panic attack.

"Kate?" he says, leaning closer. He's going to kiss me. That's obvious. And for some *inexplicable* reason, I think I want him to. "Are you hyperventilating?" he asks.

What? *No!*

I hold my hand up like a stop sign and shake my head and act like I can breathe, but, now that he mentions it, I actually cannot. There is not enough air! Everything's starting to spin. I sink onto the step and put my head on my knees, hair dangling, along with the last shred of my dignity.

What would a bad boss do?

"Can we just rewind, Hugh?" I say. "Can we start again?"

"From where?" he asks. It's a fine question. My life is such a mess that it would be next to impossible to pick a starting place for a proper do-over—one that I could bear living through twice. Or that he could.

"I don't care. Just erase what just happened," I say, hoping this is a blanket clause: *erase everything.*

"Nothing happened."

I pull my head up. Messy curls fall across my face and I catch a glimpse of myself in a mirror on the wall opposite. I am a certifiable wreck. Stricken with remorse and embarrassment.

"Just erase what I said," I suggest, into my hands this time. "About the..." *Cringe*. "The bad-boss thing. I don't know where that came from."

He laughs and sits down beside me on the step. "Really? You don't know where that came from?"

A few moments pass while I consider the question. Did this really come out of the blue? It feels that way, but it also feels like it's coming from some other, amorphous timeline. "I have my suspicions," I hear myself say. "Just need one of those police department whiteboards and a ball of string to join all the contributing factors."

"It is pretty complex," Hugh agrees. "And that's when you've only pieced together your side of it."

He has a side? I let my hands drop from my face and look at him. *What is he saying, exactly?*

"I've been trying to work it out," he says. "I've thought about it quite a lot recently."

"Since when?" I challenge him. "This morning, when I showed up on a motorcycle?"

He shakes his head. "I can't deny that delivered a bolt of clarity. But no. A bit longer than that."

It's not just the recent past that I imagine reflected in his eyes now. It's a full-length feature film franchise with multiple prequels and a cliffhanger ending.

I know what he's going to say in advance. I can guess exactly the time frame he's talking about, and it's not since this morning, or last night, or even last year.

He's going to take me back to that awful moment when I thought I'd lost him.

27

Three years ago

I've been watching Hugh in the office for days, looking progressively more unwell. Every day this week he's come in with darker circles under his eyes, slightly more unkempt than the day before. I can't imagine what could be so wrong that he'd drop his standards like this. He looks like he's losing the love of his life or he's seriously ill. I haven't asked, because it's Hugh and you don't ask personal questions, but it's getting ridiculous. Selfishly, I'm worried he's going to pieces. He's such a support to me and to Cam right now, I don't think I could bear it.

"Isn't it going to get too much for you?" he asks me in the tearoom. I'm working only part-time hours now, barely keeping the job ticking over, and we have a carer who spends time with Cam when I'm not there, for company and to stop him from wandering. It's something he hates. The more I take on, the more it seems obvious that caring for Cam *will* get to be too much for me, but I'm not ready to make that real by saying so.

"He doesn't want to go into a nursing home," I argue. "He's too young. I couldn't bear it. Stuck in there with ninety-year-olds who are more switched on than he is?"

Hugh and Cam have discussed this ad nauseam, both of them relaying various conversations about it over the months.

"This is the last thing he said he wanted—you struggling with his care on your own," Hugh says.

"But now he wants to be with me."

It's been like this all through—Cam wanting one thing, and that one thing then being overtaken by the disease and made impossible. I've been worried for weeks that he's well beyond being at work, but, mental health–wise, it's the best thing for him. Gives him purpose. So much of his identity is wrapped up in being a brilliant, academic thinker. He's clung to it. Perhaps longer than he should have.

The department has gone above and beyond to support Cam in continuing to work. They've even paired him with PhD students in a reverse-supervision arrangement for lectures. He's been teaching one of the undergrad courses for the last three years, so they've let him continue to read his preprepared content as long as there's a doctoral student on hand for any student questions. And for marking. And for anything involving higher-order thought. It's pushing the HR envelope, but everyone loves Cam. Colleagues, students, admin staff—they're all colluding to make it possible.

My phone rings, and I'm glad to stop arguing with Hugh about this.

"Ms. Whittaker?" a young male voice says. "My name's Sebastian. I'm one of Professor Whittaker's honors students."

My heart leaps into my throat.

"He didn't turn up for our lunchtime lecture," Sebastian says. "We all stayed in the room for twenty-five minutes, waiting for him.

Then we thought maybe we should split up and look for him. . . ."

"Oh, God!"

"No, he's safe. We found him wandering in the Hayden Allen building. Said he was looking for the 'Old Arts' building, but we don't know where he means."

Melbourne Uni. Where we met.

Sebastian waits with Cam in his office until I get there. When I do, I find Cam packing books into boxes. *When did this start?* This dismantling of a magnificent career, terminated decades too soon.

"I can't do this anymore," he tells me, tears in his eyes, hands shaking as he continues packing books. He means the job and, on the one hand, it's music to my ears. Nobody wanted to be the bad guy, wrenching him away from this if he put up a fight.

"I'm just so . . ." My voice trails off. *I'm so sorry, Cam.* And so scared the target on his back is getting bigger.

"Don't say it, Katie. Just help me."

While he puts books in boxes, I start to clean out his desk. On it, in addition to a massive pile of unanswered correspondence, I find what may end up being his last to-do list.

"Cameron Whittaker," it begins. *In case he forgets who he is?*

"Talk to Hugh." I wonder what that's about and how he'll ever remember, since there are no other details.

"Cancel sports channel."

Stop!

"Birthday cards."

I pick up the notebook and, underneath it, find a pile of cards, some still in plastic wrapping, others in various states of being filled out in shaky block lettering. *Dear birthday boy: You're four!*

Five.

Ten.

Thirteen.

Eighteen.

Twenty-one.

Congratulations on your graduation.

Happy wedding day!

On the birth of your first child . . .

I look up from the cards, eyes swimming, and watch him methodically packing up his beloved library.

Packing up his life.

Giving up.

And I *weep* for him.

I don't have the headspace to be worried about Cam *and* how awful Hugh looks. Nevertheless, a couple of days later, I stay back after everyone has left the office. It's Friday, so they've headed out for drinks at a pub in Braddon. Mum's home with Charlie and Cam, and I asked her to stay an extra half hour so I can have this conversation.

I knock on Hugh's office door, which swings open. He's leaning back in his swivel chair, staring out the window at the streetlights, and he's clearly thrown by me still being in the office.

"Kate, what is it?" he asks, instantly worried. I hate that that's his default response whenever I appear.

"It's you," I explain, shutting the door behind me even though we're the only two people still here. "I'm worried about you. You look terrible. What's wrong?"

Pain sears across his face. This looks really bad, and I get a feeling of dread in my heart. *Don't be sick, Hugh*. I'm alarmed at how violently I'm responding to even the idea of it.

"I don't want you to worry, Kate," he says gently. "It's true I am wrestling with something. I can't tell you what it is, though."

"So it's not my imagination?" I move around to his side of the desk, which is real estate I've rarely set foot on.

He stands up and in effect backs me into the bookcase, because there's not much room here, and nowhere for either of us to escape without invading each other's personal space. We're uncomfortably close. He searches my face, and opens his mouth like he's about to speak, but nothing comes out. I swear, if I didn't know better, I'd think he was about to cry. Strong, unflappable Hugh Lancaster. Whatever is wrong is *very* wrong.

"You look heartbroken," I whisper. Is this about the woman he's been seeing? Ruby? Cam came home from a drive with Hugh the other day and tried to relate the conversation afterward. All I got was "Hugh loves Ruby," over and over.

Recognition flashes through his eyes.

"What is it? You can trust me."

"I do trust you, Kate. I'm . . . mulling over a moral dilemma. A serious one. I'm sorry I can't be more specific."

"You can tell me anything," I reassure him.

"Not this." He moves his hands like he's going to put them on my shoulders, bore his eyes into mine, close up, and beg me to stop pressuring him. "Please," he says, a catch in his voice. "This is hard enough."

The man is emotionally destroyed. An intensity in his expression tells me I have to accept that he won't tell me why. And now there's something else. Somewhere in the furthest reaches of my soul, I can't help feeling that this is not about Ruby after all. It's somehow about me. But it's about me in a way that I don't think I want to find out. I don't even want to ask him to confirm or deny my hunch. It would push him too far, and he's already a mess. And I mean a *really* very serious mess, over whatever this is.

"I just want to hug you," I hear myself whispering, inches from his face. I mean the kind of hug Cam would wholeheartedly approve of, were he in his right mind, which he is less and less.

For the briefest second, I feel like he's going to give in and let me. We're suspended in time, in what feels like an intense, sliding doors moment I can't understand because I don't have all the information.

"I trust you to do the right thing," I say. I don't know why, but it feels relevant.

He nods, and it looks like he's using all his strength to keep himself together.

Three Saturdays later and I'm really worried I've done something wrong. The weekend after our conversation in his office, Hugh didn't take Cam to the rugby match as he normally would. Nor did he turn up the weekend after, because he took unexpected leave from work and went away. I don't know where. But I wasn't prepared for how bereft I felt without him.

They say you don't value something until it's gone, and it's like that with Hugh. I can't even articulate where he fits in my world— part boss, part support person, part friend, I guess. At least, I thought that's what we were, but I think my relationship barometer is faulty. When you're friends, you don't just skip town and not say anything. I'm trying desperately not to make this about me, but I feel deserted and hurt and terrified of even more loss.

Opening the door now and seeing him standing here on our doorstep, on a gloomy Saturday afternoon in August, really disconcerts me. He adjusts the collar on his dark coat and pulls the black scarf more tightly around his neck. He needs a haircut. His haircuts are booked a month apart, a year ahead, and I can tell he's missed one. There's even the beginnings of a beard—the type a man grows from neglect rather than personal style. He still looks haunted. Whatever the problem is, it hasn't gone away. It's grown.

"I'm sorry I left without saying anything," he says in a low, even voice.

I come outside with him and shut the door behind me, even though it's freezing cold and I'm in jeans and a light shirt because the fire is roaring inside for Cam, who's always cold these days. Hugh glances at my bare arms and frowns.

"Where were you?" I ask, searching his face for answers.

"I had something I needed to think about," he explains. "And I couldn't think about it here."

Here in Canberra? Or here on my doorstep? I don't know what the hell he's talking about, but it's making me feel unmoored.

"You still can't tell me, can you?" I observe. I'm almost hoping he'll agree, because there's only so much I can cope with at once. That said, if he needs me, I'm here. This is Hugh. One of my top people. I'd do anything for him. "Can I help you with this?" I ask. "I mean it, Hugh. You look desperately upset."

"Are we going to stand out here much longer?" he asks, while I shiver in front of him. "I'm starting to feel guilty about wearing a jacket."

He attempts a smile, but it doesn't reach his eyes, not that I'm really able to get a good look because he won't meet my gaze for more than a second. If I didn't know better, I'd read that as guilt. It's certainly secretive. What could he possibly have to feel guilty about where I'm concerned? It's about a lot more than having a warm jacket when I don't.

"Cam has gone downhill since you were last here," I say, warning him before I open the door. "It feels wrong even sharing this with you, but he's becoming incontinent. In every way. He doesn't make it to the toilet because he stands in front of it and can't see it. And he needs help understanding how to use cutlery. The occupational therapist gave me a plain black placemat with a white outline of the plate and knife and fork to help him navigate."

"Did it help?"

I can barely speak for holding back the sob in my throat. "He tried to pick up the drawing of the fork, Hugh."

My heart!

"I'm terrified how fast this is progressing. I thought we had years."

There's so much pain reflected in his eyes I can barely look at him.

"I find myself lying awake at night, willing him to have the heart attack I once dreaded so much. It would be kinder than this agony."

For once, he doesn't seem to know what to say. I know he wouldn't try to put a positive spin on this—he's more clued in about my grief than that. But he'd usually say *something*. Everything feels even more unstable.

"You don't have to come in," I tell him. "He won't remember you're coming anyway. I don't want to make . . . whatever this is even worse for you."

He looks at me briefly and stands up straighter. Takes a low breath in and out. I can almost hear the self-talk: *Get over yourself, Hugh. Think of Cam. Think of Kate.*

Now he wants to get on with it. I'm standing in the way, and he steps forward and reaches for the door handle at my back. It's been getting stuck the last few days. When it falters, he pulls back a little. A strand of my hair drags against his chin. As I reach up and untangle it, my fingers brush his jaw. His body shields me from the wind, and I feel so protected from the world in this moment, I just want to melt into it. It shouldn't feel this warm here. I shouldn't be this pathetic. I've been growing my resolve to handle the hard stuff single-handedly, since there's so very much of it coming at me. *But now he's here.*

And I'm not thinking of the hard stuff now. The usual scent of his designer aftershave is missing. In its place is something raw and rugged and far more familiar than it should be. I hope he thinks I'm cold now, the way I'm shaking.

"You need some WD-40 on that handle," he says next to my ear, still not meeting my gaze. "I'll fix it on the way out."

If I thought things were bizarre on my veranda, they're even more so inside the house. Hugh goes through to the living room and strips off his jacket and scarf and sits in an armchair opposite Cam.

Two-year-old Charlie rushes over to him and puts his arms up to be swept into his lap. "Unckie Hugh!" he says, patting Hugh on his chin, trying to work out what's different.

"Hey, mate. Nice Brumbies jumper!" He'd bought it for Charlie to wear to a game the three of them went to a couple of months ago. Giving us merch from the rugby club seems to be a theme.

Charlie snuggles into Hugh's chest, and it's like a dagger to my heart when Hugh envelops him. Lately, when Charlie's tried that with Cam, he's been pushed away, and I've had to rush in and distract him to keep him from noticing the rejection.

Cam's been asleep most of the afternoon and he's confused when he opens his eyes and finds Hugh here. But then recognition passes across his face, and he looks at Hugh like he's expecting an answer to a question he didn't ask. Not just now, anyway. It's odd.

Hugh's eyes are glistening. His upper lip is twitching. *What is this?* I notice a tiny, almost imperceptible shake of his head and a deeply apologetic look. Cam shuts his eyes, like it's too painful to be alive anymore.

I know these two men. *What are they keeping from me?*

"Can I take you for a drive, Cam?" Hugh asks, leaning forward. They don't go for beers anymore. Advanced dementia and alcohol are a bad combination. Often, on Sundays, Hugh has turned up, helped Cam into the wheelchair and into his car and they just drive, Springsteen and The Who blaring.

Cam eyes him thoughtfully. Though "thoughtfully" is becoming a problematic word. His thoughts aren't what they used to be. He fixates on things. He misunderstands. His conversation is closing in, like the four walls he spends most of his time staring at. Every sentence exhausts him—so many words on the tip of his tongue, hardly any on hand when he wants them. He can read aloud, disjointedly. It's as if the English professor within him is clinging to words for dear life, but he can't comprehend what he reads, because so much of what he's read is immediately forgotten. Even reading to Charlie the other day I noticed he repeated whole pages so many times that Charlie became incensed and threw the book across the room. It undid me. My luminous husband and teacher, losing his language.

"Go for a drive, Cam," I suggest. "It will do you good to get out."

He looks at me and glowers. "It will do *you* good for me to get out," he says coldly. The words sting. This whole time, the one thing I've been really proud of is my patience with him, right from that first incident at the work barbecue when he let Charlie wander to the water's edge and I held my anger back. It's getting harder by the day not to be abrupt with him when he asks the same thing for the hundredth time in a row, or now that he's having uncharacteristically angry outbursts like this. I remind myself that this is the disease talking. Not the person.

"Cam," I start to say, hiding how much it hurts.

"Don't you want a husband who works?"

"We're fine, Cam. We have income protection insurance."

He narrows his eyes. "I don't mean working in a job. I mean someone like him!" He points at Hugh. "He can drive and talk and make you laugh."

"Oh, that's a bit of a stretch," Hugh says.

His attempt at humor falls flat, as do most ideas in this house in recent weeks. It's wearing me down, but I'm committed to giving Cam every shred of patience that I can dredge. I kneel down beside his chair and take his hand and put it to my face. "I don't want anyone else, Cam. There will never be anyone else."

Try to remember. Please.

That's the problem, though. He won't remember it. We'll repeat this conversation, without a single word of it sticking, and, even if he believes me when I say it in real time, he'll forget it the moment it's passed. It's hopeless.

"Tell him, Hugh," I hear myself pleading, as if the information will somehow sink in with two of us on one.

Hugh looks like I've thrown him into the deep end with no warning. Cam and I watch him, waiting for his magic words. "She loves you, mate," he says earnestly, after a pause. "She'll always love you. End of story."

End of story. He directs that bit to me. It's tragic that my love life finishes here. In my more optimistic moments, I imagine I'll go on and be a mum and have a career and have friends. I'll travel and read and hopefully write again if I can ever find the will or the courage. I'll find things to enjoy, I hope. Life might even be nice one day.

But I'll always love Cam. His absence will be the eternal backdrop to everything else I do until the day I die. The second half of my life stretches so far into the distance it's out of sight across the horizon. Me here. Cam gone.

No part two.

No sequel.

It's agony already.

28

The present

Last thing I remember, I had my head in my hands, sitting beside Hugh on the steps of the beach house, each gathering momentous thoughts as waves crashed hypnotically over the rise. I'd been wrangling with more conflicting emotions than I'd have thought were humanly possible to cram into one body.

After thirty-six hours without sleep and four years without peace, safe in the company of the man who's been beside me through so much, I must have succumbed to . . . *everything*. I'm disconcerted to wake, still sitting on the steps, with a cricked neck, my head resting where it definitely shouldn't be: in Hugh Lancaster's lap. It's disorienting, except for one thing. Unconscious Kate is a liability.

I can feel the weight of his hand on my shoulder, which he removes as I stir and struggle upright, wondering why he didn't wake me or move me. I must look a picture . . . definitely not like a person who is out to impress a potential love interest.

Why am I thinking about love interests?

And why plural?

"Tried to wake you," he explains. "You were a dead weight."

Flattering.

"You don't look good. . . ." he adds.

Okay, let's agree and move on. "What time is it?" I ask.

"About midnight."

Oh! I'm hungry and cold and uncomfortable and anxious and unsettled and—very confused.

"Why don't you change into something warmer, while I stir the fire and make some hot chocolate?"

Solid plan, as usual.

There's a lamp on downstairs, but the rest of the house is in darkness. As I stand up, I'm wobbly on my feet, woozy with exhaustion.

Hugh instinctively grabs my legs and looks up at me from the step. "Sorry," he says, taking his hands off just as quickly, as if he's accidentally touched a flame. Is it because we work together, or—

I'd take it as a compliment except I'm too busy trying to work out how the heat from his fingers has lingered on my skin like a phantom touch. I've clearly been reading too much vintage Danielle Steel.

Upstairs, I sift through the bag of clothes I bought from the thrift shop and find a deliciously soft cream mohair jumper and a pair of black leggings, even though they trigger Mum's "leggings aren't pants" speech in my mind. I throw my hair, which is even more untamed than usual in the humidity, into a high bun the way I used to when I was a carefree teenager. Before *The Unraveling* . . .

That's how Grace and I always describe the period immediately following Cam's diagnosis. It's become one of our labels, and we apply it every time things go badly in either of our lives.

As I come back downstairs, I'm greeted by a scene that wouldn't be out of place in a Hallmark movie. Hugh stokes the fire as it roars to life. We could almost be stranded in a log cabin in the wilderness, holed up in the snow together for days. And if we follow the Hallmark formula . . .

"What are you thinking about?" he asks me.

"Reinvention," I say.

I don't know why that word pops into my head. Maybe it's the wholesome scene before me. Maybe it's the bad dreams and inter-rupted sleep. Maybe *The Reinvention* is an actual thing, the natural next step after *The Unraveling*. It never occurred to me that it could exist, and that one nice event could trigger an upward spiral of lovely and beautiful life changes leading toward a Happily Ever After, Mark II—whether or not a man is involved. But I'm getting ahead of myself, as usual.

"Kate?"

"Christmas movies," I admit.

"In August?"

"Well, it is winter. It's the log cabin," I explain. "The fire . . ."

You.

Hugh's kindness to me right from the start had been rolled into my all-encompassing nightmare. People were good to us, practi-cally everyone we came across, with just a few exceptions. It was an avalanche of support that snowballed out of the hospital and into our world, from the moment everything fell apart. But this was a long haul. It required the kind of persistent help that outlived most people's practical capacity.

Hugh's compassion, like Grace's, had stayed the distance. It's often colleagues who have the front-row seats when life flies off the rails. They can't avoid you.

"Did I ever properly thank you for all your support around the time Cam was diagnosed?" I ask him, out of nowhere.

He stops poking the fire, closes the glass door, and walks back to the kitchen. "You did. It wasn't anything over and above what any reasonable workplace would provide." He thinks I mean the way he rearranged my role to fit my circumstances and tweaked that as time went on.

"I don't mean the flexibility at work. I mean . . . *everything else.*" The lifts in his car. The unexpected cleaner he paid for. The way work obstacles evaporated, and still do. "The way you befriended Cam," I remind him, trying to keep my voice even.

"That wasn't a favor," he says. "Cam and I would have been friends even if you hadn't been in the picture. I still grieve for him, you know. Nothing like you do. But I loved him."

When Cam's health really declined, it became harder for me to take him places. Physically harder, lugging around the wheelchair and getting him in and out of the car. But he also became emotionally difficult, sometimes. Hugh carried on with him as if nothing was wrong, even after Cam became more confused about who Hugh was and what his role was in our lives.

"He thought you were his brother," I tell him. "Did I ever mention that?"

Hugh smiles. "I used to call him that. Brother."

I didn't know that. And I love it.

Of course he misses Cam, too. Genuinely so. I dearly want to raise that matter of their secret again, but he protects it like it's under lock and key in a safe, inside his head.

I remember something else Cam said, which had been shelved by me at the time. Hugh had dropped him off, and he'd been confused about all the interrelationships. We'd waved Hugh off and Cam had turned to me and he said, "He likes you, Red. If you weren't married to his brother, he'd want you himself."

I'd dismissed it at the time, assumed it was the dementia talking. Tried to explain I wasn't Hugh's sister-in-law but his colleague, and that he and Hugh were friends. It had been too hard and there was no point anyway, because by that stage he was permanently confused and would have forgotten all the details the next second. He was confused about everything. Who he was. Who I was. What he had to do in any given moment of the day. And I'd become one of those jaded carers unable to paint a rosy picture for newbies in the carers' forum.

"What are these?" he'd said one morning, about a year before he died. He was standing in front of a wall of books he'd previously conservatively estimated to number a thousand. Books he'd collected all his life, since he was a boy, all through school and university and through his academic career. Classics. Poetry. Shakespeare. History. Music. Biography.

"What do you mean, Cam? They're yours," I'd explained, standing beside him and trailing my fingers across the spines.

"What are they?" he'd asked again.

My eyes had filled with tears. "Cam! They're *books*!"

Books! His *life*.

"And here are the ones you wrote," I'd said, showing him a series of academic titles with his name on the spines, along with those of his various publishers, including the esteemed presses from Oxford and Cambridge Universities. I took out a copy of *Chaucer's Social Criticism*—originally his PhD thesis, later published as a book, flicked it open, showed him the pages. All those whip-smart words. I even showed him the black-and-white author photo on the dust jacket. *Nothing.*

I think that was my moment of acceptance. The man I knew was gone. He had been replaced by an increasingly unrecognizable ghost of a person, lost in his own body.

Hugh passes me a huge mug of steamy hot chocolate. Very much alive.

"You know, Cam remembered me at the very end," I tell him. "He'd been confused for months, but there was this one, final spark of lucidity and remembrance. Just as he was dying."

Hugh smiles warmly. "Of course he did. He adored you."

I've never shared that extraordinary moment of Cam's passing with anyone. "They usually forget everyone. Even their families. I'm afraid nobody will ever love me that much again, and that I won't have the capacity—or maybe the courage—to love anyone that much again either."

Hugh is in an armchair opposite, firelight playing across his face as he sips his hot chocolate. Invisible wall up, like always. Someone like him will never know what this is like. To let yourself go and fall so deeply into the life of another person that their loss almost breaks you. That it renders you simultaneously as terrified of loving again as you are of *not* loving again.

"You're like Patrick Dempsey in *Made of Honor*," I challenge him, which of course goes right over his head. "He never lets a woman stay over, because God forbid he becomes attached. Do you ever wonder what you might be missing out on with this chronic habit of pushing women away all the time?"

"Yes," he says unexpectedly. Nothing else. Just "yes." This is the problem with Hugh. You inch a tiny bit closer to him and he clams up. Grace and I had spent way too much time trying to determine why it never worked out between the two of them, despite their being perfectly each other's type in theory. She said they just didn't have the chemistry. But I think he's scared of love. Being around me so much when I lost Cam would have driven home the risk. It's too dangerous. *You might break into a million pieces, like Kate did, and never fully reemerge. . . .*

"Why didn't it ever work out with Grace?" I ask. I want his perspective now that I have hers. I'm not picking for a midnight fight. It was all just so awkward, my having introduced them in the first place. Her being my best friend. Him being my boss.

"Just didn't work out," he says. "She's a lovely person." Exactly how she'd described him.

"Yes, and she's all the things you want. She's funny, she's unpretentious, what you see is what you get. . . ."

"She's all those things, yes. I don't know what you want me to say."

"Do you know how maddening it is that you're such a closed book?"

He sighs. He's staring at me like he's trying to figure out whether to proceed. "It wasn't Grace," he says reluctantly.

"That's obvious."

"There was someone else."

WHAT?

"You just sort of threw us together, Kate. I wanted to be polite, and she really is great. I wish it could have worked out."

Hugh was very definitely single when I introduced them. At least, I thought he was. "Who else was there? Ruby?"

He looks suddenly disconcerted. "Kate—" he says firmly.

"I was convinced you were single when you met Grace!"

"I was."

"Then *who*, Hugh?"

The one who broke him?

Ah. It dawns on me now. He couldn't be with Grace because, as lovely as she is, he was still in love with Mystery Heartbreaker. Still *is* in love with her, by the agonized look on his face. Wow. She must have been something else to have led him to swear so definitely off everyone else, forevermore.

"I'm going to bed," he announces, draining his cup and getting out of the chair. "You should too. Writers' festival tomorrow. I'm meeting my uni mate in Byron late morning for brunch. Want to join us before I drop you off?"

I stand up too and take his empty mug. "I'm sorry for prying," I say. "It's none of my business."

He smiles ruefully. "It sort of is."

29

He means because it's my best friend who he dumped. Surely.

I can't afford another fitful night, trying to unlock the Hugh Code. If he wasn't ready for a relationship, he shouldn't have done what I instructed him to do and dated Grace. He is emotionally unavailable. Hung up on someone he can't have. Always will be.

Just like I'll always be hung up on Cam.

I manage to get a few hours' sleep until the crash of waves on the beach wakes me before dawn. Semiconscious, I wonder if Cam is there, waiting for me on the sand. It makes no rational sense, I know, but I crave the fleeting whisper of his soul. Those passing moments of strong awareness that he is with me, the way I'd once feel his presence when he was out of sight across a crowded room.

I creep to the bathroom, then scoop up a crocheted blanket from the foot of the bed and tiptoe onto the balcony and down the steps outside. The sandy path through the garden is cool underfoot, and I should have worn shoes, but I don't care enough to go back.

It's just me on the beach. I can see the far-off flicker of the light-house, shrouded in sea mist, and from here it feels like I'll be the first in the country to see the sun. My footsteps carve a path in the sand as I walk a little way along and choose a spot. If I was the type to meditate, that's what I'd do, but it always makes me anxious when I try. So many thoughts. So much noise in my head. So many traps. It's like a game of Chutes and Ladders.

There's one spot on the horizon slightly lighter than the rest, where the sun will appear. I've seen more sunrises since Cam died than I'd seen in my life up until then. They're a promise; no matter how bad everything is, the world keeps turning. What was Rachel Lynde's advice to Anne of Green Gables? "The sun will go on rising and setting whether you fail in geometry or not."

That used to bring me comfort during math-inspired freak-outs in high school. My current self shakes her head at the naïveté of my Teen Self. Life was going to get so much bigger and more anxiety-inducing than how badly you do in algebra, girl. . . .

"Couldn't sleep either?" Hugh says a few minutes later, giving me a fright as he arrives on the beach beside me. With the roar of the waves, I hadn't heard him approach.

"This is the free sunrise, right?" I reply, wanting to clear the tension of last night. "I'm not going to be slapped with hidden extras?"

He smiles. "There's no catch, don't worry."

We sit in silence for a long time as the tide washes in and waves crash on the sand in front of us. So much power. Unstoppable. The longer our silence goes on, the less inclined either of us seems to be to break its spell. I wanted to find Cam here, but I'm surprised to learn it's different, but just as nice, to sit here with Hugh. The thought confronts me, the way thoughts like this always do. I feel uneasy about any development that seems to push me further away from where I was when I last saw Cam, and I wrap the blanket more tightly around me—a barrier to change.

Hugh has made himself at home, leaning back in the sand on his elbows beside me, long legs stretched out and crossed lazily at the ankles. I glance at the lines of his calves, covered in a smattering of dark hair. Then I shiver and look back at the horizon.

"Cold?" he says.

"No, it's more that I'm . . ." I don't really know what I am.

"Happy?" he suggests.

It's like he's a chapter ahead all the time. I'd never in a million years have categorized myself as "happy" yet, but when I think about it, that's exactly how this feels. Being here, mesmerized by the ocean, anticipating the sunrise, I do feel . . . *something*. And for so long, I've been so flat. This is like a hopeful blip on the heart monitor after a long period of flatlining. A sign of life.

"Hugh, how do you always know—"

"Psychometric testing when you were recruited, Whittaker," he says. "It's my job to know how you tick."

I tap him on the arm. "Seriously, though. Are you psychic?"

"Just watch the sunrise," he says, nodding in the direction of the horizon, just as the first light breaks over his face. "I'm trying to have an experience with you here."

I stare at his face, attempting to decode what he just said. He refuses to meet my gaze, but the corners of his mouth twitch and it's gorgeous. *Bloody hell.*

"Concentrate, Kate. The sun is over there. Next you'll be asking for a refund."

"You said it was free. You'd better not be swindling me here, Lancaster."

He drags his eyes away from the spectacular horizon and looks at me like I'm a major pest. Which I am. But then his expression softens, and even though I've had insufficient sleep for five years and my face is smeared with the remains of yesterday's makeup, and I'm wrapped in what I now realize is a pink crochet blanket, fighting against my auburn hair, in orange half-light, I feel kind of—well, beautiful, to be honest. . . .

"I'm not swindling you," he assures me.

And, in that moment, right there, I feel myself put literally all my trust into one basket and hand it over to him, tentatively, absolutely terrified he'll drop it. I wonder if he knows how enormous this is for me. How frightening. Is he even aware that this moment is passing between us? *Is it* passing between us? Maybe it's some romance-starved figment of my bruised imagination. It wouldn't take much for me to invent a scenario here and run with it.

"What are you thinking now?" he asks.

"Psychometric testing let you down?"

He smiles.

I'm thinking I want to kiss you.

And I'm waiting for Cam to appear and interrupt me.

Or give me his blessing.

Or announce it was all a terrible mistake and he's sorry for his absence, but he's back now, so there's really no need for me to sit here on the beach at sunrise, wondering if it would be emotionally reasonable for a grief-stricken forty-year-old widow to start to fall for someone else.

"*God,*" I say aloud, as I'm hit with the naked truth.

"Thought so," he replies.

30

The sun seems to be taking an inordinately long time to rise over the ocean, but I'm not one of those people who gets up and leaves halfway through a performance. Hugh and I are watching it together, in silence. Glued to it. We're concentrating so hard, and so silently after our little exchange just then, we'll be fully qualified astrophysicists by the end of this. Anything to avoid looking at each other. I'm dreading the moment when the sun breaks free of the horizon itself, and one of us has to make the first move. Off the beach, I mean. *Get it together, Kate.*

I'm trying to think of a conceivable version of events where Hugh didn't read my mind just then, and where my mind didn't think what it thought. I need a sanitized, safe version of reality in which the impossible isn't threatening to unfold, right in front of my eyes.

Falling for someone else? *I can't.* Falling for *Hugh*? No words. None.

Although, having said that, I do seem to have words about it. Many, many words. They're all tumbling in and piling on top of one another in my astonished head as it overthinks this situation, as if it's an Olympic event. No schoolgirl with her first real crush could hold a candle to my current level of giddiness. Because no schoolgirl with her first crush could understand what this possibility feels like after the depths of hell that I've been dragged through. I've been to the place where love isn't gifted upon you gently but torn from you. Torn from each individual cell in your body in turn, one agonizing extraction at a time—torture far beyond what any human can reasonably be expected to endure. Why would I willingly place myself into a reckless position where I risk that happening again?

The sun has lifted off the horizon now. The waves are encroaching too, with the tide. The ocean is coming for us, threatening to break our stalemate. Someone needs to say something. I hope it's him. I know if it's me, I'll say something inane. Particularly as I'm now envisioning those steamy scenes in 1950s movies where the couple rolls around on the shoreline in their clothes, kissing . . .

I psych myself up to look at him. Surely it's safe? I'm not about to tear his clothes off right here like some sort of sex-starved sea monster, am I? *Am I?* It's been—

His phone starts blaring with an incoming call. Who on earth would be calling Hugh at *dawn?*

He looks at the screen and hands it over. "It's your mother."

He can't be serious. It's like the time she barged into my teenage bedroom, unannounced, the first time I kissed a boy. I have to admit this is impressive, even for her. My brain has barely dared to even *imagine* leading me into the romantic fray here with Hugh. A man who hasn't confirmed or denied his interest, now that I think about it—and Mum is already sticking her nose in, from hundreds of miles away.

"Mum?" I start tentatively, as if ducking from a moral lecture.

"Mummy!" Charlie says animatedly. "My tooth is wobbly!"

Wobbly? Is that normal at five? I can't remember when I lost my first tooth. What if it's decay? Have I let his dental hygiene lapse in my grief-clouded haze?

I scramble inelegantly to my feet in the sand and, while trying to brush the sand off myself and the blanket, I drop Hugh's phone, then pick it up and have to brush the sand off it, too, and then start pacing backward and forward in front of him, asking surreptitious questions about what Nanna thought when Charlie told her his tooth was wobbly, in an attempt to gauge whether she was startled and phoning the emergency dentist or unfazed.

"Yes, of course the tooth fairy will come!" I promise, making a mental note to research current exchange rates for teeth while also researching childhood dental development. "How exciting!"

Hugh is sitting now, trouser cuffs rolled up over his cyclist's calves, elbows resting casually on bent knees, hands interlinked like he's fully relaxed, just watching me. It is *extraordinarily attractive*, and I lose all of my bearings for a second, staggering backward a little to put some distance between us in case I'm overcome by an urge to throw his phone, and by extension my own son, into the depths of the ocean while I tackle him. In a romantic way, of course. If I could possibly manage something approximating that.

In backing off, though, I step into the water, unexpectedly, and it is *freezing*. I jump out of it and squeal in a way I haven't squealed since I was nine. I drop the phone again in the kerfuffle, but this time I catch it before it hits the water, like a fast-reflexed sporting genius. And that's when Hugh gets to his feet, walks over to me, and holds out his hand like he's about to confiscate his phone from me, but instead he confiscates me, from the ocean. He picks me up, crochet blanket and all, and carries me about thirty feet up the beach and puts me down on the sand. In the naughty corner.

"I want to tell Uncle Hugh!" Charlie announces in my ear, and I reel in horror. In the temporary departure I've had from reality, caused by the bombshell reveal that I apparently have a thing for the man, I totally forgot that Charlie thinks of him as his uncle. Because that's what Daddy called him, when Daddy was confused and thought Hugh was his brother, and not my potential future leading man in more ways than one, or Charlie's potential stepdad. I can't even begin to think how the inevitable future psychologist will start to unpack these tangled circumstances for Charlie, or indeed the fact that I've cast Hugh as stepfather of my child *already*.

Thankfully Mum gets on and asks why I'm not answering my own phone. "I tried you five times!" she tells me. "And gave up and called Hugh and how *fortunate* that you appear to be *right* next to him. At *six* o'clock in the morning, Katherine."

"Mum! We're on the beach, watching the sunrise. For fu— *goodness'* sake!"

Hugh's still standing in front of me in the sand. Watching me squirm through this phone call. Trying not to smile.

"Is it normal for a five-year-old to lose a tooth?" I ask her nervously.

"Perfectly normal, Katherine. You were precocious as a child. Lost your first teeth at fifty-eight months."

Fifty-eight months? Why can't she speak like a normal person?

"Anyway, Charlie's run off now. I don't want to interrupt your *sunrise*. I'll call you later. Love to Hugh! Bye!"

She ends the call and I hand his phone back, exhausted and nervous. It's just the two of us on the beach now, and the giant admission I carelessly implied, which I'm wondering if I can somehow retract. I'm not remotely confident, now that I replay it in my mind for the eight-hundredth time, that it wasn't all one-sided. . . .

"*God*," I had said.

"Thought so," he had replied.

Not "I hear you." Not "Ditto." Not "Me too, Kate, for the longest time. . . ."

Just "Thought so," which I'm now translating to mean "Your unfortunate and inappropriate infatuation couldn't be more obvious or unrequited."

I hope he realizes what he's dealing with here: a widow's heart. It's just like a normal heart, but it's made of a million shattered fragments, patched together in a mosaic. Reclaimed glass. Transparent. Easily broken.

In fact, just looking at his face and listening to the silence, where some sort of declaration should be, I'm worried that process is already in progress. A quick mental inventory reveals that I am unable to take on any new heartbreak at the moment. Whatever this is needs to be nipped in the bud. Stat. Cam had warned me this moment might come. He predicted I'd want to run from it, that it would fill me with guilt. And he was right. In fact, that's exactly what I'm going to do. Run.

I start limbering up in front of Hugh, forgetting I fled down onto the beach straight from bed and am in my pajamas still. And bare feet. No sports bra. No bra at all, for that matter, and this is ill-advised for exercise post-breastfeeding. I guess on the upside, nothing is leaking this time. . . .

His eyes remain resolutely focused on my face, anyhow. Eyebrows raised. "Exactly what are you doing?"

It's an excellent question, for sure.

"I want to run."

"In your pajamas?"

"Is it so hard to believe that I might want to run on the beach?"

He's trying hard not to smile. "Yes."

I hate running. Hate it hard. He knows that. I extend my pre-exercise repertoire to include dynamic stretches I've previously encountered only on Instagram reels, scrolling in bed. He frowns.

And then it happens. I can almost hear the words tumbling out of my mouth before my brain has thought them up and run a sanity check. "Mum seems to think there's something going on between us." I serve this revelation with a side of nervous laughter and something approximating a lunge. "Have you said something to give her that idea?"

He laughs at the mere suggestion. "Did you learn this particular aerobics technique when you were abducted by aliens, Kate?"

I glare at him.

"Is it an obscure mating call?"

"Hardly!"

"Because I've got to tell you, it's low-key beguiling."

I hit his arm playfully. "Will you shut up, Hugh? You're making me nervous."

"Payback," he says under his breath.

"What did you say?" I ask, just to check.

"I'm going for a shower. Then coffee. Then we've got brunch with my mate Jonesy from uni and then you've got the writers' thing." He looks me up and down critically. "Don't try your weird dancing there. It's not that kind of festival."

I make him nervous?

"And when you're talking to people, don't shrink. I've read some of your stuff."

"None of my stuff has ever been published." I hope I never left my manuscript open on the work computer.

He's backing away from me toward the house. "Relax! I've read everything you've written at work," he calls. "You can string a sentence together, Kate, and your talent is wasted on our annual report."

I make Hugh Lancaster nervous. How have I never noticed that before?

I won't shrink at the festival. Why would he say that? Do I do that? Maybe I've been so preoccupied with surviving, and bringing Charlie through his dad's death, I've forgotten about my own abilities. I feel like I've spent the last four years on the back foot, constantly in response mode, never ahead of the game.

I don't want to do this anymore. How long is it reasonable to drag out your recovery from grief until you're expected to get your act together again?

Or maybe that's where I'm going wrong. You don't recover from it. There is no "healed" moment. You just absorb it into your new life, somehow, and go from there.

31

The drive into Byron from New Brighton feels too quiet. I tell Hugh he can choose the music this time, but he says he doesn't mind what we listen to, so I play the soundtrack to the *Mamma Mia!* sequel, with the windows down, and belt along to it.

So much green in this Irish-looking hinterland. Was that conversation about Ireland only *yesterday*? I feel like I finally had my volcanic moment, in the shower. Something has definitely shifted since that eruption.

Driving into the beach town itself, the traffic slows to a crawl past boutiques and cafés, antiques stores, and eclectic gift shops brimming with wind chimes and rainbow dream catchers. It's a kaleidoscope of color and style that seems to beat to the rhythm of the drumming circles at its hippie heart.

"Did you enjoy that car karaoke?" I ask Hugh as he pulls into a parking lot near the beach.

"It was right up there with the exercise display this morning," he replies.

"Thanks!" I fish in my bag for my purse to pay the parking fee. There's so much stuff in there, I can never find anything quickly. In any case, he's got his phone out and is paying via the app, without any fuss as usual. We start walking toward the café for brunch with his friend. "So, this 'Jonesy' we're meeting. Anything I need to know?"

We wait to cross a road.

"Uni mate. Writer, actually. Used to be a print journalist in Sydney. Quit the rat race and moved here to give screenwriting a go. I think his first screenplay has just been optioned. . . . Let's go!"

We take advantage of a small break in traffic and rush across an intersection, landing straight in front of a bookshop. Fortuitous! We're a few minutes early for brunch, and I have a personal rule never to walk past an open bookshop, so I linger. Hugh looks back and sighs.

"Five minutes?" I ask him. "Come on, we've got time."

I know he loves books. But he also loves to be early. We wander along the new-fiction section, and I pick up the first two titles that jump out at me—a "perfect beach read" and "book club favorite," according to shiny stickers on the covers.

"I will buy you brunch," I offer, "if both these titles aren't about an exhausted, late-thirties woman with kids, who feels like the spark has left her marriage and longs for something more, but she can't quite decide what."

He takes the books from me, flips them over, and reads aloud.

"Felicity Page has spent the last twenty years as CEO of the well-oiled machine that is the Page-McCaffrey family of Balmain East. Married to Jock, high-flying banker and husband who's barely home, and grappling with two moody teenagers and a French Provincial homewares boutique, Felicity spends her days dreaming of the gap year she never had. When an unexpected opportunity arises to 'swap boutiques'—and families—with a woman in a picturesque French village, Felicity can't stop wondering, 'What if . . .'

Can you drop everything and travel the world on your own at forty? What if you never come back?"

"See?" I say. "And the other?"

"Vanessa O'Shea would give anything to be eighteen again," Hugh reads. "Weighed down by endless deadlines at work and swamped by a crumbling house that's less 'flip' and more 'flop,' she discovers her teenage diary and realizes she's achieved all her dreams. She has the man, the family, the career, and even the white picket fence, so why isn't she happy, the way her teenage self predicted? When an accident in the renovation leaves her with a dose of temporary amnesia, Vanessa thinks she's eighteen again. Will adulthood play out differently the second time around?"

Hugh puts the books back on the shelf. "Okay, I owe you brunch."

"I love these books, but why are they always about unhappy marriages?" I ask. "Where are all the books about happy marriages that end prematurely, leaving the protagonist desperately sad and floundering helplessly with the freedom all these other heroines dream about, until she digs herself out of the dark and creates a new path with her Chapter Two life?"

He looks at me like I fell out of the sky. "Isn't it obvious where that book is, Kate?"

No.

"Write what you know. Isn't that what they say?"

They do say that, but I'm not doing it. "I don't write commercial fiction," I explain. "I'm trying to write a literary novel. Even if I have to fight for every word. Cam told me he didn't think I'd found my place as a writer. . . ."

Hugh watches me, as if he's waiting for the penny to drop. "What would Cam have known?" he says. "He was just a professor of literature."

Fair point.

"Kate, you've got something important to say about how it's not all it's cracked up to be—this unexpected-fresh-start, parallel-universe life you're living."

"Nobody wants to read about a fortysomething widow, Hugh. Look at the shelves."

"I'd read it," he says. "Even if I'm not the target audience. Who knows? Her Chapter Two life might not be all bad in the end."

I catch his eyes for just a second, then look at the shelves. There's a gap. Definitely. I imagine it being filled with *Careful What You Wish For* by Kate Whittaker.

"People want to know you can survive the unimaginable and pull yourself onto a new path, against the odds," Hugh suggests.

I kind of like where he's going with this, but it's scary as hell to even consider it. "I'm hardly a poster girl for plan B," I argue. "In the last thirty-six hours alone I've had a domestic bomb threat, nearly missed a flight, been hysterical on a plane, and . . ." Flashbacks to my romantic admission on the beach give me palpitations. "Random calamitous ocean-side announcements," I add.

Smile lines crease at his eyes.

"What could you possibly be smiling at?"

"Just your language, Kate. I love the way you put things."

I flush with pride. Stupidly.

"And all that stuff happens to you because you're all in."

All in? Haven't I heard him say that before?

"Write the book," he rushes on. "Give Felicity and Vanessa a run for their money."

He isn't just playing here. He seems to have actual confidence that I can do it. I look again at the shelf beside us and imagine my name on the cover of a book. For the first time in years, I have to admit I feel excited about the idea of following one of Hugh Lancaster's professional instructions.

Actually, it's bigger than that. And more important. For the first time in four years, I feel excited. Full stop.

We weave our way through the outdoor tables at the café Hugh's mate has chosen. It's beachy and bohemian, with sun gods on the walls and rainbow flags depicting astrology symbols draped across the bar. Exactly the type of place Hugh would never pick, but which my inner hippie loves. I'm wearing my vintage finds—flowing skirt covered in mandalas, a white cami top, and a denim jacket, even though it's already steamy ahead of another forecast storm.

Jonesy isn't here yet, but we find a table in the shade and pour glasses of water. I close my eyes and take a slow breath, drinking in the warmth of the morning. The place smells like coconut and sunscreen and coffee and holidays, and I'm so glad we were forced to spend the weekend here. It reminds me there's a whole life outside my everyday reality.

When I open my eyes, Hugh is observing me over the menu.

"Byron Bay suits you," he says. That's all. He returns to the menu, and I feel about a foot taller.

"Every time I'm near the beach, I wonder why I don't just pack up, sell the house and all our stuff, and move somewhere new with Charlie," I confide.

He looks surprised. "Like the women in those novels?"

"Sort of. A fresh start, you know. Somewhere warmer, without any memories. Somewhere I could write."

He considers this for a second. "You serious about this?"

I think I am. Maybe. Even if the logistics of moving away from Grace and Mum break my heart. "Why, Hugh, would you miss me?"

I am a walking example of what happens when you marry your childhood sweetheart and never learn how to flirt properly as an adult. The words are out of my mouth before I can shut it, and Hugh looks taken aback. Of course he does. Inside my head lives a lawless train of thought that charges right out of my mouth.

He's about to answer me when he sees his friend across the café, coming toward us, saving us from ourselves. Jonesy hasn't even reached our table before he makes me smile. He's taken the relaxed spirit of this town and made himself the epitome of it. Surf shorts, faded neon T-shirt, flip-flops, shaggy brown hair, creases around his eyes. He and Hugh, who is always immaculately dressed, look so different that I struggle to imagine them as friends.

"Mate!" he says, hugging Hugh and pounding him on the back. "Good to see you!"

They turn to me.

"This is Kate," Hugh says. "My colleague and friend—"

Just in case I wasn't clear on the labels.

"Kate!" Jonesy says, warmly. "It's so good to meet you at last!"

At last?

He pulls me into an enormous, enveloping hug that lifts me off the floor. When I surface from it, slightly breathless, Hugh is giving him an incredulous stare.

We sit down, Hugh opposite me in his white open-necked shirt and jeans, looking a little bit spectacular, and more nervous than I've ever seen him. Jonesy sits to my left and I feel like I've known him for years. He's infectious.

"Well, this is nice," Jonesy says, winking at Hugh, who shifts uncomfortably in his seat, looking like he's rethinking this entire social event.

"Hugh tells me you're a screenwriter," I say politely. Writing. Safe, common ground.

"He tells me you're a writer, too."

He does? "He exaggerates. I do love writing though. Nothing published."

"Nothing yet," Jonesy answers, and I like him even more.

"Do you go by a name other than Jonesy?"

"It's Andrew."

"And you two met at uni?"

"First year," Andrew confirms. "We were eighteen-year-olds, living on campus."

"But not doing the same course, presumably?" Hugh did economics as an undergrad. Explains all the spreadsheets.

They look at each other like they're about to run a prepared script.

"We met through a mutual friend," Hugh explains. "Shall we order coffees?"

Interesting.

"Are you writing at the moment, Kate?" Andrew asks.

I feel exposed. "Actually, Hugh is trying to convince me to write something based on my . . . recent personal experiences. I don't know how much he's told you. . . ."

It's awkward, every single time. I don't want to make everything about the fact that I lost my husband, but if I don't mention it early in a conversation, people invariably ask me some question that lands us all in excruciating discomfort, with me breaking the news as gently as possible while they feel horrendous about having put their foot in it and I'm forced to comfort them over my loss.

"I told him about Cam," Hugh says.

"I was sorry to hear it, Kate. Writing about it could be a good idea. Some people sit on their grief for decades. They let it close in their lives completely."

I nod. Hugh turns a page in the menu sharply.

"Sometimes they become shackled to their grief," Andrew continues. "They won't take risks. They pass up opportunities that are right in front of them."

"The eggs Benedict looks good," Hugh observes, conveying this fact to Andrew in particular, as if it's imbued with a secret code. "What are you having, Kate? Smashed avo?"

"Am I that predictable?"

He shakes his head. "Only where avocado is concerned."

"I'll have the granola," I say.

"To prove me wrong?"

Andrew sits back and watches us as if he's taking mental notes for his screenplay.

"Are you going to the festival?" I ask him.

"Yeah. You?"

"Definitely. Can't *wait*. I've never been. I'm so excited!" I sound like a thirteen-year-old rambling about seeing her favorite pop star, but I don't care.

They're both smiling at me.

"What can I get for you?" a waiter asks us, looking at me first.

"I'll have a latte, thanks, and, hmm. Actually, I think I'll have the—"

"Smashed avo," Hugh says under his breath, while I say it aloud. I ignore him. "He'll have a double-shot long black, no sugar, and eggs Benedict with a side of field mushrooms. Andrew?"

"Short black and the granola, thanks," Andrew says, and the

waiter walks away to organize our cutlery. "You two have breakfast out a lot at work, do you?"

We look at each other. Not really?

"I supervise the young graduate who processes all of his business expenses," I explain.

"And you forensically analyze them and commit Hugh's breakfast preferences to memory?"

No. Actually, I can't explain how I know this. I just know it. "This mutual friend," I say, diverting the conversation. "The one you met through at uni. Who was it?"

They both sit up straighter in their seats.

"She wasn't so much a mutual friend as a girl we were both interested in when we met," Andrew says.

"Jonesy." Hugh's warning is low but clear.

I lean forward in my chair and smile encouragingly at Andrew.

"It was years later when we met her again, volunteering for an NGO in East Timor. Well, she and Hugh were volunteering. I flew in to do a photo essay," he explains.

"And?" I press.

"And . . . there's not much to say. Hugh won."

I glance at Hugh, who stares at the salt and pepper shakers like they're the most fascinating objects in the world and plays with a long packet of sugar, evening up its contents like he often does out of nervous habit. I didn't know he volunteered in East Timor. For starters.

Then Andrew delivers an innocent question that seems to hit me with the full force of a sniper's bull's-eye.

"Hugh's told you about Genevieve, surely?"

32

He has not. This is *her*. The one who broke his heart. It's written all over his face. And I'm wondering where she is now, and if she's married and has kids, and whether they keep in touch, and why I'm hot and prickly just thinking about her. Am I *jealous*? Of the girl Hugh fell for two decades ago, when he was technically a *teenager*?

He looks straight at me, willing me to change the subject, and something in his expression makes me want to rescue him. I think it's the way he's chosen me, here. He and I are the team, not he and his friend of many years.

"I met Cam at uni too," I tell Andrew. "What about you? Have you ever married?"

He laughs. "Twice. Both disasters."

I smile and touch his arm comfortingly. "They say third time's the charm, don't they?"

Hugh gives me a grateful smile across the table, and all I can think is, *Who the fuck is Genevieve?* The woman has him utterly flustered. She's got *me* utterly flustered. I start fanning myself with the napkin and it does precisely nothing. It's just pushing the humid air around. I'm actually starting to feel a bit faint. Is this the perimeno-pause? I almost hope so, because getting this hot and bothered about your boss's first love is plain pathetic. I pour a big glass of water, ensuring several blocks of ice tumble into the glass too, then I fish one out and hold it to my face.

I know. Terrible manners. It's just so cool on my cheeks, and I run it over the back of my neck and round the front and drops of icy water run down my chest and it's truly divine, particularly when there's just a hint of a breeze, enough to give me goose bumps. . . .

It's not until their conversation pauses, mid-sentence, that I real-ize Andrew and Hugh are both watching this performance. I come to my senses. Drop what's left of the ice cube into a plant to my right and dab my skin dry with the napkin.

"I thought women only did that in eighties soft drink commer-cials," Andrew observes.

Is it my imagination or does Hugh kick him under the table?

"I'm just hot," I explain, but I don't mean it the way it comes out. "Physically, I mean. *Wait!*"

I look at Andrew and shake my head, then at Hugh. "Sorry! I don't mean this the way it sounds. I'm just—"

"Hot," Hugh confirms. "We know."

He catches the attention of the waiter. "Can we have another jug of water, please? Extra ice. She's hot."

I know he's only stirring, but hearing this observation from the horse's mouth, even as a joke, is exhilarating.

"Andrew. Tell us about your new screenplay," Hugh orders, and Andrew takes the bait, because he's a writer and this is a chance to workshop his plot.

Whatever he says next, though, is a blur. I stare at Hugh and he stares at me, and I begin to think there's not enough ice in the second jug for a job of this magnitude.

The waiter brings my smashed avocado and Hugh's eggs Benedict and he scrapes half the mushrooms onto my plate without asking if I want them, which of course I do. And while Andrew provides some never-ending background noise, revealing the entire three acts of his screenplay, it occurs to me that Hugh and I, perhaps for the longest time, have been involved in a dance, choreographed by my grief. It's been me leading it, every step of the way. Always choosing the music. Always picking the pace. He's followed so closely that there have been times when it's felt like he was the one leading. The day I lost the baby. My first day back at work after Cam's funeral. First year back, probably. Each time I lost my way, everything kept turning, like magic.

And now he's sitting across from me, looking at me in a way that he never has before—not once in four years, until the airport yesterday morning. But the familiar music has stopped. The dance has faltered. And neither of us knows the new steps.

We pay the bill at the café and I excuse myself to use the bathroom while Hugh and Andrew wait outside. I'm really only in here for a break from Hugh. The man is doing things to me that I didn't think could still be done. It feels unstable and dangerous—one wrong move and we'll fall off this cliff. So many unanswered questions, some going a long way back. Way before we met, in fact.

Checking myself in the mirror, I imagine Genevieve. In my head she's impossibly beautiful. Long, luscious, perfectly straight and therefore perfectly manageable hair. Eyes so dark and deep, young

Hugh couldn't stop himself from falling right into them, never to fully clamber out.

Now he's coming up for air. Encountering me. A woman who is hot in the wrong way, and off to a writers' festival, feeling like a fraud beside the *real* writers.

As I come out of the bathroom, I can see Andrew and Hugh on the street. They're deep in conversation. That is, Hugh is deeply conversing while Andrew listens intently. He has to. Hugh's drumming something home passionately and I have a fair idea what it's about. Or whom. Their mutual crush turned Hugh's first love. The one you never get over. And the one he's no doubt imploring Andrew not to tell me more about this afternoon. *But why?*

I pause in the doorway. Seeing them like that gives me a horrible flashback to that moment in our living room with Cam and Hugh about three years ago, after Hugh had been AWOL from work for days, *thinking*. The moment was so fleeting, I almost missed it. All I know is Cam had hope in his eyes when Hugh walked in, and Hugh extinguished it. When we went to bed that night, I asked Cam to tell me what it was about, and he said he couldn't remember. It's the only time in the two years after his diagnosis that I'm sure he was lying about his memory.

Sure enough, when I appear at the door of the café, the conversation stops dead. "Talking about me, Hugh?"

He laughs. "Kate Whittaker: hottest topic in Byron Bay. Says so herself."

It's like we've met up at the school gate in Year Ten. I thump him on the arm.

"Whoa, this takes me back," Andrew says.

"To when, exactly?" I ask, guessing he's had "third wheel" experience with Hugh before.

Hugh realizes I'm taking no prisoners. He asks Andrew to excuse us for a second while we have a brief word and pulls me aside. Andrew says he'll go get the car. I sort of want him to stay. Safety in numbers.

"Kate. I know I've been secretive about Genevieve. It's not for the reason you think."

"You don't know what reason I'm thinking."

"I can guess."

"It's none of my business who you loved in your past. Or your present," I add, even though it twists my insides to voice the possibility.

"Not in the way you imagine," he says.

So he does still love her. Perfect.

"I feel like you're always keeping secrets from me," I admit.

"What secrets? I haven't told you about Genevieve, but there's a reason for that. It's too complicated to explain now."

The bottom drops out of my world. I imagine he has Genevieve and some secret family stashed somewhere. Maybe that's where he disappeared to that time when he fell off the face of the earth for a few weeks and came back looking traumatized.

"I know that look," he says. "Whatever idea you've taken and you're running with, just stop it. Wait for me to explain. Please."

"I don't understand how this is anything to do with me, Hugh." It's none of my business if he has a family of six and a minivan. He could have hordes of children for all I know. All those one-night stands. The mind boggles.

"Just please don't ask Andrew about it. He'll butcher the story."

"So you admit there *is* a story," I say. I'll whip out a notepad and pen next.

He sighs in frustration, looks to the heavens, then back at me, resigned. "Of course there's a story, Kate. I've wanted to tell you so many times over the last four years, but whenever I tried, I lost my nerve."

Well.

I never.

A car draws up beside us, and Andrew winds the window down. "C'mon, Kate. Festival time!"

There's a festival going on right here on the pavement. I am 90 percent enthralled by the trailer Hugh is playing for this epic tale, and 10 percent have my hands over my ears, too scared to hear it.

"Please," he says again, placing his hand on my arm. He's imploring me to wait for later.

"Kate, come on. Get in!"

I nod at Hugh. He always does this. Always convinces me. He's the most commanding, persuasive—

"Have a really great time," he says. He means that too. Then he opens the car door and I get in and watch him out the window as we drive off, and then again in the side mirror, because I am what, exactly? Obsessed?

Standing on the road watching us go, he looks lost. He's hoping he can trust us not to mess this thing up. The problem is he knows who he's dealing with.

33

Despite this Genevieve business, I spend the first two sessions at the festival deeply, deeply engrossed. If I've been searching for my happy place my whole life, I think I've found it. To be surrounded by people who *get* it. Storytelling. It's enchanting. Even better, I'm meeting ordinary people from vastly different walks of life, at various stages of success, from just starting out to having several books on the shelves, and they're all just willing one another on.

I attend a session called "Almost Fiction" about how to take your own experiences and pack them into a story that isn't exactly yours. It's "writing what you know" without selling your own soul. Cam died from Alzheimer's disease, but if that's too hard for me to write about, my protagonist's husband could die from a heart attack instead. Same emotional punch but not my exact life.

"Fill your book with details and anecdotes so personal and real your friends will question whether the entire thing is true," the presenter advises. "If they're not doing that from the very first chapter, you're not infusing your fictional story with enough convincing fact."

Afterward, I find myself in conversation with an editor from a boutique publishing house in Victoria. I forget I'm writing a book and fall into a chat that involves giving her the executive summary of my last four years.

"We need the voices of women in their forties," she reassures me as she passes me her card. It's not a publishing deal, obviously, but it's not a "no one wants to read that stuff" either. Maybe Cam and Hugh were pushing me in the right direction after all.

"I'm not shrinking," I type in a text to Hugh. Andrew's off at a screenwriting session and we're meeting at the bar in a few minutes. Hugh's leaving the house now to pick me up.

I see the dots on the screen, and my heart does this crazy little flip. Then I scroll back up, through literally hundreds of texts over the last four years. Not one of them had this effect on me.

Mind you, they're all about work, or my personal logistics. Me saying I'll be late in, or not coming to work at all. Him assuring me it's fine. Again. Asking if I need anything dropped off when Charlie's down with a twenty-four-hour virus, or when I am. Further back, before Cam died, they're reminding me that things will be okay. Reminding me that I will be.

Maybe I should write a book on *this*. The way we have built this—whatever this is—without a picture of the end result on the front of the box for reference. The fact that I'm even here, waiting for words to appear on a screen, speaks volumes about the state of play. This is my dream, this festival. But I'm just as excited about the idea of Hugh's incoming messages dangling on my phone. If you can't lose your head a little after you've been dragged through hell, when can you?

Andrew appears across the bar and comes toward me. "Hey, what can I get you, Kate? Champagne? Wine? G and T? Cocktail?"

I feel like celebrating the fact that we are here. "Champagne, thanks."

Hugh has stopped typing now. Obviously rethinking it. I'm fifteen again and bursting with nervous energy waiting for a boy to pass a note to me in class. It's alarming how fast you can slip into this mindset once you open the door to it.

"Here you are," Andrew says, a minute or two later, passing me a glass as I slip my phone into my bag.

"What are we toasting?" I ask.

"To Cam?" he says cautiously. "And . . . to Genevieve?"

I hover the glass near my lips. Those two hardly belong together in a toast. I can't bring myself to utter the words, so I skip that bit and gulp down half the champagne. It's barely touched my esophagus before the warmth begins to diffuse the chatter in my brain. Even then, half a glass of champagne isn't up to a predicament as steep as my own. Cam. Hugh. Genevieve. Career crisis. Thinking of selling the house, uprooting Charlie from his entire world . . .

"You know, she's no threat to you," Andrew says, and I wonder for a second if we're talking about the young woman who just walked past us and clearly caught his eye. But of course we're not. It's bloody Genevieve. Again. A woman with the power to hold two men in her thrall for decades.

"What happened in your relationships, Andrew? If you don't mind my asking." I'm eager to shift the attention away from myself.

"It was nothing to do with Gen, if that's what you're wondering."

I wasn't. But now that the thought is planted in my mind . . .

"You know, you remind me of her. Have done, ever since Hugh told me about you months ago and I looked you up on LinkedIn. Seeing you in person, I can't put my finger on what it is. Maybe it's a certain look you get. Maybe your energy. You're nothing alike, physically. She was classically beautiful. . . ."

Oh!

"Absolute knockout of a woman . . ."

Well, thanks for that comparison, Andrew. I hadn't thought I could feel any more insecure about this, but we've plunged to new depths.

By the time Hugh appears in the doorway, Andrew has shared one too many extraordinary Genevieve anecdotes, I'm a champagne and several proseccos into falling off the two-year near-abstinence wagon and I've requested "Dancing Queen" from the DJ while I FaceTime Grace from the middle of the dance floor, crying about how much I miss her.

"Remember the time we were spotted by ABBA's manager and taken backstage to meet them?" I ask her loudly, through alcohol-induced tears.

She laughs. "It was a Bjorn Again concert, Kate. Not that that stopped you from being starstruck! *Love* seeing you on a dance floor, by the way. I've missed you!"

"I miss you too!"

"NO! I've missed YOU. *This* you. The old you."

I've missed the old us. The Grace and I who'd laugh at ourselves until tears were rolling down our cheeks in dressing rooms. The friends who'd dance till the lights came on at pre-baby nights out at the one eighties-inspired nightclub in town. I'm struck by the loss of our spontaneity and lightness. The whole "Want to grab brunch? See you in twenty" thing.

"Hiya, neighbor!" Justin says, popping into the frame. *What's this?* I need to dampen my champagne-infused delight at seeing them unexpectedly together. *Keep it cool, Kate. You've retired from matchmaking!*

Seeing them play happy families for a few seconds reminds me how lovely that can be. And I realize I've been stuck in the endless purgatory of loss. Weighed down by the extra burdens of raising a child who carries the very real anxiety that I might not come home from work one day. Fearing that outcome myself. Paying bills. Being responsible. Getting on with a life that isn't plan A but couldn't in any sense be construed as a decent plan B either.

"You know 'caretaker mode' before an election?" I say to Grace, moving off the dance floor and away from the loudspeakers. "They dissolve the House of Reps and keep everything ticking over but they put the brakes on any major new decisions?"

She knows exactly what I mean. "That's only ever meant to be a temporary mode, Kate."

Yes.

Don't stop living, just because I do.

As Hugh arrives and crosses the room, and "Dancing Queen" reaches a climax, I make Grace promise to tell me everything about the new romance when we next chat, and then I end the call. Hugh looks different. It's not just the tousled hair and two-day stubble, though those do stray from his typical impeccability. It's the wildness in his eyes. As if the fight-or-flight mechanism has kicked in and he's been wrestling those demons of his—henceforth to be known as Genevieve—for hours.

He reaches me and, without ceremony, takes me gently by the wrist, pulls me back across the dance floor in silence, then toward the door and outside into the cooler air, stopping beneath a string of fairy lights hanging from a cypress pine. The distant sky lights up, followed by the rumble of thunder, and the intensity in his blue eyes almost scorches my skin as he looks at me. *Really* looks at me.

Walls down. Barriers stripped. Nothing but raw, exposed honesty between us now.

"Kate," he says, his voice heavy. "I want to tell you everything. You need to know about Genevieve."

34

Back at the beach house, waiting for the kettle to boil, Hugh looks nervous. He leans against the kitchen bench, arms crossed, staring at a spot on the cupboard while I get mugs and tea bags ready. *Wow, she's really done a number on him!*

"Is everything okay?" I ask, as waves break on the beach. I'm not sure I really want to hear the answer.

"Sorry," he says. "It's earlier. At the café. The whole . . ."

Spit it out, Hugh.

He looks straight at me. "This is exactly why I never . . ." He shakes his head and gestures at me, and at him. At *us*, if you will. I'm still lost. The kettle clicks off and he pours water into the mugs. Then we move to the couch by the fire.

My mind is scrambling to work out what he could possibly be so nervous to tell me about, and it's coming up blank. Scarily blank. This morning on the beach, which now seems like a thousand years ago, I was only just starting to vaguely admit that maybe, I don't know, Hugh and I . . .

"When Cam first got sick," Hugh begins, then falters. He inhales and expels the kind of steadying breath athletes take before the most important race of their lives. It only dials up my apprehension.

"I thought this was about Genevieve," I interrupt.

"Kate, this is going to be a difficult conversation. I know how you love those. And this isn't a performance review—"

Thank God.

"—but you have a nervous habit of interrupting."

"No, I don't."

He raises his eyebrows. "Just let me try to articulate these thoughts, okay? This is hard to say."

I zip my mouth shut, as much as that is possible, and vow to let the guy speak.

He begins again. "I first met Gen at uni, as I said, then later working up north."

"I thought this was about Cam. Sorry." I physically put a hand over my mouth to shut myself up.

"Gen was . . . well, she was . . ."

He gets a faraway look on his face, and it fills me with a type of full-body dismay with which I've not been previously acquainted. *God.* He loved her. Loves her? It's hard to tell from his expression if it's past or present tense. All I know is I have an awful, sinking feeling of inferiority. I feel like he's slipping through my fingers before he's even in my arms.

"An absolute knockout of a woman?" I suggest, and he snaps his attention back to me.

"Yes."

He looks confused.

"Andrew's description," I add, and he gives me a small smile.

I didn't sign up for this conversation and would like to request a refund at Hugh's earliest convenience. Something is knotting, hard, in my chest. I'm feeling this wrench. This heart . . . thing. *Where have all my words gone?*

"We were together six years," he explains. "You know how there are those golden couples? Sickeningly good together. Everyone wishes their own relationship would measure up?"

Yes, I know those couples. I was half of one, remember? And I get the general vibe about Genevieve and Hugh, so can we move on now?

"We lived together in this tiny one-bedroom flat. You could barely turn around. But we traveled a lot, working. It was the most idyllic, extraordinary—"

"Okay!" I interject. "Got it. Go on. . . ."

He laughs. "Kate, I might be off base here, but is it possible that you are *jealous* of Gen?"

Fine question. Pretty straightforward answer. I don't respond.

"I proposed to her in a medieval town in Tuscany. San Gimignano. Do you know it?"

No, and I've struck it off my bucket list now. Hugh was engaged? To the most idyllic, extraordinary, knockout of a woman ever to have walked the earth. *Isn't that how he described her?*

This tea is insufficient for this job, but I can't have something stronger. I need to have my wits about me for this conversation. "Can we skip to the part where you break up?"

"Oh, we didn't break up," he answers.

"What, *never?*"

He edges closer to me on the couch. I can't decide if I want to back away from him or lean in.

"Gen started getting really tired. Unusually tired, for such a high-energy woman. The type of tired where you can't stand on your feet."

I feel my eyes widen as realization dawns.

"The doctors thought it was glandular fever. Took a blood test. That was meant to come back in a couple of days. They phoned within the hour."

"Hugh—"

He puts his hand up, as if pausing for an interjection now will derail the entire story. "Immediate treatment. They started that day. Went on for months. At one point, it looked like she'd beaten it, but . . ." He shakes his head.

I sit back on the couch, suddenly needing its full support around me, and stare at him. Horrified. I don't interrupt now, because I can't find any words to interrupt with.

He waits as this information properly sinks in and my brain travels right back to the day Cam first got sick. The way Hugh first responded. The fact that he read me like a book, all through my grief, and seemed to understand what I was feeling more deeply than anyone else, often before I did.

"I thought you were psychic," I whisper.

He shakes his head. "More like a time traveler. I know grief, Kate. Intimately. So, when Cam was diagnosed—"

"It stirred everything up?"

He doesn't reply.

"It took you back," I suggest. "I am so incredibly sorry. For your loss. And for dragging you through . . . *everything*, like I was the first person this had ever happened to. But you didn't say anything. Why?"

"It wasn't about me. It wasn't appropriate at first. People are quick to compare someone's suffering with their own, and it's not about that. I just wanted to help you. Pay it forward, you know?"

I think about exactly what that meant. Hugh had been there for me in ways that floored me. Floored Cam, too, until he couldn't appreciate things anymore. I'd told him intimate, graphic details of Cam's gradual descent from vibrant husband to someone virtually comatose. I'd gone over and over the moments when Cam died, what happened, when it happened, the way his breathing changed, the sense I had of him being taken from me against my will while I grappled with a deep desire for him to be at peace. . . . How could Hugh have withstood all of this without ever once asking me to stop, or asking for an opportunity to share the burden of his own, equally tragic story?

"When I met you, at the gym—" he says.

Let's not rehash that.

"—you lot accused me of having a string of one-night stands, remember?"

To be fair, it was Purple Pants who accused him. I blush with shame on her behalf.

"Kate, that was true."

Oh, the ugly twisting in my heart is back.

"When Gen died, I knew I couldn't go through that again. That agony. The loss. It nearly killed me. And the way to protect myself from that was just to—"

"Avoid the risk."

"Yes. I had an outright ban on getting close to anyone. Decided it wasn't better to have loved and lost—it was much worse. I made a promise that I'd never put myself in a situation again that carried that much danger."

I nod. This bit I totally get.

"But what about Ruby?" I ask. I'm embarrassed to raise the office yum cha rumor, but he saw her too many times for it not to have meant *something*.

His face softens. "She turned up around the time you were throwing me at Grace," he explains, and my heart sinks. She *was* the "something personal" he was occupied with.

"You *were* seeing someone!" I can't believe he lied!

He shakes his head. "Kate, she's Genevieve's daughter."

Genevieve's *daughter*? I don't understand. How is that even possible?

"Gen and I broke up for a couple of years in the middle. I thought she told me everything, but there was one big thing she'd kept to herself."

Why wouldn't she have told him?

"She'd put the baby up for adoption at birth. When Ruby went looking for her biological mother and found she'd died, she started the search for her father."

Does Hugh have a *daughter*? Lord, this conversation is exploding beyond all expectation.

"I knew she couldn't have been mine," he goes on, quickly. "Gen would have told me that. And I confirmed it with her closest friend, who'd always felt bad having to keep Gen's secret from me. She said the only reason Gen didn't tell me was she was scared it would drive me away somehow. It wouldn't have. I would have loved that little girl."

He *does* love her. Cam told me.

"Ruby wanted to know everything about her mum. So we'd have long lunches . . ."

"At yum cha," I say. "Everyone thought you were seeing her romantically." It's mortifying to admit now.

"No," he confirms. "Just talking about Gen. I told her everything. You know, I almost wished—"

He wished she was his.

"That must have freshened up so much grief for you," I say. My heart is breaking for him.

He swallows hard. "Ruby is the image of her mother. And she's like her in so many other ways. It was a strong reminder of what I'd lost. But at the same time, this beautiful, unexpected gift . . ."

I can't believe all of this was going on and he never said anything.

"Watching you go through everything with Cam was torture at times. But it proved to me unequivocally that I was right. I couldn't lose someone like that again. I can't. I won't have it. Cam and I talked about it once—the risk you take, loving someone. And how losing Gen broke me."

Cam *knew*?

I think about Hugh's agony that time he disappeared for those weeks. I remember the conversation that passed, silently, between them when he returned. Was it too much? Watching me lose Cam? Was he giving up on us? On me?

"You couldn't stand to watch me lose him," I say quietly. "My pain was too much, so you went away."

He takes my hand carefully and studies me. "That's not why I went away. I wouldn't leave you like that. No, it was something else. Bigger than that. Something I couldn't think straight about if I was with you."

An idea takes hold in my brain. Did Cam ask Hugh to somehow "step in" after he was gone? Is that what their arrangement was about? It's exactly the sort of thing Cam *would* have done, by that point. He was desperate. And, of course, there's a part of me that absolutely recoils at the idea of it. But it's the only thing that makes sense.

I didn't want that arrangement. Didn't need it. But feel rejected anyway.

"I totally get the thing about wanting to stay on your own," I say firmly. "It's the only sensible option. I'm glad you told him no."

He looks confused.

"That's what he asked you, isn't it? To look after me when he'd gone?"

He rubs his forehead. Shakes his head. "He did say something like that at one point, and I told him you wouldn't have a bar of it, but that wasn't it. It's something else between Cam and I that I had to wrestle with when I was away. Still wrestle with, actually, most days."

"What *is* it, Hugh?" I'm so intrigued I might burst.

He puts his hand on my knee. Right on it. I didn't think such an innocent gesture could disrupt so much inside of me, and I'm grappling with that when he delivers a punchline that's so hard, I feel like I've been hit in the jaw.

"I'm really sorry, Kate, but Cam made me promise I'd never tell you."

35

I am the next of kin. Keeper of Cam's legacy. Protector of his secrets. Mother of his child!

"You have to tell me!" I exclaim.

Hugh shakes his head, uncomfortable yet resolved. "I can't. I'm sorry."

"But Cam told me everything!" I protest, outraged.

Obviously, he didn't tell me *this*. I can't work out if I'm more hurt at being sidelined by Cam just when our marriage was at its most vulnerable, or angry that Hugh is choosing to go along with the secret, all this time later.

A truly horrible thought attacks me out of nowhere. This intensely personal truth Cam shared with Hugh is something that would have hurt me. That's why Hugh had to leave town to work out what to do.

His steel integrity is unshakeable. Ironic that the very thing I most admire about him will be the thing that shoots us down. It's driving that wedge so deep between us I can't even speak. It's the idea of being excluded by the two men who I—

Forget *The Unraveling*. This is cataclysmic. End of the rose-colored filter I've had on my marriage with Cam all these years—particularly since he died.

End of Hugh and I, before he and I even begin.

I glare at him now as I stand up and pace the room. I don't think I've ever felt so . . . *silenced*. Two men and a secret so impenetrable it survives death. Hugh had better armor up, fast, because half of my rage has nowhere to go.

He's just sitting there. Watching my agony. I mean, he could fix this in five seconds flat if he'd just tell me what it is. But I know he won't. It's Hugh. You can bloody trust him.

"I shouldn't have said that," he explains quietly. "I was never going to mention it. I didn't want to hurt you like this."

Oh, right. He was just going to go through life deceiving me instead. Fantastic. Perfect start to our . . . whatever this was going to be between us.

"Why are you looking so petrified?" I ask him.

He shakes his head, as if he can't believe I'm so clueless.

"Isn't it obvious?" he asks. As he gets up and steps toward me, I back away like a skittish animal. "Kate," he says, stopping still. "I'm terrified I'm losing you."

Right. I see. Terror well placed, then.

I can't breathe in here. I grab the glass sliding door handle and reef it sideways for all it's worth. But it's stuck.

He comes up behind me and reaches carefully around my body, lifts the door off its tread slightly and budges it free. For an infinitesimal moment, his ragged breath is on my neck, and part of me implodes.

Don't lose focus, Kate.

I pull open the door and the air outside is charged ahead of the storm that's been increasing in intensity since this morning.

Good. It's a full moon. It's windy. It's moody. The sea is crashing intensely. It's like I've stepped into an external representation of what's going on inside my mind and body. Lightning strikes and a crack of thunder explodes overhead. I think I see a person at the end of the garden. Cam?

Don't be stupid.

I trudge off that way anyway. Hugh calls out to me to stop because it's late. It's dark. The storm is dangerously close. "At least take your phone, Kate. . . ."

I really don't care.

I hear the sliding door slam moments later and I know he's on this side of it. Well, I hope he can keep up.

The sand is cold under my bare feet. Every couple of minutes, the lightning flashes over the water, thunder breaks, and I see that silhouette again in the distance. It's starting to freak me out. Is there really someone there?

I check behind me and when the sky lights up, I can see Hugh, keeping his distance. He might not have seen me in a rage very often, but he knows me well enough to back off and leave me to work this out myself. Not that I can, because Cam has deserted me. Left me with no way to have this conversation. No outlet. And unless Hugh breaks his promise, I'll never know the truth.

What had Cam *done*? Something illegal? Had he cheated on me? Did Cam have other children I didn't know about? Or even just one child. That would be bad enough. What if he had a whole other family, like those people who live double lives? Is that where Cam sent Hugh? To mop up some unmentionable mess interstate that I didn't know existed?

I see the figure again. I stop trudging and stand still. Thunder and waves crash around me. Rain starts to pelt.

Another flash of light. He's still there. At a distance. Watching me on the beach.

I must be more drunk than I thought. I don't see dead people, I just feel them. I am desperate here. Torn. I want to run to him, but the pain of seeing him up close would destroy me. Not seeing him destroys me too.

"Cam!" I hear myself shouting over the cacophony of rain and thunder and ocean waves. I reach my hand out toward him. Why won't he come any closer? I feel like once I start, I will follow him forever, endlessly, never close enough, always out of reach.

This is no way to live.

I turn around, and Hugh is standing not far from me, saturated. Rain is dripping off his dark hair and his face and neck while he waits for me.

He's so . . .

Alive.

So real. So "with me," in a way that Cam will never be now.

I wouldn't be here with him if Cam hadn't died. It's that pervasive thought that occurs to me every single day. Almost everything about my existence has been rewritten because of what we've been through. I didn't ask for this. I can't change it. The longer I stay here, chasing the ghost of my former life, the shorter the next chapter of my life will become.

Hugh presents me with the cardigan that I'd picked up yesterday. He must have grabbed it on the way out, maybe as a peace offering. It's been tucked into his jacket and it's the only thing that's dry. I ease my hand through the sleeve and fish around behind my back, searching for the other sleeve until he has to help me.

We're standing so close, our breath is condensing into one cloud as we exhale. It's electric, being here in the unpredictable storm with him—every cell of mine aware of every cell of his. I'm craving him on some deep, biological level that doesn't care about secrets and betrayals and walls and professional boundaries.

Cam told me I had to move on. It was easy for him. He wasn't the one dragging himself out of bed every day without a life partner. He didn't start each new day facing a lifetime of parenting alone, where every significant and insignificant occasion is now bittersweet. School assemblies. Sports finals. Formals. Graduations. Weddings. Grandchildren. Always wanting to share these things with the only person who could ever feel exactly the same way about it. Always having to feel that way on your own.

And this extends to my own accomplishments too. I imagine writing my book and fantasize about being offered a publishing deal. But where there should be the popping of champagne in my kitchen and being picked up and spun around and kissed because Cam is so proud of me, there is nothing. A nice phone call with Mum. Maybe a hug from Charlie. Grace would take me out to celebrate, but it's not the same. Nothing is.

"Kate?"

I don't know when Cam expected me to move on. Or how. Just that he did.

Maybe he told Hugh about it. I'm not going to ask. I'm not up for another clammed-up response. In every interaction with this man from this moment on I'll feel like he's keeping something important from me. I'll blame Cam and I'll blame Hugh and it will eat me alive, not knowing. This is never going to work. How can it?

"I'm trying to think of a way to fix this," Hugh says, ever the fixer. The rescuer. The knight in the proverbial shining armor, always riding in, saving people. Often me. Mainly me, I guess. Colluding with Cam. Snowplowing everything out of my path to make it easier—except for this one obstacle, this secret, which he has the power to shift and won't.

"Tell me what I can do," he says. "I'm in an impossible situation here, like I was then. Cam trusted me. It was all for you. Always. Don't ever question how much you are loved."

"Was loved," I say dismally.

He doesn't argue with me anymore.

My arms uncross, slowly, and drop to my sides. He's gutted. And it's my husband who led to it. It's hard to stay mad at someone after he's done so much. Too much, really. I've become reliant on him, as Mum said. I think it's time to stop.

"If I'm ever going to move forward," I begin, "I need it to be on my own terms. I need to rebuild my life, Hugh. From the ground up. Quit my job. Sell the house. Write my book. Get Charlie over to the UK to see his grandparents and show him the world like Cam always imagined we would."

He looks alarmed.

"It's a lot of change," I say.

He nods. Swallows. Looks beyond my face, for once, at the wet skin on my neck, white top plastered to me under the cardigan, skirt clinging to my legs, and when his attention returns to my eyes, I know he wants me. I think he's wanted me for a long time.

I bend down and run my finger along the wet sand, making a line, then stand behind it. "I don't want you scheming to make my life easier. I appreciate everything you've done, but I need to get my act together now, on my own," I say.

He steps forward, near the line, and I put my hand on his chest and hold him back.

"I feel like this is the end, Kate. You're scaring me."

"You don't come across this line unless I ask you to," I explain. "On this side, I'm not your subordinate. I'm not someone you rescue. You're not my boss. I'm not a grief-stricken widow to feel sorry for. There's no power imbalance."

"Our power imbalance has never been in the direction you think," he says.

"I know you don't do relationships since Genevieve, and this thing about you and Cam isn't going to go away. You won't tell me, and that's your decision. I know what you're like, and I respect and loathe that about you, all at once—"

"Kate!"

"I can't see how it could work with something that monumental standing between us. I know I'm going out on a huge limb here, even suggesting you're interested in me as more than a colleague and friend, since you've danced around the topic all day and haven't actually said so in so many words. . . ."

This is possibly the most mortifying conversation of my life. I'm not holding back. Not keeping the slightest air of mystery about myself, or how I feel.

"I'm not going to be one of your one-night stands, Hugh," I announce, taking a massive leap of faith that he'd even want that.

He laughs. "Kate, I haven't had a one-night stand in a long time. It's not fair, when your mind is on someone else." He looks at me and holds his ground. And I'm flustered and confused.

"You really can't tell me Cam's secret?"

He wants to. I can see it written all over his face.

I realize I've still got my hand on his chest, pushing him away from my line. I can feel his heartbeat through his wet shirt. It's sprinting. We stare at each other, rain continuing to fall, waves continuing to crash. *The sun will go on rising and setting, whether I kiss Hugh Lancaster or not.*

I watch as my hand eases its pressure on his shirt. Grasps the wet fabric, twists it, and pulls him toward me in the rain. Toward my line. Perilously close to it. And then over it.

36

I know this is going to be our last kiss, because kisses upset Cam. He doesn't know who I am, or what I'm doing. To kiss him now feels like a violation. Even kisses like this—quick and gentle—confuse him, in the same way he's forgotten how to eat and shower and use the toilet. Every human function is beyond his grasp at the end stage of Alzheimer's.

He's sitting in his room at the nursing home, propped in one of those big armchairs with buttons you press to help you stand up. He can't actually stand up anymore, but the chair also reclines and this is where he sleeps. There are photos of Charlie and me everywhere. They ceased being any help to him months ago, but I like to think we're there if he wakes up and is frightened.

He's a shell of the man he was. Malnourished, because he's forgotten how to chew and swallow. Gaunt, with skin almost translucent he's so pale. I stroke his cheek, which was smooth after I shaved it this morning, but is now rough. The shaving was an ordeal, too, but I want him to feel better. Fresher. Cared for. Loved. Because he *is* loved, so much.

This is a long goodbye. I've been losing Cam in pieces, each progression taking part of him from me by stealth. I say goodbye each night when he's tucked up in bed at seven, and I don't know how much of him will be there the next day. Just less. Always less. I wanted to care for him at home until the very end, but it became too much with Charlie. Mum and Grace eventually convinced me my role was wife and mother, and if I could bring myself to hand his medical care to nurses, I could focus on those roles. And they've been incredibly professional and kind in here.

Cam and I have been adopted by the couple next door to his room, who are in their nineties. Without fail, whether I bowl up there wrung out and crying or reasonably put together straight from work, Claire reaches for me from her wheelchair, her beautiful face alight with genuine joy, and tells me I'm the "prettiest girl in the world." She has advanced dementia too. And Barrie adores her, the way I adore Cam. I've never felt more understood than when I'm in his presence—intergenerational kindred spirits who are *living* love in that very practical, intimate, vulnerable sense that goes so much deeper than hearts and flowers and jewelry and honeymoons. He's the father figure I've never had. I've never felt more in awe of a couple, or more envious of the length of a loving relationship.

Charlie adores them too. They're like surrogate grandparents to him. When Cam first moved in, people would ask Charlie if he was here to see his grandma or his grandpa.

"Daddy!" he would chirp, innocent of how inconceivably wrong this was, on every level. For a while, we took Cam to the special choir for residents with dementia, but their repertoire was decades out: "In the Mood" and "Danny Boy," when he needed "Blinded by the Light."

After a while, Daddy didn't know who Charlie was. "Daddy's brain is sick," I would explain. "He loves you, Charlie, so much, but his brain can't make his mouth tell you anymore."

It ruined me, the first time I said that. But children are remarkably resilient. A reality check for the awful, amid so much "normal" around us. Charlie would clamber on the bed and watch YouTube clips from ABC Kids, just like other kids running around in the aged care facility, visiting their grandparents and great-grandparents.

So Cam's last kiss is really just for me. I promise him it will be quick. He won't even notice. Leaning in to a face that isn't even his own anymore—shrunken, shriveled, blank—my eyes fill with the inevitable tears, although I'd vowed I wouldn't cry. Inside this kiss is every other one. Our first, on one of our undergraduate picnics on the uni lawns in Melbourne. The kiss he gave me through tears, straight after Charlie was born, in the delivery suite. That kiss on the bed the weekend after we lost our baby. All these kisses, punctuating a grand romance, snuffed decades before its time. He closes his eyes as I lean toward him, and I notice every breath is catching in his throat.

He hasn't said a word to me, or to anyone, in weeks. But at the moment my lips touch his, I swear I feel his soul stir. In that fraction of a second, we're Cam and Kate again, the way we used to be. Such strength between us, in this perfect, ageless, timeless, *worldless* moment.

Then I lean back and open my eyes.

He doesn't.

I stare for a long time at his beautiful, peaceful face.

And then I become aware. Quietly. Aware of my breath. My heartbeat. The million unseen, microscopic inner workings of the miracle of life, continuing to vibrate within me.

And aware of his stillness.

"Cam," I whisper, my hand shaking his arm gently, not wanting to wake him. Knowing I can't.

I trace the outline of his face with my fingers. Feel the roughness of his chin. I smooth his hair. Touch his ears. Cradle his neck in my hand, my thumb coming to rest where his pulse should be.

Panic rises within me, but it's quickly overwhelmed by a tumbling sense of peace. We sit together for ages, Cam and me.

Death and life.

Before and after.

I try to thank him . . . for what, I don't know. I just thank him, in general, and tell him I love him and I'm sorry. Again, for what? For everything. Every mistake. Each tiny hurt I may have inadvertently inflicted, ever. It feels pointless, speaking aloud to a lifeless body, when it so clearly is no longer *him*.

There's no trace of him at all, suddenly. He's just . . . *entirely gone*.

And so is the Kate that I knew. Innocent Kate, who believed in fairy tales and love stories and happy endings. Kate, who, at thirty-eight, is too young to be a widow, and who suddenly wants, more than anything, to be at the end of her own life, with her love.

I can't end it though, because of Charlie, who doesn't even know yet that Daddy has died. *Died*. What a horrible word. Charlie, who on the phone earlier tonight told Daddy he'd done another drawing for his wall and got no response, as usual. And never will now.

I'm unable to move. I sit with him for what feels like eternity but is probably a few minutes. It's only when the nurse knocks at the door and bustles in for her evening check that she finds us here. Checks Cam's pulse. Tells me she's sorry, there's nothing we can do. And even though I know that, it quashes any final hope that this is just a nightmare.

She calls her colleagues, who call a funeral director, who'll be tasked to take Cam away. Paperwork is prepared. Questions are asked. Answers are given on autopilot. It's all very efficient and administrative, and I can't take my eyes off him. My Cam. My love. My whole life. *What am I going to do now?* I've been thoroughly occupied in my caring role since a few months after the diagnosis, but that gave me purpose. I don't even know who I am without the job it has become to look after him.

"Can we call someone for you?" the nurse asks.

"It's okay. I drove myself."

She places her hand gently on my shoulder. "Someone else should drive you home tonight."

I scroll through my contacts list and find Hugh's number and pass the nurse my phone. I don't even think of calling anyone else this time. He's the one who handles this stuff best.

I can hear her muffled conversation outside in the corridor. ". . . about half an hour ago . . . she's in shock . . . thank you . . ."

And it's not until about twenty minutes later, when Hugh walks in calmly, respectfully, that the tears finally erupt. I pick up Cam's hand, my head bent, and hold it to my forehead.

His skin is already going cold.

This is the saddest I will ever be, I think.

But even this early in my fledgling grief, I suspect that's probably not true. I'm going to disintegrate.

"I'll give you time with Cam alone," Hugh says behind me.

I don't turn around. "Stay," I say in a voice I barely recognize. I don't like being alone with Cam now. But I can't leave him. I need to watch over him until they take him from here. From me.

Hugh doesn't speak unless spoken to, but his strong presence in the room is such a comfort. I say something about needing to start calling people and he tells me we'll get to that soon, it's okay just to sit here with Cam for a while.

I'm instantly terrified to go home to an empty house. I don't know what to do about anything. "Do I call in and wake Charlie up or tell him tomorrow?"

"Let him sleep. Look after yourself tonight and get your bearings."

My bearings? There can be no bearings in a life without my husband.

Charlie can have twelve more hours until his world is shattered. Twelve hours until his childhood innocence is ripped to pieces. Of course, I've prepared him for this moment, as much as you can prepare a three-year-old, but I could never quite imagine us actually being here. There's no rule book, and I desperately need one.

Grief is strange, when it happens in advance. Since Cam's diagnosis two years ago, I've been processing this loss every day. I thought the time we had to accept it would make it easier. Sudden death must be so blindsiding in comparison. But now I'm here, I'm blindsided anyway, because I never truly believed this would unfold. Never stopped hoping for a miracle, even though we were so obviously not going to get one.

Hugh passes me a glass of water. He tells me grief can be dehydrating.

I can't work out how he knows so much, but I do as he says and take the glass.

It strikes me that Cam will never need water again. He'll never need pajamas or sheets. Never a bed or a toothbrush or shaving gear. He'll never drive. Never see the stars. *Never anything.* He is finished. Done. Gone. Full stop.

"He's never coming back," I whisper, finally appreciating what grief really is. This permanent ending of a person. The end of their story. The complete lack of their existence.

I want Hugh to argue with me. Tell me I'm wrong. That I'm exaggerating. That this isn't as bad as I think.

Instead, he says, "I know, Kate. I'm sorry." And it feels like I could lose consciousness from the pain. As if everything that makes up my biology is weakening. As if I could die, too.

There's a knock at the door and the nurse introduces me to the man who will take Cam's body from here. I can see a gurney with sheets on it parked in the corridor outside the room. I've been here before when a body has been wheeled out—it's a reasonably common occurrence in a place like this, but they always shut the emergency doors to the dining room, so residents won't see anything. I hear the doors being shut now. For us.

I'm encouraged to say my final goodbyes. I look at Hugh, scared, and shake my head.

"Would you like some privacy?"

"No."

"Have you said everything?"

Said everything? We've lost thousands of conversations. Millions of words.

"We might go, first," he explains to the undertaker and the nurse. He picks up my handbag from the floor and helps me with my coat. I stand at Cam's side for another couple of seconds, put my hand on his arm, think one final goodbye, and then wrench myself away.

We walk into the corridor, and my ninety-year-old bestie, Barrie, stands in his doorway in pajamas and a dressing gown, having overheard the nursing staff. We share a momentary glance, during which he communicates his empathy at my loss, and I communicate my acknowledgment of this *awful* struggle.

Hugh deals with the code at the exit. It's all locked down in here because the residents wander, and I'm struck by the fact that Cam won't do that, ever again. Won't wander into the world. Or feel the crispness of the night air, which makes me shiver as it hits my skin. How does my body even know to continue on? To respond to the cold. To feel. To *be*?

Hugh's car is parked in a visitor's spot right near the door. The drive home passes in a blur. He asks me for the keys, unlocks the front door, and pushes it open for me.

I don't want to walk over the threshold. Cam carried me over it when we first moved in, even though we'd lived in various places before that. Such an old-fashioned, romantic moment.

"Kate?" Hugh says. "Let's go inside where it's warm."

It's not warm, though. I'm hardly ever home. Mum picks up Charlie from school each day and I visit Cam and we have dinner at Mum's place. I really come here only to shower and sleep. I've even moved Knightley to Grace's temporarily, because I was worried the poor dog was being neglected.

Hugh turns lamps on and makes me sit on the lounge and puts a blanket over me while he lights the fire. He brings me another glass of water, and a glass of wine, and says to keep my fluids up, even if I can't control anything else.

"Should I call your mum?" he asks. "And Grace?"

I nod.

"What about Cam's parents?"

"Yes, I'll have to. . . . What time is it in the UK?" They're not well themselves, and they're going to be devastated.

Hugh wants to lift all these burdens but can't. He should be out of his comfort zone but isn't. After he's coached me through making the few essential calls, he tells me there's nothing more I need to do tonight. He sits across from me beside the fire. There's total silence, except the crackling of the wood in the flames and the sound of my heart breaking.

"Is there something wrong with me that I'm not crying?" I ask after a while. I feel sick about it. I have a physical ache in my chest, as if my heart is clinically breaking. That's an actual thing that I read about. Takotsubo cardiomyopathy. Broken heart syndrome. It happens to a lot of widows.

Widows. Old women in black, wailing. Gray-haired ladies on their own at the nursing home. Women from the two world wars. Not me. Not at thirty-eight. Not with a three-year-old.

"Why can't I cry?" I ask again. Maybe if I did, the pain in my chest would ease.

"The times I'm saddest," Hugh says, "it's so deep it doesn't come to the surface at all. When I—" He falters.

"When you what?"

He looks at me and shakes his head. "I'll tell you another time," he says, and he glances at his watch.

The thought of him wanting to leave horrifies me. He stands up and I reach out and grab both his hands.

"Please stay!" I'm aware that I'm begging, but this feels like an emergency. It is one.

He squeezes my hands and lets them go. "I'm just getting you some Tylenol," he explains. "For the broken heart."

Oh, yes. Why didn't I think of that?

"Grief is a physical thing as well," he says from the kitchen. "Pain-killers can help with the impact on your body."

Of all the people I could have asked to sit with me during this horrible, defining experience, I seem to have chosen the Indiana Jones of grief. I take the tablets. Wash them down with a gulp of wine.

I need to go to the toilet, but I don't want to be alone. Obviously, I'm not asking Hugh to come with me. But what if I go in there, freak out in the solitude, and lose all emotional control? *Are these the weird thoughts I'll have now?*

I find the courage and go in and shut the door. I can't believe Cam is dead. Can't believe it. How can this be true? He was just here! Even with all the time I've had to get used to the idea that this day would come, I'm not remotely prepared for its reality.

I wash my hands, go back to the living room, and curl up under the blanket again. Hugh stares into the fire.

"I am alone in this," I say, after a long while. "*Completely alone.* Even with you and Mum and Cam's parents and Grace, it's just me, really."

"Mmm."

"Until I drag Charlie down into this hell with me in the morning."

Sweet, happy, inquisitive, carefree preschooler Charlie. I've never dreaded anything more.

37

The present

I have pulled Hugh over my line in the sand on the beach in the storm and now I don't know what to do with him.

"I didn't think this through," I divulge honestly, now that he's just inches away from me, the fabric of his shirt still twisted in my fingers, which won't seem to let him go. In truth, I didn't think *at all*. Just couldn't leave him standing there in the rain for another second.

Wanted him standing *here* in the rain, instead. With me. Even though I've just outlined all the reasons why this will never happen—particularly the fact that he won't bend on Cam's secret—and it's a watertight case.

The last time I kissed a man, he died. I don't think there's a causal link, but it's playing on my mind, obviously. That and the fact that my last kiss was more than two years ago, but it's been more like three years since I did it properly. And more than two decades since I kissed someone other than Cam—some boy at the Year Twelve formal in an unmitigated disaster that I don't have time to think about right now, due to circumstances rapidly becoming beyond my control.

Hugh takes my face in his hands. Handles it like it's precious and he's an expert. Like I'm breakable. Which I suppose I am.

"Hugh . . ."

He moves toward me, slowly, and I just stand there, waiting to receive. I can't move. I'm a flight risk. Any sudden movements, even my own, might break this trance.

A kaleidoscope of images from my life with Cam flashes through my mind the way it's supposed to just before you die. Not before someone new kisses you. But when Hugh's mouth finally touches mine, the images disappear. Warmth floods through me and he sighs as if this is something he's wanted to do for a very long time. Centuries, maybe. And I panic. Where have the images gone of Cam? *Have I lost them?*

"You with me, Kate?" Hugh whispers, pulling back and checking.

"Y—es?"

This is not something I've had the luxury of thinking about for years. It's been mere hours, perhaps since the airport just yesterday morning, when I first realized Hugh was very much a "man" with regard to me. Not just a colleague, or a friend.

And now he's kissing me for real and I'm in a zero-gravity chamber . . . *Oh my God.*

Am I doing this right? I think as his lips wander toward my neck and he pulls his face away again and smiles.

Tell me I did not say that aloud.

"Are you asking for feedback, Kate?"

Yes. *No.* God! *Am I this out of practice?*

"I thought this was meant to be like riding a bike," I say. Because how romantic. "Don't let me talk!" I suggest.

He laughs. "But," he replies, "I love the way you talk."

"Well, I love the way you kiss, apparently."

"Apparently?" He smiles again. All these smiles—it's like Christmas. "Do you think we could try this again, Whittaker, this time with your brain disengaged?"

Constructive criticism. I've taken it from him before, so why should this be any different? The man clearly knows what he's doing. All those one-night stands . . . the incredible Genevieve . . . *Gah!* I shouldn't have canceled that last waxing appointment. . . .

"Hugh, I don't know how to switch off my brai—"

He switches it off for me, finishing my sentence in a way that's unarguable. *This* kiss isn't slow and sweet and testing the waters. It's hungry. Urgent. Years in the making. All-consuming. And it's scrambling my brain and my body as my hand travels up his chest to his shoulders and neck and rakes through his wet hair and grasps it, because I need him even closer.

The deluge from the sky intensifies. The cardigan, heavy with rainwater, slips off my shoulder, and he trails his mouth down my neck, along wet skin. He grabs my waist and pulls me against him, hard. Unprofessionally. Exquisitely.

His hands move up my back in the privacy beneath my cardigan, triggering nerves and muscles that flex and arch as my head drops back, face to the sky into the torrential rain, giving him access to my throat, which he kisses so gently I have to half-feel it and half-imagine. His fingers trail lightly down my neck, drop to my chest, stop over my heart. And we come up for air, as if asking ourselves what on earth we are doing, because this is intoxicating and exhilarating. Brand new. Years old.

We stare at each other, breathing heavily. Surprised to be here, and yet not surprised at all.

"Your heart is racing," he informs me, his hand still on my chest.

"It's not used to you," I explain, and he puts his arms around me and pulls me into the most delicious hug . . . possibly ever. *How can that be?* "Will it always be broken?" I murmur.

It's the scariest question I've ever asked anyone—particularly someone who has a definitive answer on this topic from his own experience.

"Always," he says carefully. "This is not about fixing that."

I feel a major freak-out coming, but I'm just as certain I'm more centered than I have been in a very long time. "What are we doing?" I ask. We're barely halfway through our first kiss but I need to know what his intentions are and where this is heading, so I can risk-manage any potential carnage.

"I don't know," he replies.

Then we're in real trouble now.

"You always know!" I accuse him, and he doesn't answer.

"Is this the moment where you push me away?" I ask tentatively, and I feel the strength of his hug start to weaken. The ground we've clawed toward each other is lost. I'm slipping backward. Dangling over a cliff, while he holds me by the wrist and considers his choices. "Hugh, is this too close for you?"

He stands back a little, taking me in. Drowned by the rain. Steam from the heat of my body rising off my skin because of him—at least, I imagine it to be.

"Being with you the day Cam was diagnosed was too close," he says calmly. "Sitting with you at the hospital when you lost the baby was too close. The night Cam died. The next morning, watching that piercing wail of grief come out of a child's mouth, like nothing I've ever heard before or since and nothing I want to hear again."

Darling, Daddy died last night. . . .

"The time to push you away was right at the start, Kate. It's been overtaken by events."

So many events. Each of them awful. Can you base a relationship on suffering and support?

"It feels straightforward in my body," I say.

"You don't have to worry about your body."

Thank God.

"It's your head I'm concerned about. And mine."

And well might he be concerned, because my head has declared a state of emergency. Sirens. Flashing lights. Red flags. Warnings of danger being broadcast through every channel.

We've got tonight and tomorrow. Then the spell of this place will be broken and we go home. Me, to a house I've already decided to sell.

"I need to move," I explain. "Charlie and I need a fresh start, and not just another house in the same city."

"You need the beach."

"Yes. And to quit my job—no offense, Hugh—and let the equity from the house support me for a bit while I rent and write my book. Without the book, I don't think I can truly move forward with my life."

I'm pacing the sand now, threatening to hyperventilate. Is this a midlife crisis? Surely I'm too young. Or maybe the crisis already passed and this is what happens after it.

I don't know how anyone processes grief without expressing it in words. I don't know if Hugh ever really has. To have spent so long running from anything that felt too similar to what he lost— that's unhealthy. Unless he fixes himself, there's a risk he'll break my heart, and his. We can't afford that. I am not his medicine any more than he is mine.

"Kate, you're making me nervous."

"You won't ever feel completely mine," I explain. "I will never be completely yours. How does that even *work*?"

"I don't know."

"What if the secret you're keeping suffocates us?"

"I don't know what to do about that," he confesses. "I don't know how we can take this to the next step, Kate, for so many reasons. I only know I want to."

This has crept up on me. Looking back now, I can see all the signs I missed.

"I don't want to get ahead of myself, but what if we fall in love?" I ask, even though it terrifies me to express it. "How do I know you won't get spooked?"

How do I know I won't?

"This one I do know," he answers steadily. "You can trust me not to leave."

"Are you sure?"

He looks more vulnerable than I've ever seen him. "The time for me to run away from you before that happens is long gone."

38

The next morning, after the storm, I'm up early and take myself back to the beach to call Grace.

Charlie's face lights the screen. Even seeing him fills me with doubt. I'm not just risking my own heart with Hugh. I'm risking his.

"Mumma, Auntie Grace is outside talking to Justin," Charlie reports, walking over to the window. "He came over for pizza last night and we built a Minecraft city, and Auntie Grace thought everything he said was so funny. She giggled the *whole* night."

"Is that so?" I ask. This is a hopeful sign!

"I miss you, Mummy. You look different."

I am different. So much has changed, I'm scared he won't even recognize me by tonight when we get home.

"I miss you too, beautiful boy. Be good, and I'll bring you something special from the beach." *Must remember to collect some shells.* Or is that illegal? I never know.

I look at my phone after he goes, hoping it will spring forward some advice, just as Mum calls. As soon as I see her face, I start to cry.

"Oh, darling! What is it? It's Hugh, isn't it? I knew it."

She *knew*?

"Oh, come on, Katherine. Surely everyone could see it? I'm amazed it's taken you this long!"

This *long*? It's only four years since Cam got sick. Three years since we last had any semblance of togetherness. Two years since he died. I'm still so caught up in my marriage, I wasn't looking for this. And for Hugh to have been in plain sight all this time . . .

"Cam told me this day would come. Practically begged me to reach this point and let myself feel something for someone else. He said I'd want to run for the hills, and he's right. Mum, I dragged him over a line and I want to bolt!"

Hugh is worried he said too much last night about their secret. He's scared we went too far with our one and a half kisses. Granted, the second installment was quite something. My insides plummet whenever I think of it.

He'd tried to hold my hand on the walk back to the house from the beach and I'd brushed him off. Terrified of what it could lead to. I feel wretched about it now. It was me who dragged him over the line in the first place, and now he's giving me the space I insinuated I needed, and it feels like we're a million miles apart. Right beside each other.

"What is the nature of your relationship?" Mum asks, as if this is a police interview.

Lord. It's complicated. Is that a legitimate answer or is that only for social media?

"We kissed," I confide, aware that this is probably not the level of detail she requires. Nevertheless, she looks delighted. "Last night. Once. Well, twice. More like one and a half times—"

"So, you *are* in a relationship?"

I can see her mind gallivanting straight to pew decorations, bombonieras, and a mother-of-the-bride fascinator.

"Mum, look. We're not Amish. You can kiss people and not be together. You yourself told me to have a fling with a vagabond, remember?"

"Yes, but obviously I meant Hugh. Why do you think Grace and I staged this intervention?"

This *what*?

"The second we found out the flights were grounded we leaped into action. There really is only so much unresolved sexual tension the rest of us can tiptoe around, Katherine. And who could have predicted the collateral impact for Grace? Ooh, it is *thrilling*!"

What collateral impact? Is this about Justin? Mum's going full Mrs. Bennet about both of us.

"Hugh is my best friend," I say. It's news to me. And would be news to Grace, not that I'd ever tell her. He can't replace her, of course, but he's seen me through so much of the big stuff, right up close, it's unexpectedly obvious that's exactly what he is: my best and closest friend. When I try to imagine the last four years without him, I can't fathom how I'd have survived a single day.

"About last night . . ." I start to tell him, back at the house. He's standing in the kitchen, in dark blue check flannel pajama bottoms and a white tank, looking like he's barely slept. Sidenote: he is *delectable*. The tank clings to washboard abs that I'm staggered he's kept hidden under business suits all these years. Quite frankly, he's "fit AF," as Sophie would say. And he's looking at me through the rising steam of the kettle like he's thoroughly DTF in this moment—a proposal my own body would accept and pass without amendment if I let it.

"Don't apologize, Kate. I get it."

He gets what, though? The wrong idea? In the silence that passes between us it becomes painfully obvious that I'm at risk of losing Hugh altogether. But I don't know how to fix that. I'm not ready. I can't be sure he is, either. To leap straight into another relationship now, in a context as messy as ours, when I haven't really thrown myself into life on my own wouldn't be fair to either of us. I can't make a promise I'm not sure I can keep. And I wish I could look past the thing about Cam and Hugh, but it has a permanent hold over me.

Last night proved how compatible we're likely to be in ways that extend far beyond what we've ever had, but that won't fix this problem. Going there now would only make all of this even more difficult.

The idea of losing Hugh is unthinkable. Him being in my life has become synonymous with breathing.

I want to cry, but I can't. It reminds me of something from the night Cam died. What was it Hugh had said? The times he's saddest, it's so deep it doesn't come to the surface at all. He looks almost as bad as he did when he showed up on our doorstep that time, after going AWOL to think. I want to fix it. Every instinct is telling me to hug him and tell him I can't bear this.

"I didn't hold your hand last night because I was terrified of where it would lead," I explain.

"Is this meant to make me feel better?"

"Yes. Because the reality is, that kiss in the rain was . . ."

We look at each other and the chemistry is undeniable. How has it only just materialized, after all this time?

"Terrifying?" he asks.

"Exactly! Terrifying how out of control I felt. Terrifying how into you I am, Hugh."

He's listening.

"More than all of that, though, I'm terrified we're going to royally screw this up. And I can't afford to lose your friendship. It would destroy me."

I lead him out into the garden and we sit beside each other on the grass in the sun, legs outstretched, with our mugs of coffee. The day is so promisingly warm, the sun is a security blanket that I very much need to get through this conversation.

"I'm worried if I get wrapped up in you—and, believe me, after last night I know I would—I'll move straight from this holding pattern of grief into another relationship, without ever having taken any risks on my own. This is hard to explain—"

"You need to travel," he explains. "You need to make a home somewhere only you and Charlie know. You need Charlie to see you as a happy, independent mother. You need to write your book. . . ."

I do. I need all of that.

"I don't expect you to wait for me," I say, and it feels like the words coming out of my mouth are launching a personal attack on me. Like I'm kicking an own goal. Tears start to well.

He leans over and kisses the top of my head. I feel like we're seventeen and saying goodbye after a summer romance.

"I won't hold you back from any of the things you need to do," he says. "They're all important. Maybe you need an adult gap year. Sell up, travel, write . . . see what the world offers you."

I can't deny even the idea of it stirs something new in me. I need adventure. New horizons. Different challenges that don't revolve around watching a husband die.

"I need time to catch my breath," I explain. "This feels too fast. I think I'm a bit behind you. It feels like you've had longer than me to get used to the idea . . . while I've been so in love with Cam. So obsessed with his memory. So . . . *fractured*."

"Of course you have been. That's why I never said anything, all this time."

He is ever respectful of Cam and me because he's lived this.

"Kate, it took me years to even consider the real possibility that there could be someone else for me. Someone I'd actually let into my life, instead of endlessly pushing people away. You're barely two years into life without your husband. Don't ever feel rushed."

It would be easier not to feel rushed if he was less amazing. People search their whole adult lives for someone like this.

"Our entire relationship has been built on my catastrophe," I tell him. "You're instinctive with me when I'm struggling, but how will this work when I'm back on top? Are we going to be the same when I don't need you anymore? When I'm driven and decisive and accomplished and successful? Because those are all the things I haven't had a chance to aim for, and I need them like I need oxygen."

He nods, as I imagine more about how it would really be. This is all very romantic and "whirlwind" now, but it's not real life. Not when you have a five-year-old.

"When we're competing over whose work is more important or which one of us is taking school holidays off, is this going to feel so charming?" I ask.

"It's got to be better than sitting together in Emergency Departments and at deathbeds," he observes.

"Lots of couples fall apart when life gets hard. We wouldn't, because we've already made it through the worst. But, Hugh, you haven't met the woman I want to become. *I* haven't met her yet. I'm forty, and I've loved one man my entire adult life. I don't know who I am without Cam, other than the woman who lost her husband. And I don't want to be that woman anymore. I have to stop looking back."

I haven't felt this level of clarity, ever. A radically different picture of how my life could be has fallen into view. I can't unsee it.

"You're lit up," he says, his eyes a clear gray. "This is what I want for you, obviously."

This is heartbreaking. But unavoidably so. To pursue this with him now, while we're aware of this pull toward true independence, would set us both up for failure.

"You need to go," he says. "Probably as soon as possible."

Already?

"Can I take some leave?" I ask. "Organize the house? Shouldn't I see this film project through?"

He taps my foot with his, on the grass. "Look, I know I said you were crucial, Whittaker, but I'm sure I'll be able to bumble through it without you."

He makes me smile as we pull ourselves to our feet.

"Hugh, tell me you understand this is not—"

"About me, I know. It's about you. And it needs to be."

"Can I have another hug?" I ask, bereft already without him.

"Aren't you terrified of where it might lead?" he asks, teasing me, as he pulls me into one of those hugs you settle right into, until your breathing and heartbeats sync. With my cheek to his chest, closer than ever, inhaling the scent of his skin with his arms wrapped tightly around me, I want to revoke this entire conversation. I could devote myself to loving him so easily. And that's exactly the problem.

Neither of us wants to be the first to pull away. In the end, it's a mutual action and, in the disentanglement, he somehow ends up holding my hand. He brings it to his lips and kisses it, holding the kind of eye contact that conveys a primal connection for the ages.

Find your way to someone who'll love you just as much as I do.

I think we can consider that done, Cam.

39

Six weeks later

The last things to go are the neon sticky notes Cam had used to label things when he began losing his words. I remember the day I came home from work to a house *covered* in colored notes. TOASTER. CLOCK. TV. MIRROR. They were on everything. It must have taken him all day. When I walked in, he searched my face, probably hoping it wouldn't set me off—we'd learned that, with grief, the little things are the big things. It certainly winded me, but I held it together.

"You've redecorated," I said, and he pulled me into his arms as we looked at the vibrant labels around us and I tried not to cry. There'd been a time years earlier when I'd come home to rose petals scattered all over the house.

After a while, the labels hadn't worked anymore because, in addition to forgetting what things were called, he forgot how to read. I remember him standing in our bathroom after a shower, towel around his waist, hair glistening, studying the toothbrushes.

"What are these?" he'd asked me.

"Read the word," I'd prompted.

"What word?"

It was like selective blindness. Objects right in front of him were invisible. There were no words for him anymore and no words for me. I couldn't see how any person could get by without the alphabet—let alone a literature professor—but gradually words left him altogether and we could communicate only by my imagined ESP. Sometimes I liked to think he understood my thoughts as we looked each other in the eyes. Mostly I hoped he didn't. The dark circling in my brain by the time Cam had lost the power of speech was not for innocent minds. It would have broken him.

I take a quick breath now and pull the label off the hearth of the fireplace. After he died, I'd Blu-Tacked and sticky-taped the notes to everything because they were all falling off, and I couldn't bear to throw out his handwriting. But now it's like ripping off a Band-Aid and I feel my resolve slipping.

Even harder are the longer notes where Cam would capture fragments of his mind the way the rest of us might jot down a shopping list. They were innocuous at first: KATE IS AT WORK. HAVE A SHOWER THEN LIE DOWN. One day, I found one that said THE BOY'S NAME IS CHARLIE and it utterly destroyed me.

Grace and Mum had tried to remove the notes a few days after the funeral and I'd dissolved. They thought I was clinging to something upsetting, but I wasn't. These were the last fragments of Cam's decaying mind. The last thoughts he put enough weight on to want to record. Maybe it was the writer in me, but they seemed important. Late at night, beaten by insomnia, I'd sometimes pick one up and trace the letters. I was like a forensic linguist, marking the exact point in his disease when he would have written something down in this style. I could tell by the shakiness of the handwriting.

The spelling. Whether a word was held intact by the alphabet or had descended into a string of nonsense symbols.

It sounds silly, but I was always searching for a sign. Just a gut instinct I had that one of these notes would one day hit all previous communication between Cam and I out of the park. Perhaps I'd crack the code and find a love letter from Cam beyond the grave, prepared for me in advance like I was living in some sort of real-life *P.S. I Love You.*

But that didn't happen. Cam had well and truly lost the capacity to pull off a stunt that complex. I scrunch the first note now and throw it into the fire. There's nothing romantic about labels. Another two notes combust the second they hit the flames. Before long, I'm in a pyrolytic frenzy, grabbing notes off every surface in the house, throwing them into the fire, and watching them light up brightly and shrivel almost instantly. Symbolic of our relationship. And, after many tears, all the notes are burnt out, as is my hope that there was ever going to be a secret P.S., and I feel like I've torn down Cam's last-ditch attempt at holding together the fabric of our universe.

"I'm sorry," I whisper. "For everything."

By "everything," I mean "kissing Hugh." And I've no sooner apologized to Cam than I'm hit by a powerful memory of how that kiss had felt, and I have to apologize again. *Will the survivor's guilt ever end?*

Now it's almost on the market and we're leaving, the house isn't ours anymore. Not really. Charlie's been outside, saying goodbye to the backyard, and comes bustling inside now. "Hold my hand," he says, and I know this is for my benefit, not his. "Goodbye, bedroom," he says to his empty room. "Goodbye, toilet. Thank you for your service."

We both laugh. The kid's been watching way too much decluttering with me on Netflix.

As we farewell our spaces, I make sure I'm the last to leave each one. Flicking off light switches. Turning off dreams.

When we finally lock the front door and walk back up our garden path for the very last time, it's meant to feel like walking into a new future. It doesn't. It's all wrong. I should have a husband. Charlie should have a dad. I'd trade all the riches that await us overseas for just one more minute to say a proper goodbye.

The people who lose their person in an instant say they wish for that. But sometimes you miss out on it after a long illness too. You're never really sure when something is about to pass you by. There's so much focus in grief on getting through all the "firsts." First birthday without the person. First Christmas. First day of a new year they'll never share with you. Before that, though, there's a series of "lasts." And by the time you're aware of them, you've missed them. Things fade beyond comprehension. It's too late for the words you've been saving.

I bundle Charlie into the car and close his door. In those moments of quiet as I walk around the back of the car before I open the driver's door, I try to compose myself and fail. The poor child is looking for a leader and has to do the job himself.

"Don't cry, Mummy," he says as I put on my seatbelt through a blur of tears. "We're going to a party!"

Yes. We are.

My farewell from work has been organized in a private function room at a favorite Italian restaurant not far from the office, in Braddon. Everyone is going to be there. Including Hugh, to whom I've typed countless text messages since we came back from New Brighton, most of them ready to backtrack on everything I've planned and just give in to this and be with him. Somehow I've found the emotional fortitude to erase every message.

I'd planned to show up looking like a woman on a mission to rebuild her life. I'd leave no doubt that this was the right decision and would be good for us. Instead, I try not to cry as Charlie swings open the restaurant door and everyone turns in our direction. I imagine they're all thinking, "Oh my God, will Kate ever pull herself together? It's been *years*."

All the words I have imagined in people's heads since Cam died have painted a very judgmental picture. But it feels like every step you take when you're grieving is being dissected.

Be careful, they think.

Too fast!

Too slow.

Too happy-looking.

Aren't you better yet? When can we have the old Kate back, because this whole grief thing is getting old?

"Oh, you look *stunning*!" Sophie gushes. "You're so brave, Kate. Traveling the world on your own!"

"I'm going too!" Charlie pipes up, and that breaks the tension a little as I wipe my eyes and hope it was the waterproof mascara I'd used this morning.

People crowd in and hug me and tell me how big Charlie is getting and how like his father he is, and I smile and nod and thank them for their good wishes and know that Hugh is standing in the other corner, smiling and nodding and talking to our colleagues too . . . aware of me, across the room.

Bit by bit we're jostled closer to each other as if we're at one of Jane Austen's balls, exchanging social niceties with each new dance partner in turn, threading ourselves through the room until we wind up face-to-face, just as the music swells.

"Hi," I say.

"Hi," he answers.

We're constrained by a restaurant full of our personal stake-holders, who are trying not to look but at the same time can't help dragging up a pew and a bucket of popcorn and a pair of opera glasses, because God forbid they miss a single nuance of this interaction.

"Can I see you outside for a minute, Kate?" he asks, in the sort of believable tone that should win him an Oscar. I follow him outside as if we are absenting ourselves on state business. As we go, Sophie lures Charlie over with a game on her phone, and then we're out on the street, alone, in spring sunshine.

Do not ask for your job back, I instruct myself. *And do not kiss him.* Simple instructions, you'd think, but nothing about this is simple.

"It's good to see you," he says. "Must have been tough leaving the house."

The tears I've been blinking back since I got here respond to his words instantly. The house isn't the only thing it's hard to say goodbye to.

Do not cry. Do not even start, because you'll never stop.

"How have you been?" I ask, terrified that I pulled the plug on this too early, before anything was properly tested. In fact, standing here now on the path outside the restaurant, seeing the sun filtering through Hugh's dark hair, his blue eyes intense, I realize just how wrong I might have been. I'm close to calling the whole trip off in a panic and telling Hugh there's been a terrible mistake, because I think I might be in love with him . . . *know I am.*

"Kate?"

"What?"

"What?"

"Sorry?" I gasp.

"I said I think you've made the right decision," he tells me.

Oh.

"This trip is exactly what you need."

No.

NO!

You're what I need, Hugh!

"You need to breathe different air." He says it like he's been turning these words over for weeks, basting them, marinating them, simmering them in a pan until they're cooked through.

"Stop looking at my mouth, or I'm going to lose my resolve," he orders me, and I immediately need further information. Lose his resolve about what?

"I mean it, Kate. Stop looking at me like that unless you want me to kiss you."

Trick question, surely . . .

My body aches for his and steps toward him while the last shreds of sense in my mind dig in their heels and pull with all their might backward on the rope. I keep slipping despite their efforts.

Hugh puts his hands on my arms and physically resists me. "The one thing I've thought most about since the weekend in New Brighton is whether or not I can betray Cam's confidence now that he's gone," he says.

I feel myself pushing less on Hugh's arms at the mere mention of this. He drops his hands back to his sides; I'm no longer a threat. The secret is enough of a barrier to stop me from throwing myself at him. Again. Perhaps it always will be.

And that's when I realize Hugh is in an impossible place. He's trapped by his own integrity, and I'm the only one who can rescue him. But doing so will leave me in the dark forever and will leave this immovable obstacle in our path.

"Don't tell me," I say quickly, while knots of not knowing twist tighter inside me. "It's obviously important. I can't allow you to let yourself down. Or Cam."

He exhales and puts his hands on his hips, looking skyward for a minute. I know exactly why. This decision spells the end of us. A true stalemate where neither will surrender, and nothing will be won.

It feels like there really isn't any hope. We'll pretend it's okay and might agree to try this again when I get back from the *Eat, Pray, Love* thing. Maybe we'll even give it another shot for a while. But this will always sit between us, and relationships can't work like that. It will eat me up and then it will devour the two of us and turn on Charlie. I can't let him lose Hugh, too. If I can't move past this, we can't do it at all.

He pulls me into a hug and kisses the top of my head. "Goodbye, Kate," I imagine him saying into my ear, although he doesn't need to speak.

How I get through the rest of the farewell is a mystery science itself couldn't solve. How Hugh gets through a few brief, appropriate words about me when someone taps a knife on the side of a wineglass is anyone's guess. He keeps it short and professional.

"Kate, your resilience under fire has knocked our socks off. For four years, the university has benefited from your creativity, and your colleagues from your friendship. We wish you both all the very best for the adventure that lies ahead."

I manage to stand up beside him and respond. It's nothing short of a miracle.

"Thank you," I begin, my voice cracking. "You've all been nothing but supportive since Day One. Ground zero, really. I hope none of you ever has to go through something as hard as what Charlie and I have faced, but if you do, I hope you're surrounded by good people. I'm grateful to every one of you."

Especially you is implied, as I look at my former boss, and find it's him with the tears in his eyes now. He kisses me formally on the cheek and hands me a gift.

"Open it, Mummy!" Charlie says, jumping off Sophie's lap and running over. Everyone laughs.

I fumble with the ribbon and then nudge the lid off the little box. Inside is a silver pendant, made of a gemstone that glistens green and blue and gold in different lights. There's a little card in the box from the jeweler. It says *northern lights*.

"It's labradorite," Hugh says, more knowledgeable about gemstones than I would have expected. "Legend has it a fragment of the aurora fell from the sky into the stone. Thought it might keep you focused."

I think of the stars stuck on Norway on the poster I kept on my wall for all those years.

Hugh smiles. "Top of your bucket list, right? You can't work with someone for four years and not notice her screensaver. One of us had to have attention to detail."

I laugh and wonder how many other details he's logged—and how much I've missed. But everyone's flocking around me now, hugging me, shaking Charlie's hand in a grown-up fashion that delights him, wishing us well for our big adventure. Hugh steps to the back of the room and busies himself in a conversation with the restaurant's chef.

"Mummy started a blog!" Charlie announces loudly. "For our holiday!"

"Shhh, sweetie, that's really just for us, so we'll remember it."

"But we're not like Daddy," he says, as if I have come down in the last shower. "It's called 'Charlie and Mummy's Excellent Adventure.'"

I avoid eye contact with everyone. All of this, every part of it, is too close to the bone.

And just like that, it's over. Hugh walks us out.

He scoops Charlie into the air and lifts him high above our heads, where he whoops and hollers delightedly and settles into Hugh's arms for a big hug that hurts my heart. I need Tylenol again, the way I needed it the night Cam died. I wasn't prepared for how much this goodbye was going to hurt. Hadn't considered I was piling another type of grief onto the first.

"Look after Mummy while you're away," Hugh says to Charlie, who's still in his arms. Just seeing a man holding him again feels bittersweet. Hugh is purposely avoiding my gaze now, which gives me an opportunity to really look at him, and that only drives home the distinction of what I'm giving up.

"We are going away for a very long time," Charlie informs him. "Will you forget us?"

We're obsessed with memory in our house. Goes with the territory.

"I won't forget you," he says, and Charlie throws his arms around Hugh's neck again, almost strangling him as Hugh looks at me over Charlie's shoulder, reaches for my hand, and squeezes it. "I promise."

40

I cry from the tarmac at Sydney airport to the tarmac in LAX, and half the time I don't even really know what I'm crying over. It's not just about Cam. Or Hugh. It's about everything. Even the freedom lying ahead. How the customs official will recognize puffy-eyed me from my passport photo, I don't know. Ironically, we're stopping in LA to start our trip with a visit to the Happiest Place on Earth, which has its work seriously cut out for it.

The princesses get to me in the first five minutes. So smiley and perfect. Peddling lies about life and love and magic and happy endings. *Sometimes you get your prince,* I want to shout at them. *And then he is taken away!*

I miss Cam at every turn. This was never meant to be just Charlie and me. Cam and our baby were meant to be here as well. I spend the whole time queuing behind complete families, trying not to look as ripped off as I feel, while Charlie, oblivious to my sadness, soaks in all the wonder.

By the time we reach New York City and fall into our seats at a Broadway matinee, I'm starting to acclimatize. We've been here only half a day and I have fallen under the city's spell. The lights, the activity, the way the neon billboards in Times Square flash on the wall of our hotel room. Just the relentless "getting on with it," I think. And then I take Charlie to the top of the Empire State Building late at night.

"This is in that movie you like," he says.

"*Sleepless in Seattle*," I confirm.

There was a line in it that struck me. Something about people who've loved before being more likely to love again. If life was really like a romantic comedy, I'd turn around and Hugh would be standing here, surprising me. Surprising us.

But this is not fiction. And Hugh is ten thousand miles away, giving me exactly the space I insisted on.

Charlie and I look downtown toward One World Trade Center and I'm overcome at the collective grief this city has faced. So much loss on such a large scale in one morning—the families of every victim just as fractured as our own.

And yet this city's lights still dance.

Central Park still blooms.

The shows go on. Grief is absorbed into its story. And it's extraordinary.

If Disneyland was the low point, New York is a turning point for me. I realize selling our house and traveling was exactly the right idea. Being here is the fresh start of the rest of our lives.

When Charlie falls into bed after a long afternoon playing in the autumn leaves in Central Park, I take out my laptop, open a new document, and type the words I've resisted for so long.

Chapter One.

I stare at the screen for a long time, trying to work out where best to begin, pretending I know what I'm doing. Then I remember the workshop at the festival: "Almost Fiction." Write what you know, even if the details are different. And so I began to write:

If you wanted to, you could be with him in minutes.

I read that a widow's only job in the first twelve months is to keep herself alive, and I understand the achievement. Because when your husband dies, he never stops not being here. He resolutely stays away. Silent.

In the dark days immediately following his death, I couldn't imagine grief more raw than it was then, when the wound was freshly inflicted and exposed.

Back then I hadn't known that the wound would never close over. Hadn't known it would slice open, over and over again—at the sound of a song, or the sight of the perfect gift for him in a bookstore, or at a certain scent on the breeze.

Two years after his death, the triggers of grief were as acute as they were two days in. More acute, perhaps, because at two days there was the benefit of disbelief: *This couldn't be true. It's not happening.*

At two years, it is real. Embedded.

And then I found myself in New York City. A city in which my heart remembered how to beat, not just because it had to, but because it wanted to. This city scooped me from rock bottom and dragged me to the surface where I could burst through and breathe again. It showed me that maybe my world didn't end because my husband's did. Maybe there's a life beyond "widow." Maybe I wouldn't die of grief, after all. . . .

As the seasons change and the temperature cools, I show Charlie all our old haunts. Paris and Venice and Prague.

We're standing outside Cam's favorite pub in Bloomsbury, London, and I close my eyes, put my arms in the air, and spin around.

"What are you doing, Mummy?"

"She's soaking up the literary spirit of the whole of Bloomsbury," I hear Cam say. "Just like last time."

Goose bumps erupt on my skin. I slow the spinning but keep my eyes shut, a smile emerging straight from my heart and spreading through my body like sunshine. I should have known he'd turn up here. If I stay very still and very open, our energies feel so close it's as if we can almost touch in this place where love is infinite. Limitless. A transient crossover between where we are and wherever Cam might be.

My phone beeps with a message. It's a solar flare alert from the Aurora Advisory Service I'm subscribed to in Norway.

This is it. Top of my bucket list. The perfect alignment of everything that really counts. I can't help feeling on some inexplicable level that Cam is responsible—as if he controls the sun's behavior and our proximity to the best place in the world from which to see the one thing that's tantalized me most since I was sixteen years old. I touch the pendant hanging around my neck. Perhaps it's bringing us luck, infused with Hugh's ability to make things better and easier for me, ever since the day I met him.

"You always make amazing things happen, Mummy! And now you're turning up the lights!"

Turning up the lights. I remember the advice of a good friend just after Cam had died. She'd lost her baby daughter and had decided Georgie's short life would turn the lights up in her family's life, not down. It's only now that her advice is sinking in.

It's not Cam pulling the strings.

It's not Hugh.

It's me.

Every choice I make either brightens our lives or darkens them. I remember the night Cam died, and my first observation being the extent to which I was still here.

Alive.

Breathing.

This is not a fork in the road, I realize. It's just the road. There's no Story A and Story B. There's one, imperfect, meandering direction.

As our plane lands on the tarmac at night in Oslo, I imagine I can see the aurora out the window. The city lights are too bright here, but I *want* to. Reports are coming in already of strong beams in Senja, just under a two-hour flight from here.

I pull down our bags from the overhead lockers and reach for Cam's heavy winter coat, which I've brought with me. I've been wearing a lighter one of my own until now, but if I'm going to see the lights without him, I'm going to see them wrapped in his warmest jacket.

And when the coat pulls free from under someone else's bag, several pieces of paper float out of the pocket and onto my face. Pink and orange sticky neon notes, covered in Cam's handwriting.

I feel my heart thud in my chest. He must have put these in his pocket one day and forgotten about them. I'm standing in the aisle of the plane, packed in with other passengers, about to fulfill my life-long dream, and this is the least convenient time to have a grief crisis.

I'm scared I'll drop them getting off the flight, wrangling all of our stuff, and the doors aren't even open yet, so we'll be a while. My hand is trembling as I turn the first one over.

It's dated August 5. I know exactly when that was, and what an achievement it would have been for Cam to have figured out the date. It's the same day that Hugh went AWOL. My stomach lurches and I'm hot and flustered and I reach and rotate the air-conditioning vent to blow in my direction, which of course it cannot do from here.

The note reads: ASKED HUGH HE GETS GEN.

He gets Gen? What does that even mean?

The note makes no sense at all. I can't read these now, not in the aisle of this plane. I stuff the notes back into the inside pocket of the coat, my hand shaking, check that I haven't dropped any, and zip the pocket up, tight. I suspect I'm carrying the explanation of the secret between Hugh and Cam. The issue that tore both of them up and tore Hugh and I apart.

But right now, I need to make a conscious choice not to let these men and their history get in the way of the one experience I've longed for more than any other, for most of my life.

41

Sometimes you can see the aurora only through a camera. Not tonight. We can see it out of the bus window as we're driving to our hotel after the next flight.

The bus draws up to the entry and we pile out. I can barely grab our bags fast enough, race inside, check in, dump everything but the camera and our coats, and rush back outside.

It's freezing cold and we stand in the garden of the hotel, entranced as iridescent greens and purples dance quickly and silently across the sky. No one second is the same. The patterns shape-shift and, in this moment, my heart is fuller than it's ever been.

As I glance down at Charlie, I can see the lights reflected in his wide eyes. He can barely believe what he's seeing, and I love that I'm sharing this with him.

I think of Cam, and how he'd have loved this. And I touch the pendant again. Hugh's choice. But mostly I think of me, and how immeasurably glad I am that I made this happen. Put myself first. Prioritized this dream over all the others. At least this once.

I take out the bucket list from my bag, and a pen. I cross off number one on the list: *See the Northern Lights*. While I'm at it, I cross off *See a Broadway show* and *Gondola in Venice*, *Christmas Market in Prague*, and *Solo trip overseas*. Charlie's with me, of course, but I don't think a five-year-old counts.

The farther down the list I go, the more I realize I've done. *Write a book* is still there, but that's underway. *Live by the beach*—of course. I still haven't found a house, but that will happen at some point.

It's now almost midnight, and getting even colder, and Charlie's tapped out. I suggest we go inside, have hot chocolates, and get snuggled in bed. We can leave the curtains pulled back in our room and watch the lights until we can't keep our eyes open.

"I've never been allowed to stay up so late before," Charlie says, thrilled at this plan.

An hour later, he's fast asleep. I take out my laptop, sit by the window, and try to capture the vision in words. I feel like I'll never have the vocabulary to do it justice. I also can't think straight, knowing those sticky notes are in this room.

Damn. I can't leave this alone. I stare out the window some more for distraction, still astonished by the sight, and realize I'm shaking. I know I need to read the notes and put the final puzzle piece of my double-edged grief into place, even if it hurts like hell.

I take the notes carefully out of the jacket pocket and set them down on the table in front of me, in date order. And try to prepare myself for whatever I'm about to learn.

I reread the first one: ASKED HUGH HE GETS GEN. It still makes no sense. Is this about Genevieve? It baffles me that Cam knew about her before I did. But what can she possibly have to do with this?

I turn to the next note, hoping for an explanation, and when I get it, the words make me gasp. Every cell in my body seems to cave in at once. This turns my entire world upside down.

Cam had written in shaky lettering: KATE WILL SUFFER. HUGH MIGHT HELP END. BEST FOR ALL.

Understanding begins to seep into my blood and is conveyed to every extremity of my body. For long moments I am perfectly still. I know what Cam asked Hugh to do. I know why Hugh was so tortured by the decision, and why he couldn't think straight with me around. I love that he, of all people, took three weeks away to properly consider it, given it would have been absolutely illegal. Cam was well beyond the point where he could have made the decision in any state the law would regard as "sound mind." And at last I understand why it's so important to Hugh that he doesn't betray Cam's trust and tell me.

The second-to-last note confirms my fears. HUGH SAYS NO. DEVASTATE . . .

A single tear falls from my face onto the note, onto words already blurred by Cam.

I turn over the last note: THOUGHT HE WOULD SAY YES. LOVES KATE.

The attendant at the service desk at five-thirty the next morning speaks perfect English—thank you universe—because I can barely string any sensible words together.

"I need to get home to Australia," I say. "Actually, to Launceston. I can't seem to work out the most direct way out of here."

"I want to see more lights," Charlie protests, while the attendant finds the information I need.

"Charlie, there's been a second solar flare. If we're lucky, we'll see the Borealis and the Australis in one week! The Southern version is just as gorgeous—or maybe even more beautiful. Pink, purple, green, and gold. If we miss it this time, I promise we'll go chasing it together, as long as it takes us."

I am his leader now. Two parents rolled into one. I think back to the flailing mother Charlie can't remember from when he was a baby and realize how far I've come. I'm still making mistakes by the bucketload. Still in the dark about a lot of things, and I can't begin to describe how much I'm still dreading the teenage years, but there's a new confidence now. After you've been through the worst, you can handle anything the world throws at you. Hopefully even a logistical arrangement as complicated as the one I'm attempting to pull off.

As soon as the tickets are confirmed, I phone Sophie at work.

"Please don't ask questions, and *do not* tell Hugh, but I need you to book me a room at the same hotel he's staying at in Launceston this week for the conference. He's still going, isn't he?"

I was meant to be there too. My phone pinged with the reminder yesterday. I forgot to remove the event from my calendar.

"This is the moment I have been training you for during our entire time together at work," I say.

Sophie loves a conspiracy and assures me she'll get right onto it. "I'm giving this a code name," she confesses. "Project Harry Styles. Kate, you should know I am deeply invested in the outcome. The whole office is!"

"Mummy, you seem wild," Charlie says, while I throw our belongings into our bags and drag him downstairs again for the bus to the airport.

I am, I think. *Wild about Hugh.*

The fact that he would even take the time to seriously consider doing what Cam asked of him speaks volumes about his principles.

As does the fact that he couldn't go through with it. Not helping Cam, potentially making things easier for me in a way that he thoroughly understood through his own loss, nearly destroyed him. Particularly if, as seems obvious now in retrospect, he was in love with me. Not telling me eventually meant losing me, even though every step of his conduct paints him in the very brightest light.

At the airport, I put my computer, phone, and bag through the security scanner. No books this time. I'm writing one instead. I usher Charlie through first. Charlie, who has a shot now at having a mum who's not only finding her feet but finding long-term happiness, just as his dad wanted for us.

Cam's reason for wanting to end his life prematurely also speaks volumes about how much he loved us and didn't want to see us suffer his drawn-out death. The ultimate sacrifice would have been the ultimate gift, in a way. The months from August onward were increasingly heartbreaking.

What it must have done to Hugh to watch Cam deteriorate. Every step toward his death a reminder that—illegal though it would have been—he could have stepped in and cut short our suffering. All the frantic calls and meltdowns from me. At one point I'd even confessed to Hugh that I'd wished Cam was already dead, to spare him the indignity that he hated so much. Hugh will have held himself responsible for our ongoing misery—I know him. And even when I was throwing this secret back in his face, furious at him for not telling me, he kept his promise to my husband. I can't even process the caliber of the man.

"Grace!" I say. "There's not much time. I'm stepping onto a flight." I'm handing our boarding passes to a flight attendant and getting glared at by fellow passengers for being on the phone, as if nobody appreciates the urgency of this situation.

"We're all watching the live stream of the aurora here," Grace gushes. "It looks phenomenal."

"It blew my mind. But please listen. I need you to babysit."

"What? When?"

"In about thirty hours. In Launceston."

"Is this a joke?"

"Hugh will be there. Hopefully."

There's a brand of squeal on the end of the phone that I haven't heard since the nineties. "About fucking time!"

"Have some decorum, Grace, please!" I suggest, imitating Mum.

"Yes, Mary," she says, laughing. "But speaking of a lack of decorum, I have news about Justin."

"My neighbor?" I ask, playing dumb. "Don't tell me he's sold that bike?"

"My *boyfriend*! And no, Kate. I'm sure he'll still take you for rides on it."

I'm dizzyingly excited for her. And I've been away far too long. "You and Justin? Well, who could have seen that coming. . . ."

She laughs. "Stop! I thought he was interested in you first, and he said I must be obtuse if I couldn't see what was going on between you and Hugh from that first night with the grenade. Reckons it was you two who needed the bomb under you. Or the bike. Can confirm he is very much DTF, BTW. OMG."

I snort. And squeal. Our teenage boy-crazy selves would highly approve.

"Grace, I'm a mess! Or I will be after this flight. Not from the air travel for once. I've never been more nervous in all my life. What if it's too late? Oh! I have to turn my phone off. Love you. Ring

Sophie from the office about the details, okay? Code name: Project Harry Styles. Not a word to Hugh!"

I sit back and pretend in front of Charlie that I'm not sitting here stifling a multipronged anxiety attack. As soon as we're in the air and able to, I plug us both into the entertainment system and try to distract myself with rom-coms.

It always works out in the end. Isn't that what I hated at Disneyland? The perfection of it all? Yet here I am coordinating something far more logistically difficult than meeting on top of the Empire State Building, right in the middle of the indefinite period of space and time Hugh has been diligently giving me. Too much space. Now that I'm on my way home, that space feels like an impossible chasm. What if he did as I suggested and didn't wait? I have the worst case of cold feet I've ever experienced. Can I really put myself out there like this?

I switch the entertainment off. Charlie's fallen asleep and I have a glass of wine. If I focus, I'll have the first section of my book finished by the time we land. It's not great, but the bones of it are there. Something to work with, anyway, and plenty of ideas. It has been cathartic getting it out of my brain and onto the page over the last few months. I've been sending it to Grace, chapter by chapter, and she's been encouraging. But then, she always is. I wanted to write about grief, but it's landing on the page as so much more than that. Maybe because, even in loss, there's so much more to life.

42

Eight thousand words and ten thousand miles later, we're flying over Australian soil. The thought makes me cry. Or maybe it's the sleep deprivation that does it. Could be the escalating nerves. In any case, I'm a wreck as we land at Launceston Airport. I turn on my phone and get a call from Sophie. I hope everything's gone to plan.

"Okay, I know I was just supposed to arrange the flight and the hotel, but, Kate—you know that scene in *Pretty Woman* where Richard Gere is looking for her and she's in the bar in that black dress . . ."

Do I want to hear this?

"I organized a dress," Sophie explains, having gone rogue. "And a bogus meeting with Hugh at seven p.m. in the bar of the hotel. Grace is lined up to babysit Charlie. I think I've risk-managed the heck out of this, Kate. You'd be proud of me!"

"Tell me I'm not making a huge mistake?" I ask Grace, as I fall out of the airport shuttle bus and into her arms.

It had seemed so romantic in Norway. But I was half a world away from the site of potential failure. The knowledge that Hugh is in this very building is the most comforting and hair-raising information I could possibly be turning over in my increasingly anxious brain. Ironically, he's the one person who would know how to pacify me.

"The only mistake would be not trying," Grace says, shepherding Charlie into the elevator. "Now go. And have a shower! You look like you've been awake for years."

I key the card into the slot and lean on the door to my room, pull my bags inside, and fling open the bathroom door. Hanging there is the cocktail dress. Sleek. Sophisticated. Cobalt blue, "to bring out the auburn," apparently. Everything you'd expect from the office fashionista.

There's plenty of time to get ready, so I run the bath and add some of the hotel's lavender-scented oil. Hopefully it will calm my escalating jitters. I set the alarm for one hour from now, just in case. . . .

I wake up only because the water is stone cold. My phone is on the chair beside the bath, and I peer at the time. It's eight. EIGHT! Our meeting was at SEVEN. In my jet-lagged state I must have set the alarm for A.M. I leap out of the water and partly dry myself off, grab the white robe off the back of the bathroom door along with my bucket list and Cam's sticky notes, and flee the room.

Please be there, I chant as I run down the carpeted hall, wet hair dripping, and push the elevator button frantically, not that it makes any difference. Eventually I give up on the elevators and fling myself into the fire stairwell, taking the steps three at a time in bare feet, which hurts. I should have worn slippers. Who does this? Well,

Julia Roberts, obviously. But she was nineteen and stunning, and not jet-lagged to Norway and back. . . .

When I burst out of the fire door on the ground level, all eyes in the lobby turn to me. Is it really that newsworthy for a forty-year-old single mother to be running around the Grand Chancellor in nothing but a bathrobe, like a lovestruck teenager? I find the bar, which is packed with conference attendees and locals having a drink before the theater, and stand in the middle of it, spinning around, searching for Hugh.

He's nowhere. And, of course, I dashed out of my room with only the essentials, which apparently didn't include shoes, clothes, my phone, or the room key.

I've comprehensively messed this up, after so much seat-of-the-pants planning from the other end of the earth. What would Julia do? She'd talk to the doorman. He'd show her how to use cutlery properly and phone his friend in an expensive clothing boutique. But this isn't the movies. I'll have to beg the woman on the reception desk for Hugh's room number.

"I'm afraid I can't tell you that," she says. "But I can put in a call to his room."

It will have to do. It's just not remotely the Hollywood way I saw this unfolding in my mind.

"Your name is?"

"Kate," I tell her. "Whittaker." *In case he's forgotten.*

She dials a number and it rings out. "I'm sorry. No answer."

This has all been such a massive anticlimax. I thank her for her efforts and walk despondently back to the elevator bank, pressing the up button, just once this time.

The bell chimes almost immediately. The doors open and Hugh is lounging against the back of the elevator looking at his phone, shirtsleeves rolled up, loose tie, patience stretched by a "client" not turning up, no doubt. Me again.

He glances up to check that he's on the ground floor and does a double take when he sees me standing in front of him, in all my jetlagged glory: bare feet, tangled red hair falling in wet ringlets on the unflattering robe emblazoned with the hotel's logo. Neither of us speaks. We stare at each other like we've forgotten our lines, until the doors begin to shut and we both lurch forward and push them open with our hands.

He contemplates my attire and his eyes eventually come to rest on my face. "Still cavorting around in pajamas, I see."

"Technically, no," I say. "Just the robe."

He seems thrown off base by that.

"But this evening isn't turning out at all the way I'd planned," I add.

He laughs. "You're meant to be standing under a Norwegian light show," he says. "Number one on the bucket list, remember? Best display in decades, apparently. What happened?"

The elevator doors try to close on us again, and this time Hugh blocks both of them and I just stand there, reaching for my bucket list and Cam's sticky notes in my pocket. Exhibits A and B.

A warning bell starts to chime in the elevator, and Hugh takes my arm and drags me inside it. The doors finally close and it's just us. I push the number eight. Hugh's floor, according to Sophie, who I'd texted earlier. I can't remember the exact room number, but I was prepared to knock on every door, *Love Actually*–style, if I had to. There's not a rom-com I won't emulate.

"Where are we going?" he says.

"That's why I'm here," I explain. "I edited my bucket list, you see."

He looks confused, and I tighten the belt on my robe, feeling more exposed than I've ever been in my life.

"But there's something else I need to show you first," I say, handing him the first two of Cam's messages. His face shifts in recognition when he reads the words. When I pass him the third and he reads Cam's attempt to spell "devastated," his entire body crumples.

"I'm sorry you had to read those," he says, swallowing hard. I'm sorry *he's* having to.

"There was one more." When I pass the last note over, my hand is shaking, and he notices.

He reads the words to himself a few times. Then aloud. "'Loves Kate.' Cam was pretty far advanced with his dementia by that stage."

My heart quickens. *Tell me he hasn't changed his mind. . . .*

"But even then," Hugh continues, looking up almost shyly from across the elevator, "he got it."

"And seemed to be okay with it," I add cautiously. "Or is that wishful thinking?"

"It's not. Remember we'd go for those beers, earlier on? He told me one time that I needed to make sure you understood he deeply wanted to see you happy one day. He wasn't just saying it to make you feel better. He made me promise I'd try to get this through to you, if the time ever came. And then he said—"

Hugh chokes up, and I give him the moment he needs to finish what he's trying to tell me.

"He said, 'Hugh, I think when that time comes, you'll already be there.'"

Cam.

The elevator pings on the eighth floor, breaking us out of that moment, into this one.

"Shall we discuss this further in your room?" I suggest. "I left mine quickly without the door key, you see. I'd have to go back downstairs and get a spare one, and . . ."

He smiles, takes my hand, and leads me out of the elevator, down the corridor, and to the door of his suite.

"What were you saying about your bucket list?" he asks, looking for the key card in his wallet.

I gulp and pass the piece of paper to him. He reads the new words I've written at the top of the list, looks at me, hands the list back, and places his key card into the slot. It flashes red.

"I told you I don't have one-night stands anymore, Whittaker, even if having one with me is top of someone's bucket list."

I flush red. Now that he's gone off script, I don't know what to do.

"Even if you fly across the world and throw yourself at me, half-naked in a hotel elevator, I'm afraid I still can't help you with that." He shoves the key card into the slot again, leans into the door to push it open, and grabs the terry-cloth belt around my waist and uses it to pull me into the room.

"So we're at another stalemate, then?" I say. "What am I supposed to do now?"

"Well," he says, "I hired you for the superior problem-solving skills you claimed you possess in your written application. Don't tell me you exaggerated that?"

Is this a dare? Because I will absolutely rise to it.

I walk past him toward the bed, turn around, reach for his loosened tie, and pull him close. We're inches apart. I'm trying to think of something unarguably clever and sexy, but the jet lag is messing with my mind and I used up all my words in my book on the plane, which just leaves me with the option of doing something megastupid.

"Marry me?" I say, because, apparently, I have only one signature move, and I've lost all shame. All. Shame.

"Wow, Kate. You're really blue-skying this!" he says.

I rush *everything*. Proposing to Hugh was never in the plan. What must he think of me, arriving here out of nowhere, firing requests at him for a one-night stand, and, failing that, matrimony. . . .

He removes my fingers from their grip on his silk tie, undoes it, and slips it off. Then he takes two glasses down from the shelf at the kitchenette, opens the mini bar, and uncorks a bottle of champagne. He passes me a glass but leaves his on the bench and opens another button on his shirt.

It seems clear at this point he's chosen Option A: one-night stand. I'm kind of disappointed now, which is odd, given that I've had wedding bells on my mind for only the last two minutes.

But he doesn't take his shirt off yet. Instead he reaches into it and pulls out a necklace. Again, this is strange. He's not the jewelry-wearing type.

Dangling from the necklace, though, is something else.

A square-cut diamond ring.

He undoes the clasp of the necklace, takes my hand, turns it palm-up, and lets the ring slip from the chain and fall into my grasp.

"You had the aurora hanging around your neck all this time, representing your dream. I had this."

"To keep you focused?" I ask, unable to believe any of this is real.

"To keep me hopeful. I didn't want to interrupt your plans. I knew you had to take this trip, and why, but as soon as you left, I was just . . . *bereft*. Told myself it should be impossible to grieve this much for a woman who is still alive."

"I cried all the way to America. Desperately missing Cam. Desperately missing you. Wishing this whole thing wasn't so complicated."

"It is what it is," he says. He's right. It's a mash-up of inconceivable devastation and unbelievable wonder. A clash of two almost overpowering tragedies, through which hope has been pushing up quietly, tenaciously, all this time. Fighting for light. Needing just the right amount of spine-tingling courage to tip the future in a new direction.

When Cam and I had that car accident, time slowed. Our past collided with our future at an awful, agonizing pace I thought I'd never survive.

Time is warping again now, but in reverse. Everything Hugh and I have been through is being swept, suddenly, into a glorious whirlwind of all we can be. *This precious second chance.*

He glances at me for permission. Takes the ring out of my palm and hovers it over the end of my finger.

I've lost track of which one of us is asking now, but it doesn't matter. A wave of strength and confidence and certainty carries us in.

"All right, Kate, I'll marry you," he says. "Thought you'd never ask."

He slips the ring all the way onto my finger, and I'm too stunned by this entire turn of events to speak.

"You know you disarmed me the moment you threw yourself at me in the gym," he confesses, twisting the ring on my finger to check the fit.

It must be a joke, surely. Next to Purple Pants, he noticed *me?*

"Grace had just told you something awful about her fertility and that miserable relationship she was in, and she asked about you. And you'd made up some obvious lie downplaying how things were in your marriage. Grace wouldn't have a bar of it. Said your husband was delicious and how happy you were after all those years. I remember thinking, *Lucky him.* And thinking about all I lost with Gen."

I touch his arm.

"And then, when you walked into that interview and hit it out of the park, I realized all the self-deprecation at the gym was probably a genuine loss of confidence since you'd had a baby. It was refreshing after all the 'fake it till you make it' stuff everyone goes on with."

I don't want to interrupt this fairy tale he's telling me. He's looking at my disheveled self as we speak, somehow making me feel like the most desirable woman in the world.

"I didn't know I loved you though, until Cam asked me to help him. To help you. The way I felt about you came into sharp focus then. I very nearly capitulated. I realized I couldn't stand to see you go through something similar to what I'd been through. Particularly when I had the power to prevent the worst part of it."

"It never occurred to me, until I rocked up on Justin's motorcycle, that you and I could look at each other that way," I admit. "Then once I heard about Genevieve, I was overcome with this out-of-all-proportion *jealousy*. The kind you just don't have over your boss's distant flame. There's one bit I don't understand though. Andrew told me Genevieve and I were nothing alike. Said she was a knockout, if you remember . . ."

Hugh grimaces.

"Said he couldn't put his finger on what it was about me that reminded him of her."

"It's not Gen you remind him of. It's me, when I was with her. Because I'm happy again with you. It terrified me, feeling that way for a woman again. Still does. My biggest fear is—"

"Repetition," we both say at once. This path is treacherous. We cannot afford for another person we love to die.

He takes the glass from my hand, sets it on the bench, turns around, puts his hands on my shoulders, and gently pushes me back onto the bed. "It's been torture," he says. "Loving you through all of it. But when you left, I realized there was a fate even worse than your death."

"Separate lives," I answer for him. I'm crying now. Partly from everything he's saying, and partly because he's kicking off his shoes and joining me where I'm lying. He touches my face like he can't believe I'm really here. I can't believe it either. Then he smiles. That broad, rare, generous, gorgeous smile that turns me inside out whenever it's aimed in my direction. I love this man. Somehow with all my heart. The same heart that will also beat for Cam with an unstoppable rhythm until the day I die. For once, I won't over-think the mystery.

"Now, Ms. Whittaker," he says, kissing me in the longest, most excruciatingly unhurried way. "About that bucket list . . ."

EPILOGUE

Four years later

It's not long after sunset, during what we landscape and astropho-tographers call the "blue hour." I dig the legs of my tripod into the sand on the secluded beach on Bruny Island, Tasmania. While there's still a bit of light, I open the aperture wide, change the ISO, and set a twenty-second exposure, ready. I've figured out the expo-sure triangle and then some over the last few years.

Nine-year-old Charlie is beside me with the telescope Hugh bought him last Christmas. "Tell me again the order of things," he asks. We've been through it so many times!

"Grace, Justin, and the twins arrive tomorrow afternoon. We're picking them up from the ferry after school. Nanna flies in on the weekend." I look at the tall young boy standing beside me, about to turn ten. More than half his life without his dad, yet more like his dad every day.

The aurora forecast is strong again tonight, with a major geo-magnetic storm that might make it visible, at least to camera lenses, as far north as Canberra. That would have necessitated driving south of the city and finding somewhere safe to park off the Monaro Highway, or delving deep into Namadgi National Park.

It's so much easier from here. I've come to feel spoiled, knowing I can see it so close to home, so often.

We've been standing in this spot only a few minutes when the first beams of pink and purple light appear, first in my camera lens, and then in a less vivid way to the naked eye. Charlie and I squeal at the sight, even though we've seen it so many times together since that first night in Norway. I never take it for granted, living at a place where I can capture sunrises and sunsets on a deserted beach, and the aurora whenever it's visible.

The Tasmanian wilderness is so conducive to writing. I've just finished my third book. Contemporary romance is apparently my place in the writing world, not literary fiction, as Cam probably suspected all along.

Once I let go of trying to write something "impressive" and started just writing from the heart, words poured onto pages as if they'd been queued in my mind for decades. This is such an ideal place to write, in fact, that I have plans to build a cluster of three "tiny houses" on the property. We can rent them out and I can hold intimate writing mentorships and astrophotography retreats dotted through the year. There'll be a small space for the writing room of my dreams, facing south, over the beach, of course. I'll throw open the windows in summer and write with the scent of salt and the sound of crashing waves, and I'll snuggle under a blanket beside the fire in winter.

I adjust the camera settings again and take another long-exposure shot, while Charlie shows me the stars through his telescope, just as the veranda light pops on in the house behind us.

"Knew it," Charlie says. "She can't stand missing out on anything!"

We hear her before we can see her, and then two figures hove into sight on the beach, one tall, one tiny. She races up to us and throws her arms around my leg, begging to be lifted up to see the 'rora through the camera's viewfinder.

"Camryn Genevieve! You're meant to be in bed!" I say.

Hugh shrugs and smiles. "What can you do? Aurora-chaser like Mum and big brother."

Our lives aren't perfect, even under the southern lights. You can't bring together two adults and a child with shattering grief as a backstory and expect a smooth ride. We still make mistakes. We have rows. Hugh's new role with the University of Tasmania still gets stressful. I still write first drafts that convince me I have no idea what I'm doing, even several published books in.

But there's something about Camryn. She took three broken people and stitched us together as a family. She's one of the golden threads running through each of our lives. Hope, in human form.

"When is Ruby getting here?" Charlie asks.

Our second golden thread.

"She's just got to get final clearance from her doctor," I explain. "She's so close to having the baby now! But she and Hannah have everything crossed, and they'll make it."

Charlie twists his face in concentration and starts counting things on his fingers. "My stepnephew?"

I laugh. "It's a complicated family, isn't it, Uncle Charlie-to-be!"

Ruby might have been the image of her mother, but I never knew Genevieve. The more I'd gotten to know her, the more of Hugh I imagined I saw in her. The way she raked her hand through her hair in frustration. The extraordinary patience. The habit of taking the long packets of sugar in coffee shops and meticulously evening the distribution of the contents.

"Why don't you have a DNA test?" I'd coaxed him one Christmas. "Just to set your mind at ease, once and for all."

He'd resisted the idea for months. I know it was self-protection. What if he got his hopes up and she wasn't his? "We love her as if she's mine, Kate. What would it achieve?"

But something about Ruby expecting a child had tipped him over. The idea of never knowing whether this baby was his genetic grandchild would have eaten him up—and eaten up his mother too. She was positively agog at the idea of a great-grandchild.

And, of course, the result was just the miracle Hugh always deserved, so now we're officially a complex family of five, and I have a stepgrandchild on the way at forty-four and couldn't be more there for it.

"Are you free for a conference dinner on September sixteen?" Hugh asks, as Camryn squirms out of my arms and back into his. "Black-tie thing. I'm looking for a date."

"I don't know, that's months away!" I look back into the viewfinder and take a shot. "I guess so? Where is it?"

"Dublin," he says in a tone so deadpan he might as well have said it's in the local scout hall. "Thought you might be homesick."

I forget the aurora and look at my husband, with stars in my eyes and memories of that beautiful Northern Rivers hinterland, the weekend we found our way to each other. He's a little bit older and a little bit grayer than when we first met eight years ago, and so am I, but we know that every extra year is a privilege denied to the two we'll always love.

"Hugh," Charlie interrupts, his voice suddenly wavering with nerves.

We both look at him as he pulls some dog-eared papers from the Minecraft backpack he's been carrying around with him everywhere lately. He passes the paperwork to Hugh, and I notice his little hand shaking.

"What's this, mate?" Hugh says, activating the torch on his phone to illuminate the words. As he reads, he lights up with an expression more beautiful than any I've seen pass across his face in all the time I've known him.

"Adopting a stepchild," he says aloud, his voice cracking, as Charlie flings himself at him for a tight hug.

It blows my mind, in the very best way. Hugh passes me the papers so he can hug Charlie properly, and I notice Charlie has stuck a fluorescent-yellow sticky note on top of the government printout.

"I don't think Dad would mind," it says.

The tears are free-flowing now, all around. It's not just Charlie's unexpected request and everything it means to Hugh. It's the fact that he's building such an accurate understanding of the incredible man his father was.

The four of us stand together now, awestruck by the colors turning up the light in the darkness. And when I finally take a moment to glance from the aurora to my little plan B family, I'm overcome with a strong sense of Cam's nearness.

I've learned that love outlives death. It holds steady through despair. It won't fade, even as time elapses and distance increases and your world shifts. Cam's ongoing presence in my life is as fragile as the transient beams of light that dance across the sky. And as powerful. It reminds me that life is short, love is grand, and *Kate & Cam's Excellent Adventure* is timeless.

ACKNOWLEDGMENTS

When my husband died from a heart attack in 2016, I wrote his eulogy in disjointed notes on my phone at three a.m. The task felt bigger than language itself. These acknowledgments seem almost as difficult because it's not just about the book. It's about everything that happened in the seven years leading up to it, and I'd need another ninety thousand words to adequately express my gratitude for the outpouring of support we received. My heartfelt thanks to everyone who held us in your arms during our tragedy. You saved us.

Writing a deeply personal story and sharing it with the world is daunting. While much of Kate's experience is not my own (I have not found my Hugh), the grief is mine. From the moment I met Ali Watts, Amanda Martin, and the team at Penguin Random House Australia, I knew my words were safe. And I felt similarly secure when the manuscript landed in Zibby Owens's hands.

From our very first Zoom meeting, I've been swept into a wave of literary excitement led by Zibby, Anne Messitte, and the entire team, including my fellow Zibby Books authors. Special mention to Kathleen Harris and Madeline Woda, who have made the editing process a dream, and to Emi Battaglia, Sherri Puzey, and Sierra Grazia for their spectacular publicity and marketing. To Beca Kindling for her expert social media and to Graça Tito for her endless support from across the globe. Jeanne Emanuel, Bridie Loverro, Jordan Blumetti, Diana Tramontano, Lindsay Quackenbush, and Chelsea Grogan—my deep thanks for everything from tour planning, to podcasts, media pitching, partnerships, book clubs, and events. Your commitment to this book has been invaluable. To Sarah Horgan—my deepest thanks for creating such an artistic and soulful book cover.

To my gem of an agent, Anjanette Fennell, you've made my publishing dreams a reality, and I'll always be grateful for the enduring friendship that has grown out of our work together.

Gaetane Burkolter, you're my "story whisperer" and first-draft editor. You help me bring alive the skeleton of every new book. Bec Sparrow, your endorsement of this book means so much.

Amanda Whitley, Beatrice Smith, and all at *HerCanberra*, you gave my grief writing a soft place to land.

Kat, Ree, Annette, Kate, Mel, Annemarie, Cath, Fionna, Karen, Karen, Linley, Michele, Nina, and Beth—your early feedback gave me much-needed confidence. The Tuesday-night writing group, and Ness, Sal, Heidi, Tania, and Emma Z—your creativity influences mine.

Matt and the TNC team, you're a fantastic support. Jeff's colleagues and Barbara, heartfelt thanks for Jacksonville and New York.

Trevor, Elena, and Liza, thank you for your compassionate welcome into the club none of us wanted to join. Ann, thank you for lending me one of your heartbreaking stories; Megan, thank you for all of our chats about widowhood over the years. I have too many widowed friends to mention individually, but I love and admire you all.

ACKNOWLEDGMENTS

My writerly besties, Nina Campbell and Rachael Morgan, together with Anjanette—you've done more than you'll ever know in helping me reach for the stars.

Clair and Harry, thanks for all the lawn mowing while I write, and for rescuing us in myriad other ways. You're the real "hot neighbors." And April, thank you for your sparkling enthusiasm.

Alison A, for the joy with which you greet each new chapter; Ali, Al, and Lynd, for the enduring love since we were teenagers, and for reading every word for over thirty years. Sal, for all the lasagna, the gardening, and the professional advice you've given so generously—and for the late-night hot chocolates when it all got too much. And for picking me up every time—all of you.

Audrey, for every time I've interrupted our work with plot problems, for every draft you've read and every word of encouragement you've given me, I thank you from the deepest part of my heart. You are extraordinary.

Paul, Abbey, and Lucy, thanks for believing in me, loving me, and putting up with me and my distractedness.

Sarah, thank you for #KTF and for telling me honestly when it's not good enough. You're always right and you make me a better writer, sister, and person.

Victoria and Duncan, Jake and Meg—I will always love you, and not just because you're an ongoing part of Jeff in my world. Rex and Julian—thank you for being the light in our lives. He would have adored you in ways the world has never seen.

To my beloved parents, Barrie and Claire, who have a cameo in the book as their amazing selves, since the moment you taught me to read, you've supported every step. This story is a tribute to your love as well, and to Dad's endless and unfathomably patient care of Mum through dementia.

ACKNOWLEDGMENTS

Hannah and Sophie, since you were little you've watched me work for this dream. Now that you're adults, I love sharing it with you as it unfolds. The way you responded as teenagers when our world shattered is the most impressive thing I've ever witnessed, and your resilience since has been inspiring.

Sebastian, you handle life without Dad in a way that couldn't impress me more, with a maturity beyond your years. Our writing dates and mutual creative encouragement are some of the most magical and unexpected delights in my life. Dad was always immeasurably proud of you, and always will be.

Jeff, I needed to create two heroes in an attempt to capture the extent of my love for you, and even then it was impossible. You will always be more than Cam and Hugh combined. You said to "be brilliant." You said to go out into the world and get on with life. You could never have known how hard that would be without you, and how fervently I wish I didn't have the experience to have written this novel, but I hope, wherever you are, it makes you proud. You are in every word. I will always keep the light on for you. x

A preview of

PICTURES OF YOU

by Emma Grey

A new novel coming 2024

Last night's party is still throbbing in my head. As I scramble awake, eyes shut, a tsunami of remorse crashes over me. Whatever I did that made me feel this horrendous, I will *never* do it again.

The worst part is, I don't even recall having fun. But then, I normally spend Saturday nights drinking raspberry tea and debating costuming inaccuracies in period dramas with other Jane Austen fundamentalists on Facebook, so not loving a wild party isn't far off script.

I turn my head on the pillow. Pain shoots to my eye sockets. *My poor brain.* Is it true that alcohol kills the cells, or is that an urban myth? I don't actually remember drinking last night. Certainly not anywhere near enough to make the world feel this heinous.

Please don't let me have been drugged. . . .

I wish whoever owns that alarm would switch off the beeping. And stop all the clattering in the corridor. Scratchy, starched sheets bunch under my back. I wriggle to try to get comfortable and the plastic mattress I appear to be lying on squelches beneath me as an adhesive dressing pulls at the skin on my hand.

Tell me I did not get a drunken tattoo. . . .

My eyes flick open. Harsh lights bounce on stark white walls around me, punctuated by red power outlets. A tangle of cords and wires and tubes and an oxygen mask dangles on the wall above my head, where my beautiful scarf collection is meant to be draped romantically over the headboard with fairy lights. Where is the framed *Pride and Prejudice* poster of Jennifer Ehle and Colin Firth emerging from the chapel? Breanna says that poster is one of the main reasons I will never get a boyfriend. Admittedly, getting a boyfriend seems like the least of my problems right now.

I try to sit up, but pain forces me back against the mattress. I can't even clear my throat my mouth is so dry. My heart pounds and the beeping from the machine beside me gallops in tandem, alerting a woman, who rushes over, presses buttons to silence it, and looks at me kindly.

"Hello, there, Phoebe," she says, as if we're old friends. "You're awake!"

Actually, no. I can't be. This must be a nightmare.

"Where am I?" My voice is groggy, like I've emerged from some sort of swamp.

She puts a gentle hand on my shoulder.

"You're at Saint Vincent's hospital in Sydney. I'm afraid you've been in a car accident."

Oh, God. *Breanna . . .*

The nurse picks up my wrist and feels my pulse, old-school style. I can tell by her frown that it's not behaving. There's a plastic tube sticking out of my hand, leading to a plump bag of fluid hanging from a metal pole beside the bed. I notice a faded white scar on my finger where I must have cut myself, and just as I'm trying to remember the injury, a clump of hair falls across my face. Much darker than my mousy brown. Is it *colored*?

"Did you dye my hair?" I accuse the nurse, as if she's some sort of rogue hairdresser with time to administer foils and a blow-dry on her nightly rounds.

The nurse laughs. "Gosh! I'm not talented enough for hairdressing!"

Yes. I must be losing it.

"Who was I with?" I ask. "In the car?" I can barely get the question out. What if Bree is *dead*?

The nurse stops scribbling notes and hangs the binder on the end of my bed. She drags an empty visitor's chair over and sits in it, while I reel back from whatever bad news she's about to launch.

"Phoebe, I have something difficult to tell you."

A doctor who's been hovering just outside the cubicle talking on a phone ends the call, comes in, pulls the blue curtains closed for privacy, and stands at the end of my bed, like the Grim Reaper.

I feel sick.

Yes. I am definitely going to be sick. And I have a phobia of that, which makes my stomach churn even more. *I need my mum.*

"Your injuries are fairly minor," the nurse explains, even though every part of my body is blaring otherwise. "Unfortunately, your husband took the brunt of the impact."

What?

"He sustained a very serious head injury."

Everything is swimming now. The room. Her voice. My grip on reality.

"We did everything we could. . . ."

My brain is doing cartwheels. She must have mixed up those records. Walked into the wrong room?

"Phoebe, I'm deeply sorry for your loss," the Grim Reaper adds.

Er, thanks? It's not *my* loss. Relief washes over me that it's not Bree who is dead, but some fictional man.

"I'm not a teen bride," I argue. I'd tell them my views on marriage—that it's an archaic, patriarchal trap that made sense only in Jane Austen's day—but they look like they're struggling to comprehend the fact that I'm a teenager. Teachers always say I speak like an adult. It's because I read so much. . . .

The two of them exchange subliminal communication and the nurse scurries off. The doctor sits on the chair now and smiles at me. It's a smile that says *We're sending for reinforcements.*

He makes polite conversation, avoiding the topic of my imaginary husband and asking other things, like how old I am and where I live and what year it is.

"Have I been abducted by aliens?" I ask. I've been watching old reruns of *The X-Files* lately and freaking myself out. An alien seems more plausible at this point than a husband.

He laughs. "No, nothing like that! You're just a little confused."

I'm not at all confused. They just have their information wrong. Hospital administration debacles happen all the time. I see it on *Days of Our Lives*. That's my comfort watch when I'm writing essays. Bree doesn't know how I can concentrate, but I find it harder to focus without daytime soaps unfolding outrageously in the background while I study.

What's ridiculous is that they think I'd get married at my age. Or at any age. It's probably not even legal.

When the nurse returns, she's brought a woman, who introduces herself as a psychiatrist. Perhaps she is here to walk the nurse and doctor through their delusions.

"Hello, Phoebe," she says. "How are you feeling?"

"A bit sore, but otherwise normal." I realize I sound unnaturally chirpy, like a person trying to convince the authorities they should start filling out the discharge forms. Must dial myself back.

"We're just a little bit concerned about some things you're saying," she says.

"There's nothing wrong with my memory. I can literally remember what I ate for lunch yesterday in the canteen. A sausage roll with sauce and a packet of choc-mint carob buds. The canteen doesn't sell proper chocolate. We started a petition about it but got nowhere. I eat so much junk food—I'm just lucky I have an amazing metabolism. I eat like a horse and I'm a size four!"

I pat my stomach through the thin sheet as if to demonstrate said overachieving metabolism, and that's when I realize something is very wrong. There is . . . *more of me* than there was yesterday. I lift up the sheet to investigate. Yes. Thicker thighs. A gentle roundness where washboard abs should be. Are they . . . stretch marks? What has *happened* to me in this car accident? It's like I've been redistributed in my own skin!

I look back at the psychiatrist, who is studying me closely. "I'm not a size four," I admit. "How did that happen?"

I envisage having been in some sort of coma. Maybe they fed me through a tube and gave me too much sustenance for my activity level. Perhaps the car accident triggered my metabolism to go into shock, and of course lying around on this bed for weeks or months, I'd be out of shape. . . .

"When was my accident?"

"Yesterday," the nurse replies.

I look back at my body. And that's when the boobs hit me. What's going on here, then? I mean, I had boobs yesterday, obviously, but not like *this*. I must be a C cup!

"Where have the extra two cups come from overnight?" I demand to know. They all glance at the single plastic tumbler on the bedside table beside the water jug, struggling to keep up. I don't correct their misassumption that we're suddenly discussing drinkware—I'd sound insane.

"Phoebe, how old do you think you are?"

"Sixteen?"

The psychiatrist puts her clipboard down on the bed and clasps her hands, rocking back and forth in her sensible shoes, as if she's playing a caricature of herself in a medical sitcom.

"I know this might come as a shock," she begins. "But according to your driver's license, you're twenty-nine. Now, don't be alarmed. Temporary confusion can be common after a blow to the head. . . ."

Blow to the head?

She's rambling on, but I've stopped listening. There is no way that I am twenty-nine and married. Or whatever it's called when your husband is dead. Widowed? I can't be. I would never have *gotten* married. And I don't even have a driver's license. I was going for my learner's permit next holiday. . . .

"But I'm opposed to marriage," I tell them. "I am one hundred percent a career girl. I haven't even finished Year Twelve. I can't be *twice my age*."

Another curl falls across my face and I sweep it away, then grab it and look at the color more closely. It's definitely not my natural shade. But Mum won't let me color my hair. Not even pink for crazy hair day. She's got this boring theory that we're born with the hair that most suits our skin tone.

"Can you get me a mirror, please?" I ask. The nurse retreats to the station out in the corridor and comes back with a compact from her handbag. She passes it to me, and I flick it open and stare at my reflection.

"*Fuck!*" I say. "Sorry." The apology is a force of habit. It's an immediate detention if the teachers catch you swearing. . . .

It's not just the brunette waves. There are tiny lines around my eyes and mouth. They're not full-on wrinkles, but they're unambiguously carving a discreet and determined path across my face. The other thing is everything is slightly blurry. I squint at my reflection.

"Here, would you like your glasses?" the nurse asks.

"Oh, I don't wear glasses," I answer, just as she passes

me a pair of stylish Prada frames I couldn't possibly afford that bring everything into perfect focus.

And by "everything," I mean the unbelievable set of facts that I appear to be an adult woman with fine lines on my face, additional pounds on my frame, extra cups in my bra, and a dead husband I never wanted.

ABOUT THE AUTHOR

Emma Grey is an acclaimed writer, photographer, professional speaker, and accountability coach. She has been writing fiction since she first fell for *Anne of Green Gables* at fourteen and is the author of the young adult novels *Unrequited: Boy Band Meets Girl*, *Tilly Maguire and the Royal Wedding Mess*, and the nonfiction book *I Don't Have Time* (coauthored with Audrey Thomas), as well as the parenting memoir *Wits' End Before Breakfast!: Confessions of a Working Mum*. Along with composer Sally Whitwell, she cowrote a musical based on her novel *Unrequited*, titled *Deadpan Anti-Fan*. *The Last Love Note* is her debut adult novel.

Grey wrote *The Last Love Note* in the wake of her husband's death. It's a fictional tribute to their love, an attempt to articulate the magnitude of her loss, and a life-affirming commitment to hope.

She lives just outside Canberra, Australia, where her world centers on her two adult daughters, young son, loved stepchildren, and stepgrandchildren, writing, photography, and endlessly chasing the aurora australis.

@emmagreyauthor

www.emmagrey.com.au

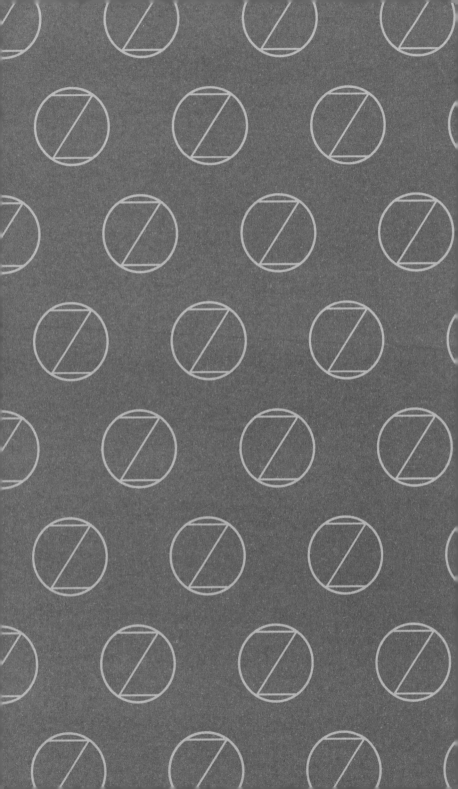